SCREAM FOR NOW

Bob Howard

ISBN-13: 978-1-945754-02-9

Cover art by Lorena Martin of Premade Ebook Covers

For Dawn, the woman who believed in me
when I said I wanted to write a book.

ACKNOWLEDGMENTS

Writing books can put you in touch with people around the world. I remember an evening when I was contacted by a reader in England, and while I was chatting with her on social media, I was contacted by another reader in Australia. That has been one of the real pleasures of being read. I've heard from readers all over the United States, and I have to admit, I value all of them, but I feel like I've made friends with the people who have stayed in touch. Kevin Hammermeister and Tim Harrelson, you two are right there at the top of the list, but I hope the rest of you know how I feel about you. I can't list everybody here, but each and every one of you is appreciated. Phyl Lamattina, I was just looking at your post about your leg. When you said it has been a rough year, you weren't kidding. I'm going to predict that 2020 will be an incredible year for you, so hang in there.

I've made a new friend this year. His name is Shin Saikyo, and he lives in Tokyo. Shin has earned my respect quickly because he's a master of the English language. Anyone who has learned a second language will tell you that American English has some difficult rules, probably because we have such a diverse history. Shin has been helpful by catching some of my rule violations that all writers try to avoid. I welcome Shin to my circle of friends and hope he chooses to continue to be my friend and to read my work.

To all of my readers, I want to tell you it has been an incredible experience to write for you, and I give you credit for my successes. When I was contacted by Tantor Media this summer and asked if I would consider a contract to produce the series on audiobooks, my first thought was that it couldn't have happened without your support. Thank you so much.

South Carolina

Jetty

Northern Dock

Mainland

Moat

Mainland Dock

Mud Island

Atlantic Ocean

Jetty

Fort Sumter

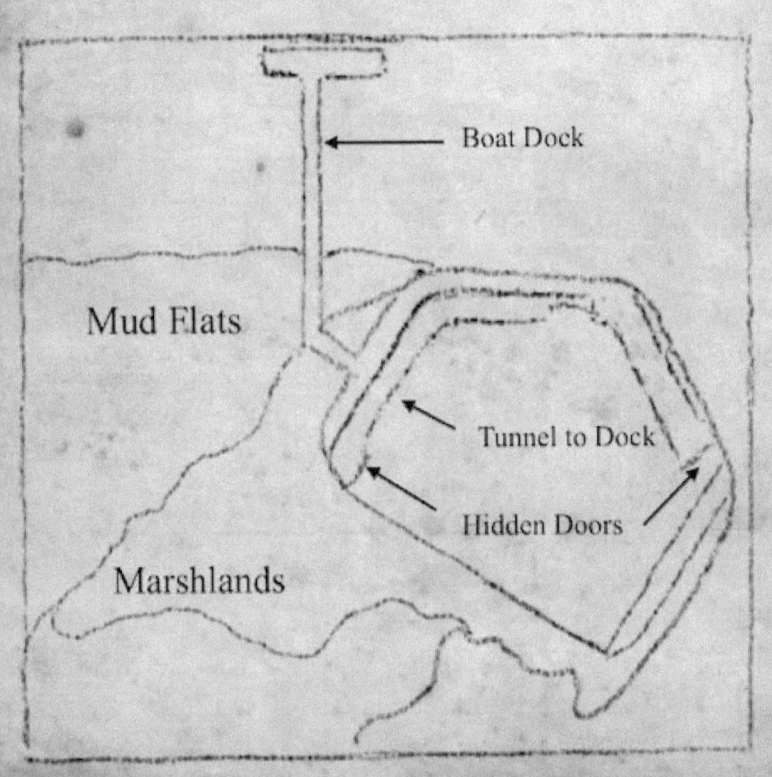

1

Wet Season

Before the Decline

The South American wet season was dragging on for much longer than usual. At least that's what Salem Townsend was thinking when he pushed his flat-bottomed boat away from shore. It was just one more reason he was considering going back to the States and giving up on his plans to earn his doctoral degree by presenting new research that would prove the crab-eating fox was really extinct. He would show that the species of *Cerdocyon thous* that ranged over most of Brazil, Venezuela, and Colombia was an entirely different species. After two years of rain and bugs, he was ready to start over with a thesis that didn't place such relentless demands on his body. Not to mention his love life.

Marcia Townsend, his wife of four years, had been understanding when he explained where he would be going and for how long, but the letters from home had become less frequent, and he had been reading a distant Marcia in between the lines. The distance wasn't strictly geographical. The letters were so impersonal she might as well have been writing about the weather. As a matter of fact, she had on a number of occasions. He felt like he could tell her a thing or two about the weather.

The boat slid smoothly across the water, and the rain made a steady pattering sound on his slick poncho and the aluminum boat. Despite his thoughts about quitting, he got back into the moment and was watching the slippery banks that resembled a picture of the moon. Tiny craters were everywhere, and Salem knew that the crab population was exploding with all this rain. Even as he watched, the pockmarks in the mud popped bubbles at the openings as crabs came to the surface. There would be something else watching those bubbles from the dense forest, and when enough crabs came into the open, he could expect to see their grey and brown bodies dart from the trees and snap up the tasty crustaceans before they could retreat into the mud.

When Salem had told Marcia where he was going, he had painted the experience as a once in a lifetime opportunity. It would be like a vacation in southern Venezuela, and he would come back healthy and tanned, ready to publish his findings and guarantee them a better life.

"Some vacation," he mumbled.

He was about a minute from rowing ashore and calling it quits when he saw the motion in the bushes. Something was getting ready to make its move, and Salem got his camera ready. There was more motion on the left and right sides of the place where he aimed his lens.

The crab-eating fox had been an opportunistic feeder, and so was this new species. They would eat the meat from small animals or carrion, but during the rainy season they hunted the plentiful crabs. If they paid any attention to him at all, he would be surprised. As they hunted he expected them to keep a wary eye on him at the most.

The rain came down a bit harder and made it difficult to focus on the shadows that moved in the trees. He knew the pictures weren't going to be very clear. Shooting pictures in this much rain was worse than shooting in heavy fog, and he hadn't been able to afford the special camera that would have been right at home in this much water. He would have to move closer to shore. There was no current pulling him away from his spot, so at least he didn't have to pull in an anchor. A couple of slow and easy strokes with his paddle made him coast a little closer to the bank.

"That should do it," he said under his breath. Any closer, and he would scare the crabs and the foxes away.

From his new position, he could see that there were several furry bodies under the low bushes. As a matter of fact, there were far more than he had ever seen. The crabs were also more abundant, and that could account for the extraordinary number of eyes that were regarding him with interest, but it made him nervous that the eyes were on him instead of the crabs that were darting between the tiny craters.

Salem gently sat his camera down on the seat of the boat and picked up his paddle for a second time. He didn't think he had taken his eyes off of the trees, but he must have when he reached for the paddle, because there was a fox standing on the muddy bank when he put the paddle into the water. It was standing as still as a statue, and Salem could have sworn the stare that the fox had fixed on him resembled the stare he had seen on their faces when they had identified their next opportunity to eat.

"Why are you looking at me? You should be looking at those things running around by your feet."

Come to think of it, the crabs weren't acting like they usually would when their predators showed up. They weren't running for their holes in the mud. They were emerging above ground in large numbers and migrating toward the water. The surface of the tidal stream was usually glassy, and the rain had hidden it from him at first, but now he could see the tiny ripples in the water as the crabs swam toward his boat.

Salem turned his body left and right on the seat and stared into the water on both sides of the boat. He saw that the ripples were everywhere.

"Why would the crabs get in the water when the foxes were out in the open?"

He knew he was talking to himself, but he had been using that as a tool to make himself think through the arguments of his thesis.

His head snapped up in the direction of the opposite bank. A dozen or more foxes were standing out in the open facing his way, and even from a distance he could see the crabs running across the mud and disappearing into the water. The foxes were ignoring their favorite food.

His paddle was almost pulled from his hands. He had dipped it into the water when he saw the foxes appearing from their hiding places and had forgotten about it until now. When he raised it, it was heavy with the small crabs. They were clinging tightly using their tiny pincers. Salem had to shake it and even bang it on the side of the boat to make them fall off.

"So much for stealth."

Normally he would have seen the foxes dive for cover when he started banging the wooden paddle against the aluminum boat. It sounded like he was beating a big drum, and it was loud enough to sound really out of place in this wilderness. If anything it did the opposite, and he watched with surprise as the banks became crowded on both sides of the stream. He estimated that he was at least forty or fifty feet from one side and twenty feet from the other. He didn't particularly like the way the crabs were acting, but the usually shy foxes were being a touch too curious about him. Despite the crabs immediately clinging to his paddle when it went into the water, he stroked several times to get his boat more into the middle of the stream. As he did, his boat moved downstream at an angle from where he had been, and the foxes on both sides jostled with each other for position and moved with him.

He had to beat the paddle against the boat for a second time, and the fine hairs on the back of his neck crawled when he saw that the banging caused the foxes to become agitated. Some of them made a yelping noise that was like a high pitched bark, and they half-heartedly jumped into the water where it was shallow. They immediately ran back onto the banks, but it was as if they were testing the water to see if they could come after him.

"That's absurd," he said.

The sound of his voice caused more of them to bark, and they snapped angrily at each other. Salem saw the way they curled back their lips, and for the first time since his arrival in South America, he was afraid. If he wanted to prove this was a new species, he could start with their behavior. The crab-eating fox was a shy creature. They mated and stayed with one partner, and they got along well with other pairs of mates. It was rare to see them attack each other, and there was no alpha in the group. The foxes on the banks of the tidal stream made him think they were all rabid.

Salem was so intent on the behavior of the foxes that he forgot about the crabs until one of them closed its pincers on the tender piece of flesh between the thumb and index finger of his left hand. It felt like his hand was set on fire, and a scream escaped his lips before he could stop it. The crabs held onto his paddle when he pulled it out of the water, and a large number of them fell into the boat.

Salem was on his feet without even thinking about it. He alternated between the crab that was causing him pain and the ones that were trying to go up the legs of his pants. Every time he stomped one of his feet there was a loud crunch, but the boat was rocking so much that he had to grab the sides with his hands. When he did, more crabs latched onto his fingers.

He stood up again and grabbed at the hard little bodies that were covered by his blood. They were slippery, but he indiscriminately tore them free and threw them back in the water. He didn't even care that he ripped off large chunks of his own flesh at the same time, and he was no longer even aware of the foxes. If he had been, he would have seen that the smell of blood had whipped them into a frenzy. They were swimming to the boat.

Free of the crabs that had shredded his hands and no longer finding more with his feet, Salem snatched up his paddle and stroked the water as hard as he could. He hit a swimming fox on the head as he made the third stroke, but he didn't slow down. On both banks more excited foxes were coming out of hiding and jumping into the water, and Salem knew his life was on the line. They ran along the bank and got ahead of him before diving into the water. Salem absentmindedly told himself to remember they were doing that. He had never known a crab-eating fox to think ahead quite that way.

Something reminded Salem of his supply bag. He had never needed it, but now was a good time to use the Glock that had been recommended to him by a man at the store where he had loaded up on provisions. He might not be able to shoot all of them, but he had never seen a fox hang around if it was being shot at.

Salem sat down in the boat and shoved his hand into the pack. The grip felt like it belonged in his hand, and he pulled the gun out and took aim in one motion. It wasn't hard to hit one because there were so many, and the explosive crack was followed by the yelp from a fox.

The results were beyond his wildest hopes as the foxes all reacted as one. They disappeared from the banks just as quickly as they had arrived. Those that were swimming toward his boat reversed direction and swam furiously after their fleeing mates. Just to be sure, Salem fired another round. He missed everything, but the exodus continued. The crabs were still climbing his paddle, but he could deal with them better now that he had the upper hand. He beat the paddles against the boat and made sure none of them had succeeded getting in with him. After he was sure he was in control, he paddled upstream staying in the middle just to be safe.

His camp was just over a mile from the place where he left his boat. He didn't plan to return, so he didn't bother to tie the boat to anything. He kept his Glock in his hand and ran the entire way, but the bleeding on his hands had stopped, and the pain was making him concentrate on where he put his feet. His camp came into view sooner than he expected.

He had a long way to drive, and the roads were bad, but the old Jeep was in good condition with a full tank of gas. He threw his gear into the cargo area without packing and expected to be jumped by foxes until he pulled the door shut behind him. That was when he finally lowered his eyes and examined the damage to his hands.

A crab's pincer was still embedded in his left hand, and he pried it free with a pair of surgical scissors from the first aid kit. The kit was always under his seat, so he had painfully pulled it into his lap. He fumbled with the bandages and the disinfectant until he had secure, if not perfect, bandages over the worst parts of each hand. He would have preferred to let the wounds get some fresh air, but he pulled on a pair of leather gloves to give the bandages more support. He was surprised at how much better the gloves made his hands feel, and for the first time since it had started, he thought he would actually make it home.

******

It took almost four days for Salem to drive to the coast. Political tensions in Venezuela were too high for him to be seen by the Venezuelan military. If he ran into them, he was likely to be detained, and that wasn't what he needed. His body was in trouble. He had a blinding headache that was sending out bursts of pain through the backs of his eyes. He winced every time he felt a new jolt, and the last thing he wanted was to be stuck away in some under funded third world hospital. At least that was his perception of the local medical care system.

A detour east took him out of Venezuela into Guyana, and he drove to the city of Timehri. His plan was to board a plane at Cheddi Jagan International Airport. Their security checkpoints were so bad that twenty dollars was all the passport anyone ever needed. Not that he didn't have a passport, but he wanted to move through customs as quickly as possible. He put his Jeep in long term parking and paid in advance for a week. No one would get suspicious about the abandoned vehicle for at least twice that long, and he didn't plan to return to pay for the extra week. He put together a carry on bag of things he wanted to keep and one suitcase to send through checked luggage.

In line he hoped no one paid any attention to the sweat stains on his clothing. He had been able to change out of the dungarees and denim shirt with the blood stains, but it was so humid that he was sweating profusely. He sniffed at his shoulder and realized that he smelled worse than he looked. There was no way to hide a week without bathing or showering, and his face was a dirty mess of hair that needed to be washed if not shaved. He avoided eye contact as much as possible getting through the ticket line. When he headed for the boarding area he kept as much distance as he could between himself and the other passengers.

Salem wiped a sleeve across his forehead, and it came back so wet that he knew it was more than the weather. He put his hand back on his forehead and felt the heat radiating from the skin. The pounding in his head seemed to be right under his hand and he held it there for a moment too long. The pressure of his hand felt almost as if it was holding back the pounding. Like someone would be able to see it if he took his hand away.

"Señor?"

Salem jerked his hand down in surprise and found the customs agent was talking to him.

"Are you sick, Señor?"

The man was regarding him with a wary expression and had his hand held out for Salem to give him his passport. His mental lapse was going to cost him. Salem shook his head and discreetly surrendered his passport, but not before managing to slide another twenty dollar bill into the little folder. The agent took it and visibly relaxed when he checked the contents. He made a small show of inspecting Salem's carry on bag and gestured toward the boarding gate. He gave Salem a friendly smile and showed two rows of rotten teeth. Salem gave a weak smile in return and accepted his bag from the man. That forty dollars was most likely more than the man had made in weeks or even months.

The plane was overbooked, and there were so many people crammed inside it that Salem was sure they were selling standing room. For once, though, he was almost grateful because the man who was shoehorned into the seat next to him was grossly overweight and definitely overcooked. He was sweating more than Salem, and the smell made Salem feel nauseous. Despite becoming claustrophobic and sick to his stomach, Salem was invisible to the other passengers because he was pinned against the window. He just had to keep from throwing up.

The first leg of the flight was short because of a layover in Miami, and it felt like the plane was landing as soon as it had taken off. Salem started worrying about getting through customs as soon as the plane stopped at a boarding gate. Getting out of South America was easy compared to getting into the United States, but as it turned out, his new friend in the seat next to him was all the distraction he needed. A little oversight involving a package of white powder in the man's carry on bag was enough to take all of the attention from Salem. It was neatly wrapped up inside his spare underwear, and he no doubt thought the customs agents would avoid those unsavory items. He was wrong, and Salem passed through customs without problems. He was careful to stand up straight and not to touch his hot, sweaty forehead. He also reversed his tactics and tried to make eye contact with everyone. It hurt to look at people, but he succeeded in making them avoid his gaze.

Rather than running the risk of offending someone by getting on the next flight, Salem decided to rent a car and drive the rest of the way. The young woman at the rental counter carefully pointed out that there was a penalty if the car wasn't clean when it was returned. Salem thanked her for bringing that to his attention, but he was already thinking about making yet another change in his plans.

He really should have asked her where he could find the nearest hospital, but he didn't think his fever had anything to do with his headache, and he didn't think his headache had anything to do with his hands. Instead of the hospital, he made a mental concession and asked where he could find a hotel. Maybe a long shower and some sleep would make him feel better, and he could quit worrying about what people were thinking. The woman couldn't resist the obvious answer.

"This is Miami, Sir. You won't have to go far to find a hotel."

Salem learned that she wasn't kidding because hotels were everywhere around the airport. He checked into the first one he came to, and thirty minutes later he was filling the bathtub with hot, steaming water. He wasn't sure he could stand up as long as he needed to take a shower, and the idea of soaking was too enticing. He sat on the toilet and peeled away the bandages on his hands. That was when he discovered that it was the smell of infection he had mistaken for body odor. The skin came away in sheets with the bandages, and he almost screamed from the pain.

When he finally stopped sobbing, he forced himself to move his swollen and cracked fingers enough to undress. He held his hands in front of his chest like a doctor who had just finished scrubbing up for surgery and stepped into the hot water. His fever made him shiver with chills as soon as he had both feet in the tub, and he couldn't wait to get the rest of his body warm. His mistake was in thinking that would include his hands, and he let them both drop to his sides in the soapy bath.

This time he did scream, and the pain surpassed anything he had ever known. The shock combined with his fever caused him to pass out, and for good measure he hit his head against the side of the tub just before he slid under the surface of the water.

******

The housekeeping staff found Salem Townsend the next day. He had been in the tub for at least fifteen hours, and the preliminary cause of death was listed as drowning under extenuating circumstances. To the Medical Examiner that meant it was being investigated for foul play due to the trauma on the side of his head. The police also wanted the forensics staff to determine what had happened to his hands. The official report said it appeared as if he had put his hands into a paper shredder.

It didn't take the police department long to put together their case. His passport and drivers license gave them everything they needed to know about who he was and where he was from. The letters in his personal belongings meant they would be contacting his next of kin for positive identification, and flight information told them where he had come from. They had a wealth of information to work with, except for one thing. No one had ever seen injuries like those on the man's hands.

The Medical Examiner had been identifying injuries for almost thirty years, and he wanted to believe the deceased had mangled his hands in some form of machinery, but he couldn't find the pattern that always gave away the type of machine. Machines operated at high speeds, and they inflicted injuries by repeatedly striking the same body parts before the victim could withdraw. In this case, the hands didn't appear to be crushed, so they had most likely been withdrawn, but the puncture wounds were too random for them to be made by a machine.

It was one of the uniformed officers who had arrived ahead of the

Medical Examiner who provided the observation they needed. He recalled a tragic accident involving a man who had ignored warning signs about alligators. He had his arms extended outward over a pond of water when an alligator grabbed his hands. The man's friends had rushed to his rescue, grabbing him around the waist and pulling as hard as they could. They got him free, and he kept his hands, but they were torn beyond repair.

Armed with this observation the Examiner asked his associates if they would agree that animals had caused the injuries. He sent photographs to friends and colleagues around the country and asked for opinions. Ironically, a pathologist at the Medical University of South Carolina in Charleston recognized the injuries first. It was ironic because it was already known that Salem Townsend was returning to his home in Charleston when he had checked into the hotel in Miami.

Dr. Grace Williams at MUSC compared the photographs to pictures taken at a recent autopsy of a man who had drowned near Myrtle Beach. His body had been in the water for over four days, and the blue crabs had gotten to him. The difference between the two cases was that her victim had the same puncture wounds all over his body, but otherwise she was sure it was the same wound.

When the identification of the wounds arrived from MUSC, the Miami Medical Examiner had just received the toxicology reports. It was unfortunate that the victim had soaked in a bathtub overnight because the hot, soapy water had cleansed the wounds very well. He would have preferred to see them in their worst condition in order to know how long ago the injuries had occurred. He had also expected to find bacterial infection present in the wounds, and tissue samples confirmed his suspicions.

Something else caught his attention in the lab reports. He sifted through the file that had grown impressively fast and found what he was looking for in the forensic interviews. They were almost duplicate entries, but from separate examiners. He had to wonder if it was likely that a man studying a species of crab-eating fox would be severely injured by crabs. He guessed it was possible if the man somehow got too close to the food supply of the foxes.

Cause of death was still listed as accidental drowning, and the extenuating circumstances were described as severe lacerations to the hands inflicted by South American crabs. The Medical Examiner included an observation that it appeared possible that some of the tissue around the puncture wounds had been exposed to necrotizing fasciitis, otherwise known as flesh eating bacteria.

The Examiner recommended that the findings should be forwarded to the CDC, but in the bureaucracy of his office it wasn't unusual for paperwork to be buried by more pressing issues, and he would never know that the file wasn't forwarded to the CDC as he had instructed.

******

Over the next few days there were a series of deaths that were not known to be connected to Salem Townsend until much later. The customs agent in South America had a raging fever and died after several days of burning agony. His wife didn't tell anyone about the terrible sores he had developed on his back, and no one suspected anything more than just another viral infection that wasn't treated early enough. The coroner in the small South American city had never personally encountered flesh eating bacteria, but he was aware of it, and he would have been alarmed to find the victim was suffering from both viral and bacterial infections.

It wasn't until the coroner in Des Moines, Iowa notified the CDC of a man who had died from an unidentified viral infection that the pieces started to come together, but the missing files and delays in reporting caused them to be slow to respond with efforts to quarantine people who had been in close contact with him. His morbid obesity was thought to be the cause of his inability to fight off an infection, but they didn't find the bacterial infection until the autopsy. It was also not documented that he had recently flown from South America to Miami.

The red flags started flying when the Medical Examiner in Miami was hospitalized due to a high fever, dehydration, and virulent sores at random locations on his body. The forensic interviewers sent by the CDC reviewed his recent cases and quickly discovered the unreported case of the man with mangled hands. They traced the path he had followed and started locating passengers who had been on the plane with Salem Townsend. They also placed the young woman from the car rental agency in quarantine.

Before the connections were made that led back to the crabs on the banks of the Essequibo River, over a hundred people were either directly or indirectly exposed to the infections carried by Salem Townsend.

The Decline Begins

Kamarang village sits near the border of Venezuela in Guyana but is in disputed territory claimed by Venezuela. Despite its remote location, it boasts a small hospital and an airstrip, and is not as cut off from the rest of the world as most villages in the region. Routine flights are made to Georgetown, Guyana less than two hundred miles away on the coast of the Atlantic Ocean, and tourists who are willing to forego amenities find their way to Kamarang in search of cheap souvenirs.

Sheleza Persaud had been the head nurse at the small hospital for twelve years, and during that time she had never seen a more curious illness than the symptoms displayed by the young man who had stumbled into the waiting room three days earlier. She had seen fever, infections, weeping sores, and all manner of injuries caused by contact with wild animals, but what had happened to the unidentified man was still a mystery.

She had been on duty when he literally fell through the front door. A patient who was leaving had pulled it open from inside just as the young man appeared to reach for the handle on the door. The patient was apologetic and had attempted to keep him from falling but was unable to stop his momentum. To everyone's surprise, the young man tried to bite an orderly who had rushed to his aid. A wrestling match had ensued in which a guard helped the orderly overcome the man but not before both of them had sustained bites to their hands and forearms.

The man had been strapped to a bed behind privacy curtains away from the other patients, but all eyes were nervously watching those curtains where the man could be heard struggling against his restraints. An eerie sound escaped his lips in a continuous moan as if he didn't have to take breaths of air. The doctor on duty concluded that it would be better to ease the nerves of everyone by having the man sedated, so he ordered a morphine drip. The needle was taped to the back of the man's hand and the drip started, but to their dismay the clear liquid wasn't being drawn into the vein.

Sheleza had no explanation to give the doctor when he asked her if she had inserted the intravenous device properly. She told him the resistance she felt as the tip of the cannula slid into the vein felt unusual, and no blood had escaped into the line when she opened the valve. When he asked her what was so unusual about it, she said it was like the vein was filled with very thick blood or mud.

Dr. Michael Khan had only been in the small hospital for a year, but he was well known by doctors in Georgetown and respected for not quitting when he encountered problems.

"Nurse Persaud, draw a blood sample from another location and send it to the lab. Let me know as soon as the results are back."

Sheleza gave him a nod and prepped a syringe to draw samples. Without being told how many, she decided that four vials would be enough. Dr. Khan went to see how the security guard and orderly were doing. The rapid onset of their fevers was disturbing. He found them in separate rooms and was surprised by the rapid deterioration of their respective conditions. Both had fevers and were sweating profusely. Their pupils were dilated, and neither were responsive to questions. He checked his watch and saw it had only been fifteen minutes since he had last spoken with them, and at that time both were responsive. It was less than an hour since they had been bitten.

As a precaution, Dr. Khan instructed the staff to put restraints on both men and to draw blood samples. Sheleza met him as he was coming out of the quarantine area and told him she had been unable to draw blood from the first patient, and he suspected he would not have been able to draw a sample from the other two if he had waited much longer.

It was against hospital protocol, but he went to his tiny office where he picked up his phone and put it to his ear. He used his other hand to flip through an old Rolodex to the number for the Centers for Disease Control in the US. He knew he was supposed to notify Georgetown Public Hospital, but he had a feeling that time was important, and he couldn't afford to wait for approval to call the CDC.

2

Where We Were

Six Years After the Decline

It had become a popular insider joke at Fort Sumter. If you were an insider, you knew what it meant. If you were new, not an insider, no one would tell you what it meant until you proved yourself successful on a supply run. Of course, being successful on a supply run meant more than finding supplies or coming back alive. It also meant you didn't get someone else killed.

The question would always come up when a new survivor was discovered. As strange as it seemed at times, our scouting groups were always finding one or two people hiding in a building, perched in a tree, or sleeping in an abandoned vehicle. Most of mankind was gone, but here and there individuals managed to keep from being bitten and somehow found enough food and clean water to last over six years.

"Where did you want to be when it started?"

That was the question. This time it was Jean who was asking a new couple. They were sitting in the main dining hall eating something that resembled a pot pie, but it was cooked in a crock that was just big enough for one serving. It was the standard first meal that was given to survivors, and the only thing that slowed them down when they started to eat was how hot it was. Turkey, ham, Swiss cheese, cheddar cheese, and an onion broth baked inside a crust. It had come straight from the oven to their table, and both the man and woman were already wide eyed in disbelief at the quality of the food.

Jean gave them a moment to let the question sink in then asked again, "Where did you want to be when it started?"

They kept eating, but the question always got the same reaction. Most people repeated it word for word with emphasis on 'want'.

Of course it was all a setup, and for the life of me, I don't know how it got started. Over a mouthful of the delicious food the woman told Jean she wanted to be anywhere except where she was. That was actually a better answer than we usually heard. If they weren't repeating the question back as if they hadn't heard it correctly, they were usually saying where they had been when it all started.

Jean said, "You didn't have some place you wanted to be when it started?"

People who hadn't taken a real bath in months or years, people who hadn't eaten an oven baked meal in years, and people who hadn't felt safe for years didn't dwell on where they had wanted to be on that first day. Somehow they had only fixed in their minds where they had been, and when they ran into other living souls, that's the information they traded. Where they had been, not where they wanted to be.

The man fell for the setup first.

"Why, where did you want to be?"

"With Ed."

Jean stood and left the table before either of them could get an explanation. I heard the man ask the woman, "Who's Ed?"

I hadn't met them yet, so they didn't know I was Ed, but even if they had known who I was, they wouldn't have known why everyone answered the question the same way.

The truth was that I had turned into somewhat of a folk hero by the joke, and I guess that's what kept it going. It wasn't a funny joke by any stretch of the imagination, and it wasn't meant to be, but it was the only sensible answer if you were an insider. On the day it all began, anyone with any sense would have wanted to be with me. I was the one who had a shelter. I was the one who had enough supplies to last for years and had a shelter that could protect me every day of those years as long as I stayed inside. If I had stayed inside, I would still be safe, and I wouldn't have put a dent in the supplies. But if I had stayed inside, it was likely that the dirty, starving man and woman eating their hot food only a few feet away wouldn't be here. None of them would be.

I had inherited the shelter from a man I called my uncle, but the relationship was more complicated than that. We were mostly related by the way we thought, as uncle Titus liked to say.

Titus Rush had become rich over the years, but you wouldn't have known it to look at him. His long gray hair tied back in a ponytail was a trademark on him. He always needed a shave, and relatives joked that he was born with a bushy mustache, but none of them ever gave him credit for his keen sense of humor and incredible genius. I did, and that's why he left everything to me.

Uncle Titus believed that the end of civilization was going to happen at any moment. Not any day, but any moment. He even managed to convince the right people that it was coming, and even though he had enough money to build his own shelter, he had convinced the federal government that they should fund the construction of almost three dozen shelters. They built them for him, and they were stocked to the ceilings with food, water, and all the comforts afforded to politicians. Some had saved people, but some sat empty. Others we didn't know about yet.

The end came as suddenly as he had predicted, but unfortunately it came after Titus died. It was unfortunate for him, but not for me...not for Ed. I inherited his personal shelter and sealed myself inside as the world around me died. That's the short version. Let's just say I was in the neighborhood when people started killing each other and the world was consumed, literally and figuratively, by a virus. If I hadn't been in the neighborhood, most of the hundreds of people enjoying lunch in this cafeteria wouldn't be alive, and the only thing any of them could say about where they wish they had been on the first day was, "With Ed."

Even though I was sitting by myself in the cafeteria, I was surrounded by friends and family, and I was probably the one person in the cafeteria who was recognized by everyone except the new couple. And since that joke had taken on a life of its own, everyone who passed by my table with their tray of food made sure the couple heard them say, "Hi Ed."

There would be time for me to get to know the couple. As a matter of fact, I already knew a little about them. Being an insider, I knew everything that was happening around Fort Sumter, and I knew every story of survival in the room except theirs. For now, I felt like they should be left alone for a bit so everything around them could soak in.

After their meal, they would be intercepted by escorts who were watching from a distance. They didn't know it, but the escorts were waiting for them to push their crocks away after every crumb was eaten. Then the escorts would try to time their approach perfectly and introduce themselves. The couple would be taken to private quarters where they would be told to enjoy their baths or showers and to get some rest. They would get a very casual explanation that they only needed to pick up the phone in their room and call the operator on duty if they had a problem, and that included medical care.

The orientation of new survivors was well orchestrated to ensure the safety of everyone around them. They had already been inspected for bite marks, but there was no inspection that could guarantee their minds had not been damaged beyond repair. Certainly they were traumatized, but we had learned over the years that some survivors would snap without warning. We considered them to be lucky when they were rescued along with someone they already knew because they had time to process everything by talking about it in private.

Then there was the other danger. We were willing to take in anyone who wasn't bitten, but sooner or later they would be survivors from Patriots Point. It wouldn't be a surprise to find that they were spies from the secretive base of operations only a short distance away from Fort Sumter across the harbor. Over the next few days, the couple would be carefully interviewed by Army and civilian medical personnel to see if their survival stories were the same and if their health matched their stories. From what we could see, the people at Patriots Point were at least well fed.

The couple seemed to be done eating and were just taking in their surroundings. I was spoiled to the point that I couldn't really imagine what it was like to fight to survive day after day and year after year. If they were for real, they had to feel like it was too good to be true. There had to be a catch.

A group of soldiers sat down at the same long table with the couple. They gave them their space, but they all exchanged friendly nods and greetings. The man leaned toward the soldiers who were all keenly aware that the couple was being gradually acclimated to their new existence. They knew what they could or could not say.

"Can I ask you all a question? Who's Ed?"

The nearest of the soldiers answered, "He's the guy we all wish we had been with on the first day of the infection."

The escorts timed their arrival perfectly and intercepted the couple before they could pursue the question any further. I saw one of them wink in my direction.

* * *

******

As they left the table and dropped off their dishes to be washed, the escorts began their well rehearsed explanation.

"Now that you've had something to eat, it's time for you to get cleaned up and get some rest. I'm sure you wouldn't mind some fresh clothes for a change. While you were eating, we took the liberty of stocking your room for you. I hope I guessed your sizes correctly."

The escorts were both women this time. They were dressed in civilian clothes, 'civvies', as the military liked to call them, but they were both highly skilled in hand to hand combat. They were two of Captain Miller's soldiers, and they were fanatically loyal to their boss. If the couple turned out to be spies from Patriots Point, they wouldn't learn anything important from their escorts, and they weren't going to be able to overpower them.

The man had been doing most of the talking for the couple, but the woman finally spoke up.

"This is just a bit much. Don't misunderstand, we're grateful and all, but what if we want to leave?"

They had walked from the cafeteria through a hallway that appeared to be a main artery through the underground city. It resembled the concourse of an airport. Then they had ridden in an elevator with polished brass trim until getting off on a floor that looked like it belonged in a five star hotel. Rich carpet, mirrors, paintings, and above all else, clean.

The soldiers did their best to appear unfazed by the question. The one who had just spoken was tall with black hair pulled back into a ponytail that bounced like she was just another college kid on her way to her next class.

"You're not prisoners here. Your door won't be locked, and if you want to leave, just use the phone to call the operator. Tell whoever answers that you want to leave, and it will be arranged. You'll be given a few days rations and transported to a relatively safe location of your choosing."

They arrived at a door made of rich wood, and the second escort inserted a key. As soon as she unlocked the door, she turned to the woman and offered her the key along with an understanding smile. She didn't mention the cameras located at the ends of the hallway and in the elevator, nor did she tell them about the motion sensors.

Both escorts stood aside to allow the couple to enter the room first, then they followed closely behind. The leader of the pair was Brenda McIntyre, and even though her partner, Staff Sergeant Tonya Archer, was the same rank as her, one soldier in each escort pair was always in charge. It was also her responsibility to start the real interview process, and it began with making newcomers comfortable enough to give information about themselves. It had gotten to a point that we had to be very careful. So far, we were sure everyone we had rescued was not a spy.

"You'll find everything you need to clean yourselves until you feel human again, including a small fridge with some essentials in it."

"How can all of this be here?" asked the man. "After all these years of waking up every time something steps on a twig. After all these years of starving? How could all of this have been so close to us?"

"Mr. Corrigan, that's what we'd like to know from you, and we're going to offer you a trade. In return for your story, we're going to keep you safe, warm, clean, and fed."

"What do you want to know?" asked the woman.

"It doesn't work like that," said SSgt. Archer. "We're going to leave you now. You see that computer over there? Just turn it on and follow the instructions on the screen. Take your time, answer the questions, and tell us your story."

The escorts left the couple, and despite the overwhelming evidence they had already seen that meant the room was safe, Phillip and Denise Corrigan looked under the bed, checked the closets, and pulled back the shower curtain. If anyone was watching, their behavior would appear to be perfectly normal.

******

Our Information and Technology personnel expected to see the remote access indicator activate between one and two hours after the new survivors were situated in their private quarters. That was the average. They were ready to begin their questions as soon as the Corrigans logged in. To the survivors it seemed as if they were taking a survey, but they were actually answering carefully worded questions customized just for them. The story of their survival gradually unfolded.

The Corrigans had been married for five years. Educated, healthy and they kept their youthful bodies by working out and cooking together. They were such a perfect fit for each other that friends teased them about it. They were the same height and each had full brown hair and hazel eyes.

It was the second marriage for both, and they had just begun talking about the possibility of starting a family. There were still a few things they both wanted to do before taking on the responsibility, though, and one of them was to visit a few of the vacation spots they had heard so much about but never seen for themselves. Charleston was the first stop on their list, and they had only been in town for three days when the world ended.

They had tried to rent a place in a bed and breakfast on South Battery between King and Meeting Streets, but they found that even during off-season months they were all booked. They had hoped to have a view of the historic White Point Gardens, known as The Battery to locals, but when they checked into their hotel on Market Street, they weren't disappointed by the view of the city rooftops. They didn't realize at the time that if they had gotten their original bed and breakfast that they would have become the breakfast. The polite young man who had carried their bags to their room had also given them suggestions about places to visit, and his recommendation to eat lunch on Shem Creek was the reason they were on Mt. Pleasant when the sirens and horns blared from rescue vehicles and fire engines.

It couldn't have been a more beautiful day. They were sitting at a corner table on the veranda of the restaurant watching shrimp boats and private fishing boats come and go in such precise paths that it could be called a graceful dance. The waiter had delivered a large platter of boiled shrimp and oysters on the half shell along with their second round of Bloody Marys. They had passed on the crab dip and she-crab soup appetizers because the waiter had discreetly told them he always recommended the freshest seafood, and the shrimp and oysters had arrived only an hour earlier.

Phillip Corrigan expertly pinched the shell from the shrimp and dipped it in cocktail sauce. It made a slight crunch when he bit into it that signaled a perfectly cooked shrimp, and he nodded in satisfaction. Denise sat across from him and had a clear view of the mouth of Shem Creek. Her right hand was holding a tiny fork that she had used to pry an oyster loose, but she held it only a few inches from her face. Her forehead had deep furrows that he interpreted as pain, but before Phillip could ask her if something was wrong, her hand began to shake, and the oyster dropped onto her plate. Denise had her eyes fixed on a spot behind her husband and he turned to follow her gaze. What he saw didn't make sense.

The restaurant next to the one they had chosen was also dealing with a brisk tourist business, and their outdoor dining area was at eye level to Denise Corrigan. Since they were at a corner table, there was nothing blocking her view of an unpleasant exchange that had developed at a table along the railing of the other veranda. She had seen a man knock his glass off the table followed by the waiter deftly intercepting the liquid as soon as it hit the wooden floor. What she couldn't understand was why the man, who had been seated with his back to her, had then fallen from his chair on top of the waiter's back. The waiter appeared to be just trying to push the man off of him, but his efforts changed from pushing to something better described as violent jerking. It was like his legs weren't working together, and they jerked in tremendous spasms as his scream rose above the rising sounds of the customers.

The man who had fallen on the waiter suddenly stood to his full height and stumbled backward into the railing behind him. As he did, he was turned by his own feet that were tangled in the legs of the waiter, and he didn't stop until he was facing directly at Denise. There was no way to explain the brilliant scarlet blood that ran in a cascade from his face to his waist. That was when Denise had dropped the oyster. It had all happened so fast.

Phillip was turned in his seat and only about thirty feet from the other railing, and he locked eyes with the customer covered in blood. For a reason that would only become obvious over the next day, the seemingly enraged man had reached for Phillip with both hands as if thirty feet was close enough. He flailed both arms wildly as he reached, and they watched in horror as the man flipped head first over the railing, dropping onto the hood of a parked car.

The Corrigans did what anyone else would do in the situation, and that was proven by their fellow diners on the veranda. They all rushed to see what had happened when the man landed. At first there was stunned silence. Then came the screams from Denise and a few others as the man astonished everyone by rolling from the roof of the car onto the pavement. For a second time in the last few minutes, he stood to his full height.

On the dining area of the other restaurant the people had reacted the same way. With the exception of those who were tending to the injured waiter, the customers and staff were all pushing to get a better view of the man who had fallen. The screams from both restaurants became background noise as a fire engine and paramedics arrived at the same time. The pandemonium that followed offered no answers to the people who were screaming to know what was happening, but it became obvious that the Corrigans had chosen wisely when they had selected their restaurant over the one next door.

The screaming next door seemed to rise higher than the sounds of the sirens and the screaming around Phillip and Denise. There was more pushing and shoving, and a section of the railing broke away. A waterfall of people poured through the opening as some fell and some jumped. Almost last to come through and drop onto the pile of people was the waiter who had been attacked by the customer, and he had his teeth buried into the arm of a woman. They fell together, and to Phillip it seemed that the waiter was more interested in maintaining his grip with his jaws than he was with the impact of the fall. As soon as they rolled off the pile of patrons who were scrambling to either help friends or to escape, the waiter crawled onto the chest of the woman he had been biting. The eruption of blood seemed to reach everyone who had fallen around them.

The Corrigans kept answering questions on the computer about that day and what happened after the restaurant. Phillip had wisely held his wife back to allow the crowd to flee ahead of them. In the pushing and shoving that followed the bloodbath at the other restaurant, more than one person was pushed to the ground by the stampede of customers. Even the exits from the parking lot became impassable as cars rammed each other and fights broke out. They eventually became so entangled with wrecks that people abandoned their cars and ran.

There was plenty of reason to run. The customer who had attacked the waiter had moved on to attack anyone close enough to reach, and the waiter had joined him. As people were dragged to the ground and bitten until they stopped their struggles, other victims receiving medical help from firemen and paramedics were grasping the startled rescuers by their uniforms and pulling them closer. Then they bit their exposed faces and necks. In a matter of minutes there were as many attackers as there were customers running for their lives. If there was a saving grace, it was that the attackers moved slowly. They were clumsy and fell down easily, and the Corrigans dodged their hands to reach the main highway.

With no way to retrieve their car from the parking lot they crossed Coleman Blvd and sought help from anyone who would give it. Traffic was still moving, but it was obvious that it might not be for long. No one was heeding red lights or stop signs, and there were even cars using the lanes on the wrong side of the road. As cars collided with each other, the drivers cursed and shook their fists, but they didn't waste any time before driving away. There was one exception when a driver got out of the car that had suffered the most damage. He pulled a pistol from his belt and shot the driver of the other car twice. Then he pulled him into the street. The driver's wife was hit by another car when she jumped out to help her husband. She was most likely unaware of anything from that second forward.

Despite earning angry shouts and blaring horns, an elderly couple from New Jersey pulled to a stop in front of the Corrigans and offered them a ride to the Mt. Pleasant police station. It seemed as if they might at least make it that far, but as they got closer to Houston Northcutt Blvd where the map said they would find the municipal center, traffic came to a complete stop.

Up ahead on Coleman Blvd they could see the bridge over the Cooper River. The sun was reflecting off of thousands of cars and trucks in every lane. Unsure of where to go to reach safety, people on Mt Pleasant were making their escape by going over the bridge to reach I-26. On the other side in Charleston, the people who could see that I-26 was already a snarled mess were making their escape to Mt Pleasant. In the light of day it was obvious to the Corrigans that no one would be going anywhere in either direction, and as they watched they could see that people were running between the cars. From their vantage point they could see it all. There were still people trying to move forward to cross the bridge, but the running people soon took on the appearance of a tidal wave that was pouring down from the towering bridge. They watched in fascinated shock as the tidal wave of people literally crashed into the wall of people going the other way. The tidal wave was slowed for only seconds as it washed over hundreds of families.

It all seemed to happen in slow motion, and later as they answered the questions on the computer screen, they had to ask each other about that day to see if they were remembering everything correctly. They weren't sure if there had been noise at first, but as they were coerced into remembering what they had wanted to forget forever, they remembered that it had sounded like a college football game crowd that had erupted into one long, loud, and sustained cheer. But it was screaming and crying.

When Phillip and Denise turned back from the melee in the distance, it was to tell the elderly couple that they should hurry to the police station only two blocks away. They turned in time to see them disappearing in another tidal wave of people that was flowing toward the municipal center. The elderly couple was practically carried by the wave in that direction. A hand grabbed Phillip's arm, and he yanked himself away out of reflex. The hand was covered in reddish and yellow grime that looked like it had just been inside a freshly killed chicken, and as soon as Phillip broke free, the hand reached for Denise.

Denise screamed for Phillip to get the man off her, but he had already grabbed the man by the hair on the back of his head. It seemed like the right place to grab him, and it proved to be very effective to not only pull him off of Denise but to redirect him away from both of them. Phillip steered the man to the right until he was pointed directly at an ornate wrought iron fence. When he shoved from the back of the man's head, he was only trying to push him hard enough to make him fall, but Phillip was shocked to see a metal fence post erupt from the middle of the man's skull. Phillip's first impulse was to be upset that he had just killed a man, but that impulse didn't last more than a second before the crowd washed over him and his wife.

It was their turn to be swept away by the people who were running for their lives, and the one place everyone wanted to be was the police station. They were in a sea of people, and their heads seemed to be bobbing, rising above and sinking below the surface. Phillip managed to catch the outstretched hand of his wife barely in time as he was almost pushed off his feet. Falling down in the stampede would mean death under the feet of what was now a crowd of thousands. Someone else grabbed his other arm, and he pulled hard to free himself of the grip out of reflex. He found himself face to face with a teenage girl as he reeled her in close to him. Her pleading eyes locked onto his, and she begged desperately for him to help her. Phillip gripped more tightly to his wife while pulling hard on the unknown girl's arm. He somehow managed to draw them closer together until his wife was able to help by catching her fingers in the material of the girl's shirt. Holding tightly to each other, they just focused on keeping their feet under them and went with the flow of the crowd.

As if the entire event wasn't already unreal, a new sound blended in with the screams and shouts. Up ahead where the sea of people was already cresting against the municipal center there was a popping noise. Phillip had the insane thought that someone was making popcorn, but he immediately replaced it with another insane thought. Someone was shooting into the crowd, and in the split second when he realized he knew that sound, the teenage girl released her hold on him and Denise. They held onto her as long as they could, but they reluctantly let go when they saw her hair was matted with blood. Almost as if they had the same thought, Phillip and Denise immediately shifted their hands from the girl to each other. They held their bodies as close to each other as they could and ducked their heads lower. The popping sound became a steady rattle.

They could see no rhyme or reason to the shooting because there were so many people who were attacking rather than escaping, but the shooters were doing the best they could to tell them apart. Somehow the Corrigans found themselves at the front of the crowd, and they were pulled as much as they were pushed through a line of blue uniforms. They didn't stop to watch as they scrambled to safety along with dozens of people into the depths of the building. The sound of the battle was behind them, and then there were more doors closing behind them. They weren't sure how far they went, but eventually the only sounds were coming from the people who had come inside with them and a police escort.

The Corrigans were surprised to see how much time had passed since they had started answering questions and typed into the computer that they would like to take a break. There was no response to the question, but a new window opened on the screen that had the same appearance as the previous questions. The only difference was that every question was related to where they had been since the first day, and how had they had survived. Phillip typed that they weren't going to answer any more questions until someone answered something for them.

There was a longer pause that stretched out enough for Phillip to decide that he wasn't going to get any answers if he kept filling in the boxes below the questions they had for him. He sat back from the computer and crossed his arms. Fifteen minutes later a text box appeared with the question above it, "State your inquiry."

"Now we're getting somewhere."

Phillip typed three words.

"Who is Ed?"

Scream for Now

3

Spider Web

North of Charleston
Six Years After the Decline

Jed Ambrose noticed the difference before his friends at the colony. The spiders were changing, but when he thought about it, why shouldn't they? Everything else had changed. What he noticed was the way the meanest spiders didn't seem to be hiding. Some of the people in their camp didn't agree, but most of his friends said if someone who grew up in the country thought the spiders were different, you could believe they were different.

He and his friends had survived for six years by moving constantly, but they never let themselves get too far from the territory they knew the best. There was plenty of room to move in the forests, and they quite often found themselves to be right back where they had been the year before.

The northern banks of Lake Marion was where most of them had been raised, and from the beginning they used their knowledge of the lake and the dense trees to at least outlast the dead that seemed to have an endless supply of replacements.

Spiders weren't exactly new to South Carolina, and if you learned where they liked to live, you could avoid them. Growing up in Cross, South Carolina, Jed had seen his share of brown recluse and black widow spiders, and it was their predictable habits that spared him the scars and fevers from their bites. One predictable thing about them was that they had always hidden from people.

As an African American child from the country, Jed loved the isolation of his small community. His parents had taken him to Charleston a few times, but he preferred the woods around Lake Moultrie. If weather permitted, he would be fishing on the Tailrace Canal at the headwaters of the Cooper River every day after school, and of course he was there all weekend. He loved catfish the best, but whether he knew it or not, he was becoming educated in the ways of outdoor survival at a young age. While he caught food necessary to live, he avoided the habitats of the spiders, snakes, and alligators.

He recalled passing by a campsite on the way to the Pinopolis dam at Lake Moultrie and seeing a young family at a picnic table. They were cooking on a charcoal grill and had set up a beautiful table of food that would be tempting to any kid with a healthy appetite. The family had mistaken his interest in the table as wanting some food, and they asked him if he wanted to join them. He almost forgot why he had stopped and stared at them, and he was ready to accept the invitation. At the last moment when they moved aside to give him room at the table, he remembered what it was he had stopped for.

"Did y'all check under the table for spiders before you used that table? Them poisonous ones like it under there."

There was a mad scramble as the three children and the mother literally fell off the benches backwards. The husband rushed to lift them out of the dirt and to inspect them for spiders. He stood them up and brushed at their clothing as if spiders would fall out. The mother was on her feet screaming and stamping as hard as she could.

While they carried on, Jed moved into position with a long tree branch. He reached under the table with the tip and circled it around the wooden boards. He pulled it back out covered with a big mess of spider webs and a long legged spider angrily attacking the branch.

"Brown recluse," he said with satisfaction and a big smile.

He held it out in the direction of the horrified family, and they scattered for a second time.

"My daddy told me that you should always turn a picnic table and benches over and check the bottom for spiders before you sit at it."

"Are there anymore?" asked the father. His voice was much higher than he wanted it to be.

"Yessir. There's always some more."

Jed helped the man turn over the table and benches. It was safe to say they were having more fun when they were ignorant of what they were sitting with, but they were close to making a trip to the emergency room. There were brown recluse spiders under both benches, and their webs were full of newborns. Thousands of baby spiders hung within inches of the children's bare legs.

Years later Jed found himself standing on the northern side of the big lock gate at the Pinopolis Lock. He wasn't close enough to see down into the water and would have to go much further to see over the one hundred foot drop, but what he was able to see at the top was something that bothered him tremendously. He knew spiders, and something was making them do something he had never seen before. They were almost agitated, and he wondered if the thing that was causing the ringing in his ears was bothering the spiders too. The ringing had been driving Jed crazy for weeks.

From where he was standing, he could tell it was a spider web, but he didn't recall ever seeing one that big, not in his entire life. He could also tell it was a brown recluse web by the disorganized way it was spun. It was like a giant, off-white cotton ball that had been pulled apart. He thought about that picnic table from long ago and imagined that if he threw the table into this web, the web was big and thick enough to stop the table from falling through it to the water below.

At the age of forty Jed thought he had seen it all in his small rural town, but then the infected showed up. He had organized the members of his church and set up a small militia that had worked hard to protect their families. They had pulled together as a community and managed to survive without help from the outside. That had worked for the first five years or so, but over time they were forced to go further on each supply run, and they had lost people. Their population only got smaller, and it had become a greater burden on him and a few others to find supplies for the rest of the community.

Now Jed was confronted by this new development and didn't know what had caused it. Only a week ago he had crossed the dam at this point to reach the other side of the Cooper River. It had been a useful escape route they had all used from time to time. With little more than a narrow walkway and safety railings, it was difficult to cross it if you were afraid of heights.

If you were being pursued by the infected, all you had to do was go out to the walkway and cross the very top of the lock gates. It had been easy to block both ends with rope so that people could climb over, but the infected would crowd around the walkway until they fell over the edge into the water below. Now that walkway was barely visible under the mass of webs. In some places he couldn't see the walkway at all.

Jed checked the trail behind him to be sure there were no infected today, because his escape path was temporarily closed. The buildings near the top of the dam were the only cover available, but the advantage was that he could see further than if there had been trees. He knew he had to go out to that web to see why spiders had built it out in the open like that, and he didn't want to get trapped there. The sun was out from behind the clouds, and there was only a slight breeze, but it was way too quiet. Jed knew that the animals in the forest would stay quiet when it wasn't safe to make a sound, so he strained to hear anything. No moaning and no breaking of branches under the clumsy feet of the dead, but that didn't mean they weren't there. He wished again that his ears didn't ring so much.

"Sometimes the stupid things just stop and stand still," he mumbled out loud.

He thought again that he shouldn't have gone out alone, but it was his turn. He couldn't make someone go with him just because he was having a bad feeling about it.

Like many people, Jed could recall the unpleasant experience of getting a spider in his hair or somewhere in his clothing. If you were going to live in the south, you were conceding that sooner or later it would happen to you. When he was six he had woken up in the middle of the night to find a large wolf spider taking a shortcut across his pillow. His screams had made him the victim of merciless kidding for several days, and his big brother said he screamed like a little girl. His scalp itched just looking at that messy web. There was debris in it, and even from a distance he could see things moving through it. As he got closer he could make out more details, and it made him sick to see that spiders were adapting to the new world order. There were birds stuck in the web.

Jed couldn't believe his eyes at first. Birds flew into webs when they stretched between trees, but he had never seen a web stop a bird. Sometimes they had to land and strip themselves of the sticky webs, but they always got away. He imagined that somewhere in the Amazon there were spider webs that trapped birds, but not in Cross, South Carolina.

The brown recluse didn't try to build webs that would capture prey. They made webs for the sole purpose of retreat. That's why they were such an ugly mess. If it was a maze through which only they could navigate, then it was a successful web. The difference with this web was that it was just so big that it was hard for things to avoid it.

He followed the safety railing out as far as he could go, but he was boxing himself in. He kept checking the trees behind him, and even though he couldn't see anything moving, he was sure they were there. They would come for him if they saw him, so he watched and waited for five full minutes before going closer to the web. When he inched closer again, he could see some larger dark shapes further down inside the web. It appeared that birds weren't the only victims of the spiders. There was an assortment of small forest animals. Possum and raccoons were always rooting around in human habitats, so he wasn't really surprised to see them wriggling around inside the cloudy mess of sticky silk. It must have been windy since the web was built because it was full of leaves too. He didn't know what went through the mind of an animal, but he could imagine that was a horrible way to die, especially if you could see the spiders coming for you.

Now he was within a couple of feet from the web. Where it covered the safety railing Jed saw that the aluminum poles were almost invisible because the web was so dense. What he wanted to see was how far down it went.

He was at the top of the lock gates. The lake was seventy-five feet below the level of the river, and the last time it had been operated, the water level inside the lock had been lowered to the height of the river. Apparently, someone was trying to come upriver to the lake, and the gates had not yet been opened. The water level was almost a hundred feet below where Jed stood to peer over the edge. He was sickened by what he saw at the bottom, and he suddenly understood why the web was at the top of the lock. It was also at the bottom and everywhere in between. The web was over one hundred feet deep since it included the railing at the top of the lock.

At the bottom there was a writhing mass of infected, and if he hadn't seen them yet, he could certainly smell them. There must have been several thousand for them to be able to fill the bottom of the lock so completely, and from what he could tell, the web was fastened to the bodies of the infected. The spiders were already feeding on them at the bottom. It didn't look like they would be getting to the small animals any time soon.

There was a cracking noise behind him, and he knew without looking that he was in trouble. He turned and backed up at the same time, and as his hip bumped into the railing, he recoiled in panic. He could see dozens of spiders dropping down on silver threads as they tried to get away from his intrusion.

Jed began swatting at his pants, whether there were spiders there or just his imagination, he felt like he had to get them off his body as fast as he could. As he swatted he turned in circles, forgetting completely about the noise he had heard behind him. The infected dead that was reaching for him leaned forward and missed as Jed twisted out of its way, brushing at an imaginary spider. Two more steps forward, and the infected was shoulders deep into the dirty, tangled nightmare that Jed had only brushed against.

Jed was in the process of removing his shirt because he thought he felt a spider go down his collar and crawl to the middle of his back. He had seen the infected go by and kept one eye on its progress while trying to undress and check his surroundings for more infected. He could hear a mewling sound coming from somewhere but didn't know it was coming from him. He had been amused by the family at the picnic table, but that was a few little webs. This was the one from a movie he had seen, but it was even bigger.

His fears were confirmed when Jed saw a large brown recluse run out of the shirt he had thrown to the ground. He knew he hadn't been bitten because the bite of a recluse was usually painful. That didn't make him feel better at the moment. Jed reached up to his head with both hands and ran his fingers through his short hair searching for spiders he was sure were there. Having confirmed he had bumped the web hard enough to get them on him, he was positive he would find more.

The infected dead had waved its arms around in the web and come away with a sizable amount of dirty strands that clung to its face and upper body. The infected didn't know a web from cotton candy, and it didn't care that its head and arms were covered with the eight legged creatures that lived in the web. It did care about the living being that was making strange noises as it dodged around pulling off its clothes.

It got its balance under control and took aim at Jed. Two steps forward and then a third, and it was practically on top of him for a second time. Jed was horrified when he saw the infected making another pass at him, but this time Jed also saw that he wouldn't be able to defend himself without getting into close quarters with the infected, and that meant getting those spiders on his arms.

Jed fell over on his back as the infected leaned with all of its forward momentum following Jed to the ground. If Jed hadn't acted fast enough and pulled his feet up in front of his own chest, he would have wound up on his back with the infected on top of him in an embrace. If he didn't get bitten by the infected, he would definitely get bitten by the spiders that were desperately trying to crawl away from the intruders.

He was also screaming, and if he didn't really scream like a little girl when the wolf spider was on his pillow, he was doing it now. With his feet planted on the chest of the infected, he pushed with every ounce of strength he had and sent it flying backward. Its feet were off the ground when it hit the safety railing below its waist, and its body flipped in a somersault several feet into the web. Just as Jed had expected, the fall was stopped only a few yards below the railing, and he felt sick at the thought that it could have been him. Even as he watched, hundreds of small spindly bodies were climbing toward the infected dead.

Jed was pulled back to reality when he realized he wasn't alone. Almost a dozen infected had him blocked from getting out of the corner he had so stupidly let himself be forced into, and they were steadily making the corner smaller. He backed toward the railing again, but another glance toward the gap in the web where the infected had gone through was enough for him to know he would rather go down fighting than squirming while insects searched for the openings in his face. He could see they were doing just that to the infected, finding its nose and mouth to be easy targets.

Jed only had his long bush knife with him, but he had managed to stay alive with less on a few occasions. He also knew better than to attack a line of the infected dead by going toward the middle of the line, so he wrapped his shirt around his left arm and went toward the last one on the right. That way he was able to throw up his left forearm as he went around it. He felt the grip of the infected on his shirt and for the first time in the last hour, he also felt like things were going his way. As the infected pulled on the shirt, he pushed while letting his arm spin over and under the shirt allowing it to unwrap from his arm.

"Keep the shirt," he yelled as the infected fell backward into the path of the others.

Jed used the opportunity to break into a full run. He was surprised when he ran straight into six of his best friends as they came around the corner of the nearest building. He was elated to have come close to dying only to break away from the spiders and the dead, and he quickly described what he had seen. His friends all wanted to see what he was talking about, but he didn't want any part of it yet. In the end they won, but only because it made sense for everyone to know just how bad it was.

Seven of them could handle a dozen of the infected on a bad day, and they made short work of the fragile bodies of the infected. With them out of the way Jed led the way and pointed at the top of the lock gates from a safe distance. It didn't take long for them all to be cautiously peering over the edge and shouting about what they could see from the top to the bottom.

"What are we going to do about this?" asked Jed.

"What's that mean? Why do we have to do anything about it?"

The questions were asked by so many of them at the same time that it was hard to tell who actually said it, but Jed turned his attention to Ben Kinlock, someone he had known since before the first grade.

"We need that walkway to get to the other side of the lock, especially if we're being chased by something."

Ben wasn't totally convinced that they needed the escape route, but even if they did, he was having issues with what they could do about it.

"What you gonna do, Jed. Take a stick and go mess up that web?" asked Ben. He wasn't trying to make fun of Jed, but his question got plenty of laughs.

"Here you go. Here's a big stick."

One of the guys was quick to get a branch and start stripping off the small twigs along its length.

Jed had been panicked earlier, but listening to the good natured teasing from his friends made him relax a bit, and along with the break in the tension came clearer thinking. He smiled and held up his hands in mock surrender.

"Okay, y'all. I get it. You think it's funny because it didn't happen to you, but I'm serious. Do you guys actually want to let this thing keep getting bigger?"

The group of men all took turns getting close to the edge and getting a good view of the infected dead below, but once they had seen the scope of the problem, they asked Jed the one question that put the issue to rest.

"How do you plan to knock down a web that size?"

Jed ran every possible way of destroying a spider web through his head. He even considered a version of using a big stick. He pictured how much web they could get rid of by dropping tree branches into it, but he couldn't picture doing enough damage.

"We could throw in some branches but set them on fire first," said Ben hesitantly.

Ben seemed like he thought everyone would make fun of the suggestion, but Jed thought it was a great idea. He slapped his friend on the back as he passed him, and everyone else got into the spirit of the project. Within a few minutes they had a large pile of branches near the web. It would be easier if they had some gasoline with them, but a little bit of quick planning showed they could do a reasonably good job without it.

After the pile of branches was big enough, they brought some of the heaviest branches over to the web. Jed explained that they could throw the branches in that would sink the farthest through the web and then set fire to the branches with the most leaves on them. Hopefully, they would fall far enough into the web that they would set fire to the heavy branches.

It worked like a charm. One of the heaviest branches made it at least half way to the bottom, and they tried to land more branches right on top of it. When they threw a burning branch through the hole they had punched in the web, it was the web itself that acted like gasoline. The fire raced through the thin strands in all directions, but the important thing was that it set fire to the heavy branches. The smoke also did its job. One sure way to get rid of spiders was to smoke them out, and there was an incredible amount of smoke.

Jed wasn't sure what he was going to do about the spiders on the walkway to the other side of the lock, but the smoke took care of that problem. He had worried that the spiders would cling to the underside of the walkway when they destroyed the web, but the plumes of smoke were so huge that the spiders could only try to get out of it as fast as possible. Of course that was enough to scare all of the men as the spiders tried to swarm over the edge and run past them on the ground. The men hastily set up a narrow firebreak a few feet back from the edge that worked quite well as thousands of spiders ran through it and ignited.

By sunset they had cleared their passageway to the other side of the lock, and it was time to get back to their camp. The women would be wondering where they were. Before leaving Jed told them all that they needed to check the walkway every day to see if the spiders were rebuilding the web, and if they were, they could destroy it before it covered the whole area.

Jed studied the bodies at the bottom of the lock and for the first time he was able to go further out onto the walkway to inspect the railings for spiders. It was a good day as far as he was concerned, but he was still uneasy about this new development. He couldn't get it out of his mind how unusual the behavior of the spiders had been to start with.

"Do you hear something funny?"

He faced Ben when he said it, but he asked the question loud enough for everyone to hear.

"I wasn't going to mention it," said Ben, "but I've had this awful ringing in my ears all day. Is that what you're talking about?"

"Yeah, that's it. It's been driving me crazy, and at first I thought I'd hit my head or something, but it's too loud to be just inside my head."

Some of the men were covering one ear and listening, and everyone was quiet for a few seconds. One by one they all agreed that it was something in the air, and one of them said he thought that it was bothering their dogs back at the camp.

"Do you think that sound is what has the spiders acting so strange?" asked Jed.

******

The small church outside of Cross, South Carolina had been their gathering place since the infection began. And it was crowded tonight. There was good visibility in all directions even at night, so they were able to bring together the leaders of small bands of survivors to make plans. They had some growing problems that couldn't be ignored any longer.

There were ten different groups represented at the meeting, and the apocalypse had broken down barriers that had existed for centuries. People who were almost enemies before it began were now doing their best to keep each other alive. They were still living in their own territories, but they were coming together to share information.

"That's crazy," yelled one of the men from Jamestown. "The spiders may bite people, but they don't eat them."

"I never claimed that they eat the infected," said Jed. He didn't let his voice get as loud as the guy who yelled at him because their relationship was too fragile. "I said they had them trapped in their web, and they had built the web all the way to the bodies at the bottom of the lock."

"Why is it crazy?"

The question came from a woman who lived closer to the coast in McClellanville. Jed knew she had been a retired teacher who had a small place on Bulls Bay. She had received word of this meeting and traveled two days to be here. She needed to let the others know that the infected were all flowing south toward Charleston as if something was calling to them.

"I've seen spiders eating road kill before. If given the opportunity, they'll eat anything that gets stuck in their webs, and I've been seeing some big webs between trees."

Jed appreciated her coming to his defense. Some of the groups were still a threat to turn on the others and take their supplies, and alliances were only good as long as people weren't desperate.

He continued, "The web across the lock at Pinopolis is the biggest one I've ever seen. It covered the entire gate. We burned it down, but we've gone back every day since just to keep it from getting built as high as the walkway over the top. If we can't cross there, we have to go around the lake, and that ain't easy with all them infected doing the same thing."

"Does anyone have any decent food they would trade?" asked an elderly man who was very pale. He made everyone nervous because his group had been living off of crab meat and oysters, and no one was going to trade for those.

"We're all low on food, Jack. That's why we're having this meeting. We're trying to figure out what to do. With all them dead things walking through the area like it was at the beginning, we can't get near any of the places where food might be, and everywhere else is picked clean."

Jed was careful not to let himself sound like he was talking down to the old man. He had become a bit too sensitive when everyone had ganged up on him about eating crabs.

"I heard there's people in Fort Sumter and on that aircraft carrier in Mt. Pleasant," said Mrs. Wortham. "The word around McClellanville is that some of the survivors down there were locals. Maybe they would help us if they knew we were here."

"And just how do you propose to contact them?" asked Jack.

Mrs. Wortham was not to be easily pushed around by the cranky old crab-eater.

"Use your imagination, Jack. We've seen their helicopters and the seaplane too many times for it to be a coincidence. They must have some kind of setup near Murrell's Inlet."

The meeting went on for another hour with the entire discussion revolving around where to find supplies, but it was becoming obvious that everyone felt like the best place to search was not at any of the old Wal-Mart stores that had been picked clean years ago. As unlikely as some of them thought it was, they had to find out why the helicopters kept coming back to the barrier islands. They decided that they couldn't send everyone or they might seem like a threat. At the same time, there was so much distrust between the ten groups that they didn't believe someone would share what they found. They put it to a vote and selected one person from each group to go on an expedition. If they found the hidden supply base used by the people at Fort Sumter, they would try to make contact with them peacefully. If they wouldn't share what they had, the survivors would vote on how to make them share.

The meeting broke up just before midnight when the sentries reported the infected were passing through. It was no surprise that they were headed south. What was always a surprise was the numbers in the small hordes. It seemed like there was an endless supply of the infected. Just when they thought they had killed them all, more arrived. Jed guessed it was because there were survivors in small pockets everywhere, just like his group. They managed to stay hidden long enough to make it through the first days, and they managed to find food and uncontaminated water for the six years since, but they gradually ran out of food and luck.

4

Preparations

Six Years After the Decline

While the largest of the hordes had marched with relative ease down I-26 from Columbia, a massive horde had been decimated on I-95 by the natural barrier of Lake Marion. The sprawling body of water claimed thousands of the infected that didn't successfully walk onto the interstate bridge that crossed the lake. They were bumped to the left and right as the horde advanced on the four lanes and kept walking forward until they were forced into the water. What remained of that horde was still an unholy parade. For every one infected dead that walked into the water, a hundred crossed the bridge. They followed I-95 and picked up speed when the leaders of the horde heard the sound of the dead marching down I-26. The two hordes merged about fifty miles from Charleston and became one family.

The horde grew in size and then dwindled again when smaller natural barriers caused logjams. As expected by those who knew about the horde, the dead became mired in the swamps on both sides of the interstate. The horde was so immense that it even acted as a barrier to the infected dead that were pushing from behind. As they became stuck in the mud and brackish shallow water, others walked across their backs, and then they took their turns to become stuck.

Eventually, the unthinking, uncaring forces of the infected filled in the swamps, and the thousands of dead in the back of the horde spread to the sides and walked over them onto the solid ground of the Lowcountry. The vanguard of the horde had outdistanced its slower members by staying on the centerline of the interstate. They had marched onward without slowing until they came to obstructions caused by long ago collisions of cars and trucks, but the sheer size of the undead horde caused them to push through the vehicles as if they were cardboard and paper. Even the concrete barriers that had been placed across the interstate in the early days of the infection were pushed aside as if they were nothing more than a nuisance.

At a rural overpass the advance scouts from a group of survivors near Charleston had traveled up the interstate to get as much information about the oncoming horde as they could. Unlike other overpasses where scouts had crouched behind concrete walls for too long, only to be encircled by the infected, this group of scouts was surprised to feel the road move under their feet. The wall of infected was so dense that it pushed against the concrete supports that were worn with age and vehicle damage. As it pushed, the concrete groaned along with the infected. It groaned and even screamed as metal bars were pulled free of their rusty holes. Metal began to twist and pull apart in protest as cracks appeared in the asphalt.

Of the twelve men in the scouting party, three escaped because the collapse of the overpass crushed the infected that would have killed them. A temporary setback for the horde would be too strong of a description for the survivors. As the road fell away under their feet, they surfed huge chunks of concrete as it slipped sideways, and then they ran for their lives. They ran through the infected that had moved ahead from the sides of the horde, overtaking and then leaving them behind. If they made it home, they collectively planned to tell their enclave of survivors on the other side of the Ravenel Bridge it was time to leave. Nowhere was safe against this many of the infected.

After more than five years since the beginning of the infection, there were very few people alive who had not seen a horde, but this time there were very few people left to talk about this horde after it had passed through. In the narrow strip of land that sits between Lake Marion and Lake Moultrie, no one was left to describe what they had seen. Most of the people who still lived along the canal connecting the two lakes had run across the bridge on Highway 45 and didn't look back. Even those who had planned to blow up the bridge were too disorganized to get it done before the infected arrived. When they saw the shambling mass of infected all along the opposite banks of the canal, they knew there were too many to stop. All they could do was run. Thousands more of the infected fell into the canal and were carried by the current toward Lake Moultrie, but it was once again only a fraction of the number that crossed successfully. The Pee Dee horde, as it was called by those who saw it and carried the word to others, took advantage of a dry season and used the stretches of solid ground between country roads to cross large distances in less time. As they moved, they converged with the horde on I-26, and the numbers swelled again.

The last natural barrier protecting the Lowcountry and Charleston were the dense wetlands of the Francis Marion Forest. During the Revolutionary War, it was the territory that had given the famed military officer his nickname as the Swamp Fox. Over two centuries later, it was still unforgiving land and water that was proving to be the same trap for invaders. This time the invaders were an army that dwarfed the British forces that eventually forced the Continental Army to retreat from South Carolina, but history was repeating itself as the last survivors fled before the unrelenting infected dead. The countryside to the west of the Cooper River was swarmed as Moncks Corner became more populated than ever in its history. Soon they would be winding their way through Goose Creek and joining with the infected army as it engulfed Summerville.

The infected were forced to separate where the interstate was divided by safety barriers, but the deafening sound was amplified until it could be heard in all directions. Swarms going in the same direction heard the other swarms, and despite being apart from the main horde, they acted as if they were together. All roads leading to Charleston were filled to capacity.

******

It was strategy time at Fort Sumter. Regular meetings were being called by either the Chief or Captain Miller. Not since the first day of the infection had any of them seen so much activity out on the roads and even in the sky. Several small planes came and went from Patriots Point. When they took off, they always left to the north, as if they were avoiding the air space near Fort Sumter. When they returned, they did the same thing, not that it wasn't expected by anyone in the island shelter.

The helicopters at Fort Sumter were kept ready for rapid response if there was ever a threat from Patriots Point. The Army mechanics even did some retrofit work to install heavier machine guns on each door. They were Navy helicopters best suited for transport or rescue, but that didn't stop them from being converted into gunships. They were still hopefully just a deterrent against attack from their neighbors at Patriots Point, and the Army hoped they wouldn't be needed for more than that. Captain Miller and the Chief had both maintained the belief that living people could be united in their common cause, and that was survival against an enemy that they knew would never relent. They could only be destroyed.

The increased strategy sessions were the result of their own long range reconnaissance toward Columbia. The helicopters had made regular flights toward the state capitol. It was only a little more than one hundred miles, but every day saw the helicopters return after less time because the horde had progressively drawn closer. They also never returned with encouraging news. The horde was so big that when the photos from above were shown to the survivors back at Fort Sumter, everyone had to sit down, and silence fell over the crowded room. Almost the entire population of Fort Sumter was present, and we could have heard a pin drop.

Captain Miller couldn't have been more somber when he spoke, and the lump in his throat betrayed a small loss of composure.

"Comments?"

One of his Lieutenants was the first to speak, and her words were a reflection of what everyone else was thinking.

"There's no way they can get across the harbor to us......is there?"

She searched the faces of everyone in the room, but all she saw was what must have been written on her own face.

Captain Miller said, "No, not a chance, Lt. Harrelson, and if you're wondering if they can come in the back door, even a horde that size is going to be fragmented once it reaches the city. Charleston is a peninsular city, and much like Florida you don't have to go far in three directions to reach water."

The Chief accented the point made by Captain Miller by standing and walking over to a big map of Charleston on the wall of the conference room. He reached up and put his finger on a spot someone had already circled in red.

"This is the T. Allen Legare Bridge, also known as the Ashley River Bridge. It's actually two bridges next to each other, as most of you know. We're going to change the face of the map by opening both of them. Just to be sure, we're going to open the bridge to James Island, and the bridge over the Stono River onto John's Island."

Captain Miller joined the Chief at the map and took over.

"There were some objections, but we've come to the conclusion that stopping this horde could turn the tide on the infected. We can't even estimate how many infected are moving this way, but I think there were less people at Woodstock, and that was a half million."

"Why do I get the feeling you're about to stun us into silence again?" asked Kathy.

Kathy had been a rookie police officer in the days before the infected dead. She wasn't a seasoned officer yet, but her supervisor had written on an evaluation that her cool, level headed behavior made her appear to be more experienced than she was. She was also the best looking police officer any of us had ever known. Her full blonde hair made her stand out in the crowd.

"You know me too well," said Captain Miller. "We're going to blow up the fixed spans over the Ashley River where West Ashley connects to North Charleston and the bridge on I-526, the Mark Clark Expressway."

He had been right. The room was silent again, and I saw that Kathy had her mouth hanging open.

I leaned back in my chair and took in the faces around me. I had known most of them for years now, but the faces I sought in the crowded room were the original Mud Island family. Some had been with us almost from the beginning, and some had joined us later, but the Mud Island group was a tight knit bunch.

I had a laptop open and was chronicling the events that would, as the Chief said, change the map of Charleston. It would no longer be connected to most of the surrounding area. Water would define where people went, and it would certainly decide where the infected went. The heading of my notes said, "The Journal of Ed Jackson, Mud Island Survivor." It was a bit dramatic, but then again, my wife was always saying I was too dramatic.

My eyes found Jean where she sat with our son Josh and some of the children born at Fort Sumter in the last five years. She was still just as cute as the first day I met her, but like the rest of us, she was formidable with a machete when we went into the field. Jean wasn't smiling, but I couldn't see anyone in the room who was.

Tom was sitting next to Kathy, and ever since we had gotten back from New Orleans, it was no surprise that Molly was sitting with them. I didn't think Tom would ever get over almost losing Molly when she ran away. It was bad enough that her boyfriend, Sam, had died. Tom would have been destroyed if she had been killed too. Tom was a former baseball player. He was tall and muscular, and his jet black hair was a contrast to Kathy, but they made a perfect couple.

Speaking of perfect couples, Hampton and Colleen were sitting with Cassandra and Sim. Across from them were Olivia and Chase. No matter where I turned in the room, I saw perfect couples I would never have met if not for the end of the world.

Cassandra saw me watching them and waved. Then she winced a bit. She was still healing up from being shot by the madman who had killed Sam. I allowed myself a small amount of satisfaction in knowing that the Chief had disposed of him in the Gulf of Mexico.

The Chief's voice pulled my attention back to the front of the room.

"When Charleston was established as a settlement, the people chose a site further up the Ashley River than the present day location of the city, but it was the need for bridges that kept it from expanding outward. There are plenty of them now, and destroying them will be turning back the calendar. If we could just open them all, that would be enough, but the fixed spans have to go."

"What about the Don Holt Bridge on I-526?" asked Hampton.

Hampton was from Georgetown and had been living only a few miles south of my shelter on Mud Island. We met him on the road as we were trying to get back to the shelter from one of our less successful trips to Charleston. We had taken a bullet in our plane and were lucky to meet him and his friends. One of his useful talents was his memory for every road or waterway in South Carolina, and he also had some experience with blowing up bridges.

"I think you know we would blow that bridge up if we could," said the Chief. "As a matter of fact we planned to ask you if it was possible, but there's another problem. The people from Patriots Point have been using it. Their patrols have been keeping it clear of the infected by making routine sweeps."

Hampton nodded his understanding of the answer.

"That would prevent us from planting enough high explosive charges to bring it down. It's a solid bridge, so it would take a lot. Any chance we could use our heavy duty GROM or GROM/B weapons?"

Most of the people in the room knew those were weapons we had liberated from the Air Force Base, and the fact that we had them was something that had kept the people at Patriots Point from being too threatening toward us.

"How much of the horde will detour over that bridge?" asked Hampton. "The infected population along the coast was severely decreased when we cut off Georgetown from the Lowcountry."

One of the helicopter pilots stood up and raised his hand to speak next. Even after over five years from the time they broke away from the remaining military forces at sea, Captain Miller's men showed the discipline to be respectful.

"For those of you who don't know me, I'm Lt. Harper."

He blushed a bit when everyone laughed. There were a few good natured cat calls at Harper because he introduced himself. There were about three hundred and fifty people in Fort Sumter, and everyone knew everyone else by name.

"Anyway, we've been flying over the Georgetown area getting an idea of the infected population. We've seen them go in the water upriver and then wash up on the other side and start walking. There were also a few isolated pockets of people who somehow survived but then were overrun. We tried to reach a group of about twenty, but they were carrying wounded, so we had to back away."

Hampton asked, "So, your assessment is that there's still a sizable population of the infected between Georgetown and Mt. Pleasant?"

"Yes, Sir, and growing. I think a lot of migrating survivors are getting trapped in that area. They got flushed out by the big horde, and then when they holed up in the area south of where the bridges were blown up by your people they got caught."

Even after five years, there were still survivors being flushed out of places that were safe for a while, but Titus Rush, the man who had left me with the Mud Island shelter, had said safe places were like oysters. Sooner or later someone figured out how to pry them open.

The Chief got our attention and drew the conversation back to the main topic.

"We've covered why we have to blow up the bridges, and why we can't blow up some. It's time to move on to when. We have good intelligence, thanks to our pilots."

He gestured toward Lt. Harper, and there was some polite applause. He nodded appreciatively at the crowd.

The Chief continued, "What we know is that a horde has formed for whatever reason, and it's moving this way. We have the safest place in Charleston to be, and no matter how we break it down, we don't see a way for this horde to reach us. The only threat we see is that the sheer numbers will make some of them wash up on the mudflats around Fort Sumter. To keep them from getting behind us, we're going to take out and open some bridges. Any questions?"

One hand went up in the middle of the crowd.

"Why don't you call them zombies, Chief?"

Captain Miller tried to hide his smile by yelling, "Dismissed."

The soldier who asked the question managed to lose himself in the mass exodus.

"Did you put him up to that, Jim?"

The Chief was staring down Captain Miller, but even he was grinning.

Captain Miller avoided answering by calling over the squad leaders who were going to fly out to the bridges. There would be a group briefing followed by a break-out session for each group. Everything had to be planned and then picked apart, especially since we didn't know if the people at Patriots Point would try to stop us. The soldiers going along were well trained and could deal with the infected, but we didn't know the Patriots Point people well enough to know if they were trained at all. Someone over there had to be experienced with combat, judging by how quickly they had set up a safe zone.

I caught the Chief's attention as he was working his way toward Iris Mason. She had missed part of the meeting because she and Bus, our best doctor, had been wrapped up with some information that had been brought back by one of the patrols. A helicopter had dropped the patrol off on a long distance reconnaissance near Atlanta, and they had managed to reach the Centers for Disease Control. No one could stop the rumors from circulating throughout the shelter that they had been on the right track toward finding a cure. The men had come back with several computer hard drives, and the Army doctors couldn't hide their excitement. Captain Miller had dished out some reprimands for loose talk, but even he understood. He just expected discipline.

I had to practically shout over the crowd that was filing out.

"Chief, I have a suggestion. I'd like to arrange the evacuation of nonessential personnel and children to Mud Island until this is over. The horde isn't moving that way, and as far as we know the Patriots Point people don't know about that shelter."

The Chief had an expression on his face that he couldn't hide. I had gotten to know him well enough to know I had struck a nerve about something.

"As far as we know," he said. "It's hard to miss from a plane

46

because of everything we have parked at the dock, and their Cessna's have been coming in from that direction. Jim speculated to me just this morning that he thinks they've been keeping tabs on Mud Island."

That wasn't what I wanted to hear. I would feel better with Josh and Molly somewhere else when the horde arrived.

"Maybe we could send a few people to Guntersville," I added. The reports we had from the shelter in Guntersville, Alabama were that the settlement above the shelter had been operating well with a little support from the Army. They hadn't lost anyone to the infection for three years at least.

"Not a bad idea, now that you mention it. We can kill two birds with one stone. Bus and the Army doctors want to make a quick stop at the CDC to be sure nothing was missed. We can take the kids to Guntersville and then hit Atlanta on the return trip."

I was relieved to hear him agree, and I knew Jean would be too. Even though it was tough to be away from Josh, knowing he was safe inside a mountain five hundred miles from Charleston was a relief.

"If it's okay with you, I'll get it arranged," I said. "Thanks, Chief."

We had named our son after the Chief, so he was the last person who needed to be thanked, but he gave me an understanding smile anyway.

******

Bus left for Guntersville with the children in his trusty de Havilland Beaver. Radio contact was spotty at best, so we might not know for sure that they had reached his shelter safely, but the plane was sturdy, and they were going to an area that was surrounded by deep lakes. The survivors in Guntersville would be sure they were well protected, and it was still better than having them here with so much happening.

All four helicopters left at the same time, and even though we were always concerned about what Patriots Point would do while our defenses at Fort Sumter were depleted, we didn't have time on our side, so we didn't have the luxury of keeping helicopters at home. We had to get the bridges blown or open before the horde got too close. As a matter of fact, they were too close for comfort already. The helicopter that was sent to blow up the bridge over the Mark Clark Expressway reported back that the leading edge of the horde was only about six miles from that exit on I-26. The Chief had one of his usual good ideas when he got the news.

When the crew got the call from the Chief to set the charges but wait to blow up the bridge, they were surprised, but they knew he always had something in mind. Some of them had been there when he had used the Sikorsky like a giant weed-whacker on the infected at the airport. He was quick to explain, and they were relieved that his idea wasn't quite that crazy.

The Chief told them to wait until the horde was entering the interchange from I-26 onto I-526 and then blow the high explosives. Even though there was some distance between there and the bridge, there was a chance that some of the horde would break away from the main group to follow the sound of the explosion. The crew of the helicopter liked the idea enough to ask if they could stay behind to see if it worked. They were given the go ahead as long as they had the fuel and could stay out of harms way.

The other crews weren't having any real problems because they only had to deal with small groups of the infected that were drawn to the sound of their rotors. Even though there were plenty of them, the infected had a long walk up the bridges. At the two drawbridges the mechanics worked quickly to set up power lines to the controls, and within minutes they were raising the bridges. A few of the infected had reached the spot where the Folly Road bridge met the asphalt. Two went up with the bridge and then fell with predictable results onto the pavement after the bridge had reached its maximum height. The rest that reached the span that had lifted into the air before they arrived just walked right over the edge.

The helicopter that was sent to demolish the West Ashley bridge had the hardest job. Even though they could land in the middle of the bridge, it would take a lot of explosive charges to bring down the fixed span. They were carrying two squads of men so they could cover both sides of the bridge for the infected that were sure to make the long walk up to the middle. The bridge was so elevated over the water that it would take them a long time to make that walk, but there wasn't a good reason to make the demolitions experts rush the job. It would be bad news if the bridge blew up but didn't become impassable.

The Navy VH92A helicopter wasn't the fastest or most agile craft for this type of mission, but it had plenty of room for troops and a high reliability track record. The pilot sat the aircraft down quickly to give the men more time to complete their mission, and instead of lifting off, he stayed on the bridge with the rotors turning on idle. The noise was guaranteed to draw the attention of infected dead on both sides of the bridge, but the soldiers were happy to see the nearest of them was at least thirty minutes away. There was no need to waste ammunition at that distance, but the soldiers would have been glad to practice their sharpshooting skills. They decided to take up their positions closer to the infected, eliminate them, and then withdraw to higher ground as the number of infected increased, but only if they had to.

They had just finished placing their charges when the two squads began to open fire. Sizable groups of infected gathered on both sides of the bridge, and the soldiers concentrated their fire on the closest of them. They were surprised and not at all disappointed when the radio call came out to both squads to withdraw to the waiting helicopter and be prepared for immediate liftoff. As they boarded the craft they were told they had new orders to rendezvous with the VH92A that was sent to the Mark Clark Expressway. They didn't know what was expected of them yet, but they were told to come in hot.

The squad Sergeant asked for clarification and was simply told they would know what to do. When he was told not to waste time blowing up the bridge, that they could come back later to finish the job, he had a better idea of what it meant to go in hot.

The flight was only four minutes from liftoff when they could see the scene at I-526. The other VH92A was in the grass in the middle of the interchange. Concrete lanes snaked away in all directions, but they didn't block the incredible view up I-26 toward Aviation Avenue. The pilot hovered for just a moment as the copilot snapped pictures on a digital camera, but they hurried to get on the ground. For some reason that they couldn't yet understand, the squads from the helicopter on the ground had deployed in a straight line and were walking toward the solid wall of infected dead. As they walked, they were carefully selecting targets and firing. Twenty men and women were laying down a withering assault at targets that didn't try to dodge the bullets, so they were making an impressive dent in the wall.

As they landed the doors flew open before they were on the ground, and they were unloading to support the other squads. They were surprised to be delayed at all, but they stopped when they were met by the pilot of the idling helicopter. It was Lt. Harrelson, and she shouted above the sound of the rotors to identify three friendlies who were between them and the horde.

"Did she say friendlies?" yelled one of the Sergeants.

The other squad leader held up three fingers, and they passed the word to their squads as they ran to join the others. When they arrived at the shoulders of the first two squads, they scanned the swaying bodies of the infected dead in the distance, and they were amazed to see three men running as hard as they could. The men were making a final sprint after having run a marathon to stay ahead of the horde, and it was fair to say they were running out of gas.

******

After the overpass had collapsed under their feet, they had zigzagged through the stumbling infected dead that had no idea there were three warmed blooded, living people in their midst. The men sprinted when they were in the clear and stopped to catch their breath only when they were far enough ahead, but they could never run far enough or fast enough to get away from the sound of the horde. They had given up on running with their rifles after the first ten miles. All they were was extra weight, and it was becoming clear that they would never outdistance the infected. It took them hours to realize that the reason they couldn't gain any ground was simple. They weren't being chased by the same infected anymore. As they ran, the dead emerged from the trees, the side roads, and the exits, constantly keeping the distance between the men and the front of the horde where it had been the entire time.

When they stopped to rest, one of them told the other two if they stopped for too long, they wouldn't have to worry about the horde catching up with them. They would have to worry about the infected in front of them. They dropped all of their gear except what was left of their water, and they ran again, trying to keep a steady pace. Several times they saw infected ahead of them. When they did, they ran as quietly as possible and got as close to the opposite side of the interstate as they could. It was almost a fatal choice twice when they ran straight toward the places where new infected dead were coming out of the woods onto the interstate. Also, running across the median instead of straight ahead was the same thing as adding distance to their marathon run.

It seemed like they had been running forever when they reached the crest of the interstate just past Remount Road. They knew that over the crest ahead was the big interchange with I-526, and even though they still had to run a long way to reach the Don Holt Bridge, they were in friendly territory and had a good chance of running into one of their patrols. When they saw the helicopter idling in the grass, their first reaction was that they were saved. Then they weren't so sure. They saw soldiers spreading out on either side of the aircraft, and they had their weapons aimed in their direction. It wasn't until they opened fire and the bullets hit the wall of infected behind them that the three men were sure they weren't the targets.

5

USAMRIID

1969

Capitol Hill was a place where deals were made. Those who couldn't get rich got elected to Congress, and those who were rich courted politicians for the passage of pet bills that would make them richer. It was no secret to anyone, and the key to getting what you wanted from your investment was finding someone who needed campaign funds and had a senior position on one of the powerful committees. The problem was that there were so many powerful committees. If you couldn't line the pockets of someone on more than one committee, you might not get the return for your investment you expected.

Then there was the Cold War to deal with. There was so much paranoia in the population that people were passing up on the swimming pool for the kids in order to build fallout shelters for the whole family. If the bombs fell and radiation carpeted the suburbs, the way to keep up with the Joneses was to have a shelter big enough for the grandparents.

Politicians had families too. It was no small wonder that they worked together to devise a plan for shelters that would protect them from the hardships of survival after a nuclear war. No single goal was more effective at bringing them together across party lines, and it wasn't long before the President learned about it.

He had always expected to be kept safe if someone pressed the buttons that would bring the human race close to extinction, but when he found out the extent to which the government was willing to go, he was quick to sign off on bills that made certain committees even more powerful than before. The more power they had, the easier it was to hide the purchases made by donors who wanted in on that life insurance policy being sold by the government. That special policy that included being safely tucked away during and after a nuclear war.

It started out that way, and it was supposed to be a secret, but for every person that knew a secret in Washington DC, there was someone who's job was to expose secrets, and along the way to have some secrets of their own. The intelligence community in the nation's capitol was the best in the world at learning the secrets of other countries, but they never forgot the value of the secrets being kept in their own back yard. They learned about the shelter program right from the start, and the jealousy behind closed doors was the source of an invisible wall that went up between Congress and the CIA. To complicate matters even more, as administrations came and went, members of the intelligence communities became politicians so they could keep their secrets and insurance policies. If politicians and their rich friends could be protected in shelters, the intelligence community expected the same benefits.

The government came out of the Cold War with secrets but no obvious need for shelters that would protect them from a nuclear apocalypse. There were rumors that the politicians were still building shelters and selling seats, but the intelligence community wasn't interested in outsourcing the shelters to survivalists. Instead, they channeled their funds into the development of a plan to support their own efforts if there ever was an apocalypse, no matter what type apocalypse it was.

One of their most ambitious plans was to join forces with the people who would be on the front lines in a different kind of war. Every threat assessment pointed straight to biological warfare, and the only way to survive a biological apocalypse would be with the help of the Centers for Disease Control and the United States Army Medical Research Institute of Infectious Diseases, better known as USAMRIID.

Present Day
* * *

Six Years After the Decline

The Chief showed his wealth of knowledge as we watched the blue and white single engine plane descend toward Patriots Point. The pilot approached his runway not much higher than the trees, and we wouldn't have spotted it if we hadn't already been watching Patriots Point. We also couldn't hear him above the storm that was rolling in from the Atlantic. It wasn't going to be a big one, but the dark sky and the wind hid the plane's approach well.

"It's a Quest Kodiak," said the Chief. He remembered everything anyone ever told him, and I didn't doubt Bus had told him about that particular plane. Both of them were pilots, but Bus was a walking encyclopedia on single engine planes.

He had his elbows resting on the brick wall of the old ramparts to keep steady. I was only two feet away on the other side of him.

"Perfect plane for short take off and landing. For a moment I thought it was a Cessna 208 Grand Caravan."

I was propped so much like the Chief that I could have been his shadow. Both of us were so intent on the plane that we had forgotten Tom was there.

"Good thing it wasn't. Those can be modified to shoot Hellfire missiles," said the Chief.

"Quest made that thing convertible into a float plane. Do they have a boathouse over there that can lift it for refit then lower it into the water?" I asked.

The Chief raised an eyebrow in my direction. I could tell he was impressed that I had been doing some homework.

"I imagine so. They covered the facilities at the marina before we got a good picture of that part of the complex."

The plane disappeared into an area we knew was part of the golf course, and we stood up from the wall where we had been leaning. It was funny to see us the same height when we were using the binoculars and then so different when we stood up. The Chief towered over me, but then again, he towered over all of us except Tom.

"It's been over four months since we sent Randal over there," Tom said.

It was more of an observation than anything. I was thinking about how Randal had accepted the job as if it was no big deal. We didn't know if we were sending him to his death or if the people would see it as a golden opportunity for some useful information about us, but it was likely to be both.

The Chief had the faintest frown lines appear on his forehead when he thought about Randal. When I had asked him once if he was going to do the same thing to Randal that he had done to Stokes, he had gotten the same frown. I didn't press him for an answer, but Kathy told me later the Chief thought it would be fitting to take Randal to the cemetery and bury him. We all knew what the Chief had done to Stokes, but that was the end result of a fair fight, and the Chief had been angry. When he was calm he wasn't likely to actually bury someone alive, although I wasn't quite so sure about Randal because he had been the one who helped Stokes bury Molly and Sam. Stokes buried Iris on his own, and that debt was settled.

The Chief let out a deep breath and said, "I don't think things worked out so well for Randal over there. That's why we didn't send someone over there who we would have worried about. If they had set fire to him and shoved his boat back into the harbor we wouldn't have tried to put out the fire. At least we know we can't send someone else."

I was about to say more, but I caught the signal Tom gave me to drop it. If the Chief had something bothering him, Tom was likely to pick up on it and let the rest of us know. The Chief told his most intimate thoughts to Iris, but he talked with Tom about things that were eating at him. Tom had warned us that the Chief was worried about the arrival of the horde. He wasn't worried that the horde could reach Fort Sumter. He was worried about what the people at Patriots Point were going to do if the horde overran them.

Despite Tom's silent warning for me to drop the subject of sending someone else over to Patriots Point, there was one more thing that needed to be discussed. I saw Tom cringe, but I asked the Chief anyway.

"Any concerns about that couple who managed to survive on Mt. Pleasant without getting killed by the infected or captured by the people at Patriots Point?"

The Chief wasn't always easy to read, especially if he was about to pull a practical joke on someone. I was one of his favorite targets because I was a lousy poker player, but this time he didn't scowl or smile. He really did have some concerns.

"It's worth keeping an eye on them. I'm not saying at this time, but I find it hard to believe anyone survived on Mt. Pleasant without help. For the time being I'm going to focus on the horde, but keep an eye on them. If they're spies we should treat them well and see if we can turn them."

"You mean we find a way to let them go back to Patriots Point as spies for us?" asked Tom.

"Something like that," answered the Chief, "but think about it for a second. What would they report back that Patriots Point doesn't already know? It would be like a Russian spy reporting back to the KGB that America was powerful. As a matter of fact, that's what we want them to know."

I could tell the Chief had been giving it some thought, so I didn't push him with more questions about it. We quietly went back to our own thoughts.

The Ravenel Bridge had been barricaded so well that there was no way the horde would get through by crossing the bridge from Charleston. His experience with the current in the harbor made him believe the horde wouldn't be able to flood the harbor with so many of the infected that they would make it to the Mt. Pleasant side in the water. Whatever it was that was eating at the Chief, it wasn't something he could explain, but there was something that made him think the infected dead would force the people at Patriots Point out of their fortified corner of land, and they would come to Fort Sumter, the one place the horde couldn't go. It was more of my own thinking that I had borrowed from my uncle. Patriots Point was an oyster waiting for the right chain of events that would lead to it being opened, but my thinking didn't include one oyster attacking another.

We climbed down from the wall and worked our way across Fort Sumter to the side facing the tidal plain between us and Morris Island. It was high tide, and the moon was nearly full, so the mudflats were completely under water. It was only a couple of feet deep, but if the horde managed to get onto James Island behind Fort Sumter, there would be a lot of infected stuck in the mud. The timing of the full moon was working in our favor.

"Why are you so worried, Chief? We've got the best place to be, and even if the people at Patriots Point decide to attack, all we have to do is shut the doors. Captain Miller even had his people reinforce the emergency entrances. As of today after we go back inside, the only way into or out of the shelter will be the back door over on Morris Island, and you know what it would take to open that door."

"I don't know. I guess it's just an old habit of mine to worry about everything."

As if the Chief needed evidence to make his point, we heard the high pitched turboprop of the Quest Kodiak as it sped toward us. This time it flew over the fort only a few feet above the walls. The only reaction we could have was to hit the deck. The guards had been instructed not to fire upon the planes from Patriots Point unless the planes shot first, but this was the closest they had ever come.

The plane was by us so fast that the Chief and I were scrambling to get our binoculars trained on it.

I said, "No markings at all. Not even a number."

"That was a message," said the Chief, "but I have no idea what they were saying."

We all knew it had something to do with the horde, but we would need more direct actions to know what they were trying to tell us.

I couldn't help making a guess, though.

"I think they know where our helicopters are right now, and they haven't seen the Cormorant in months so they took a chance to get a closer look."

"I think you're right," the Chief said without lowering his binoculars, "and he just changed course toward Folly Beach. That means he's spotted where we parked the Sikorsky when it got back from opening drawbridges."

When we decided to seal the hidden entrances to the shelter, it meant we would have to use the back door to reach the helicopters. It was fairly safe from the infected because the water between Folly Beach and Morris Island was deep, and the current was too strong for most swimmers. Not to mention the sharks and crabs that sat around waiting for their next big meal. A few well placed guard posts were spread around the island, and aside from the sand fleas, it was a good plan. It wasn't something I would say in the presence of the soldiers who had to stand guard there because sand fleas were just plain mean.

We watched the Kodiak veer south and dip lower, so it was obvious that the pilot figured out that we had established a new landing area near the lighthouse at the tip of Morris Island. It had been inevitable that the move would be discovered, but we had hoped it wouldn't be before the horde arrived. Now that they knew, it was a possibility that they would attack that landing area if the infected breached their defenses.

"It was always our weakest point," said Tom. "We can't have it both ways. We could try to protect the helicopters at the fort, but we would run the risk that they would penetrate the shelter through the hidden emergency exits. By sealing the exits we can protect the fort better, and the big door at the back entrance is impenetrable. I hope we don't lose the helicopters, but better to lose them than the shelter."

******

Across the Harbor from Fort Sumter

Marshall Sayer was in the worst mood he could remember since the beginning of the disease that had brought the world to its knees. It was officially known to his organization as CEL Day, or Contagion: Extinction Level Day. Since that day he had a firm grip on the throat of every problem to cross his desk, and he couldn't understand why he lacked so much information on this particular day. Information was what made governments rise and fall, so why were his people having so much problem giving him answers? That was the question he kept asking himself.

Thirty years in the government had caused his hair to thin, but it hadn't taken a toll on his health the way it seemed to on politicians. Everywhere he looked, he saw politicians getting fat and lazy while the people of the health and research community, or Secret Society as he had named them, stayed fit and ready. He had risen quickly through the ranks of the US Army Medical Research Institute of Infectious Diseases, or USAMRIID, by always keeping his eyes on the goal, and that was to be the best at his job. He was ruthless and mean by nature, but he calculated when it was time to be either way, and when it was time to put on the politician's face. He didn't reach higher rank by climbing over the backs of the people ahead of him, he moved them out of his way. He was good at his job, and despite losing his blonde hair, he had a youthful, smooth face.

Today he wasn't feeling very likable because no one knew what had happened to the patrols. There were seven patrols in the field, and none of them had checked in. He had even sent one of his planes to see what was happening, but other than spotting the Fort Sumter executive helicopter close to the lighthouse, there wasn't anything worthwhile to report. They got some new pictures of the horde, but that wasn't exactly news.

Ted Atwater opened the stateroom door as he knocked on it. He was the only person who Marshall trusted enough to let him do that, and he didn't abuse the privilege. It had to finally be something important enough for him to do it now.

The stateroom had been the captain's quarters on the Yorktown. It had been restored and nicely furnished when the World War II aircraft carrier was a tourist attraction at Patriots Point. It was also highly defensible from attack. For one thing, they had lived up to their reputation of being secretive, and as far as he knew, no one knew that the former Director of USAMRIID was the person behind the operation of the base at Patriots Point. He had control of a large swath of land from the Arthur Ravenel Bridge all the way to the State Ports Authority on the Wando River. He had supplies, men, trucks, weapons, and almost anything else he wanted or needed. That's why he found it so hard to believe that the Senator had helicopters. Every time he saw one take off from Fort Sumter he would ask Ted why the Senator had helicopters and he didn't. It didn't make him feel better when Ted told him the Navy VH92A's had been delivered to the Charleston Air Force Base by CIA operatives working for him and had been originally intended to be delivered to Patriots Point. Somehow the Senator had stolen them away from him.

Marshall constantly told Ted he would trade almost any intelligence to find out how that old Senator Harold J. Thornton III had gotten to the helicopters first. All he could figure was that he had brought some good people with him when he was evacuated from Washington DC on CEL Day One. Maybe it was because he was in the Presidential line of succession, and he had been at the White House when they evacuated. Marshall didn't plan to let Senator Thornton take over the Oval Office, so he could have his helicopters for all he cared.

"What have you got for me, Ted? Make it good, because right now I don't feel like the Director of USAMRIID. If I was, I would know a lot more than I do."

Ted had been his assistant for five years before CEL Day, and had been the one who suggested Patriots Point to him when they moved their operations out of DC. He had handled all of the logistics, and Marshall didn't ask him how he did it. They were so quiet when they took over their new home that they didn't even draw the attention of the military. Of course there were some issues with the locals.

On CEL Day One it had been total chaos everywhere, so it was no surprise that the Yorktown had been used by the locals as a place to hide. Almost two hundred men, women, and children had hidden in the ships at the Maritime Museum, so USAMRIID had to engineer a peaceful takeover. Ted had not only kept it peaceful, he had made it seem like the federal government had rescued the unprepared survivors. The only issue that arose was what to do with people who had been bitten, and Ted had devised an ingenious plan for them. He had a hospital set up in the destroyer that was parked next to the Yorktown, and bite victims were taken there. Families were not allowed to stay with the victims, but by separating them, there was less conflict when the victims died.

The entire operation was coordinated by Ted because he had placed operatives in the State Ports Authority in advance. The international health community had received a warning of some form of disaster from foreign assets and set plans in motion before it was too late. Trucks were dispatched from the ports into a designated area where they were used to set up the defensive perimeter around Patriots Point, but they weren't empty. Not only were they used to close off the area, they carried weapons and supplies that were enough to get them all through the early days of the infection. Once they were in place they went quiet, and they stayed that way until they could expand without resistance from the military or survival groups like the ones that were constantly showing up at Fort Sumter. The survivors who had been at the Yorktown on the day the infection began were put to work. If they wanted to stay and they wanted to eat, they didn't complain.

Ted had the smile on his face that he got when he had good news.

"That redneck from Fort Sumter finally gave us something useful."

Ted paused for effect. If he had a fault that Marshall didn't like it was his tendency to stretch out the drama. He tried unsuccessfully to keep the impatience out of his voice.

"Don't make me ask for it."

"The Senator isn't in charge over at Fort Sumter, or at least it appears he's not."

Marshall almost came out of his chair, but he stopped himself in time. Ted was too good at his job to yell at him over something so trivial.

"How is that useful to us, Ted? So we've been wrong about who's running things over there. We know there are military and civilians working together. We know they have helicopters that belong to us, but I really don't care who's in charge."

Ted was always ready to bounce back if something made him look bad, so he also tended to keep something in reserve. Since his information didn't get Marshall excited the way he had expected, he didn't skip a beat.

"Some of the patrols are checking in. The big horde is still moving this way, but that's not a surprise. It's just good news that the patrols are alive."

"How many have checked in, and was there anything they learned that we didn't know?"

Ted knew Marshall wasn't going to be happy with the answers to both questions, so he avoided the subject by going back to what was happening at Fort Sumter.

"Most of them have made radio contact, and that's nothing new, but the redneck says he heard his guards talking about the food and what they were showing at the movie theater one night, so the shelter at Fort Sumter must be bigger than we ever expected."

It almost worked. For just a moment Marshall forgot the original question. He had a movie theater on the Yorktown, and the food wasn't bad, but before CEL Day it was common knowledge around DC that the shelters had been much more extravagant than the taxpayers would have appreciated.

"Ted, if you can't give me anything useful from our patrols the next time you come to my office I suggest you don't bother to come at all. Now go get me something, and while we're talking about your failures, have you heard anything from your people on the inside?"

Ted had almost made it back to the door, and he stopped without turning around to try to find an answer that wouldn't sound worse than the truth, which was indeed another failure. He hadn't heard a word from his spies, which wasn't necessarily bad news. It just wasn't good news.

"Forget I asked," shouted Marshall.

Ted knew when it was a good time to get out, so he did.

Marshall waited for a few minutes and then decided it was time to go down and see the redneck himself. He went out through the same door as Ted, but he immediately went down through the decks. The brig was down in the storage levels well away from the populated parts of the old aircraft carrier. It was also near the labs.

Each deck that Marshall passed through was more and more in need of restoration. The lower decks gave the appearance that they were as they had been when the ship was towed out of mothballs years ago, and there were no plans to make it suitable for tourists. That was just part of the disguise, though. When they had decided to set up a secret base inside the Yorktown, they had to make it appear to be for a different reason than research on highly infectious diseases, so they had FEMA stockpile their equipment and other supplies in the lower decks as if it was a relief center. If there was a hurricane and someone tried to access the crates of supplies, they could easily claim it was a government mixup of some sort.

Marshall reached the lowest habitable deck and crossed through a maze of passages until he came to a watertight door that gave the appearance that it hadn't been opened since World War II. When he pulled it open, the rusty corridor was bathed in brilliant white light. He stepped through the door into pristine labs that were filled with all of the modern equipment needed to do delicate research. It was almost silent despite the fact that there were at least thirty people working at their stations. They were all wearing starched white lab coats with the exception of two who were just about to enter the biohazard lab. They were dressed in state of the art protective suits that would allow them to work with a series of dangerous pathogens that USAMRIID had on site.

The researchers hardly even noticed Marshall Sayer as he passed through the labs, not because they didn't respect their boss, but because they had been trained to believe distractions led to careless handling of dangerous materials. If he found one of them to be more interested in him than their work, he would have them removed. Besides, Marshall didn't come down to see them in the first place. He was looking for the Russian scientist they had brought into their fold on CEL Day.

Anton Mikhailov had been visiting the American labs when the infection began because there had been reports of a new pathogen in Central America. The Americans had accused the Russians of introducing the pathogen into the river basins of Venezuela when they had boldly stationed troops in the country during political unrest. Ever since that time the US had been trying to pry them back out of the country. When the CDC had been called in to investigate a strange virus that spread quickly through the area, they were surprised to find the Russians were already there investigating the same thing.

The Russians uncharacteristically welcomed the intervention by the CDC and even USAMRIID. They claimed they were not responsible for the virus, but they were eager to find its source, especially since some of their researchers had already been exposed and quickly died from it. In their typical fashion they failed to mention that some of the infected workers had returned to Russia before becoming ill. The

Americans quietly closed the Russian labs in Venezuela and transported everything back to the main research facilities at Fort Detrick, Maryland. Unknown to anyone except themselves and select people at the CDC, they brought back everyone they knew of who had been exposed to the pathogen, even the ones that appeared to have died and then become reanimated.

Doctor Mikhailov didn't know what his fate would be after the Americans arrived because he had discovered there were secrets within USAMRIID that were being kept from the US government. He was surprised by the lack of oversight because he had seen how dangerous the pathogen was. He was even more surprised when Marshall Sayer, the USAMRIID Director, had informed him of secret bases operated by the research facility in populated areas. Mikhailov went along with Doctor Sayer because he had no choice, but his eyes had been opened to the fact that there were secrets in the American government similar to those found in his home country. It was fortunate for him that he did, because he was evacuated first when the infection raced around the world.

"Where is Mikhailov?" Sayer asked one of the lab techs who was only noticed when things went wrong. The man nervously pointed at the biohazard lab, and he realized he had just missed the Russian as he had entered the sealed chamber.

Sayer walked over to the observation window and saw that the Russian and an American were working with one of the infectious subjects they had brought aboard to study. They were removing tissue samples and body fluids to attempt to identify locations in the body where the infection was present. So far they only knew the same thing everyone else did. A bite was the primary means of transmission. They suspected that there were instances when the infection was spread through the food chain, but they couldn't explain why it was only in certain species. Crabs could pass along the infection, but they hadn't identified any fish that could, even though they fed on the bodies of the infected just as the crabs did.

Inside the biohazard chamber, Mikhailov went about his work as if he didn't know he was being watched, but he had seen the Director enter the labs. He had hoped he would get inside the highly restricted area before Sayer arrived, and he was satisfied that he was going inside just as Sayer walked into the labs. The man wouldn't expect him to come out soon, and a small smile appeared on his face when he saw Sayer leave only minutes later. Mikhailov believed the man was dangerous and that he would get them all killed with his obsession to control the infection.

6

Colony

Present Day
Six Years After the Decline

People found ways to survive if they had a few things going for them. The biggest thing was luck. No one doubted that close brushes with death were the new normal, and anyone alive could recount the many times they had almost died. After surviving close calls, the way to survive the next one was to take what you had learned from the near miss and put it to good use.

The last close call had driven the colony out of their previous sanctuary, and even though they knew it before, they knew they would have to find a way to be sure the infected couldn't reach their new home. They wanted to help the other groups search for the supply depot they thought was somewhere near Murrell's Inlet, but they had to postpone what they wanted in favor of what was more important.

The island Jed was searching for was originally connected to land. It had been an oxbow in the Cooper River south of the Pinopolis Lock, and over the years the river had eaten a straight line through the narrow strip of land until it broke through to the other side. There was a shabby old foot bridge that appeared ready to fall down under the weight of the next squirrel to cross it, but it was where Jed and Ben wanted to go. They had searched for this island before, but it didn't show up on any maps until satellite photos became available on the internet. They tried to find it just for fun in the days before the infection. Now they were searching for it to help their people survive. The beauty of this location was in the fact that the oxbow could only be entered by crossing the Cooper River first. It was shaped like a thumb pointing upward, and the infected would only find the old bridge if they decided to go north. The dead didn't seem like they were interested in going north anymore.

Jed went over the bridge first, and he could feel it swaying under his feet. He wondered what was holding the bridge up and his unspoken question was answered when he spotted the ropes that were wound through the boards. The bridge looked more shabby than it was. It was deceptively reinforced by the ropes, and the swaying just added to the deception. Jed made a mental note that they would need to rig the bridge to be able to fall if a horde tried to cross it. The river was about twelve feet below him, and the current was swift enough to keep the infected from climbing back onto land if they fell in. This island was just what they were hoping it would be. Ben followed Jed across, and as he caught up with his best friend, he pointed at the far end of the bridge.

"All we have to do is block that end. The infected would never know we're here. We could even have campfires and clay ovens cooking without them seeing us."

Jed nodded his agreement. Swift current, steep banks, thick trees, limited access, and way off the beaten path. The island had everything they needed if they could get enough supplies to it.

There were no real roads that had been cut through the forest, but the legend of the island was that it had been a hiding place used by survivalists. A trail about as wide as a sidewalk meandered through trees from the base of the bridge and came to a dead end in the middle of nowhere. More accurately, it came to a dead end in the middle of the island. When Jed and Ben stumbled onto the path and literally disappeared only a few feet from the view of the bridge, Ben asked Jed if he was thinking what he was. Jed had nodded.

"You still marking the trees? Can you find this place again?" asked Jed.

"You bet. We're not going back for the others yet, are we?"

Jed shook his head from side to side.

"We need to find out if this is the place we heard about."

Rumors had circulated through the coastal towns for years about a stash of supplies hidden by a local man who was preparing for the end of the world. Some of those rumors said he owned some land that included an island formed by an oxbow in the Pee Dee River, some said the Santee River, and some said it was on an island along the coast. There were even rumors that there were several such treasure troves of precious food, weapons, and medicine.

Jed took off down the path in the direction he knew would take him into the center of the oxbow. There was a big, looping turn in the river, and Jed felt like it was either the path used by someone to reach their favorite fishing hole, or it was something much more mysterious. Thirty yards later he knew it wasn't a fishing hole. It just came to an end. The trees were close on three sides, close enough for Jed to extend his arms outward and touch trees with his fingertips as he turned in a circle.

Ben laughed at his friend who was acting more like a kid than someone who was trying to survive for another day, but Jed had always been the thinker when they were together. He wasn't always right, but he always had a good reason for what he thought.

Jed was in his second turn when he saw what he was looking for.

"Deer stand."

About ten feet into the trees was a well disguised ladder that went up to a covered platform on a tall tree.

"What kind of hunter puts a deer stand in an oxbow?" asked Ben.

Jed pushed his way into the bushes toward the ladder as he answered.

"A hunter who isn't looking to shoot a deer. It's more like a watchtower."

Both of them knew what they were doing in the woods, and shooting a deer in an oxbow was a quick way to lose a deer in the water. If the deer didn't go down on the first shot, there were no clearings where the hunter could hope for a second shot, and the deer would hit deep water if it ran in three directions. In this case it was four sides, and the deer wouldn't use that rickety bridge. If it could somehow run out of the oxbow, it would have dense trees where it could hide.

Jed dropped his backpack and climbed quickly. He made a second discovery when he reached the top. The platform curled around the tree so he could get a clear view in all directions.

"Hey, Ben. Go through the trees to the river. I want to find out if I can still see you."

Ben disappeared into the trees, and Jed lost track of him

immediately. He rotated in his loft about twenty feet high and couldn't find him again. He could see the opposite bank of the river on all sides of the oxbow, but the trees were so close to the river that he couldn't see the banks on the island side.

"This would be an easy place to defend," said Jed out loud.

"What?"

Ben was standing below his tree.

"I said this would be an easy place to defend. We would only have to build traps and barricades along one side. The banks are too muddy and steep for the infected to climb out of the river. The water is deep, and the current is strong enough to carry them right around the oxbow island."

"If someone buried supplies here, it won't take long to find them," added Ben.

"How far did you go?" asked Jed.

"Straight through to the river. Didn't see nothing except an old gravestone."

It took everything Jed had not to laugh. He didn't want his friend to be embarrassed, but the odds of a gravestone marking an actual grave on an oxbow island this far from the beaten path were slim. He went through the trees where Ben had gone and walked right to it. The bushes were so thick that Jed could see the path that Ben had made.

The grave looked old. As a matter of fact, it was so old and eroded that he couldn't even tell where the dates had been. He ran his hand across the cold stone and didn't find any indentations that would give him a clue. He shook his head as if he was denying something.

"No, this gravestone is wrong, Ben. It's all wrong. There's no wind through here, no dust beating on it when the storms blow through. The rain can only drip down at it. I don't think anyone was ever buried here. I think this stone was put here just to make people think that it was a grave."

Ben wasn't too excited about digging up a grave, but he didn't stop Jed as he retrieved his camping shovel from his backpack. Jed eagerly pushed the tip into the black topsoil and very quickly had a tall mound next to the hole. He was rewarded by a scraping sound on the top of something flat, and he moved his shovel until he located the edge of a large sheet of metal roofing. He had to be careful not to cut his fingers on the sharp, rusty edge of the metal, and he was excited by the discovery.

"This isn't a grave," he said.

Ben wasn't feeling like he was disturbing the dead anymore and joined in at the edges, clearing away dirt all the way around.

"Too shallow to be a grave," he said, "and no roots growing across it."

With two of them attacking the hole together, two edges and then three were uncovered. They got shoulder to shoulder and slipped their hands under the edges at the same time. On three they lifted together, and the metal lid came free with no trouble. They found themselves staring at waterproof tarps arranged in rows, and they eagerly dragged the first bundle from the hole. They laid it next to the pile of dirt and found where it was sealed. When they opened it, they could hardly breathe.

"You ever shoot a rifle that looks like this?" asked Ben.

"I've never even seen one of these in real life," said Jed. "Just on TV. They're AR-15 rifles. I think they're supposed to be common or something. It should be easy to find ammunition for them if they are."

"You don't think there's any in that hole?"

"I hope so, but I won't get my hopes up just yet."

There were eight rifles in the bundle, each one individually wrapped in clear plastic. The plastic was also sealed so no moisture would get in.

"I'm sure we're going to get a lot of practice just shooting at the infected, so we won't need to really teach anyone how to shoot these," said Jed.

They moved to the ends of the next bundle and carried it free of its hiding place. It was also full of rifles, and it was a relief to know they were going to have enough of them to protect the colony.

Any concern they might have had about ammunition was dispelled by the next four bundles in a row. Whoever had buried this cache of weapons believed in keeping it simple. There was one type of rifle and one type of ammunition, and there was plenty of it. According to the labels on the tightly wrapped packages, there were thousands of rounds. The same was true for the Smith & Wesson 9 millimeter M&P handguns that were in the next four bundles.

Under the weapons and ammunition they found antibiotics, medical kits, pain killers, and an unbelievable supply of morphine. There were several people in the colony who had become skilled at battlefield medicine. One had served as a Corpsman in the Navy and had done three tours in the Middle East. They could probably count on her to teach them how to shoot the AR-15s as well.

Over the next two hours they opened bundles and did an inventory of the gear. Jed wrote everything down in a notebook they found in a briefcase along with other office supplies. He didn't know how much use he would get out of paperclips and rubber bands, but he felt a strange bit of nostalgia when he handled the items. There were military issue MREs, candy, cookstoves, Coleman lanterns, fuel, matches, lighters, flashlights, batteries, hatchets, tents, fishing equipment, flares and flare guns, water purifying kits, short range radios, salt, sugar, coffee, and most surprising of all, night vision goggles. Whoever had hidden this treasure planned on surviving a long time. Jed told Ben that he hoped their benefactor was alive and well somewhere. They kept doing their inventory even after it got dark enough to light a lantern so they could go back to the colony with a complete list.

When they finally finished, Jed had almost filled the notebook. He sat back and peeled the wrapper from a candy bar. He savored the first bite and seemed to be studying the treat as he chewed.

"Something wrong with it?" asked Ben.

"No. I was trying to remember if they tasted like this before. How could I have forgotten about chocolate?"

"You put it out of your mind."

When he finished enjoying the last bite, Jed reached for an AR-15 and unwrapped it. He loaded rounds into a magazine and inserted it into the rifle. He was pleased that it was all common sense, and he had no trouble loading one of the handguns. When he held it up to show Ben how easy it was, he saw that Ben had given in to temptation and was unwrapping his own candy bar.

Ben saw that Jed was watching him and grinned.

"I could smell yours while you were eating it."

The snap of a twig made them both freeze. Jed reached out and closed the fuel valve on the Coleman lantern that had bathed them in warm light as the sun had gone down. The temptation to keep it lit was too strong, and the darkness was so close in around them that whatever was out there would see them long before they could see it. Neither of them said a word. Until they knew what was out there in the dark, there was nothing that needed to be said.

The snap came again, Jed locked in on the position of the sound. He was straining his senses so much that he realized he could smell Ben's candy bar. Whatever it was that was moving, it was somewhere behind Ben. Jed remembered that the night vision goggles were about eighteen inches from his left foot. He allowed himself to bend at the waist and reach into the dark packages. He squeezed each of them one at a time until he felt the irregular shape he was searching for. The plastic around the goggles was soft and flexible, so there was no sound as he slowly unwrapped them and eased them toward his face. He thought he heard a faint whisper from Ben, just barely loud enough to be heard.

"Jed?" There was a tremble in his voice.

He wanted to tell Ben that he was going as fast as he could without making noise, but he sensed there was more motion behind his friend. Saying anything at all could be a death sentence for Ben.

The straps of the goggles went over his head and he adjusted them in front of his eyes. When he powered them on there was no sound, but the green light was almost bright enough to make him dizzy.

Every movie or TV show Jed had ever seen where someone used night vision goggles made it seem like it was the easiest thing in the world to do, but he was disoriented. No one had ever told him that he had to focus them to a specific distance and then get used to what he was seeing. They could give him plenty of advantage over someone who wasn't wearing them, but they took away a lot of his depth perception, and everything looked like it was stacked on top of things that were closer to him.

Jed's eyes were facing to the right of Ben, and he turned to sight in on his old friend so he could get his bearings. He saw Ben raise the candy bar to his mouth and silently take a big bite. It was like watching an old movie before high definition. Everything was flat. He also saw that Ben must have moved over slightly to lean his back against the stump of a tree. The tree seemed awfully short to be as wide as it was, and Jed felt like there was something wrong with what he was seeing.

Ben's arm lowered back to his lap, and it helped Jed to understand the depth a little better. He felt like he wanted to ask Ben something. When had he moved over to lean on the stump? Had there been a tree stump by the grave marker? He didn't remember seeing any. So what was Ben leaning against?

When Jed focused the goggles a bit more, everything took better shape, but without depth perception it was hard to tell Ben from the stump. Until the stump moved.

Ben felt the movement at the same moment that Jed saw it. He turned his head without turning his body and looked at the place just above his right shoulder. Jed saw Ben's head lean backward away from his own shoulder as if he was trying to focus his eyes on something that had just landed there. He had stopped chewing his candy bar, and his mouth was open like he was going to say something.

Jed didn't know for sure what was sitting on Ben's shoulder until it leaned toward Ben's face. It took shape when it was only inches away and its mouth opened wide. In the bright green light the black outline of the head and the gaping mouth converged with the clearer face of Ben, and his scream broke the silence.

Jed remembered later that in the split second between the scream and the sounds that came from the Smith & Wesson in his right hand that he hoped Ben had screamed in fear. He didn't think about the gun. It was just there. He raised the gun as if it was an extension of his arm, aimed, and pulled the trigger repeatedly. Everything in his vision disappeared. He didn't know what he had hit, but Ben was gone, and so was the tree stump.

The smell of the gun shots had replaced the sweet smell of chocolate, and Jed remembered just in time to flip the goggles off of his face before lighting the lantern again. The warm glow came back to their little place in the middle of the trees, and Jed saw Ben wasn't moving. There was something next to him, but from the angle where he sat, he still wasn't sure what it was. He stood very slowly and held his breath as the scene became clearer.

He didn't know how many shots he had fired, but his aim had been good enough to put several rounds through the right ear of the infected. It had landed on its left shoulder facing Ben. Its head was destroyed, but its mouth was still open with its teeth bared.

Jed stepped closer with his eyes fixed on Ben's unmoving body. He was praying that Ben had passed out or was just staying very still, paralyzed with fear. He knew how stupid it was to hope such a thing, but at the moment, hope was all he had. Another foot closer and Jed saw there was no hope. One of his shots had gone to the right and must have killed Ben instantly. His eyes were open, and he appeared to be looking straight into the face of the infected dead that was about to sink its teeth into him.

No one should have to die looking into the eyes of an infected, and even though he knew Ben was already dead, Jed reached for his eyelids to push them shut. It wasn't until Jed dropped to his knees that he was able to see the two curved rows of puncture marks in the center of his friend's face. The lower teeth had torn into Ben's upper lip and pulled it almost to his nose. The second row curved down across the bridge of Ben's nose onto each cheek. Jed knew that his one stray bullet had killed his friend, but if he hadn't shot him accidentally, he would have been forced to shoot him on purpose, and that would have been worse for both of them.

Jed sat back on the damp ground and wept for his friend just like he had when they were kids. They had been there for each other through every broken bone and every illness, and when one felt pain the other felt it too. For the next two hours, Jed felt the pain just as if he had been bitten in the face, and he seriously considered putting the gun to the side of his head to experience the same life ending pain of a bullet the way Ben had. It would be over fast. All he had to do was lift the gun. Through the rest of the night, the pain became numbness, and Jed just stared at nothing.

At sunrise the light filtered slowly through the trees until Jed became aware of his surroundings. He wondered about the lone infected dead that had killed his friend.

"Correction," he said out loud. "Would have killed him if I hadn't."

His voice sounded like it belonged to someone else. The words were dry and strange sounding with the trees being so close. That made Jed lift his head and try to see between the thick growth.

"Where did you come from?" he asked the crumpled mound that was slumped only a foot from Ben's head. Jed could see why he thought it was a tree stump. It didn't look much different even in daylight.

Jed pushed himself from the ground. His legs shook, but he ached from spending the night on the ground without a sleeping bag or at least a blanket. He put his weight against several small trees and focused his eyes on the infected. There was something about the body that wasn't right.

A few weak steps in the direction of the bodies was all he needed, and he realized the infected must have approached them by crawling on the ground. Both legs were twisted and pointing away at unnatural angles like it had fallen off of a building and landed badly.

Jed turned his head and his eyes searched the trees for the platform. He looked too low at first and saw that the watchtower was higher than he had thought at first. It was more than high enough for someone to break both legs if they fell. Jed had no doubt that's what happened and that the man had been alone when he fell. He had died out here and then crawled toward the sound of living men talking. He felt guilty to be relieved that the little island was really as safe as he first thought. He mentally buried his guilt as he buried his childhood friend and the unknown man who had left his treasure for the colony.

******

The colony had been on the move for almost a month, but they tried to stay in the general area above and to the east of Lake Moultrie. They had become nomads, breaking camp every day and continually moving to outflank the infected. They even camped in the same places they had used weeks before. Wherever it was safe, they set up camp again and only did enough work to the area to last a short time. Sometimes they sent out hunting parties to find supplies, and they had to move out before the hunters returned. It was never a cause for concern, because the hunters already knew where the colony would have gone.

They had mostly been raised in the area, so they felt like they had an advantage over the dead. All they had to do was stay one step ahead of them. For some unexplainable reason, the dead seemed to be migrating to the south, and a fair number of them walked straight into the water of Lake Moultrie and the Cooper River. All the colony had to do was move out of the way and not get caught with their backs to the water.

Jed had returned with the bad news about losing Ben, but as was often the case, he had been lost in pursuit of a better existence for all of them. Sooner or later they wouldn't be able to get out of the path of the migrating infected, and they would be forced to go in a direction they didn't want to. They were also getting tired. They needed to find a place they could defend. This new place had the added bonus of the supplies that Jed and Ben had uncovered. It was the legendary cache that had been buried by a survivalist. Jed had come back with two boxes containing four dozen candy bars. There were forty-five people in the colony, and most of them had forgotten what it was like to bite into a piece of chocolate and caramel. They chewed in silence and whispered their thanks to Ben.

It took a full day for Jed to catch up with the colony, and it took three more days for them to work their way back around to the other side of the Cooper River. Jed had already crossed the top of the Pinopolis Lock twice, once with Ben and once by himself. Each time had been unnerving because of the spiders. He was careful not to touch the railings for fear that he would get into a new web he didn't see. When he led the rest of the colony across, he had passed the word down the line that everyone should do the same. He only hoped no one noticed how nervous it made him. Seeing the mass of bodies at the bottom of the lock was made worse by the spiders, but with the warm weather the experience was enhanced by the overpowering smell.

There were no complaints, though. The thought of a supply cache that contained weapons and food was a strong motivation, and the memory of the candy bar had everyone moving with purpose in their steps. After crossing the top of the Pinopolis Lock, they turned south and followed the west bank of the Cooper River toward their new home. Jed made sure he was up front when they arrived at the swaying old bridge, even though he had occasionally let the colony move out ahead of him. He was prone to doing head counts to be sure they hadn't lost anyone, and he liked knowing everyone by name.

The last time they had all filed past him on the trail he had actually been surprised when he noticed how diverse the colony had become. A few years ago, they were almost all African Americans from the town of Cross. Now there were an equal number of blacks, whites, and Hispanics with a few Asians thrown in. They were from every small town in the area, and some were from other states. It was amazing the way they had all come to regard each other as family, and when they started calling themselves the 'colony' they had felt as if they truly were related. They also finally accepted Jed as the leader with no reservations. The only sadness he felt as he greeted each of them by name was the lack of children. There were only six in the entire colony. Everyone in the colony had experienced that awful loss, and the six children still alive had belonged to parents who didn't survive. There was no shortage of adults willing to care for the children, but to say it was a family that had known pain would have been an understatement.

At the bridge he told Ella, one of his neighbors from the old days, to stop just inside the trees on the other side and wait for everyone else to cross. Then he had them cross one at a time to keep the swaying from dumping someone in the river. He pulled aside Terrance and Javon, a pair of cousins from St. Stephen, and told them he wanted them to help him pull together some large tree limbs to barricade the entrance of the bridge. Charles joined them, and they were able to gather some heavy logs to brace the branches. When they were done, they pulled the barricade into place behind them and crossed over to their new home.

Home it was. For the first time in years, they weren't moving out the next day. It was almost sunset, and everyone was tired, but they marveled at how the outside world seemed to disappear. They couldn't see across the river once they reached the center of the oxbow island, and they knew no one could see them. They posted watches just inside the trees at the edges of the forest, and it felt like a special occasion to have a campfire burning at night.

Jed put a couple of people in charge of the supplies. There were whispered praises to God as they checked the inventory and decided what would be in the first meal that was to be served from the MREs. It was a source of strength to know many of them still had their faith despite their losses.

Some of the men organized a work crew, and even though the light was beginning to fail they silently went about clearing the center of the island. The brush and small trees they removed were carried toward the outer perimeter of the island by anyone who wanted to help. By adding it to the already dense trees and undergrowth, they became even more invisible to anyone who might be watching from the banks of the river. The clearing grew, and the campfires were skillfully hidden behind new piles of dirt. In a little over an hour the colony took on the appearance of a permanent settlement.

Even Jed didn't expect the biggest bonus of the night. As if they didn't have enough to rejoice about, they had dug a fire pit right into a second cache of food and other survival gear buried only a few yards from the first one. It would take days to inventory the variety of canned goods and sealed military surplus meals. Tents were unpacked and erected in a circle around the clearing, and even though a light rain started to fall, there were only smiling faces in the colony.

A tent was pitched in the center of the clearing for Jed and the other recognized leaders to gather and make plans. As they tiredly sat down in a circle, some couldn't resist stretching out on their blankets as if they were on a family camping trip. They kept their voices low, not wanting to forget that they would always be in danger, but the temptation to cheer was unbearable. Men and women taking their turns at feeding the colony came into the tent and passed out food. Rationing could begin later, but on this night everyone got a full meal as a reward for making the difficult trip. A woman came in and passed out candy bars for dessert.

Jed started the meeting of the leaders with his usual light hearted comment.

"I guess you're wondering why I asked y'all to be here tonight."

Good natured laughter was muted but widespread.

"Tonight we rest and mourn the loss of my oldest friend. Tomorrow we start over again in our new home. We'll do the things we need to do to make this place even safer than it already is, but we need a longterm plan. We need to find out why the hordes are all moving toward Charleston. We need to find out what's happening at Patriots Point and Fort Sumter."

7

First Contact

All the soldiers knew for sure was that the three men were living, breathing people, and they were running toward their firing line with thousands of the infected building a wall of flesh behind them. As each soldier sighted in on that wall of flesh, they had the feeling that they couldn't miss what they were aiming at. It was a target rich environment. They couldn't miss hitting something, and even a bullet to the body of an infected dead up front was enough to cause a pile up. The bullets slammed into them and drove their bodies backward causing temporary chaos and giving the three desperate men a better chance to make their last sprint to safety. Of course it was a matter of pride for the Army sharpshooters to hit the infected between the eyes, and after the initial barrage they settled into a rhythm of firing and acquiring a new target that was almost as precise as a well directed orchestra. More and more infected were going down with headshots.

The three men were exhausted, and even though these weren't their friends who had come to their rescue, they were alive. They could deal with being captured because it meant they would live awhile longer. From their point of view in front of the groaning horde, the distance between them and safety seemed to be miles, but before they knew it they were staggering through an opening between the soldiers. No one stopped firing until the order was given, and by that time the trembling trio of scouts had been escorted by medics who helped them climb aboard one of the helicopters.

The medics did what they would have done for anyone. As the soldiers withdrew from the firing line and boarded the aircraft, the medics were checking the vital signs of the men, and someone had wrapped them in blankets. As the helicopter lifted away from the ground, friendly faces surrounded them and welcomed them to safety. When they thought about it, they realized they should have expected nothing less, because in a different time they had been comrades in arms. As everyone quickly learned in the helicopter, the men were former soldiers as well.

That was one of the first things the Sergeant learned once he had been assured that everyone in his squad had boarded the helicopter unharmed. He had gotten a report over his radio that the other craft had completed its mission without casualties, and it was returning to the Ashley River Bridge to finish setting its charges. That meant they could detonate their explosive charges and watch to see if it caused the horde to turn toward it. The pilot increased their altitude until they could see the bridge and the horde at the same time, and the Sergeant gave the word for them to transmit the signal that would hopefully take down the bridge while distracting the horde.

It was a spectacular sight. With no urge to see the bridge still intact after the explosion, they had used twice as many charges as they needed. There was no doubt that the bridge would be gone when the cloud disappeared. At the moment of the explosion all eyes turned toward the bridge, and the crew cheered with satisfaction. Their eyes stayed on the bridge as the smoke and debris settled, and a long gap appeared in the roadway over the river. It was doubtful that there would ever be a bridge over that part of the river again.

Hopeful eyes turned away from the bridge to the horde, and the crew saw something they had never seen before. The horde had come to a complete stop from shoulder to shoulder on the interstate. It was as if there was an invisible line across all eight lanes, and only the infected could see it. They stood behind that line and turned their heads in the direction of the great cloud of debris that rose above the trees in the direction of the Ashley River.

"Come on. What are they waiting for?" asked the Sergeant to no one in particular.

The helicopter was hovering high enough not to distract the infected from the explosion, but gradually the heads of the infected began to turn back toward the road ahead of them. One by one they moved forward as if the explosion had not happened, and within a few minutes it was obvious that none of them were going to go in that direction. Any hope the crew had that the horde would march into the Ashley River was gone.

The Sergeant asked the pilot to radio in and inform Fort Sumter of the bad news and to make them aware that they had three guests on board. The pilot acknowledged the request, and the Sergeant turned to the three tired men.

"Where are you from, and can we give you a lift?"

The Sergeant had been too busy to find out who the men were up until that moment, but he wasn't so busy that he missed their hesitation. He also didn't miss the look they all exchanged before one of them spoke up.

"You'll find out soon enough, Sergeant, so I might as well tell you," said one of the men. "We're from Patriots Point."

The Sergeant was disappointed by his own lack of judgement when they had landed to rescue the men. If he had followed protocol, he would have had the men searched for bite marks and weapons. There had been enough time. As the one who had spoken to him slid his hand out from under the blanket, the Sergeant saw he had plenty of reason to be disappointed. The man had a grenade in his hand, and the pin had been pulled from the handle.

"No need to panic, Sergeant. All we need is a ride home. You can leave as soon as you drop us off."

"Do you expect me to believe that?"

The Sergeant tried to act natural just in case any of his men saw what was happening and tried to intervene.

"No, but you have my word. Now, just let the pilot know that he can land on the deck of the Yorktown."

The pilots preferred that communications took place through the radio headsets, so they were surprised when Sergeant Graham squeezed into the flight deck, but they knew by the grim expression on his face that there was a problem. He only spoke loud enough to be heard as he explained the predicament they were in, and they understood why he didn't use the comm system. One of them gave him a nod when he was done, and he knew they would make Fort Sumter aware of the situation.

******

* * *

Captain Miller and the Chief were both summoned as soon as the call came in, and they knew they only had a few minutes before the helicopter reached its destination, but as they soon learned it wouldn't have mattered if they had an hour. There was nothing they could do to stop the helicopter from being hijacked. The best they could think of was that Sergeant Graham should tell the people at Patriots Point that they were under orders to bring the men back to the Yorktown as a gesture of good will. It was doubtful that they would buy it, but it was the only thing they could try. Even with over twenty men and crew on the helicopter, there was no way to overpower someone who was holding a grenade. They sent the message to the pilot and wished them all good luck.

On board the Navy VH92A Sergeant Graham made an announcement to the soldiers and had everyone stow their weapons. He stayed as calm as possible and assured them that he was acting on direct orders from Captain Miller. There was a little grumbling at first, but he stared down the soldiers who had something to say.

"Everyone listen up. You might take someone out, but you can't do that and put a pin back into a grenade. Besides, even before we rescued these gentlemen from certain death, we were under orders to deliver them to their own people, whoever they were. Captain Miller gave those orders, and now he has given new orders in light of the danger to everyone in this aircraft. Anyone have a problem with that?"

Sergeant Graham locked eyes with the man holding the grenade and hoped the man paid attention, especially to the part about saving their lives.

"Can we get the frequency and call sign for your people so they don't shoot us down when we land at your base?"

"That would be a really good idea, Sarge."

He nodded at one of his men who immediately went to the flight deck to give instructions to the pilot. He stayed where he was over the pilot's shoulder and watched as they quickly descended toward the Yorktown. The landing was as smooth as an elevator coming to a stop, and the crew opened the doors immediately, obviously having been ordered to do so.

It was a bad moment for Captain Miller, the Chief, and everyone else who gathered in front of the monitor that displayed a close up view of the deck of the Yorktown. Knowing he would have to see his men file out of the helicopter with their hands behind their heads made Captain Miller furious. They had been with him for years, and they felt like family to him.

The Chief wasn't used to the helplessness he felt. As a matter of fact, the last time he had felt this way was when Allison had died. He felt responsible for her death even to this day. If you asked him why, he would say that the infected dead under the steps should have bitten him, or that he should have seen it in time to keep Allison from being bitten. Either way, no one could convince him it hadn't been his fault. Now, he was second guessing their decision to rescue the three men.

Both of them were so busy being angry and blaming themselves that they didn't see Kathy standing only a few feet away with her arms crossed.

"When you two get done feeling sorry for what happened, let's start working on a plan to get them out of there. We still have a lot of firepower and some very well trained people just waiting for your orders."

They glared at her, but they knew she was right.

"Sorry, guys. I know you needed to get that out, and no one expected you to feel good about it. It was a rescue mission. Anyone would have done the same thing if they had any decency. We just need to learn from the mistake and figure out how we're going to crack open that oyster over there. If playing nice doesn't work, we need to make them pay the price."

"Good speech," said the Chief.

Captain Miller nodded his agreement.

"What would your SEAL training recommend for this kind of operation?"

"We have all kinds of options, Jim. We can go in underwater or by force, but they will expect one of those. I don't think they'll expect a night parachute rescue."

"Do we have parachutes?" asked Tom.

"Already on it," said the Chief.

He got the attention of the soldier who was manning the radio and took the liberty of telling her to contact the helicopter that had gone to the Ashley River Bridge and tell them to detour to the Air Force Base and find some parachutes.

The explosion that rocked the Yorktown wasn't large enough to be heard or felt at Fort Sumter, but it came as such an unexpected surprise that the Chief and Captain Miller both reacted as if it had happened nearby. When their minds connected the dots between the flash of light and the billowing smoke that was swirling in the wind from the helicopter rotors, they understood that their well trained soldiers had taken matters into their own hands.

It was difficult to tell what was happening because they hadn't seen what had happened in the moments before the blast. They didn't know who was where, and they realized they had taken their eyes from the screen in front of them long enough for anything to have changed.

The helicopter was lifting away from the deck, and someone was firing small arms from the open door. As a matter of fact, there was a withering barrage of rifle fire pouring from the aircraft onto the deck of the Yorktown. From what they could see, there were no shots being fired from the ship toward the helicopter.

The VH92A seemed to lean over toward its right side as it lifted away from the carrier deck, and the angle increased as the helicopter banked so hard to starboard that it appeared to be out of control.

The Chief felt Kathy frantically squeeze his arm from behind as she tried to see what was happening, and he obliged her by letting her get in front of him. She got there just in time to have the same reaction as the two men as each of them was sure the helicopter was going to lose its rotors when they passed within inches of the safety lines that had been installed around the flight deck. The safety lines flew away from the whirling blades, and the helicopter fell over the edge of the ship toward the water over eighty feet below.

Anyone who was watching on television when the second plane hit the World Trade Center would say they thought everything was moving in slow motion. The same could be said about watching the helicopter making that fall. The trio watching from the control room in Fort Sumter was silent, and none of them were breathing. Then their eyes grew wider.

What had become tears in Kathy's eyes were quickly wiped away as she joined the Chief and Captain Miller when they began to shout words of encouragement to the pilots of the helicopter. As impossible as it appeared to be, the helicopter was falling, then laboring against the tremendous forces of gravity as it fought to stop its downward motion. Then it was hovering for a split second only inches from the water that was being whipped into the air by the turmoil above. Then it literally sprang upward with as much power as the pilot could give it.

The firing had stopped when the helicopter went into its steep bank, and from Fort Sumter they could see that someone had managed to close the crew door. If they hadn't, the soldiers would have spilled onto the carrier's deck or in the water before the pilot could get control. As the spinning rotors of the aircraft drew further away from the smoke on the ship, it became thicker at the side of the superstructure that rose from the starboard side of the carrier. Something was on fire there, and the smoke was becoming thicker and blacker as they watched.

"Captain Miller, Sir."

The radio operator was holding up a microphone in the Captain's direction, and he had a broad smile on his face.

"We have radio contact with the crew, Sir. Lots of bruises and bumps on heads from that wild take off, but no real injuries. One possible broken arm on the soldier that closed the door because he didn't have time to get himself secured."

"Tell the pilot we don't have time to give out medals right now, but they all deserve a steak in the mess hall tonight."

The radioman was happy to relay the word.

"I can't wait to debrief Sergeant Graham," said Captain Miller.

******

The debriefing was as interesting as they had expected it to be. When they were done and able to piece together the individual accounts of the pilots, Sergeant Graham, and each of the soldiers, it had come as no surprise that their escape from the carrier had been the result of circumstances becoming perfectly aligned, followed by the quick thinking and fast reactions by everyone.

They were only met on deck by a handful of men holding weapons, and they were so focused on their own three men as they got out of the helicopter that they were rushed away ahead of their captives. They totally forgot that the only reason the soldiers couldn't use their weapons was the hand grenade. Once they were separated from the helicopter crew and soldiers, the hand grenade was no longer a threat to them. That was the perfect alignment of circumstances. The fast thinking and quick reactions followed when the Sergeant pulled his handgun and shot the man with the grenade and just as quickly shot the nearest captor. His soldiers grabbed for weapons and decimated the other captors while the pilots did what they were trained to do.

There wasn't time to assess the situation on the carrier where the fire appeared to have spread to a fuel source. It may have been supplies or anything else, but whatever it was it burned easily. The men on board the helicopter didn't have time to see what it was or what was happening from the moment the wheels came off the deck, and as the Sergeant described it, most of them were in a pile against the inside of the starboard door. If Corporal Langdon hadn't closed it, Sergeant Graham guessed the helicopter would have been considerably lighter after dumping everyone overboard.

Once the initial adrenaline rush began to wear off, the Sergeant had managed to climb up front to thank the pilots for their fast reactions when the grenade had exploded. He also wanted to see if they had observed any useful intelligence because the pilots had the best view of the people on the carrier before they staged their escape. They both had the same information, and it was a curious observation. They reported that the people who had come onto the deck from the door of the superstructure wore uniforms, but they weren't military. Both pilots agreed that they were dressed like security guards, and their training was basic at best.

The pilots of the helicopter were shown a recording of their harrowing escape, and they watched in stunned silence. They knew they had to let the helicopter fall off of the carrier and generate lift at the same time, but they probably wouldn't have tried it if they had been given the time to think about it first. They went wide eyed when the rotors passed within inches of the safety rails and the deck, and they gripped the arms of their chairs with white knuckles as they watched the helicopter win the battle over gravity just as their wheels got wet.

"Curious," said Captain Miller. "They were so disorganized that they didn't even try to shoot at the helicopter. If they had used the RPG they had in the boat that day in the marshes, they couldn't have missed."

"My thoughts exactly," said the Chief.

Kathy added, "These people can't be military. Who do you think they are?"

One of the communications officers in the control room interrupted with some bad news that wasn't entirely unexpected. Nonetheless, it would have been nice to have short range radio contact just a bit longer this time.

"Sir, radios are down again. This time I'm not sure we're going to be able to get them back. We've been patching into new satellites every time we've lost the last one, and I don't think there are any left in orbit we can use."

Captain Miller nodded at the man without showing any concern, but he was worried. Without radios, they couldn't coordinate with the other shelters.

"See what you can do about short wave connections, Private. We haven't always had satellites and cell towers."

As the pilots had watched the recording and the debriefings were done, the control room had become a bit more crowded. The rest of the Mud Island survivors began to gather in the room to see what we were going to do next. We were facing the threat from the biggest horde since the apocalypse began, and we were confused about the people at Patriots Point. They were the enemy, but other than having assets we had to wonder what kind of threat they posed to us.

The rescue of the three men followed by their skyjacking of the helicopter had been unplanned, but the information we had gained about our neighbors at Patriots Point had been invaluable. They were undoubtedly paranoid, but they had not displayed any hostility until today. When they had the opportunity they hadn't functioned well enough to pull off what should have been an easy capture of the helicopter and prisoners.

"I have an idea," said Hampton. "We should get someone inside their operation."

The Chief nodded, "Good idea. I'll go. I think I can get in easier than anyone else."

More than one of us laughed, Tom put into words what we were all thinking.

"Maybe we can get one of their security guard uniforms in your size, Chief."

Almost everyone in the room tried to volunteer, but Hampton was arguably the most logical choice. He would blend in the best, but he also had that mixture of talents that gave him the best chance of getting back out alive. After some debate there was a gradual acceptance that we couldn't all go, but after I had volunteered, I had a moment of self satisfaction at the thought that I wanted to go and could have been as good a choice as others might have been.

I thought to myself, "Ed Jackson, former nerd gamer. Husband, father, zombie slayer, and wannabe spy."

When I snapped out of my private world, I found that plans were already in motion. Infiltration appeared to be easy because there were so many places that could be weak spots in their defenses. It was once and for all decided that Hampton would fit in better at the State Ports

Authority because it turned out that he had actually worked at the docks when they had hired temporary workers. He knew his way around the cranes and the container ships. Besides, there was so much activity around there that one more person wouldn't be noticed. There weren't any new ships coming in and waiting to be unloaded, but the people at Patriots Point had them working on something. We just needed to know what it was.

Over our usual collection of maps and digital satellite photos we searched for places that would be spots where Hampton wouldn't be seen as he entered the area. We knew they would have plenty of security because they couldn't let any infected get inside their defenses. We also had mountains of scouting reports that had been collected ever since we had discovered the existence of the secretive people living over there.

They were collecting containers from ships for all kinds of reasons. Some were obvious reasons such as food and medical supplies. With hundreds of thousands of containers to search, they needed an army of people to inventory every container at three different terminals. Most were already offloaded from ships, but there were still a half dozen ships with as many as ten thousand containers on each one. We had to choose our insertion point carefully, but it was only a matter of time before we found the perfect spot.

We turned our attention back to the Yorktown and watched the black smoke rising away from the ship. A fire fighting team had extinguished the blaze, but the smoke was still too thick for us to see anything useful.

******

If Marshall Sayer was having a bad day before, it was nothing compared to what he felt like after hearing the helicopter had been captured and then escaped. Ted Atwater had conveniently disappeared to another part of the ship while Marshall was venting his anger. Anton Mikhailov wasn't aware of what had happened yet, so he didn't know to make himself scarce the way Atwater did.

"Where's Mikhailov?"

His usual way of storming into the lab didn't surprise anyone, so they didn't even look up from their work. Mikhailov was just disappointed because he couldn't get away this time.

"Maybe you can give me some good news. No one else in this ship of idiots has anything good to report these days. Those fools made it all the way back from patrol just to get themselves blown up by one of their own grenades."

"Is that what that was?"

Mikhailov only had a little of the information, and it had come from the guards who had shot one of their own men. After one of them had died in the gunfire that had followed the explosion, he had turned and had almost bitten the others. He couldn't believe that years later people were still being caught off guard and being bitten by their friends. He also couldn't believe they didn't restrain the man and deliver him to the lab. He needed more test subjects, especially those who had died by means other than a bite wound. He had plenty of test subjects who had become infected by being bitten, but he needed more that had died of other causes and then turned.

"Yes, that's what it was," snapped Sayer.

Mikhailov didn't look up when he asked Sayer if he would mind reiterating to his men not to dispose of dead people because he needed them in his lab.

Sayer stopped short and stared a hole into the back of Mikhailov's head.

"I guess I can take that to mean you don't have any good news, either."

It was more of a statement than a question.

"If I have a breakthrough, you will be the first to know," mumbled Mikhailov.

"In case you have lost track of time, doctor, you've been working on a cure for over five years. I'm starting to feel like you're just making sure that you're safe while the rest of us are putting our own necks on the line."

The sarcastic remark didn't faze the doctor in the least bit. He knew full well that Sayer didn't do anything that would risk his own neck. He had most likely been one of the safest people in the world since CEL Day One.

"We have learned something you might find interesting," said Mikhailov. "It's not a cure, but it is interesting."

Sayer perked up a bit. He didn't have to answer to anyone, so he wasn't under any pressure to produce results, but he was driven by his own success. Anything that wasn't known before would be interesting to him. He would at least be able to revel in the fact that he knew something that other people didn't.

"Well, don't just sit there and wait for me to ask. Spit it out."

Mikhailov let out an exasperated sigh and explained.

"The pathogen can be transmitted from one human to another through body fluids. That includes any fluid that goes from an infected person to a living person."

Sayer interrupted, because there was something he always wanted to know.

"We already know that, doctor, but at what point does a person become contagious? If they get bitten but haven't died yet, are they able to infect someone else?"

Mikhailov wished he could tell Sayer he was a moron.

"I won't be able to test that question until you tell me to try it on living subjects. So far we have only done tests on subjects we knew to be infected. This isn't Auschwitz."

Judging by the last part of his answer, Sayer understood Mikhailov to be insinuating that he wouldn't test that question by knowingly infecting living subjects. If someone was bitten already, he had gladly run tests on them, but only because he knew they were going to die. It would be a horse of a different color if he asked Mikhailov to infect someone who had not been bitten by exposing them to a bite victim who was still alive.

"Okay, well how else do you propose to find the answer to that question?"

It was obvious to Mikhailov that Sayer would authorize testing on human subjects if he asked him for permission, but he wasn't that far gone himself. He stood up and faced the man as closely as he could.

"We will only find out if it happens and we are aware that it has happened," he said slowly and deliberately.

Sayer heard the menace in Mikhailov's voice and tried to think of something he could say to gain the upper hand again.

"So, if that wasn't your interesting news, what was it you wanted to tell me." He was relieved when he remembered he had changed the subject on the doctor, and he could steer him back again.

Mikhailov turned back to his lab results and his notes and found one in particular.

"In layman's terms, there is only one animal that appears to be capable of carrying the infection without itself becoming infected. Furthermore, it appears that it can also spread the infection by inflicting bodily injury to humans."

Mikhailov paused to judge whether or not Sayer was following him.

Sayer said, "Doctor Mikhailov, talk to me like a student in his first year of biology classes, and I'll authorize those human trials."

Judging by the expression on Marshall Sayer's face, Mikhailov had very little doubt that he was insinuating that he would be the first test subject. He decided to take the director a bit more seriously.

"I have been studying the blue crabs that are so plentiful here, even around the ships at Patriots Point. We can go outside with a net and literally scoop them out of the marshes at low tide."

Everyone had seen them clinging to the bodies of the infected dead, so it was no revelation that the doctor would study the effects eating the dead flesh would have on the crabs.

"I have learned that they are not infected by eating contaminated flesh, but their bodies preserve the pathogen in a manner that allows them to pass it along to people. They do so by inflicting wounds or when they are themselves consumed by humans. It just takes longer for the infection to kill a person who ingests it through their digestive tract. I have not yet discovered why the infection is passed along by inflicting a wound. Perhaps it is causing the crabs to produce a toxin that carries the pathogen or perhaps it is simply a matter of the pathogen clinging to the body of the crab."

"That would mean the pathogen is incredibly virulent," said Sayer. "Most viruses don't live long outside of their hosts, but you're saying it's possible this pathogen can live for hours or days on the body of a crab that's immersed in salt water."

"Correct. I don't have much data at this point because I don't have any baseline information, such as the amount of pathogen the crabs are exposed to or when the crabs became infected."

"Or how long the crabs had been in the water after they were exposed," added Sayer.

"Yes. Exactly."

Mikhailov was getting a little excited by the discussion because something told him there was something relevant about the fact that the pathogen affected humans but could be carried by arthropods.

"What I have been thinking is that I should find another arthropod that can be managed more easily than crabs because they wouldn't need to be in salt water," continued Mikhailov.

"Like what, insects?"

"Insects are such a diverse group of arthropods. We need to work with a smaller group, such as arachnids."

"Spiders?"

As a scientist Marshall Sayer knew that he should be able to at least hide his distain for the eight-legged creatures, but his experiences as a child had shaped his phobia just the same as it had for millions of other people. Just the thought of them made his scalp itch.

"Yes, spiders. We can create a contained environment for them and control their exposure to the pathogen. Then I can dissect them to see if the pathogen has survived in their bodies, and I can even learn if it has evolved in any way."

Sayer couldn't help putting his thoughts into words.

"Too bad we can't have them bite people to see if they get infected."

Anton Mikhailov mustered up the strongest expression he could to show his revulsion at the thought, and Marshall Sayer recoiled from him enough for him to become defensive. He put up his hands in surrender as he backed away.

"I wasn't seriously saying we should, just that it's too bad that we can't."

Judging by the expression still frozen on Mikhailov's face, that hadn't helped. Sayer took it as his cue to leave, but as he turned for the door, he added one last thing.

"I think that's a fantastic idea, doctor. Use whatever resources you need to collect your specimens. Talk with Reynolds about taking you into the field if you need to find their colonies."

"Spiders don't live in colonies."

"Yeah, well whatever. Just go ahead and find where they do live."

Sayer was out the door, and both men were glad the conversation was over for now. Mikhailov was at least satisfied that he could begin testing another group of arthropods to see if they could carry the pathogen, but as he thought about it, he realized it would be better to hope that spiders couldn't. As for where spiders live, Mikhailov didn't think he would even need to leave the ship to find them. There were plenty of neglected areas of the old aircraft carrier that were perfect hiding places for spiders.

8

Swarms

Kathy remembered sitting in a boat with the Chief at night. They were passing the time waiting for sunrise at the Coast Guard Station by just chatting about things that had happened to them. Her mind didn't seem to want to stay in one spot as it flashed back to an earlier time when they were all sitting in a raft at night at the mouth of the Stono River. That was back when 'all of them' meant her, the Chief, Ed, and Jean. Then their group had grown again, and they were moving through the snow in Columbus, Ohio toward the President's shelter. They had seen some terrifying and amazing things, but when she tried to remember what had been the worst time, she thought of the heat in New Orleans, and how they had dug frantically in the cemetery to rescue Iris Mason.

She held one hand out in front of her in the dark. There was so little moonlight that she could barely see her fingers, but sometimes the clouds moved out of the way, and the water reflected the light back at her. She counted off on her fingers as she named the places they had been.

"Ohio, Minnesota, Alabama, Louisiana...."

"Don't forget North Carolina."

Kathy might have been more startled because she didn't expect anyone else to be outside on the beach with her, but the voice belonged to Iris Mason, and it had a way of cutting through the darkness

92

without being intrusive. Besides, they were in friendly territory, if there was such a place. There was no way an infected would have been able to get close enough to attack her, and there was very little chance of there being an infected on this stretch of beach in the first place. The Morris Island lighthouse loomed out of the water about thirty yards to her left, and the island behind her was occupied by hidden sentries guarding the new helicopter landing area.

"I was just thinking about you. How could I forget North Carolina?"

Kathy patted the blanket next to her indicating that she wanted Iris to sit with her.

"Beautiful night," said Iris as she sat down. She gestured toward the ocean in general. "What's that over there?"

"Folly Beach. You haven't been out here before?"

"After New Orleans, I didn't want to leave the shelter for the rest of my life. Remember, I was used to living underground because I had to for five years. It's taken me a long time to venture away from the Chief's side."

"That's where you belong," said Kathy.

Iris peered into the darkness, and she could just barely make out the shape of a man walking toward them on Folly Beach. He had the familiar stumbling lurch of the infected. He was too far away for him to see them, but sound carried at night, and he could probably hear them.

Iris lowered her voice out of instinct and asked, "That doesn't bother you?"

She gestured toward the infected, but Kathy had seen it too.

"It used to. It bothered me the way they don't care what happens to them when they set their sights on their prey. They walk into fire, into the water, and over the edge of cliffs with no worries while we cling to our lives."

"That's because we have lives to cling to, but you already know that."

A small chuckle was her way of letting Kathy know she was trying to lift her spirits a bit.

Kathy couldn't help but smile because she did know why the living cared about what was happening, and she also knew Iris was just trying to help her keep her head together. It wasn't just a fear of dying anymore. Now it was a fear of becoming one of them.

"When I was with the Chief and Jean on the Atlantic Spirit we were physically close to the people as they died. They had both been on the ship before me, and I didn't think we would leave Charleston alive. It was a close call at the cruise ship docks, but then the three of us were elbows deep in people who had been bitten. Things are so different now. Now we keep our distance."

Iris studied Kathy's profile with the dim light behind her. She was impressed by Kathy's classic beauty even through the years since the infection began. She didn't need makeup to look good, but she also had a way of making everyone feel comfortable around her.

"You have something really eating at you tonight, don't you?"

Kathy seemed to go into herself as if Iris had never been there. She snapped out of it and found Iris waiting patiently for her to come back.

"Oh, I'm sorry, Iris. What did you say?"

Iris didn't ask again because she knew Kathy was going to realize what she had asked the first time.

Kathy put her hands over her face and said, "I'm so embarrassed. You must think I'm being rude."

"Not at all. You have something on your mind. Care to share it with someone?"

"You're right, something's really bugging me."

Kathy turned to give Iris her undivided attention, but just as quickly she was on her feet walking toward the water. Iris was surprised by how quickly the emotion flooded out of Kathy. So quickly that it was making Kathy practically explode with energy.

"You see that infected walking into the water like it thinks it can just walk right over here to us? That's the tenth one in the last thirty minutes, and my guess is that it's been going on longer than that. And you know what? I don't think it's because I've been sitting over here. I think it's because something is calling them from over there."

Kathy was turning so fast that Iris could hardly keep up with her, but she ended by pointing back in the direction of Fort Sumter.

Iris was confused.

"Why would someone from Fort Sumter be calling them?"

Kathy shook her head. "Not Fort Sumter. Patriots Point."

Iris had forgotten that Patriots Point was in a straight line from where she was sitting but on the other side of Fort Sumter.

"How are they calling them?"

"I need to talk with the Chief about that, but I'm not the only one who has developed a whopping case of tinnitus. I've heard a lot of people complaining that they have ringing in their ears."

Iris seemed to be thinking about it but agreed.

"I thought it was just because I was getting old."

"No, it started a long time ago. I can't say exactly when, but it was there for a long time before I started feeling like it was coming from somewhere over by the bridge. I think they have something over there that's making the infected all come toward Charleston."

"You think it's got something to do with that big horde coming this way?"

"I do, and the proof is right over here. Every infected on Folly Beach has been walking into the water trying to get to Patriots Point. At first I thought they were trying to reach me, but I'll bet if one of them made it across the water from Folly Beach to Morris Island, it would walk right by us and keep going until it walked into the Charleston harbor."

As if to accent her point, there was a splash over on the beach behind her as another infected dead walked too far out into the current. Its head bobbed on the surface for a few feet before it disappeared for good.

Iris had always been a surprise to anyone who had gotten to know her. Before the infection she had become the chief of security on a cruise liner with the same job as Chief Barnes. That job had showcased her talents as a ship's ambassador as well as a supervisor. Her striking silver hair and her tall, slender stature carried with it an aura of confidence. She could single handedly de-escalate any situation that had already gotten out of control, but if she got there first, it would never reach a boiling point. Before the cruise ship she had worked as a professor at the University of North Carolina where she was able to share her critical thinking skills with young people. All in all, she was one of the main intellectual assets of the Mud Island family.

"If you're right, we need to find out why someone would want to summon the infected into one area, but as sinister as it sounds at first, isn't it just as likely that they're doing it to eliminate the infected?"

Kathy didn't answer immediately, and Iris waited patiently. That was one of her ways of making sure people thought through their own beliefs. She gave them time to think about their answers when she put forth an opposing view.

Kathy hadn't leaned in that direction. One thing made it seem evil to her, and that was the fate of anyone alive who might be in the path of that massive horde. People were surviving when confronted by small hordes, but this one was like a plague of locusts, and it didn't just consume everyone in its path, it absorbed them.

"I can't bring myself to believe there's anything good about summoning the largest horde in the world to one small corner of humanity," she said. "If the purpose is to destroy them, someone must have thought it through, and they would have decided that the living people in the path of the horde were expendable for the greater good."

"I see your point," said Iris. "History is full of examples that support your theory. Sacrifice a few to save many. If it's the decision of the few to sacrifice themselves, then it would be noble, but too often it's the decision of someone in a position of power who's deciding the fate of the people who are being sacrificed. Is that what you suspect is happening?"

"It has to be. They didn't conduct a survey before they started doing it. They just decided that as long as the victims are faceless, it's okay to just give them a memorial service and a statue or something. Most likely not even that much."

"Okay, if they are summoning them, whoever they are they must be well funded and not entirely stupid. They would have had an existing infrastructure to begin operating right after the outbreak of the infection. That would narrow down the list of candidates to the military and the federal government."

"Or the combination of the two," said Kathy.

Iris did as Kathy had done earlier. She held up her hand and started counting off agencies with her fingers.

"The CIA, Homeland Security, FBI, FEMA, Department of Defense, ICE, ATF, DEA, CDC, or even more likely two or more of them together."

A pair of dark silhouettes was approaching at a leisurely pace from the direction of the tunnel entrance that led to the steel vault door of the shelter. Ever since they had decided to seal the doors at Fort Sumter and use the backdoor as the main point of access, the inhabitants of the shelter had taken advantage of the opportunity to enjoy the night time air of the beach. The air around Fort Sumter usually smelled like the marshes and the thick pluff mud. The air on the beach was fresh and clean on the best nights, and it was mosquito heaven on the worst nights.

Kathy and Iris stopped talking and waited for them to draw closer before resuming. They expected it to be friends, and the dark pair didn't walk like the infected, but they were always going to err on the side of caution.

"This must be ladies night out," said Iris when she recognized Janice and Colleen.

"Mind if we join you?" Colleen always had a smile on her face since teaming up with Hampton, and she flashed it in the direction of Kathy and Iris.

"Not at all," said Kathy. "I would have brought wine and cheese if I had known we were going to be doing this."

"I feel like this must be the calm before the storm," said Iris.

Janice asked, "What's that mean? I had enough drama on that oil rig. Are you expecting something?"

The newcomers dropped to the blanket with Kathy and Iris, and Colleen handed Kathy a bottle.

"I brought my own."

Janice produced a sleeve of plastic cups, and they eagerly passed them out.

"Now we can discuss this situation in a more civilized manner."

"Whatever that means," said Colleen. "Are you two talking about something specific or just rehashing the old stand-by question about where the zombies came from."

Kathy and Iris did a mock double-take in the direction of Fort Sumter.

"I don't think the Chief heard her," said Kathy. "This is something I think all of us have wondered about, but it has a new twist."

Iris added, "Kathy thinks there's something over at Patriots Point that's summoning the infected to Charleston. That's why the horde is coming this way."

"Wait a minute," said Janice. She had both hands in the air in front of her as if she was telling something to stop coming toward her.

"Are you saying those things can still hear? I mean, I knew they could hear something because if you make a noise near one it will zero in on you, but you're telling us they can be called to you from a long distance? But I don't hear anything, so that would make me more stupid than a zombie. Someone is using a 'zombie-whistle', and I don't even hear it."

"But you do hear it," said Kathy. "You just haven't realized it yet. How long have you had ringing in your ears?"

"I always thought it was something in the power systems of the shelter, sort of like a hum or vibration or something," said Iris. "I lived inside the shelter below Ambassadors Island for five years, and there was always a persistent hum from the generators. I guess I just got used to it and pushed it from my mind."

"Well, I've slept better at times. It was always so deathly quiet on the oil rig, but now that you mention it, there's something here that keeps me from falling asleep sometimes."

A series of splashes on the other side of the inlet made them all look that way. At least six infected had walked into the water and were being swept away by the current.

"That's been going on for hours," said Kathy, "and if we could still go topside at the fort, I would go out with binoculars and watch the Battery over at White Point Gardens. I'll bet they're trying to walk to Patriots Point from there and dropping into the Cooper River. Until the horde arrives Charleston could win the safest city in America award because the infected are all drowning themselves."

"Do we still have a camera aimed at the Ravenel Bridge?" asked Colleen.

"Why didn't I think of that?" asked Kathy. "I'll bet the ones that aren't swimming in the river are walking right to the source. Thanks for the wine."

She was up and running toward the tunnel without even noticing that Colleen, Iris, and Janice were all right behind her.

******

Captain Miller was in the tunnel when he saw the four women coming toward him on the golf cart. It was moving at top speed, but the way they were gripping the handrails made him think they were willing the machine to go faster. He didn't have to hold up his hand to stop, and they actually fishtailed toward him.

"Are we under attack?" he yelled.

They all talked at once, and this time he had to hold up his hand to restore order.

"One at a time. Kathy, you first."

"We think Patriots Point is calling the infected."

Kathy was panting as if she had been running instead of riding.

"Calling them how?"

Despite wanting to stay as serious as he could for Kathy's sake, Captain Miller couldn't stop himself.

"Did they figure out how to use cell phones?"

The expressions on the faces of the four women made him hold up both hands this time.

"Hey, don't shoot me. Do you know what you just said?"

"Okay, let me rephrase it. We think Patriots Point has been sending out some kind of signal that only the infected can hear, and it's making them all come this way. It's the only way to explain the behavior of the infected. We want to get a look at the camera views of Charleston to see if the infected are trying to reach Mount Pleasant."

"There isn't room for me to join you on that cart. Go ahead and I'll catch up with you. When you get there, tell any of the pilots you see that I want a crew in the air over the Ravenel Bridge as soon as possible, and see if someone is available to make a run over Folly Beach."

Kathy didn't waste a moment, and the way she and the others burst into the control room was enough to create the sense of urgency they needed. Two pilots and a flight crew got to the vault door just as Captain Miller arrived, and he explained in as few words as possible that he needed to find out what the infected were doing near the bridge and along the coastline of Charleston. Then he remembered to add Folly Beach.

He joined the ladies at a computer terminal that was connected to the cameras and saw that Kathy was already zooming in as far as possible along the Battery at White Point Gardens. She had a remarkably clear image that showed several of the infected searching for an opening in the railing that ran along the edge of the park. Where the railing ended, there were dozens of infected dead walking into the water. At night they were silhouettes against what little light came through the clouds from the moon, and they could imagine that it would be a shocking view in daylight.

"I wish our radio signals were as reliable as our cameras," said Captain Miller.

"I wonder how many have already gone into the water," said Colleen.

"I can't get a view of the bridge from high enough to see over the railing, but I'd bet anything there's a parade going up the bridge from the city," said Kathy.

"I ran into the pilots, and I told them to get some good intel on movements of the infected, but I also told them to get some good pictures of the bridge. If you are right about what you said, they would need to be broadcasting their signal from somewhere high. There couldn't be anywhere better than the bridge itself. One question, though. Have you sorted out why they would be calling the infected to come to them?"

"She thinks they're exterminating them," said Iris.

Captain Miller was speechless for a moment. If it was that simple, the military could do the same thing. They could sit off the coast and draw every infected within range into the Atlantic, Pacific, and Gulf of Mexico. They could even do it along the Great Lakes and every major river in the country.

"I haven't been able to explain why they're doing it by themselves if that's what you're wondering, Jim. It would only make sense to me that they would want to use their zombie-whistle from a location that was completely safe and would do the maximum damage to the infected population."

"You got it right before, Kathy, back on the beach when you said they must've realized they would be eliminating the infected, but they would be sacrificing every living person in the path of that horde. I saw it for myself when I followed them down the interstate, and whoever they are, they knew they didn't have the ability to warn everyone in the area first, so they just went ahead and did it."

"My God," said Jim. "The military would have spent a few weeks or months evacuating people in the path, and then we would've drawn them through unoccupied areas."

"Exactly," said Iris. "That may also explain why they didn't come to you for help. They knew you would order them to stand down until it was approved up the chain of command."

The helicopter appeared in their camera view for a few minutes, and they watched its progress as it hovered at the base of the bridge on the Charleston side. Radio communications had been sporadic at best, and Captain Miller even speculated that the signal being sent out to the infected dead was so powerful that it was interfering with their radio signals. The helicopter eventually peeled away from its position and flew in a direct course for the landing area beyond Fort Sumter.

Thirty minutes later the photographs were uploaded into their computer, and even in the darkness, startling images of the bridge were displayed on the wall-sized monitor. Thousands of infected dead were on the bridge already, and the main horde hadn't even arrived yet. They were laboriously walking up the steep on-ramps and converging before tackling the slope of the main span of the bridge. The helicopter had rotated where it hovered and gotten them a three hundred and sixty degree view of the area, and when it faced north they could see the incredible wall of the infected less than a mile from the exit to the bridge.

"Will the bridge support that much weight?" asked Janice.

The Chief arrived just as the question was asked, and combined with the images on the monitor, he easily guessed what they had been doing.

"I was just about to send for you," said Captain Miller. "Our resident geniuses figured out why the infected horde is coming to Charleston."

Tom, Hampton, the Chief, and I had been making plans for the next day when we would take to the air to watch the progress of the horde. We would also be trying to assess how many of the infected would be going into the rivers now that the bridges were either destroyed or open. We had gone to find Captain Miller because we would be using his men and helicopters. Whatever had delayed him from meeting with us, we figured it had to be something important, and the control room would be his likely location.

"Of course they did," said Tom. "Brains and beauty."

Normally his comment would have elicited a few remarks back from the ladies, but they were so caught up in their new revelations that they let it pass.

Kathy gave the Chief a quick breakdown of her theory, and his face was like cold stone at the part about the people trapped between the horde and Charleston. Iris had told him what it was like when she had followed the horde. She had told all of us, but at night when they were alone, she had woken up screaming, and each time it was because she had dreamt she was on the wrong side of that mass of evil. If it had been a nightmare to her, we could only imagine what it was like for the people who were in its path.

"It's too late to help those people now," he said in a sober voice, "but I think we should treat what those people have done as war crimes."

Captain Miller said, "I can't exactly act on behalf of the military. I may be charged with war crimes myself, but in the absence of civil authority, I would support that position, Chief. We can cross that bridge when we come to it."

Iris was nodding in agreement.

"You've got my vote, but like you said, it's too late to help the victims. We have to let those people play out whatever it is they have in mind. We're safe out here at Fort Sumter, but I have to wonder if they've thought this thing through to a logical conclusion. Are they completely safe?"

"I think they are," said Hampton. "That bridge is bigger than the one we blew up in Georgetown, and when it was packed with the infected, it would have stood like that until the end of time if we didn't blow it up. They've blocked it well enough to keep anything from crossing it, so I think we're about to see a spectacular display of the laws of physics."

"We'll know at sunrise," said the Chief. "Which law?"

"The one about an unstoppable force hitting an immovable object."

The Chief nodded.

"If you're right, the horde will be forced to spread left and right, and the railings will get packed with the infected. It will take hours for them to get packed tight enough against the railing on the right side to make it buckle, but sooner or later it will break."

"What about the left side?" I asked. "There's no pedestrian railing on that side."

"All guesswork," said the Chief, "but I think the pileup on that side will get so deep that it will force the infected to fall over the concrete barrier further down the bridge by Charleston. Think of it like this. They get jammed up against the barrier built by Patriots Point under the set of towers closer to Mt Pleasant. The pileup backs all the way past the towers on the Charleston side and then slopes downward. The infected get directed toward the sides because they can't go uphill at the center. They fall over the concrete barriers, and the pedestrian walkway instantly starts a new parade. Thousands of infected dead march past the jammed up horde until they meet the barrier. That's when the railing gets tested."

Janice asked, "And do you have a guess for the strength of that fence? It's about eight feet tall, but it doesn't look that strong. I don't think anyone ever expected it to have thousands of bodies packed against it."

"Exactly," answered the Chief. "When it goes down, I expect bodies to fall through the opening for several days."

The thought was staggering. Sometimes it was hard to remember these were people, and they had to be eliminated, but this was going to be a massive thinning of the infected population. The prospect of how it would change the world gave rise to one more question.

"It's a sacrifice, isn't it?" said Kathy. "The few people caught in the path of the horde are being sacrificed for the greater good of the people who survived at Patriots Point."

I couldn't help adding, "And arguably anywhere else including us."

Kathy gave me a withering glare that made me lower my eyes to the floor, but the Chief came to my defense and was quickly seconded by Tom.

"They would use that logic, Ed. As a matter of fact, they'll want us to thank them when we finally meet."

"What have we learned from the photographs about the signal they've been sending? What did you call it, a zombie-whistle?" asked Captain Miller.

No one missed an opportunity to call them zombies just to get a reaction out of the Chief.

Before the Chief could say they weren't zombies, Kathy answered by moving a pointer across the screen to the section of the photograph that included the massive V shape at the top of the bridge on the Mt Pleasant side. Even in the darkness they could make out the circular outline of a parabolic dish.

"I want to shoot a missile into that thing just to stop the ringing in my ears," said Kathy.

The Chief could be unreadable in a poker game, but there were times when we could all read his emotions just as if he had them written on his forehead. The anger he was feeling as he stared at that dish was obvious.

"They knew what they were doing when they turned that thing on," he said. "Look at the size of that thing. A lot of work went into getting that array up there, so they must've known they were condemning survivors to death."

"We have sporadic radio contact with the helicopters," said a soldier wearing a headset. "It isn't clear, but it's good enough to understand. They confirm hundreds of infected in the downtown area are finding their way to the Cooper River and walking right into the water. Folly Beach still has stragglers walking into the ocean at the tip of Morris Island, but it appears the dead population of Folly Beach is almost zero."

******

There was no reason to expect the infected to be capable of experiencing emotions, but sometimes it was easy to interpret their sounds as pain or their reaching hands as pleading. The overall feeling we got when we studied the pictures of the swarms of infected walking toward the bridge was a projection of how we felt to have that incessant ringing in our ears. It wasn't drawing us to the bridge the

103

way it was the infected, but now that we knew it was there, it was easy for us to wonder if it was agitating them as much as it was us. Another question came to mind, and that was how much research had been done by someone on the infected to learn that they responded to specific sounds. Whoever was doing the research must have unlimited resources, as well as time and safety.

We all stared into the darkness across the harbor at the black hull of the aircraft carrier. The darkness was symbolic of whatever it was that was going on inside that ship. Someone was conducting experiments that would ultimately benefit mankind and its struggle to survive, but whoever they were, they were doing it at a great expense to humanity.

9

Gravity

At sunrise we were ready to fly. We had the Sikorsky packed as full as we could, and the whole 'Mud Island Family' was along for the ride. Iris was the newest member, and the only one missing was Bus. Janice had spent so much time alone on the oil rig that she found it difficult to leave the company and safety she found in the shelter, so we understood when she chose to remain at Fort Sumter.

Our first pass over the Arthur Ravenel bridge was in hope of catching a glimpse of our adversaries on the other side of the barrier across the bridge, but whoever they were, they had skillful engineers. The cargo containers that were stacked six rows deep and four rows high formed a precisely made rectangle across the bridge and along the sides back toward Mt. Pleasant. That end of the rectangle was open and the center was clear of vehicles and debris. We could see windows cut in the walls of the containers, so it wasn't hard to imagine that the inside row all the way around was empty and used as a fort. The remaining containers had most likely been filled with extra weight to keep the infected from pushing them out of the way.

There was no movement on the Mt. Pleasant side of the bridge, but the first of the infected had already arrived at the barrier. They were milling around as if they didn't know what to do next. High above their heads the signal that was calling to them was still sending out whatever it was that they could hear, and now that we knew it was there, we were sure it was causing the incessant ringing in our ears.

We slowly hovered toward the bottom of the bridge to watch the main procession as it arrived. The horde was so densely populated that it tried to spread outward every time that it passed through a choke point. The individual goal of every infected was something invisible that kept pulling them in the same general direction as before, but the pressure to expand was just like water through a garden hose. A 'spray' of infected was shoved out of the choke points in a wide pattern. Wherever the horde had also managed to have smaller groups traveling parallel to the main group, the spray of infected sent reinforcements that made those groups swell in size.

One such group split away from the main horde at the intersection of the highway with the roads that merged onto the bridge. Just like other major entrances and exits on the interstate, most lanes were heavily littered by rusting vehicles that had become snarled in traffic on those final days and nights. Thousands of people from neighboring cities and towns that shared the escape routes all converged on the spot with the same idea that they would be safe if they could only get onto the other side of the bridge. Most of them would never know that there was nowhere to go that was safe. Even within hours after it had begun, it was over for most people.

The infected swarmed between the rusty cars and collected in the lane that had been cleared by the people at Patriots Point. That gave a path to the leaders of the horde, and they gained some speed. At first it caused them to become slightly more spread out, but their damaged and decaying bodies slowed their progress again, and the slope of the bridge caused the dead up front to be pushed from behind. As they were pushed, hundreds of them were redirected toward the sides of the bridge, and we watched an unexpected development begin. The pedestrian path along the side of the bridge didn't wait for a backup to force the infected onto it. Instead, a stream of infected veered toward an opening in the concrete barrier and walked unobstructed up the bridge. When that opening in the barrier had been made was a mystery. It was such a subtle change in the landscape that we hadn't noticed it.

"There goes the neighborhood," the Chief said over the intercom system.

The largest hordes we had seen since the first day had always been frightening. It would leave me speechless to see hundreds of the infected walking together in a group. I guess the first horde was the one the Chief and I saw walking down the coast from Myrtle Beach toward Georgetown. It was a narrow highway with heavy forests along the way, so it was probably hundreds of infected dead. Then there was the horde we flew over when we ventured away from the shelter for the first time. It was marching toward the Naval Weapons Station as if it knew that was where they would find the largest number of living people. That one was probably a few thousand. The horde by the airport had been a few thousand, but that one was such a close call that I didn't care how many there were. We were too busy running.

I pictured a crowd of people the same size trying to get a glimpse of a presidential inauguration, and I couldn't. The horde that arrived on the Ravenel Bridge made Woodstock look like a local church Sunday picnic, and there were people who believed that famous event was over a half million people. The interstate was a solid mass of movement on all lanes, and since the infected were only following the call of the signal being sent from the top of the bridge and not using a map or GPS directions, the surrounding area below the interstate was covered with a drab colored blanket of infected that flowed through every path it could follow.

Infected that had wandered the city streets near the famous military college, the Citadel, were drawn by the same beacon of sound, but only a few would reach their desired goal. If they were near the onramp of the interstate when it started, they joined the parade and found their way to the bridge. Far more crossed Morrison Drive and followed the buildings and fences until they found openings that would let them walk into the Cooper River.

The Chief came over the intercom and said, "Some of them have to be coming from the Ashley River area. That means they ignored the explosions on the bridges in favor of the zombie whistle."

We all knew what he was doing, but it worked anyway. He got everyone to at least chuckle for a moment. He was serious about what was happening below us, but he was hoping to lighten the mood just a little. There was no way he would ever agree that the infected were zombies, but he had admitted he was amused when he had first heard the beacon referred to as a zombie-whistle.

As if someone had thrown a switch that was guaranteed to change the mood inside the aircraft, something caused a thumping sound on the fuselage of the sleek Sikorsky helicopter. It was only once, which was both good and bad news. One thump meant the possibility of one bullet instead of several. That was the good news. The bad news was that it was never a good idea to be shot down, but there wasn't a place below us that had ten square feet that wasn't occupied by the infected. We all went silent and waited for the Chief and Kathy to review all gauges and indicator lights for warnings, and at the same time the Chief put the helicopter into a steep bank away from the area. He had to choose right or left and hope he picked the right one. If there was a shooter below us and the Chief turned the wrong way, we would be more exposed to the next shot.

The Chief chose to bank left and go west toward the Ashley River. It was far less populated with the infected. He leveled out and shook his head in Kathy's direction. She reported that she saw no warning lights and all checks were normal.

"How stupid can a shooter be to give away his position in the middle of so many infected?" I asked over my headset.

"There's no scale to measure that much stupidity," said Jean.

The left turn had brought us back around toward the river as planned, and the Chief turned again to bring us on a course for home, but he descended earlier than we expected and sat the helicopter down just past second base in the minor league baseball stadium. Tall grass was flattened by the burst of wind from the rotors, and we threw open the doors knowing that the Chief had chosen to land for a visual inspection. He would need us outside watching for infected that may have been trapped inside the stadium.

Joe Riley Stadium, or 'The Joe' as the locals called it, was a small park, but in its time it had been perfectly located with a view of the Ashley River and the T. Allen Legare Bridge, which was at the moment pointing straight upward where we had put it. The Joe had been a picturesque addition to a quaint city, but the empty seats were littered with remains that told the story of survivors in the early days of the infection. On second thought, if there had been a game in progress when it all started, the litter told a different story. I tried to imagine it as I panned the sights of my rifle across the rows of seats, the dugouts, and the tunnels that led to the concession areas.

"I saw a news report that said an aid station was set up here," yelled Jean over the sound of the rotors. "It was when we finished boarding at the cruise terminal. The reporter was saying not to take someone to the hospital if they had been bitten, but to take them to the baseball stadium on Lockwood Drive. I guess this is where they meant."

"Why would they tell people to do that?" yelled Cassandra. "I know the hospitals became dangerous as soon as the first bite victim arrived, but a baseball stadium full of them was like falling into the lion pit at the zoo."

Kathy pointed and yelled, "The city police station is on the other side of that fence. When I was sent over to the cruise terminal, a whole squad was sent over to the ballpark."

We didn't need to hear more because the story had been the same everywhere. The police had been sent here to protect people, but they had undoubtedly been forced to turn their guns on the first bite victims in order to stop them from biting their own families. Then they had been forced to turn them on everyone including some of their own people. It would have been a duty assignment that decided whether they lived or died, and Kathy was feeling the weight of it as she stared in the direction of the left field fence where the police station had been.

"Incoming," yelled Cassandra.

We had fanned out on both sides of the helicopter while the Chief did his inspection, and everyone stayed at their designated post, but those of us facing the area over the visiting team dugout and third base had the best view of the infected that were coming our way. The railing wasn't high enough to stop them from falling onto the field, and there were a couple of small gates that opened directly from the stands.

The Chief gave the all clear signal before we had to open fire, and we were able to climb aboard before the infected reached us. As we lifted off, we heard Kathy's low exclamation over the intercom. Almost all of the infected still wore the tattered remains of their police uniforms.

"They've been here for years," said Kathy.

******

In the early days of the infection, everyone lost someone or something. At least it felt that way. Whether it was a family member or a friend, I didn't know anyone who hadn't lived through the pain of seeing someone they loved die. Before the arrival of the infection there were so many different ways to die, but since it began it was almost always the result of being bitten by an infected. Statistically speaking, winning the lottery jackpot had nothing on dying in a helicopter crash. There were likely to be some military units operating around the world, and they would run a greater risk than before the infection due to lack of routine maintenance. After all, we had one of those units living with us, and they flew three Navy helicopters. Still, there couldn't be too many civilians running around out there with an executive class Sikorsky loaded with weapons.

The Chief didn't see any obvious damage when he inspected the helicopter. It was even possible that there had been no one who had shot at them, and the damage was really just a malfunction. We so often thought of him as a miracle worker, but this time he would have needed a miracle on the level of parting the Red Sea to know that the engine was about to fail. If it had failed fifteen minutes sooner, we would have crashed into the interstate right into the horde of infected. If I had been given a choice between hearing the engine shut off as we were clearing an outfield fence or from our usual altitude of a few hundred feet, I would take the fence every time.

The Sikorsky lifted from the ground under full power, moving forward as it moved upward. The nose tilted downward as it always did, and the deafening thump of the rotors was as strong as ever....until it was just gone. There was still the feeling of moving forward but only because gravity had taken over.

I have this vague memory of hearing the rotors cutting through the air, but they weren't turning fast enough. Going from a full power take off to a totally stalled engine made me feel like I had gone instantly deaf. We all had our eyes locked on someone. Mine were locked on Jean's face, and I remember a simple question there.

"What?"

The Chief had used the helicopter like a yard tool to mow down a horde of the infected at the Air Force Base. He used a seaplane to spray fuel on a horde that had Captain Miller and his men surrounded, but he couldn't defy gravity.

The helicopter tilted over slightly to the left as the Chief fought to get the nose higher. The miracle, if there was one, came in the form of a charter bus that was parked across the street from the stadium and pointed straight at the left field fence. Instead of falling from twenty-five feet we only fell twelve feet. Our momentum was at a down angle, and because we hit the second half of the bus, the impact was mostly in the form of sliding. If we had hit toward the front, we would have crushed the bus because we were so heavy, but the rear of the roof collapsed as we slid against it and unceremoniously dumped the helicopter right behind the bus. When we fell from the roof we landed on the concrete dividers between the parking spaces, and it appeared that I got the most serious injuries in the form of something that popped in my shoulder and a mild concussion.

It went from quiet to an ear splitting shriek in a half second, and my only immediate memory when I opened my eyes was that question on Jean's face. I didn't remember where we had been or where we were going. I didn't understand why we were sitting so close to a fire, and I didn't know who was screaming. Jean was cutting my safety belt, and someone was lifting my left arm above my head.

The door was above me instead of to my left, and I knew I was in the Sikorsky, but the impact had punched in my side of the fuselage so far that the table between the seats had been torn from the bolts that held it to the floor. When someone tried to lift my right arm up to the waiting hands of the Chief, I was the one who was screaming. Passing out isn't always a bad thing.

******

I came to when the wind blew the cloud of smoke straight back to us on top of the helicopter. Something about the acrid smell of burning plastics and fuel made me react as if someone had shoved smelling salts under my nose. Even though my right arm wasn't useful, it would make it easier on everyone if I was at least using my legs.

No one was missing as far as I could tell, but there were so many of us, and everyone was moving. We had to get away from the crash site for obvious reasons. There was a pillar of smoke billowing away above the aircraft, but it changed directions with the wind. Along with the toxic gases in that black smoke was a tremendous amount of heat, and the Chief was yelling for everyone to get away before it could blow up.

I don't know if someone led everyone to a safe place on the other side of the charter bus or if we just followed the leader, but when the helicopter exploded the bus saved our lives for a second time in one day. We still felt enough of the concussion, but the blast was far worse on the back of the bus than it was on us. The rear wheels lifted off of the parking lot pavement, and the bus hung in the air for a few seconds before it slammed back to the ground. A second explosion turned the bus into an oven when its own fuel tanks ruptured and sent a fireball from the back seats that raced to the front of the bus and blew out what was left of the glass. Despite getting knocked down by both blasts, we were back on our feet and running for the ball park. With a little help from Jean on one side and Tom on the other I was able to make it back across the street without doing more damage to my shoulder.

The gates to the ballpark were made of sturdy metal bars, and chains were threaded around the middle poles. It was anyone's guess if they were chained shut in order to keep the infected out or if they had been put in place when it had become a failed treatment center. Either way, there were infected dead on both sides of the gates.

We followed the Chief as he ran along the left field wall that we had just flown over only a few moments before. He was heading for center field, and all I had to do was glance behind us to understand why he had chosen that direction. There were a few infected dead ahead of us, but there were dozens behind us. They had been crossing the big open field that was used for parking at ball games, but the helicopter crash had drawn their attention. So much for our theory that the zombie-whistle was making Charleston a safer city.

The parking lot was still packed with cars that had undoubtedly carried bite victims to the designated treatment area on the first day. Wooden barricades still blocked the streets as the police had tried their best to deal with the throngs of people who had arrived with bloody towels wrapped around their wounds or carrying loved ones who were already dead. Now the infected were being called from every corner of the city and were trying to reach the east side.

"Why are there so many of them?" yelled Jean. She sounded winded from helping me get away before the bus blew up. "Shouldn't they have been gone a long time ago?"

"We just opened the Ashley River bridges yesterday," I said. "These infected have been pouring in across those bridges ever since they started hearing whatever it is they hear."

"We should have waited one more day to crash."

She didn't say it very loud, but somehow Hampton heard her.

"Remind me to make a point of that to the Chief once we get somewhere safe. Where's he going anyway?"

Just as Hampton shouted his question, the Chief turned and scaled the center field wall like a squirrel going up a tree. I didn't see the handholds that he used until I was practically at the spot directly below him. I shouldered my rifle and supply bag and helped Jean reach the first metal rung. She was so short that she couldn't lift her foot high enough. I heard her ask the Chief as soon as she was climbing how he knew about the ladder. He disappeared over the top of the wall as he answered, but by then I could see the obvious answer.

There was a narrow ledge along the edge of the big scoreboard in center field, and the rungs allowed fast access to that ledge.

One by one we reached the top rung, and I found that the Chief had tied a rope to it. He had thrown the rope over the edge so we could easily descend the inside wall into the ballpark. Maybe it would have been easier for me if my shoulder wasn't screaming in pain, but I eventually made it over the wall.

For some reason I expected to see a ballpark inside the fence, not the overgrown field of swaying grass and scrub brush trees. Even though we had landed inside a few minutes ago, it looked different from my perch above the center field wall. Nature had moved into the small ballpark.

"Toss your bag," he yelled from below.

Jean was already hitting the ground next to him, and as I dropped down the wall, Hampton was throwing his leg over the top. Tom was the last one to come over, and by that time a sizable horde of the infected had been grabbing at his legs as he began climbing.

Kathy had reached the top rung ahead of Tom, but instead of dropping over with the rest of us, she reached for the ledge in front of the scoreboard and pulled herself into a sitting position above Tom. She braced her feet along the top of the wall and pressed her back against the scoreboard. She had her hands free to pull her rifle around in front of her and take aim. I couldn't see what she was shooting at, but she couldn't miss, and judging by the number of times she adjusted her aim and fired, it must have gotten crowded around Tom by the time he was able to climb. The last few shots were more out of anger than necessity. They had almost gotten her man, and she was taking it out on all of them.

Kathy shouldered her rifle and smoothly made the transition from sitting on the ledge to sliding down the rope. Her feet were barely on the ground before she got her arms around Tom's neck.

"It was that close?" asked Colleen.

Tom could only nod. I couldn't recall ever seeing the expression he had on his face. Tom had always been a leader, and when he had his game face on, his expression was deadly serious. Whatever it was that happened on the other side of that wall, it had scared Tom enough to make him turn pale. As Kathy held him close, his eyes were darting from face to face over her shoulder.

The rest of us weren't ignoring the infected that had seen us in center field, but we weren't giving them the immediate attention we would normally have shown. They were still a long way from us, and the closest wasn't out of the infield yet. It was the frightened look on Tom's face that had us all on edge. Hampton took aim at the infected that was passing second base and shot it. He turned back to Tom before the infected even hit the ground.

Iris was behind the Chief when she put her hand over her mouth. I saw that her eyes were aimed lower than mine, and I followed them down toward Tom's feet, and I saw that there was a huge, dark stain on his faded jeans. It began at the right knee and ran down the front of his leg all the way to his foot. Tom wasn't pale just from fear. He was pale from a loss of blood. The audible gasp that escaped from behind her hand made everyone glance at Iris and then back to Tom's leg.

Kathy supported Tom's weight, but she realized he wasn't just hugging her. He was losing consciousness and probably already in shock. She lowered him to the ground as the rest of us rushed in to help her. Tom towered over the rest of us, and as strong as Kathy was, they were going to fall hard if we hadn't reacted in time.

Most of our usual crew was along on this disastrous trip, nine of us besides Tom, so we worked well together. The Chief didn't need to tell us what to do. Most of us broke away from the group and took up defensive positions with our weapons aimed into the ballpark. We each had our emergency packs, but we had lost a lot of our gear in the crash. There wasn't time to retrieve anything important before the explosion, so we knew we would have to secure the stadium and then inventory our supplies. Ammunition would be counted and then equally distributed. In the mean time, carefully aimed shots were critical until we were able to assess how many of the infected were inside with us.

Jean had taken over the medical crisis while Kathy tried to talk Tom into staying conscious. Iris was assisting Jean to expose the injury and to get an answer to the question that was written on all of our faces. We all needed to know if Tom had been injured in the crash, or if he was bitten as he made his escape up the center field wall.

"How many infected?"

The question from the Chief wasn't directed at anyone in particular, and it didn't matter if the answers were the same or different. We all needed to know how bad it was going to get, and more importantly whether or not we had to waste ammunition.

"Fourteen," I answered.

"I count sixteen," said Hampton.

"Same here," said Colleen.

Colleen was standing next to Hampton, and they were focusing their attention toward the first base side of the field. I was more toward the center of the group. Cassandra and Sim seemed to be joined at the hips, and they reported eighteen already on the field over by third base. The front gates were on the third base side, so we all expected more to arrive from there.

I saw Iris and the Chief exchange glances. She was shoulder to shoulder with Jean, and I could tell she only took her eyes off of Tom so she could use them to tell the Chief something. I saw what she was telling him too, and what I got from it was a worried message from her to him. It wouldn't do us any good for me to assume the worst, so I was holding out hope that his injuries had been from the crash. There was a lot more blood soaked into the pants than I would have expected from a bite.

"Can he be moved?"

The Chief did his best to make it a question and not a demand, but the urgency in his voice was clear. Before he could decide how we were going to attack the problem, he had to know if we were leaving someone behind to cover Jean, Iris, Kathy, and Tom, or if the whole group could move together.

"He's not stable yet," answered Jean. "He's still losing blood."

His next words were more of a command, and we all knew why he did it. Kathy and Iris were too valuable in a fight, whether it was hand to hand or guns.

"I need one shooter here to cover Tom and Jean. Everyone else form up into one team of eight. We'll take the third base side first and work our way toward the center of the park. If we hear Kathy start shooting, it means infected have reached the infield. We'll double back to clear them out and then go toward first base. Any questions?"

Kathy had heard the Chief and was glaring at him. She wanted to stay with Tom, and she knew what the Chief was doing. She also knew he was right. Comforting Tom wasn't going to be of much help if we didn't secure the ballpark before it got dark. We still had several hours left in the day, but there was always the possibility that there was a breach somewhere and that the infected would keep coming into the stadium.

The Chief had made a concession by assigning overwatch to Kathy instead of taking her along with the main group. I had a feeling that he was going to change the assignments if she didn't acknowledge his orders soon.

There was a tense moment, but it ended when the Chief held her rifle out in her direction.

"Hold your fire until they reach second base. We might need the ammo."

Kathy took the rifle, and Iris pulled her machete from the straps holding it on her backpack. Jean gave Iris a reassuring nod to let her know she could take care of Tom on her own and then turned toward Kathy.

"Trust me."

Kathy's nod was barely perceptible, but it was enough. She rotated her body and went into a shooter's sitting position as she brought the scope to her eye.

The Chief didn't need to tell us what to do. As he shouldered his rifle and pulled out his machete, he led the way toward third base. We had done this before, and we knew not to get too close to each other. So far, we hadn't gotten ourselves hurt by getting in the way of someone else's swing.

Every time we move toward a group of the infected with our machetes at the ready, I think about the early days when the Mud Island family was much smaller. Tom's wife, Allison, had insisted on going with us when we left the shelter and within minutes we were swinging machetes at the infected. Allison had been so scared that she had dropped to the ground. At least that way no one had to worry about cutting her head off.

Since that day we had refined our attacks as a group, and we even practiced forehand and backhand rules. In order to avoid an accidental injury from a machete, the left side of the formation used forehand swings, and the right side used backhand swings. That way we were less likely to hit someone behind us with a follow-through if we missed our target. We also practiced starting our swings without using a pitcher's windup. No one ever let their blade cross behind their own body.

The Chief and I were in the lead with him on my left. I matched his speed as we moved toward the infected, and since I knew he would be swinging a forehand toward the infected closest to us, I automatically veered to the right. I was grateful to do a backswing because it hurt far less than a forehand. As the first infected went down, the Chief changed course to his left to intercept the next one. The rest of our group followed the person in front of them, and if someone had been watching us from above, they would have thought we moved from side to side like a snake.

We had seen other people attacking the infected, and they always got strung out in a line shoulder to shoulder. Before long the blades would be flying from the left and right, and they were lucky to come away from the fight with all of their own arms still attached. Using our method of attack we drove straight into the middle of the infected that were already on the playing field. There were more in the stands, but we would have plenty of time to deal with them.

A shot rang out behind us just as we were getting into position to dispose of the infected that were falling over the rail on the front row. It was a low wall, so the infected walked into it and immediately did a head first summersault. Their brittle bodies made loud snapping sounds as decayed bones shattered on impact, and the sound of the gunshot was so similar to the breaking bones that we almost didn't hear it.

We all turned out of reflex. No amount of practice would make us so disciplined that we could forget that three of our family members were left behind in center field. The distraction almost cost us because we had moved too close to the wall to take our eyes away from the infected. They seemed to suddenly pour out of the stands down the third base line. One of the rotting bodies fell in a perfect, rolling dive, and its momentum caused it to fall forward as it came to a standing position like a gymnast. The combined dive, roll, and fall put it within an arm's reach of the Chief. Its bony, skeletal fingers wrapped around his right forearm, and he reacted with a violent backhand swing.

The Chief wasn't the kind of soldier to lose his composure or forget the rules. A mental lapse by him was rare, so I was surprised to see that the only thing between me and his incoming machete was the scrawny neck of the infected. The problem was that the weight of the infected was holding his arm down as the machete whistled through the air, and I knew the force behind that swing was going to keep the blade coming across in my direction. The sharpened steel edge hit the fragile neck, and the head disappeared so quickly it might as well have been a baseball sitting on a batting tee. The head disappeared, but the blade kept coming at me.

Hampton saw the same things that I had, but instead of becoming a spectator like me, he reacted. He dove from behind me and hit my legs at the knees. I collapsed under his weight and heard the sound of the machete as it went by.

What happened next was a little confusing to me, but the situation became crystal clear when Kathy snapped out of her loss of composure over Tom being hurt. The last thing any of us had expected was to see our own personal superhero face down in the dirt. Seeing the Chief sprawled on the ground caused us all to freeze for a split second, but then we all moved with purpose. We formed a semi-circle around his prone body and faced outward. Instead of machetes, our rifles were swept from our shoulders, and we began clearing away the infected with abandon.

Kathy had somehow gotten to the middle of the half circle and lifted the Chief's head from the ground. By the time we had the advance of the infected reduced to random movement in the stands, she had discovered that the Chief had been operating on autopilot. He had a huge lump on the top of his head that he must have gotten in the crash of the helicopter. Iris stopped firing first and helped Kathy to turn him over. I saw that she wasn't crying, but her face was the same pale, ashen color as the Chief's. Judging by the color of his skin and the size of the lump on his head, I doubted that he would even remember that he came within inches of decapitating me.

10

Chaos

There are times when the best plans just go to pieces. We probably adapt better than most people or we wouldn't be able to count ourselves among the survivors of the infection. We had lost people along the way, but for the most part those we had seen die were also those who needed the most protection. Alone they couldn't have survived without the help of the group. It was safe to say that the Chief was one of those survivors who would most likely still be alive even if he had never met any of us. If he had met someone else, they would be his family, but we were the lucky ones. We were here because of him.

I had told myself countless times that I would have survived easily if I had locked myself into my shelter and just stayed there, but when I faced facts, I knew that I would have become starved for the one thing that was missing in the shelter. It was a little light on human companionship. I've sometimes wondered how long I could have lasted alone in the shelter, and when I've been honest with myself, I lasted as long as I could without people. When the Chief, Kathy, and Jean arrived in their life raft, I was totally glad to see them. I needed them to come along when they did, and if they hadn't found me, I would have done something dumb like go looking for them. Not them specifically, but someone.

When Kathy found the lump on the Chief's head, she gasped loud enough for all of us to hear. We had been shooting nonstop, and our ears were ringing, but her gasp might as well have been as loud as the shooting. The lump was already changing colors and Jean was breaking out an instant cold pack from the first aid kit. Iris had taken over with Tom, but Jean was already moving back to him.

"Someone keep that compress on the Chief's head while I take care of Tom," she said. "How did he even climb over the fence back there, let alone lead the charge against the infected?"

I was the closest to them, so I dropped to my knees and put one hand over the compress. It was cold, and I was grateful for the little things at the moment. Grateful that Jean was a Registered Nurse, and grateful for first aid kits. I could have wished that we hadn't crashed or that no one had been hurt, but I chose to say a silent prayer of thanks for the fact that we could treat the injuries. Maybe it was my way of hoping that the injuries weren't worse.

Jean motioned for Kathy to come help her, and Kathy practically jumped to her side. Up until that moment, Kathy had appeared to be unable to move from the spot between the two men that she loved, one as a father and the other as a companion.

"Here, hold this."

Jean directed Kathy's hand to the cloth she had pressed against Tom's leg, and as soon as Kathy put pressure on it, Jean was threading a large, curved needle.

"Is there anything I can do?" asked Iris.

Jean pointed at something in the first aid kit and Iris immediately saw Jean wanted her to sterilize the needle and the wound. Iris poured some alcohol on a sterile gauze pad and passed it to Kathy. She took the gauze and glanced at Tom's face. Jean was lifting one of his eyelids and shining a small light into his eye. She nodded at Kathy, and Kathy lifted the bloody cloth away, quickly replacing it with the gauze. If Tom had been conscious, he would have reacted.

Iris had sterilized the needle by the time Jean was ready for it. Jean moved with skilled hands and made the first stitch so quickly that the wound didn't have a chance to release much blood.

"The wound is a straight line, or close to it," she said. "It must've happened in the crash. If it was a bite, we wouldn't be able to stitch it so well."

"It couldn't be a bite on top of a crash wound, could it?" asked Kathy.

Jean shook her head. "We've both seen enough bites to know the difference. You're just worried. Give Ed a hand with the Chief while Iris and I finish this up."

Kathy was lost for a moment. She realized she had totally blocked out the fact that the other main man in her life was also unconscious. She gave Jean a weak smile and a quick kiss on the cheek.

When Kathy joined me at the Chief's side, she wanted to take a look under the cold compress. She winced when she saw it.

"We need to get these two into a safe place. Where do you suppose that would be?" she asked.

I had already been thinking ahead to what we were going to do, and I knew it had to be somewhere that could be totally closed off, but every place I thought of also had the unsavory possibility of being a dead end. Not to mention the fact that the Chief and Tom were two big guys. We were in for some really heavy lifting.

Sim knelt down next to us and cleared his throat.

"When we holed up in the airport we were lucky to have supplies, but the main thing we had was a way to seal ourselves in where the infected couldn't see us. As long as they couldn't see us, we were able to spread out through a large part of the airport. Unless we have another rat invasion, this place should be safe, but that means cleaning out anything else that's moving in the ballpark."

"I'll second that," said Hampton. "We can start a sweep, and then we can stay away from the places where they can see us from the outside. Unless we find a big hole in the walls or fences, we should be able to manage this."

Hearing Sim and Hampton lay out a strategy was just what Kathy needed. She realized that she knew Joe Riley ballpark better than any of us. As a rookie police officer she had been able to catch a few games when she got off work, but even before that she had been to plenty of games. She had never seen what was hidden behind the dugouts and the locker rooms, and she hadn't ever gone up into the press boxes and the party suites, but she knew there wasn't anything complicated about making the place safe.

I said, "If we can close off the locker rooms from the outside, we won't even have to worry about what's inside them."

"If they're already closed, I can't think of a good reason to open them," said Sim. "We sealed a lot of rooms with the dead inside them at the airport. Then when the rats came through they always found a way to get inside the rooms. By the time we came back out of the airplane, the rats had cleared all the rooms for us."

I think we all thought of the same thing at the same time. There had been a rat invasion in Charleston too. Probably were rat invasions in every city to some extent. Some were worse than others. After the rat population got too large they turned on each other for food, and the balance of nature took over. Then the dead went back to work trying to find more survivors to bite.

"Do you think the rat swarms got to the infected inside the rooms below the stands?" asked Colleen. She had been listening to us while standing guard with Cassandra.

Sim said, "There were infected walking around inside the park." He gestured toward the stands where we had just shot a few dozen of the infected that had walked toward the sound of gunfire.

"Only one way to find out," said Kathy. "Sim, would you be okay to stay behind with Jean and Iris?"

Kathy started to add that she hoped he wasn't insulted, but he stopped her.

"I know, I know. I'm a navigator. Just take care of my lady for me."

Cassandra flashed a big smile at Sim. In a firefight there would be no contest as to who I'd rather have by my side. Cassandra had been the only survivor on a ship that was jammed full of the infected. She had to fight the infected and the living at the end. Sim had survived by being smart, but Cassandra had survived by being a warrior.

"Should we move the Chief and Tom out to the center field wall before we go?" I asked.

Everyone was in agreement that the grass had grown tall enough to hide them if they stayed still, so we carefully lifted the Chief's huge body and carried him to the fence. It took all of us, and we were winded by the time we got back to Tom. Just to make it easier, we all helped to carry him as well. Everyone went to work on some bushes nearby and then dragged the branches into place. Unless they stood up and shouted, it wasn't likely that any of the infected would wander out and find them.

With our injured friends well hidden, we followed the outfield fence toward the stands in right field. With Cassandra in the lead we climbed over a low wall and began our search for any infected dead that were trapped inside the park.

The place was a mess. There were barricades in places that gave us a good idea of how badly things had gone in the beginning. Not that we didn't already know, and not that we hadn't seen the same things in other places, but it was obvious that what had happened in Joe Riley

Park had happened a long time ago. The infected we had seen and shot from our position in the outfield were likely to be the only infected we saw unless there were some trapped in the bowels of the stadium.

What bothered us the most about the signs of long ago chaos and death was the signs that the place had never stood a chance to be the refuge it was thought to be. The infection had overwhelmed the hospitals so quickly that people actually tried to retreat to the ballpark. The evidence was the line of ambulances that were backed up against the closest gates. There were walls. There were steel gates in solid steel fences, and they closed against brick walls. There was food, lights, and police protection. We could even imagine how the mayor and his family had rushed up the front steps before the gates were pulled shut. We could see his limousine next to the ambulances, and someone had even taken the time to tape up a makeshift sign on an office door proclaiming it as belonging to the Mayor of Charleston. It was chaos at the start, and it was chaos at the end. Sadly, those two days hadn't been too far apart.

We searched through several vending areas and found doors that led to restricted areas where fans could never go. We had to use flashlights for far longer than we would have wanted, and everything appeared to move when shadows crept through the rooms. There was that ever present smell from what had happened here a long time ago, but there was that other smell of something that had happened more recently. Patches of dark black blood and blood that was still closer to red.

Even where there hadn't been death, there was still the rot. The smell of spoiled food and decay was long gone, but now there was the smell that comes from lack of use. Sewer lines poured methanol gas into rooms that had been closed for years, and sometimes it was enough just to pass by rooms and leave them closed. We weren't staying, we just needed to be sure it was safe until the Chief and Tom were back on their feet.

I think we were all surprised to find how much time had passed when we finally emerged from the interior of the ballpark. It was raining and had been for a while. The gloom made the debris that accumulated over the years look even more sinister.

Kathy held up her hand with the signal for everyone to stop. Cassandra was still in the lead, and it made us all nervous that she wasn't the one to signal danger. We all stood completely still and just listened. There was nothing. One by one we made eye contact and everyone gave the same slight shake of the head to say we didn't know what had spooked Kathy.

Cassandra held up one hand to signal move out, but when it was half raised her eyes found something. She kept it half raised and raised her other hand to match it. Kathy was next in line, and her eyes followed Cassandra's. Her head was tilted back so she was looking at something beyond and above Cassandra. Colleen, Hampton, and I watched her raise her hands. None of us could see anything ahead in all of the debris, but it was obvious that Cassandra and Kathy were in agreement about surrender.

It wasn't a loud voice, but it was very clear as it carried through the concession concourse of the ballpark.

"The rest of you need to be as smart as the ladies with their hands up."

I managed to zero in on the spot where Cassandra had spotted something, and I saw the barrel of a rifle with slight movement behind it. To the left was another rifle. From somewhere behind me there was movement, and I wanted badly to face it rather than to have an infected dump saliva down the back of my shirt before ripping me open. I was almost relieved when I heard a voice come from the spot.

"Don't turn around. Everyone ease your weapons to the ground then lace your fingers behind your heads."

Rough hands grabbed me even before I could sit my rifle on the ground, and a sack made of coarse material was pulled over my head. I could see a little light through the material, but only enough to see that we were overwhelmed by a group twice as big as ours. I heard muffled commands and grunts as the others were handled as roughly as me. Someone was kicked, and I was pretty sure Kathy kicked one of them. Then it was quiet.

Several hands lifted me, and I realized I must have been knocked out for at least a few minutes because I didn't remember my hands being tied behind my back. If I couldn't feel the hands gripping my skin as well as my clothes, it would have felt like I was floating. Then it was lighter through the material of the cloth until I felt like I was falling. I landed on top of something I recognized as human bodies. I panicked because all I could think was that I had been tossed onto a pile of dead people.

There was a loud sound that had to be doors closing, and then the sound of an engine starting. I felt the body directly under me squirm. All I could think of was getting away from the body I knew must be an infected that was trying to get into position to bite me. The problem was that it could see me but I couldn't see it.

I pushed myself up against something that had to be a metal wall behind me, but the whole room seemed to bounce at the same time, and my feet left the floor. When I landed, my right knee hit something hard, but my left knee was buried into soft flesh. I heard someone exhale all of their breath and cry out in pain. It was Kathy.

"Kathy," I yelled, but I was too late. She must have gotten her balance just as I realized who it was, because there was no way for her to stop the head first shoulder tackle that was coming my way. She crashed into my midsection with tremendous force and slammed me against that metal wall behind me. Then I could hear her when she understood who she had just rammed into.

"Oh no, Ed? Is that you?"

All I could manage was a weak, "Uh huh." I was in a heap on the floor.

"I'm over here," said Colleen.

"Are you guys done beating up on each other?" That was Hampton's voice somewhere.

"I owe somebody a knee," said Cassandra. "Does everybody have a bag over their head?"

There was another big bump that knocked us around on the hard floor.

"I think we're in an ambulance," said Kathy.

"Maybe," said Cassandra, "but this thing rides like one of those personnel carriers we had in the Army."

******

"Great. I just felt a couple of raindrops."

Jean held a palm out and checked the clouds above. She instantly had a few heavy drops splash across her hand. The patter of the rain sounded like a whisper coming closer in the grass surrounding them.

"Can anyone see us from the stands or the press boxes?" asked Iris.

She raised her head higher so she could see the rest of the ballpark.

"I don't think so," said Jean, "but it always looks better from the low ground than it is. That's why everyone always tries for the high ground."

"I get it, but I think we can pull a small tarp tent over us and still be safe. The light's getting bad, and the tarp is the same color as this grass and small trees. If something or someone doesn't see us putting it up, I think we'll be fine."

A few more heavy raindrops convinced Jean that it wasn't much of a risk, and she helped Iris tug the tarp out of the canvas bag it had been squeezed into.

"This should help," said Sim. He crawled out of the deep grass dragging a relatively straight pole. "We can use it as a way to raise the middle of the tarp."

Working together they managed to get the tarp in place as a makeshift tent over them and their two friends.

Jean said, "I'm worried about how long they've been unconscious."

"Not much else we can do. At least we had enough stuff in our first aid kit to stabilize them. It also didn't hurt when you found someone had the sense to pack antibiotics and syringes."

Sim ducked out from under the tarp, and they saw their ceiling sag down slightly. He came back under with them just as quickly.

"What did you do?" asked Iris.

"I put a couple of light branches from a bush on one side. From the press boxes it should look like a big bush. It should also help the rainwater drain off on one side too."

The Chief let out a low groan, and in the dim light under the tarp they could see he was doing his best to get his elbows into position to push himself up.

"Stay down for a minute, Chief," said Iris. "If you sit up too fast you might wind up flat on your face. Better to stay on your back until we get you oriented."

"What... happened? Where... are we?"

He was definitely still groggy, if his voice was any indication. The words were slurred and pauses between words made him sound drunk.

Iris lifted the compress from his head and shone her small flashlight on the lump. It was still ugly, but it wasn't nearly as big as it had been.

Jean leaned in closer and checked the reactions of his pupils.

"Much better. I think you're going to be okay. What's the last thing you remember?"

The Chief reached up with his right hand and gingerly touched the lump on his head.

"How did that get there?"

"You hit your head when we crashed, and somehow you managed to climb a ballpark fence and attack a few of the infected before you got it through your thick skull that you were hurt," said Jean.

He eyed her suspiciously, as if she was making it up.

Iris leaned in closer.

"Hey, remember me? What's that last thing you remember."

"I was trying to make the helicopter hit the top of a black charter bus."

"Wow," said Sim with admiration. "You do better on autopilot than a lot of people do on purpose."

The Chief looked at Sim like he had no clue what he was saying, but then he realized there was someone else lying on the ground next to him. He leaned back away from the prone body as if he was focusing his eyes by moving. That bothered Jean and Iris.

"Tom?"

The Chief tried to stand but understood immediately they were under a tarp. The rain was doing a steady patter on the other side. He moved forward over his friend, forgetting his own injury for a moment.

Jean said, "He's sedated, Chief. He got a nasty cut on his leg either in the crash or crawling out of the wreckage. We had to sew him up. We think he's going to be okay, but he lost a lot of blood, and he's been out for a long time. That part we're worried about."

"Crawling out? He wasn't bitten, was he? I think I remember some infected around the place where we crashed."

Iris answered gently as she put one hand on his arm, "We don't know for sure because we didn't know either of you was hurt until we got inside the ballpark. He was the last one over the fence, and the infected had followed us all the way from the parking lot across the street. He didn't stay conscious long enough to tell us how it happened."

"We have to get him back to Fort Sumter."

When he said it, the Chief realized he was only talking to a few people.

"Where's everyone else?"

Sim answered for everyone, "We don't know. They went to clear the rest of the ballpark. Iris and I stayed to provide cover for Jean while she treated you two. We haven't heard any shots, and they've been gone for over two hours."

The Chief got that look on his face they all recognized. He was mentally walking through the ballpark, visualizing the concourses, the vending areas, the stands. He knew there was far more to a ballpark

127

than what meets the eye. That wasn't just empty space beneath the bleachers, and the suites were spacious even in minor league parks.

"Two hours," he repeated. "It could take twice that long if they wanted to be thorough, but they wouldn't really need to go into some places. It's not like we were planning on hanging around here longer than we had to."

Jean didn't think the Chief was ready to go out on a search and rescue yet, but she had to say it in a way that the Chief wouldn't just automatically dismiss her.

"There aren't enough of us to go after them yet. I don't think we can split up until Tom is able to walk."

The Chief was visibly recovering, and they could see it. As his senses came back to him, so did his ability to think through the problem.

"The three of you were standing guard over two of us. Now you only have to protect one of us. I'll be okay out there on my own. Is it dark out there yet?"

The Chief lifted back a corner of the canvas tarp and saw it was twilight, and the steady rain made it seem even later.

"Darkness and bad weather," he said. "Two of a Navy SEAL's best friends. You guys stay here. If I don't come back by tomorrow morning, I want you to assume I won't be back. Make your way to the city marina and find a boat that will get you back to Fort Sumter. Remember the entrances to the shelter have been sealed, but you know where the cameras are located. Let them see you and then hole up somewhere until they can send a chopper for you. You know they're searching for us by now, so they'll be watching the surface of Fort Sumter."

"I'm not assuming anything. We can wait here for you to come back," said Iris.

"You said it yourself. Tom needs real medical care, and it's going to take all three of you to get him out of here."

"We could argue the same thing," said Sim. "We need you to help us get him to a boat."

"Well, I don't feel right about the rest of our group being out there overnight, so I'm going after them. Like I said, I should be back before morning. Hang onto this for me."

The Chief held out his rifle to Iris. She hesitantly took it.

"I'll want that back from you, so try not to lose it or get any dirt in the barrel."

The grin on his face was too much for her to resist. She had to give him a grin in return.

"If you don't come back for it, I might just have to use it to hunt you down."

"You can do that if I don't come back, but I'll see you by tomorrow morning."

The Chief gave Iris a hug with his big arm wrapped around her neck, hiding their faces from Jean and Sim. The kiss he gave her made her feel limp from head to toe, and she was fairly sure they could tell. When he let her go, it was hard not to fall over even though she was sitting under the low tarp. The Chief gave the others a wink and ducked out into the rain.

******

For a big man, the Chief could move like a ghost. The rain and gloom from the sun setting gave him the cover he needed to be able to reach the stands with confidence that he hadn't been seen. At the same time, he was acutely aware of every shadow. Where it was when he first saw it, and where it was when he checked it again. His memory for details had been honed over years of training and combat as a Navy SEAL, but he had said many times that enemies were predictable, and the infected dead were not. If one was nearby, you didn't know what it was going to do.

It was easy for him to find where five people had climbed out of the tall grass into the stands, and he saw they had chosen well. They were able to stay under cover as soon as they were in the seats. When he found their footprints he knew they had picked up moisture and dirt, but he could tell they had also walked through dried blood. Since they weren't trying to hide their tracks, he wouldn't subtract any points for being easy to follow. As a matter of fact, he was counting on them being easy to find.

Something caught his eye in the mess of footprints that made him freeze. He went from being cautious to being ready to fight in a split second. There was a pattern to the footprints that told him within reason which set of prints was in the lead, and which set of prints belonged to the person bringing up the rear. There was a footprint that didn't match the others, and it was on top of the prints he had established as belonging to the last one in line.

He studied the print, and it appeared to have been made with force.

The Chief raised his eyes slowly and saw that someone had dropped down from above after his friends had passed by. It didn't take long to find more prints that followed the first one from above, and he wasn't sure how many there were.

There was a time to track and a time to follow, and the Chief picked up his speed. There was a place where the tracks went inside the building under the stands, and he hoped they weren't still inside because it had to be really dark in there. His eyes scouted ahead where he could see fresh tracks at a door that might be where they came back out, and he decided to bypass searching inside the building. If he hadn't moved to there, he wouldn't have reached the corner in time to see what was happening up ahead.

He was never one to go around a corner without a quick look, and he wasn't about to start now. He was tempted to dive on the back of the man closest to him, but his glance around the corner told him that wouldn't go well for his friends. Uniforms made it easier for him to do a head count in the moment that he had exposed himself, and there were so many that he couldn't come up with an accurate total.

His friends were surrounded by uniforms, and the bags over the heads of Kathy, Ed, Hampton, Colleen, and Cassandra meant they wouldn't be able to help themselves. As quickly as it seemed to happen, it was over just as fast. When he glanced again, he saw the backs of the uniformed men as they rushed his friends blindly down a flight of stairs. A few cautious steps forward, and he was in a position to see them roughly thrown through the open doors of ambulances. When they drove away he saw he had been wrong. They weren't ambulances. They were BATT-T armored personnel carriers.

******

"Shut up or I'll put two bags over your heads."

The male voice didn't have to sound rough or even mean. The close proximity of it was enough to silence us. I think we all assumed we were in the back of an ambulance or EMS type vehicle, and there was separation between us and our captors. The way we were being tossed around was making us disoriented, and I wasn't sure where the front of the vehicle was until I heard the voice.

"What do you want with us?" demanded Kathy.

The voice didn't answer the question, but after several moments of silence a second voice said, "If anyone is more comfortable sitting, there are bench seats along the walls."

I was leaning against something that didn't feel like it was a bench seat. That meant I was either up against the back door or against the front seats. I didn't know which was worse, the possibility of falling out of the back of the bouncing vehicle or being within inches of our captors. I scrambled away from where I was and turned what I thought was sideways. I pushed myself up using just my legs and was surprised that the seat was actually padded.

"Well, I am impressed," said a sarcastic voice. "They're all smart enough to choose comfortable over uncomfortable."

The two voices joined each other in a laugh.

"Where are you taking us?"

No one could say that Kathy would ever give up, but her questions didn't seem like they were getting a rise out of the unknown men.

I felt a tap against my foot and knew it was someone's boot. We had collided with each other so much that it could have been random, but we had all learned Morse Code as a survival skill, and the boot tapped out one of our key words. Capitulate.

Sometimes it was too much work to tap out a whole sentence, so we had key words that meant entire paragraphs. The Chief had chosen the key words, and they had to be words that couldn't easily be mistaken for other words. In this case, capitulate meant that we had no choice but to go along with our captors. We had also agreed that anyone could initiate the keyword messages, and if we were in disagreement about the key word we could tap one word back. Object. The paragraph written for this key word said it wasn't necessarily a surrender. It was meant to cover situations where we would be more likely to die if we didn't at least give in for the moment. I didn't tap back that I objected.

After the key word was given to my left foot, I moved my other foot to the right. I made contact with a solid surface and rubbed against it. As I expected, it had to be the back wall of the vehicle, and thanks to the information provided by one of the men up front, I knew there would likely be someone directly across from me...unless we all tried to sit on the same side, but that would have evoked even more laughter up front.

I slid my foot forward and felt my boot bump into something that immediately moved away from my foot. An instinctive reaction by someone blindfolded. I slid further forward and began tapping as soon as I made contact. The foot stayed close enough this time for me to pass along the message, and there was no objection. For now, it looked like we were going for a ride.

11

Phillip & Denise

The Corrigans felt at home at Fort Sumter with the exception of a feeling they were being watched. Maybe it was because they were, but it was more likely that they didn't have experience as spies before they were chosen by the people in charge at Patriots Point. They had heard stories about the radicals at Fort Sumter, and even though they had seen nothing to support those stories, they felt like they were being sent into a lion's den without protection. The Army and the civilians they had met were all so nice, but that's what they had been told to expect...a total act. Still, it wouldn't hurt to tell their story about that first day over six years ago.

The nightmare of that long first night seemed like something out of a bad dream, and it had taken its toll, especially on Phillip. So far the worst thing about the people of Fort Sumter was that they were making the Corrigans relive it. Reliving it was making his chest hurt. His heart had pounded wildly that day. More wildly than he believed possible. The shotguns and nine millimeter handguns had made their ears ring for hours, but somehow they had been pushed along with dozens of other people down several flights of stairs until they reached a floor of rooms with prison style doors. There was no choice but to allow themselves to be locked in. They were afraid there would be no one left alive who could let them out, but the people with the keys also had the guns.

With nothing left to do except wait for rescue, they had huddled with the other survivors and shared their experiences of that first day, and they all had the same story. They were going about the day with no clue of what was about to happen. Most of them had watched as their families were slaughtered before their eyes. Some of them had seen their family members doing the killing. One man had been unable to stop sobbing since they had arrived. A witness saw him kill his own wife after he had pulled her off of their two children. Then he was forced to defend himself from the children. No one wanted to hear the rest of the details.

Everyone around them was afraid, but Phillip was deathly pale. His lips were blue, and he was drenched in sweat. Someone said they thought he was having a heart attack, but he thought it couldn't be. He was only thirty years old and had been in good health. A lady who had been pushed inside with them dug through her pocketbook and pulled out a slender cylinder. Through the ringing in his ears and the pounding of his heart, he heard her say something about him being allergic to something, maybe some kind of shellfish like crab or shrimp. It hadn't made sense, but whatever it was in that cylinder, it had done the trick.

He had learned since then it was an Epi-Pen, and for some reason the epinephrine had worked. But he knew there must have been something else because his heart still hurt sometimes, and he still turned pale and began to sweat whenever the stress got too bad. Needless to say, the stress level of living in the infected world was enough to make his heart hurt on a regular basis.

It was hours before a police officer came back to the locked door that opened into their corridor, and the only good news he brought with him was that he had keys. They were startled when he appeared at the doors and came inside, but it didn't bother them at all when he locked them behind himself. No one wanted those doors to be unlocked, even for a moment. Then he gave them the bad news. It hadn't gone well up on the ground floor.

The officer explained that the area where they had been sheltered wasn't a holding cell for prisoners. It was under renovation to expand the evidence room. The evidence stored there would be for high profile cases, so there was additional security. That's why there was a cell door across the main entrance and on the doors of the individual rooms. They had running water and a restroom, but there was no food or other amenities because the work had been in progress. If it had been finished, there would have at least been a snack machine and a coffee room.

The people in the basement, thirty-six not counting the police officer, had already found the restrooms but they hadn't found anything else they considered useful. There were a half dozen blankets in a closet, and those were given to the most needy. Everyone had insisted that Phillip should take one because of how sick he had been.

The officer got everyone together in the largest room and told them the building had been locked down. There were only a few officers left in the rest of the building, and they were in scattered rooms watching over small groups of survivors like themselves. If they could get the opportunity, they planned to move everyone from the other groups into the basement along with any supplies they could locate in the building.

Someone asked when that might be, and the officer said he didn't know. It all depended on what they were told to do by the military. He said that martial law was in effect, and a few things had gotten back to him before they lost communications. People outside at night would be shot.

The officer left them with no food and very little hope but gave the keys to the steel doors to one of the men who appeared to be taking the situation well. The man had been attentive and calm, and the officer encouraged them all to follow his example. He left them with the promise that the police department was ready to meet the crisis head on. They never saw the officer again.

There was no cell service. That added to a sense of growing fear that they were trapped in the basement of the police station, and everyone constantly checked their phones to see if they could call for help. There wasn't a television or radio in any of the rooms, just small construction supplies and new fixtures to store evidence.

Through the first night they heard gunshots on the floor above theirs. They expected to see the door from the stairwell fly open at any time, and after some discussion, the consensus was to use their small supply of blankets to cover the bars that separated them from the other side of the corridor. It was a false sense of security, but one thing they all agreed on was that the infected could open a door with a panic bar on it just by falling against the device that was intended to save lives during a fire. The door to the stairwell had a panic bar on the other side. If they heard the door open, they would stay quiet until they knew what was on the other side of the blankets.

Hunger became the primary motivation by the following morning. They had taken turns standing watch at the blankets draped across the bars, and a faint sound had everyone holding their breath. They thought it was something in the stairwell, but they weren't positive. When the sound wasn't repeated, they weren't sure what it meant, but they decided they would all sleep better if they turned off the lights. It was a good theory, but no one slept.

Lack of sleep and hunger made people get restless, and a few of the more vocal men voiced their concerns about waiting for the officer to come back. It escalated fast, and the calm man with the keys to the doors was no match for people who decided they had waited long enough. He tried to reason with them, but he barely managed to get out a sentence before a fist hit his front teeth.

Being afraid causes angry people to get angrier. It wasn't enough to hit the man in the face and take the keys from him. They also had to kick him. Phillip wanted to help the man, but it was shocking how many others joined in on the kicking side. Even after they had the keys there were a few kicks to his ribs, and some of the mob laughed when the man begged them to stop. Phillip and Denise held each other and watched helplessly.

Once the keys were liberated from the beaten man, a guy who could have been a lawyer or a stock broker took over and led the way to the door. They pulled the blankets down, and he reached his arms through the bars. The crowd around him pushed against the steel door, and as the click of the lock signaled the door was unlocked, they surged forward. The man's arm was still through the bars as he was pushed along with the door, and his scream of shock and pain was lost in the cheer from the dozens of people who suddenly gave in to the claustrophobia that had gripped them through the night. Their fear burst from them as they stepped on anyone who fell down in the rush to leave.

The screams from the man with his arms trapped through the bars rose even higher when the bones in his arm snapped, and they served as fuel for the rising panic. People who hadn't rushed the door joined the others. Phillip and Denise retreated into one of the evidence cells and pulled the door shut. It didn't lock, but the crowd in the main room wasn't interested in them as they hid behind the door of the newly installed evidence locker.

Silence descended on the bottom floor of the police station as the crowd of survivors disappeared one by one into the stairwell. The door swung shut as the last of them went through, and the Corrigans waited a few minutes longer. When they emerged from hiding, they saw that the only people left with them was the man who had been beaten by the crowd and a woman who was tending to his cuts and bruises. Even the man who had unlocked the door was gone.

"Can I help?" asked Denise.

She didn't wait for an answer. She tore off a strip of blanket and rushed to a sink where she soaked it in cold water. She brought it back to the woman who gratefully accepted the gesture.

"How bad is he hurt?" asked Phillip.

He was asking the woman, but the man answered for himself with a grimace.

"I've been worse, and believe it or not, I'm probably better off than those people. If I'm right, none of them has thought about what they're going to find when they get to the top of the stairs. I hope some of them make it."

He held out a hand to Phillip.

"Alex, and this is Grace."

Phillip shook his hand and told them their names, but he was amazed that the man was so calm and good natured after what had just happened.

"You're a lot more forgiving than I would be right now. A few more kicks and you could be lying here with a punctured lung. We're also not much better off than we were before. There are just less of us to feed."

Alex laughed and immediately grabbed his ribs.

Grace said, "Thank you for staying behind with us. We don't have much longer to wait."

Before Phillip could ask what she meant, they heard the commotion in the stairwell. It sounded like a crowd of people.

"The key," said Alex.

Grace seemed to know what Alex wanted her to do. She ran to the door and checked the lock.

"It's still here."

She pulled the door shut and reached through the bars to turn the lock. After she retrieved the key she backed away just as the stairwell door burst open. People spilled through the door on top of each other, and the noise they brought through with them sounded like the previous night. Screams and cries for help filled the air, but there was something else. There was a groaning sound that was almost louder than the screams.

The first few people slammed their bodies against the door and shoved their arms through the bars. They pressed their faces as close as they could toward Grace and begged with wide eyes for her to let them in. Grace took a few more steps backward, but the Corrigans could see that it wasn't because she was afraid. They turned to Alex with a mixture of fear and pity but didn't know what to do. These were the same people who had brutalized Alex just a few minutes ago.

Alex said, "I would if I could, but we can't let them in."

A bald man in a heavily stained suit was straining to reach Grace. He was pleading in a voice he had most likely never used before now, but it suddenly became even more shrill and desperate sounding. His hand continued to grasp at the air in front of Grace, but his back arched when someone pressed against it, and his chest pushed even harder at the gap between the bars. It looked like he was trying to push his overweight body through the three inch opening. The woman next to him did the same thing only seconds later, and they saw a pool of blood collect at their feet.

From inside, the Corrigans couldn't see what was happening beyond the people who were trying to get in with them, but they could see the stairwell door was still open. They saw it open further and then retreat toward closing but never quite making it before it would be bumped open again. The groaning grew louder, but then the screams would take their turn again. Through it all there was a rank smell that was suffocating. A copper smell mixed with the smell of human waste.

Grace turned to face the Corrigans, and it was at that moment when Phillip understood she and Alex weren't surprised by anything that was happening. There was something about their calm acceptance of watching people turn into the blood thirsty creatures that were biting anyone that was still alive in the chaos. They had expected this.

The screams diminished as the living succumbed to their wounds. The floor was slippery with blood, and the creatures that were constantly slipping and falling down were no longer human. The Corrigans didn't know what disease those people had, but they appeared to be hungry, judging by the way they took over from the living who had been reaching through the bars. They were pressing their faces where the desperate people had been, but now they were groaning and reaching with a different, longing desperation, and as they reached they snapped at the air with their teeth.

The four people on the inside of the bars wore such different expressions on their faces. Phillip and Denise were horrified. They held each other for safety and comfort while Alex and Grace were strangely watching as if they were studying the bloody faces…as if they were observers. Phillip had an eerie feeling that Alex and Grace knew what was going on. He was just about to say as much when there was a new sound behind the wall of crazed faces at the bars.

There were voices, and in between the words there was the steady popping from automatic weapons. The crowd around the door fell away one at a time until there were no more standing, and unfamiliar uniforms filled the corridor. Heavily armed men wearing some kind of breathing gear and protective gloves were dragging the bodies away from the door, making a clear path. Grace stepped forward and handed the key through the bars. One of the men took it and unlocked the door.

******

During the previous night, while the Corrigan's hid with three dozen people below the streets of Mt. Pleasant, a battle raged between the police and thousands of citizens who converged on the municipal center. The living people only wanted protection, but in the darkness the police couldn't tell them from the blood soaked people who outnumbered the living.

The municipal center had been moved from its original location after it was flooded during Hurricane Hugo in 1989. Its present location was chosen because it was convenient to the major arteries that spread out across the city and led to the bridges that crossed the Cooper River. Over the years the two bridges had been replaced by a much larger bridge that could accommodate more traffic. No one could have guessed that these changes would put the Mt. Pleasant police department at the center of a battle for survival.

As the chaos erupted on the bridge, the swarm of people driving away from Mt. Pleasant abandoned their cars and ran from the infected. The infected moved slowly, but the living could only run as fast as the logjam of people in front of them. They all had the same idea…get to the police station.

On the other side of the massive Ravenel Bridge, thousands of people were escaping from Charleston with the same belief. If they could just make it to Mt. Pleasant, the police station wasn't far. All they had to do was reach Patriots Point where there were bound to be other people who could help them. Safety seemed to be within an arm's reach until a convoy of tractor trailers emerged from the darkness of a parking area at Patriots Point and lined up across the lanes, separating Patriots Point from the chaos and closing off any chance of escape to the Yorktown. The drivers abandoned the cabs of their trucks and were collected by an armored vehicle that followed closely behind them. It had oversized tires and the truck drivers had to be helped to climb up to a hatch on top.

Terrified families froze in shock when the armored vehicle drove straight into the crowds of people who had already abandoned their cars. The oversized tires made the strange looking vehicle bounce as it rolled over cars and the unfortunate victims inside them. As quickly as the trucks and the armored vehicle appeared, they disappeared back into the Patriots Point complex. The barricade of the bridge caused the flow of humanity to drain like rainwater over toward the traffic that was trying to exit from Mt. Pleasant on Highway 17, and the result was a total standstill of progress in any direction. What had been a slowly moving exodus in both directions became as congested as an outdoor rock concert, and the darkness only added to the illusion as the shadows of people were almost enough to blanket the headlights.

The mass of bodies swirled as the momentum of the crowd on one side made the tide turn in favor of the escapees from Charleston. If the remaining police officers at the municipal center had been able to see what was coming, they would have understood the futility of their efforts and tried to save their own lives. Too late they retreated into their building where they came face to face with the infected that had died after reaching safety. The officers didn't know who they had been saving.

Throughout the building the injured were dying, and as they died they turned on their rescuers. People who had been hidden in the holding cells for their own protection found themselves trapped with the infected. In one cell a man who had died sat up and groaned. Everyone in the cell with him screamed and shook the bars of the cell door, but when the dead man put his feet on the floor and stood, the others tried to get behind each other, pushing women and the elderly to the front.

There were cells to the left and the right of the cell with the dead man, and the people in them were putting as much distance between themselves and the bars of the middle cell as they could. It was as if they were afraid the dead man could pull off a second miracle in one day by bending the bars to get into the cell with them. The people in all three cells were screaming, and with as many as twelve people in each cell, the screaming was deafening.

The infected stood still for several seconds, just long enough for the people trapped with it to wonder if they were actually going to get a break. Maybe this one was different and couldn't see them. It lifted its head and aimed its milky white eyes toward them, and the screaming and shoving became even more frantic. It took one step forward and stopped. Something bounced off of its head and landed on the floor. It was a water bottle.

A young man in the cell on the right was reaching through the bars and waving his hands at the infected.

"Hey you...hey. Look at me," he yelled at the infected that stood only a few feet from him.

A groan escaped from its mouth as it took a few steps toward the young man. Both hands lifted out at the Good Samaritan who was risking his life for people he didn't know. As soon as the infected reached toward him, everyone in all three cells began to scream. It was as if they were sure it would get him, so people began screaming for him to get away from the bars. Even some of the people in the cell with the infected were yelling at him, but as the distance between the two became shorter and shorter, he kept his arms between the bars and shouted taunts at the creature that used to be human.

Before the infected reached the bars, everyone was shocked when the young man struck first. His hands shot forward, and he grabbed the infected by both cuffs of its jacket. He yanked the cuffs as hard as he could, and the infected slammed into the bars face first. The young man held onto the jacket cuffs that had easily slipped past the hands, and he tied the loose material of the sleeves into a knot on his side of the bars. The infected was pinned safely against the bars inside a straitjacket. 0

The screams turned to cheers, and when they died down, the young man yelled for everyone to listen. First, he wanted to know if anyone else was dying in the cells, or if anyone was bitten. There was a general commotion as everyone in each cell turned to assess who their cellmates were and whether or not any of them had been bitten. The reports were almost simultaneous as someone in each of them spoke up and said no to the questions. Secondly, he asked if anyone had weapons or something that could be used as a rope. The next infected to reach through the bars might not be wearing a jacket.

As frightened as everyone was, the last part of his question earned him a round of cheers, but one at a time the cells reported that they had no weapons worth mentioning. There were a couple of pen knives and a pair of scissors. It was amazing how many people had fingernail clippers, and one woman offered up her keychain can of pepper spray. Someone politely thanked her but added that they didn't think pepper spray would work on the infected.

With the only infected safely tied to the bars, everything settled down. The celebratory mood after the capture of the thing subsided, and the people began talking about what was going to happen. The holding cells were only supposed to be temporary, so there weren't even sinks or toilets. That posed a difficult question because the officers who had put them in the cells hadn't returned.

Because the young man had been the only one to take positive steps to deal with the infected, people asked him what they were going to do. He didn't have a clue and told them as much. He said if it was up to him, he would have preferred to not be locked into a cage without food, water, or even a toilet. His resignation was a bad sign to the others, and a cloud of despair settled over the three cells. It was deathly silent until people began crying, some softly and some with wracking sobs.

After an hour of feeling defeated, someone started screaming that they wanted out. A woman went to the door of her cell and yelled for help. She kept it up until a few people joined in, and before long all three cells were once again in an uproar.

Something slammed against the outside of the wooden door that led to the main hallway of the station. The sudden noise made everyone stop yelling, but all eyes were on the door. There was a squeaking sound from the other side. Those closest to the sound tilted their heads, cocking their ears toward the sound as they tried to identify it.

"We're in here," yelled an elderly woman who had been yelling for help.

The door was slammed into again. This time they saw the door move in its frame, and there was no mistaking the fact that something had rammed against it. The squeaking sounded again.

One of the men with his head cocked toward the door snapped his fingers.

"I've got it. You know that sound that you make when you wash a window with a rubber squeegee? That's what it sounds like. The other side of the door must be wet."

The man was satisfied that he had figured it out until the elderly woman at the bars asked, "Why would somebody be using a squeegee on the other side of the door?"

She screamed when the door was slammed into for a third time, and this time it opened. It wasn't the jolt of an infected hitting the door that made it open. The handle was the type that only needed to be pushed down far enough. The answer to the question about the squeegee was easy to see. The other side of the door was slippery with blood.

An infected fell into the room, and it reached for the first cell even before it got up from the floor. The door had almost swung shut in time, but a second infected stumbled into the room and walked past the first one.

The occupants of the first cell didn't need to be told to back away from the bars, and just for good measure the occupants of the other two cells did the same thing. Everyone was packed against the back walls of the cells. Everyone was also screaming again.

Both of the infected went to the first cell and reached as far as they could through the bars. The young hero in the middle cell yelled as loud as he could for everyone to be quiet.

"Stop screaming."

He waited for everyone to settle down before he said in a much more normal voice, "Listen to me. Two of you take off your belts. Catch their hands and tie them together."

The occupants of the cell eyed the waving hands as if he had told them to grab snakes. The idea of touching a dead person who was waving his arms at you was revolting, and he could see them trying to time the grab. He understood that these were people who couldn't put together a playground set without written instructions.

He used a voice that was calm and almost soothing.

"You don't have to rush it. Take your time. Just move closer until you're just out of reach and grab one by the wrist. Get control of it and then grab the other wrist. You can do this," he coached.

A tall man eased closer to the two infected until he was directly in front of the one on his left. The grimy hand was still wet with blood and waved only inches in front of his face. The man wrinkled his nose, clearly able to smell the stink coming from the hand. He glanced across the middle cell at the young man who was standing dangerously close to the infected that was in a straight-jacket.

"You've got this. Get the first hand at the wrist with your left hand and the other wrist with your right. Pull in and then together. You...

yes, you." He was pointing at another man who was still hanging back with the group by the wall. "Get your belt off and put it around the arms when he pulls them together."

The second man hesitated but eventually forced himself to step forward while taking off his belt. He didn't want to be close enough for the second infected to grab him while he helped to subdue the first one, so he squeezed around by the bars of the middle cell.

The taller man made his grab and held on. What surprised him was how easily he was able to grab the second hand, and it was simply because the infected didn't have the mental capacity to understand that the person that held its wrist was the same person it was trying to reach. He was also surprised by how easily the other man completed his assigned task. The belt was tossed over both wrists. He caught the loose end, pushed it through the buckle, and drew it tight.

Everyone cheered for a second time. The taller man and his assistant threw a high-five at each other and missed. Neither of them had ever been coordinated enough to do a high-five, but they were too pleased with themselves to let it bring them down. They were both filled with so much bravado that they were ready to take on the infected.

They got another belt from a cellmate and restrained the other infected. This time they had better aim for their high-five, and their hands slapped together. They had no sooner finished when there was another resounding thud at the door.

"How many belts do we have?" asked the taller man.

There was a nervous laugh from a few people, but it wasn't loud enough to cover the sound of retching that came from the back of the group in the first cell. A woman was doubled over at the waist, and her hair was drenched with sweat. People moved away from her, but her husband moved between her and the others.

"She's fine. She just needs a little water. We both had to run so far to get here."

The other occupants spread out toward the sides of the cells and wore skeptical expressions on their faces.

"She's got a bite mark on her arm," said one lady.

A collective gasp went up from all three cells, and someone yelled from the third cell that they lied when they said they were okay before. An argument quickly arose from all three cells about hiding bites. Was anybody else hiding a bite? Was anybody else sick? Shouldn't everyone have to take off their clothes so no one could hide a bite? And general shouts from people who valued modesty over their lives that they weren't taking off their clothes for anyone.

The woman in the first cell fell from the bench that ran along the back wall of the cell. She landed hard, but it was doubtful that she felt pain from the fall. She was too busy convulsing on the floor. Her husband tried in vain to hold her still, as if that would ease the minds of everyone in the cells. Some people began to cry, but once again it was the young man who intervened.

"Put her hands through the bars, fast," he shouted. He pointed at a pair of men in the middle cell and yelled, "You know what to do."

Since the woman wasn't trying to bite anyone yet, the men in the middle cell made fast work of tying her hands together.

"We can't keep doing this," said a woman in the middle cell. "We don't have enough belts, and we don't have enough room to tie everyone to the bars."

"I'm more inclined to be out of here before we run out of belts," answered a man in cell number three.

"Okay, Houdini. Let's see how you do it."

The sound of a large number of people came from outside the door, and they knew they weren't the infected because they were shouting. The door opened, and this time the man holding it open didn't fall through. He stared in disbelief at the number of people in the cells.

"What did you all do to get yourselves arrested on a night like this?"

"Nothing, get us out of here."

It seemed like they all yelled the same thing, and the man held up a ring of keys.

"Got these from a policeman who was eating someone down the hall."

He avoided the two infected that were tied with belts to the bars of the first cell and quickly unlocked all three. The occupants poured past him into the hallway, and they ran even though they didn't know which way they should go. Most of them just didn't want to be in a jail cell any longer.

Those who made it outside the doors of the police station found themselves to be in the middle of a dark nightmare. Those who stayed inside searched for places to hide, and none of them found what they were looking for. Every hallway had infected wandering around, and when some of the frantic survivors eventually found a group of armed police officers, they saw that one of the officers was bleeding from a serious bite on his neck, and his friends were trying to save him.

The tall man from the first cell who had successfully tied the hands of the two infected hid for several hours in an office. He found some bottled water and power bars in one of the drawers and hungrily washed them down. He knew he couldn't stay in the police station, but maybe the water and food would buy him the time he needed to get away.

He slipped out of the office in the early morning and ran as silently as he could along a carpeted hallway. When he came up behind a man who was hiding behind a desk, his heart skipped a beat. He recognized the shirt and jeans the young man in the third cell had been wearing.

"Oh, man. Am I ever glad to see you?" he said as he dropped to his knees next to him. His shoulder bumped against the young man.

The young man turned away from a body on the floor. The body of a woman whose blood was smeared across his face.

12

Pandemic

Zero Hour - Beginning of the Decline
Contagion Extinction Level Event - CEL Day One

"Are you one hundred percent sure?"

Marshall Sayer had a habit of making people repeat themselves. It was his way of telling subordinates he didn't believe them or that they'd better be right. Dr. Grace Williams didn't appreciate his little tactic.

"Of course I'm one hundred percent sure," she answered. "That's why I called you."

She thought to herself but didn't say out loud, "I also called you to make you squirm."

Instead she said, "I hope you have a plan for how to deal with this."

"Of course I have a plan," he snapped.

For good measure he hung up the call and wished for the good old days when he could hang up on someone by physically slamming the phone into the cradle. He didn't have a plan despite what he had said. All he had was a plan for how to survive it, not how to stop it from spreading. This was one pandemic that couldn't be stopped. No vaccines, no quarantines, no cures. It was also supposed to be no exposure, but obviously something had gone wrong there.

On the other end of the phone Dr. Williams considered calling him back. She hated politicians who were bosses over doctors. Some were smart enough to understand the complexities of medicine and were even reasonably able to converse with doctors on the same level, but they never seemed to realize the full scope of making a mistake in this business. Someone had made a mistake, and now this thing was in the wild. It was a virus that couldn't be contained without eliminating a significant percent of the population, and after that was done, there would need to be fundamental changes to how the remaining population dealt with death. Everyone would have to die twice.

Grace had found a corner in the building where she was out of the way and could make some calls without being interrupted. She had been wearing her white lab coat when she started for the city, and she didn't bother to take it off when she abandoned her car. A pretty woman at forty, despite a few extra pounds, she was constantly being asked by men if they could help her with something, and she finally realized she looked somewhat out of place dressed like a doctor and wearing red high heels. Her auburn hair was loose and resting on her shoulders, so she drew plenty of looks from the men who rushed by.

"Ah, what the hell," she said as she hit his number again. "You better answer."

Grace was about to say something about personally doing something surgical to him when he answered.

"I don't need you hanging up on me when I call with bad news. I want to know what kind of plan you have to contain an outbreak of this thing."

Sayer kept the phone to his ear, but he pinched two fingers together between his eyes and across the bridge of his nose to relieve the pressure he felt there. He had already lied by saying he had a plan ready if this contagion got loose. Grace would recognize the lie as soon as he tried to make it up. A plan on this level needed a lot of funding, but most of all they needed permission to make the hard decisions that no politician could make.

He was just about to admit as much to Grace when he had an epiphany. If they were right about this disease, there wouldn't be anyone left to blame it on him.

"We take shelter until it burns itself out."

Grace couldn't believe she heard him correctly. What he was proposing was that they just sit back and let the population of the world go back to levels before the Stone Age. The only survivors would be people who could be so isolated that they were self-sufficient and unable to be exposed to the pathogen. It reminded her of an article she had read about a guy who believed the only way to survive an apocalypse was to have a shelter that was impenetrable, and that you should go inside that shelter, lock the door, and never come out.

"What do you plan to tell the President, Marshall? My bad?"

Sayer paused just long enough for her to guess the answer.

"You don't plan to tell him, do you? While Washington melts down in the chaos you created, you plan to escape to an island somewhere."

"Face the facts, Grace. You said it yourself. The only way to stop this thing was to eliminate all of the potential hosts. People are the hosts, so if we're going to survive this thing that we haven't even had the chance to give a decent name, we have to look out for ourselves first. Once it burns itself out by eliminating most of the population, we can rebuild by living off of the supplies and manufactured goods left behind by an overpopulated world. The more people it eliminates the less we have to share with."

Grace was appalled by how insensitive Sayer was, but it wasn't like she didn't think this was going to happen. Once they discovered this virus and recognized it for what it was, she knew it would show up outside of containment and couldn't be stopped. They barely had time to start looking for a cure when Salem Townsend practically gift wrapped and delivered the virus to Miami. Along the way he gave it to fellow travelers and people working in airports. Before anyone even discovered his body and what had killed him, there were probably over a thousand people cultivating the disease like human test tubes.

"We're calling it Brachyura CEL," she said.

"What?"

Sayer was expecting Grace to tear him apart, not get on board. With smug satisfaction he realized that she was facing reality, and he could think of worse people to survive the apocalypse with.

"I get to name it," she said. "I should name it after you because you're as uncaring and heartless as this disease, but you'd take it as a compliment. Brachyura is the biological name for crabs, and the contagion is an extinction level disease, so Brachyura CEL."

"Nice. I like it. Are you still in Charleston?"

"Where else would I be? This thing is spreading like wild fire. The news stations hardly know where to start because emergency reports are coming in from everywhere. They're opening shelters. Hospitals are announcing that they can't take anymore patients. The airport has canceled flights that are sitting on the runway full of passengers. I just left my house in Mt. Pleasant and was headed for MUSC in

Charleston, but traffic is already sitting still on the bridge."

"Where are you right now?"

"Well, I already saw a guy carjack a family's SUV, and I might be the only person without a gun, so I stopped at the Mt. Pleasant Police Department. I remember you did a briefing last week and you mentioned this place for some reason. It's getting crowded fast, but I can hold out for a bit. Can you send someone to get me?"

Sayer had a special barking laugh when he was feeling particularly pleased with himself, and even though it grated on her nerves, something told Grace that this time as she listened to him laugh it was for her benefit.

"Already got that covered, Darlin'. Find the Desk Sergeant and tell him you want to speak with Alex Reeves. He's the public relations guy for the Police Chief there. Tell him to look after you, and we'll take him under our wing when we get there for you. Now, let me get out of here while I still can. See you soon."

Being from the South, Grace had been called 'Darlin' her whole life, but she still didn't like it when Marshall Sayer said it. He made her feel dirty. Nonetheless, he was going to pull her out of something that was starting to take on a strong resemblance to a third world civil war. She wasn't exaggerating about the guns. People used to grab the family photo albums when they were told to evacuate. Now they grabbed their gun collections.

The Desk Sergeant was behind something more like a counter at the bank, and he ignored her despite the attention she was getting from everyone else.

She cleared her throat and said, "Excuse me, could you…"

"I'm busy, Ma'am. Take a number and have a seat over there." He gestured toward a packed waiting room where at least a hundred people sat with little numbered tags between their fingers. He called a number, and at least half of the people checked their numbers, probably for the tenth time or more.

"I don't have time to wait over there, Sir."

"Then have a good day, Ma'am."

He didn't even look up as he dismissed her.

"I need to speak with Alex Reeves."

"Who's stopping you? He's standing right over there."

Grace glared at the officer and pictured herself grabbing him by his collar and dragging him over the counter, but the man he had pointed at was walking away toward an elevator. She didn't want to miss him and get stuck dealing with the Desk Sergeant again, so she ran after him. Grace was beginning to feel like time was slipping away. The bustling crowd of people and the faces of the police officers were taking on a sense of urgency. She decided to cut to the chase as quickly as possible.

"Mr. Reeves, I'm Dr. Grace Williams, and Marshall Sayer from USAMRIID said to talk to you. He said to tell you to look after me until he gets here, and he would repay you by giving you a seat on the bus."

It was apparently the right thing to say because his expression changed from indifferent to totally interested.

"Right this way, Dr. Williams."

He took her hand and led her to the door of a stairwell. On the way he waved over an officer and asked him where they were putting people to keep them safe. The officer told him they had been putting them in offices and holding cells, but they were ready to start sending them down to the new evidence room.

"See you there, Henry."

He gave the officer a light slap on his shoulder as he went by with Grace in tow.

******

The Present

The oxbow was exactly what they had hoped it would be. Hidden deep in the forest on an island in the middle of a river, they could go undetected for years if they were careful. They had an abundance of supplies unlike anything they had found ever since the Walmarts and grocery stores had been stripped bare. All this was theirs, but something was bothering Jed.

More deer stands were built on the island so they could have a good idea of what was in the woods at all times. When they saw an infected on the other side of the river, they knew it was just a matter of time before it would go into the water and not come back out. From time to time they saw movement in the woods near the hanging bridge that connected their safe haven to the mainland, but if an infected came near the bridge, there nothing to draw them across that was stronger than whatever it was that was calling them to the south.

Despite the safety they enjoyed for the first time in years, Jed was sure something was happening, and he suspected it was the spiders. It finally came to him when he saw a spider fall from a tree. He didn't recall ever seeing a spider do that before, and as he watched the spider run across the ground he noticed that it was moving in the same direction as the infected.

Jed didn't know what he expected to find, but he became restless and decided to go back to the Pinopolis Lock to see if the spiders had taken control again. It only took a couple of hours to get there because the southern bank of the Cooper River was free of the infected. Any that had been in the area had left weeks ago. When he had gone far enough to be able to see the railings across the top of the lock, he could tell even from a distance that the spiders had expanded their territory. The entire walkway and the railings disappeared under a gray and brown web that was so thick it could have been mistaken for smoke. He eased closer but didn't plan to disturb the web. He just wanted to find out what was bothering him about the spiders.

It was because he was being cautious that he stayed alive, but he almost walked straight to his own death. He was an experienced woodsman, and true woodsmen watched where they put their feet. Jed's eyes were constantly moving between the ground and the huge web when he saw something move on the ground. Actually, he thought the ground moved.

There was no breeze, but if it had been windy, there would have been a reason for the gusts of dirt blowing around like little dust devils. Jed took a few steps backward and watched with his mouth hanging open. Right before his eyes he saw the spider web from the Pinopolis Lock spreading across the ground, and it wasn't just the web...it was an advancing army of baby spiders that were building the dirty web that was more like brown cotton candy being spread across the ground.

"Millions...there must be millions of them." He said what he was thinking out loud.

Jed circled the growing mass of spiders and web that was doing something he had never seen before. There were so many spiders that he could see the web expanding, and he knew what that many spiders could do to a man. Forget being eaten by them. It would be a very painful death to be bitten by that many spiders at one time. It would feel like fire running up the legs and across the torso, and by the time they reached the arms, neck, and shoulders, the victim wouldn't be conscious to feel them filling his mouth, nose, eyes, and ears. Most people feel like there's a spider in their hair if they see one hanging from a ceiling in their house. That feeling would be real in seconds if they stayed awake long enough after stumbling into this nightmare.

Jed saw that an infected was getting to experience it firsthand. He thought this one must've had something wrong with its ears because it hadn't been following the rest of the horde to whatever it was that was making them all go south. Jed had decided it was a foregone conclusion that something was calling the infected to go south to Charleston. He knew there were whistles that only a dog could hear, so why not whistles for zombies. It would be funny if it wasn't so bad for everyone caught between the zombies and the whistle.

The infected was already on its knees, rotating at the waist as if it knew where the attacks were coming from. It had been a woman, and Jed could tell she was a recent casualty judging by how intact her body was. There was nothing to show how she died that Jed could see, and the only reason he was sure she was an infected dead was the indifference she showed to the unbearable pain a living person would be experiencing. If she was alive, she would be screaming, and Jed was shamefully glad. He wouldn't have been able to stop himself from running into the middle of the web to help her, and he would be dead too.

Something interesting happened. The infected stopped rotating at the waist and faced directly at Jed. Even though it meant putting her hands into the smokey colored web and millions of spiders, she used her hands to push herself from her knees to her feet. Then she stumbled in his direction. Jed was confused until he remembered that the infected didn't feel pain even if they were being eaten. This one was bringing more than the threat of a single bite to him, and he couldn't wait for her to get that close.

Jed wasn't one to waste a bullet, but if he ever needed an infected dead disposed of beyond his reach, it was this one. He unslung his AR-15 and carefully put a single bullet into the woman's forehead. When he lowered his rifle, he saw the web at his feet was approaching as if it was crawling. This time he backed away further and faster, but he still had to know one thing.

He ran in a big curve until he was almost parallel with the lock that he and his colony had cleared of the webs only days before, and he saw more than he expected. The web wasn't spreading in all directions. It was only spreading in the same direction that the infected were all walking. Whatever was calling the infected was also calling the spiders.

"A zombie whistle and a spider whistle?"

From where Jed stood, he could see the dam from the side, and the web overflowed the dam and hung down toward the water in the canal. It was like a kitchen sink that had been filled too full with water and dishwashing suds.

"No," he said. "It looks like the dam grew a gray beard."

He wished he could see over the edge of the lock to see how full it had gotten. There must still be infected falling into the lake and then washing up against the lock, especially if one had made it this far to Jed's side. He kept an eye on the web that was still spreading across the ground and worked his way toward a small cluster of buildings. One of them was tall enough to give him at least a little better view of the inside of the lock.

When he was closer to the buildings he saw a sign that said it was a training center for firemen, and the tallest structure was used to test their skills running up and down flights of stairs wearing their heavy gear. It must have been built just before the beginning of the infection because Jed never knew it was there. He knew the other side of the two huge lakes better than anyone, but he hadn't spent as much time on this side. It was a good thing that the tower was to the west of the Pinopolis Lock. If there were any spider webs on it, he wouldn't take the chance to climb it.

He was winded by the time he ran up the tower stairs, and he had a new admiration for the men and women who had done it for a living. If there were any left alive and he had the chance to meet them, he would have to tell them about this.

When he reached the highest platform, Jed pulled his binoculars from his backpack and focused on the lock. What he saw made him want to be sick. He felt his stomach acid rise in the back of his throat. Something had gone wrong at the lock, and if he was right, there was about to be a terrible disaster.

If it was six years ago, he would have found a computer and searched for anything that would tell him how much pressure the gates of the dam could withstand. Everything raced through his mind at once. How deep is the water? How much pressure is there on the dam? How many millions of gallons was he looking at? Most of all, he wanted to know what would happen if the dam broke? How far downstream would the water travel?

One thing he was sure of because he had seen it for himself. The water level of the lake was higher than he had ever seen it in his whole life, and as he watched he saw it lapping over the top of the dam. Worse yet, it had already broken through the first gate, and the place he and the colony had crossed that was full of bodies of the infected was now full of water. Science was never Jed's strongest subject in school, but for the first time in his life he wished it was.

He shut his eyes and thought about something that made him feel tired, like he wasn't sure he could take much more of the deaths that he had seen. Watching his best friend eat a candy bar and then dying minutes later was something that seemed to be sitting at the front of his mind, and every waking moment since then he had been forced to look past it. Forced to ignore it because his life and the lives of others had to go on. What other choice was there? Jed knew that he had taken it personally, and he knew he was taking responsibility for all of the people in the colony. That's why he felt so much dread at the moment. Something told him he was about to lose someone again.

When he opened his eyes, he knew instinctively what he would be able to find if he could search the internet. The dam was going to break, and it was going to break soon. Millions of gallons of water would be released with more pressure behind it than he would be able to calculate even if he knew how. And the worst part was that he didn't need to do the math to know it would send a raging torrent of water and bodies speeding downriver toward the colony. Water and bodies…and spiders.

If he was winded when he reached the top of the tower, he would normally be winded running down so many flights of stairs, but he didn't notice. He made the last turn on the stairs and took so many at the same time that he could have sprained an ankle or even worse, broken a leg. He gave the ground covered with spider webs a wide berth and ran as hard as he could, and he prayed that he could get there in time.

He heard the sound of the dam bursting long before he felt it. It sounded like a massive cannon or the explosion of a large bomb. Even after the initial sound waves rocketed past him, the rumble of the water escaping in such a vast quantity was enough to make him feel it in his chest. The vibrations reached his feet not long after, and it was strong enough to make him change course away from the river of water that grew like a huge fist getting ready to smash everything in its path.

A glance back toward the river made his heart sink. He saw it pass by in the narrow canal that fed the Cooper River, and it was like seeing a tsunami from the side. It rose into the air higher than any wave he had ever seen as it rushed downstream. He knew he would never make it in time. His only hope was that the people of the colony would hear it coming and evacuate the oxbow island. Better yet, if they heard the explosion in the watchtowers they had built and everyone was warned in time, they would have plenty of time to get everyone across the bridge and away from the riverbanks. They could even gather up some of their new supplies as they evacuated.

As he became more and more winded, counting the seconds and the minutes since he had seen the wave go by, he started to understand that it had probably already reached the island. He was still close to a half hour away from the bridge, and the wave only had to travel in a straight line. His mind pushed him on, and it even created scenarios in which the water crested and dissipated before it reached the island. He could visualize it so well. The water would crest the banks on both sides of the river. It would lose all of the energy that had built up as it pressed against the dam. By the time it reached his island, it would be nothing more than a river that was running at a faster pace.

Then his mind filled in the painful blanks. All of those bodies in the water…all of those bodies would be carried like dangerous debris, some being pushed ahead at high speed and some being carried along in the current. When the bodies reached the oxbow, they would fill up the place where the water passed under the hanging bridge, the river would swell in the curve of the oxbow, and the wave would wash over the island. Even if it didn't totally flood the colony, it would deposit how many millions of spiders, and how many of the infected? They would be dead, but just like the spiders, they would be biting.

Ten minutes from the island he was still trying to find a place where he could turn north to head for the hanging bridge. Before the dam broke he would have been able to go straight for the bridge, but now he was being forced to run his parallel course because the water had crested so far above the banks that it had flooded fields almost a mile from the river. If it was flooded a mile away, what was it like at the center?

He instinctively knew that he wouldn't reach them in time to warn them.

******

The colony had all three watchtowers manned, and they were

concentrating on the wooded areas on all sides of the river. The newest tower was the tallest, and the man seated at the top had a view for miles to the south where he could see smaller hordes closing in behind a larger group that had already been formed by small groups catching up with the others. He thought it was absolutely great that they were all leaving the forests.

To his left he had a clear view downstream on the Cooper River. The only real reason to watch that area was to keep track of traffic. They needed to know if there were still many infected walking out of the woods and falling into the river. To his right he had an equally good view upriver. He tended to check that direction more often than downstream because anything that fell into the river could wash up onto the island. The bank of the island on that side had been fortified with sharpened stakes that were buried in the mud. If something washed up, it was likely to become impaled on the stakes, and they could dispose of it before it could reach solid ground.

There was a boom in the distance upriver, and the watch immediately focused his binoculars on the river to his right. The watch heard it in the second tower too, but he didn't have the angle that would let him see the water too far upriver. They got the attention of the man in the third tower and all he could do was raise his hands and shrug his shoulders to let them know he had no idea what it was.

Anyone who lived in South Carolina before the infection when there were the occasional earthquakes knew that it was common to hear a booming sound rather than to feel the vibrations, and the watch pulled out a notebook and checked to see what time it was. He made a brief note about what he had heard, put the notebook back in his pocket, and put the binoculars back to his eyes.

When he saw that the water was cresting the banks of the river, he knew something was terribly wrong. They weren't experiencing heavy rains, so there was only one reason the water level would be rising. He realized that the level wasn't just rising, it was rising very fast. There was also a large number of bodies in the leading edge of a wave that was moving ahead of the rising water, and he felt the blood rush from his face when he saw that the wave was growing in height. Judging by the speed and size of it, the wave would reach them in five or ten minutes at the most.

Among their newly discovered caches of supplies they had found flare guns. For obvious reasons they couldn't be used for many situations, so the watch captains had agreed on the meaning of different colored flares. If the flare was green it meant living people were coming, and they would send armed squads to the bridge. If the flare was blue it meant infected were near and to send the squads to the bridge with the likelihood that they would need to shoot the infected. If the flare was red, it meant to climb a tree as fast as possible. The watch chose red.

The flare would have been more visible at night, and the reaction time of the colony was slowed by the canopy of trees blocking the view of the sky. Word of mouth wasted precious seconds while members of the colony were forced to convince the others that they saw a red flare. People reacted much faster when the other two towers also shot red flares. Over forty people found trees and climbed. Some climbed the watchtowers because they had ladders and the platforms could hold several people. No one was left on the ground by the time the wave washed over the island.

They were like people on news programs back in the days before the infection, and even on the first few days when people thought they could climb to get away from the chaos. They gasped with surprise when they saw the water cross over everything below, their supplies, camp sites, tents, food, stoves, and everything they had so gratefully uncovered on the island. Those people who could see the upstream side of the oxbow watched with shock as the bodies of the infected piled up against the dozens of sharpened stakes that had been shoved into the mud. The stakes did their jobs, and as bodies were added to the growing piles, more bodies were stopped against them. Hundreds of the infected squirmed and wrestled to free themselves from the tangle. Their arms and legs waved in the air, and their jaws snapped at each other.

A few of the bodies were pushed over the piles by the water, but they could be dealt with later. They were so waterlogged that they weren't going to be a threat. None of them could walk, and they weren't strong enough to lift their soggy arms and crawl. There was also enough water that the current under the bridge lifted some of the bodies onto the bridge. That was going to be more difficult to dispose of, but it could be done. The problem was that they also piled up under the bridge until no more could pass through. On the oxbow curve around the island the bodies were deposited in such large numbers in the first five minutes of impact that they clogged the river like a drain. A dam formed across the first curve in the oxbow, and that forced more water to cross the island instead of going around it.

The colony members didn't know how long they would need to stay in the trees, but they knew they couldn't go down until the current decreased. From their places of safety, most of them couldn't see that the oxbow had become blocked, so that meant the river would probably continue to build in height against the wall of bodies until it crested the island permanently.

As they passed word from survivor to survivor, it was the watch captains who had to make the decisions. Jed was away from the island, and Ben had died, so the colony turned to the watch captains to tell them if it was safe to climb down into the shallow water to try to retrieve supplies before they were lost forever.

It was impossible to work together to make the decisions because they were spread too thin. One of the best known and respected families in the colony was the Lee family. Two brothers, a sister, and two cousins made them one of the largest families. Needless to say, they had been more considerable in number when the infection began. When Jason Lee began to climb down, his brother and sister were close behind. Their decision caused others to do the same. Before long almost everyone, over forty people, were either knee deep in the rushing water or barely above it.

Everyone thought Maureen Lee screamed because there was an infected dead in the water, and the instinctive reaction of her brothers, her cousins, and every other man was to rescue her from the infected. That was why they let go of their trees and rushed in her direction.

Then there were more screams. Even the people who were still above the water screamed. They let go and fell into the water as other colony members mindlessly tried to climb the trees to escape the pain they felt on their arms, legs, backs, necks, and in their hair. They wildly scratched at their skin and tore away bleeding strips along with handfuls of hair. Many were already trying to breathe past swollen tongues. Some from the allergic response to spider bites, some from the venom, and some from the spiders that were biting the insides of their mouths.

There was some cooling, momentary release from the fiery agony of thousands of spider bites as the victims fell face first into the rushing water, but it was short lived. When they tried to stand up again they found that they couldn't.

It was over in fifteen minutes. That was all it took for the screaming to stop. Then there was only the sound of the rushing water and the groaning from the piles of the infected on the upriver side of the oxbow island.

Mark Howell had stayed in the tower after climbing up to join the watch who was the first to see the onrushing disaster. He could tell by the strength of the current that it was going to stay bad for a long time, maybe even forever. The water was rapidly changing the course of the river. The oxbow island was becoming nothing more than a submerged sandbar with trees sticking out of it. In a year, there would be no evidence that there had ever been an island there. Mark knew that was just the same story in the history of every river. The one thing that was different about this story was the webs that were forming so fast below his feet that his view of the water below was already blocked.

Thirty minutes later the web was less than a foot below the tower platform, and Mark said a prayer of thanks for having brought his gun with him. One shot meant he wouldn't suffer, and he wouldn't become an infected dead.

13

Rescues

At dawn the gray sky and steady drizzle made their joints ache. Sim rolled over and lifted a corner of their makeshift tent. The light that filtered through the tall grass and shrubs was faint at best, but they had made it through the night undetected.

"Why aren't we wet?" asked Jean.

They didn't have a weather resistant tent and had used a tarp to erect their only protection from the rain.

Tom mumbled something about baseball fields having really porous drainage so the fields would dry faster between games.

Everyone else jumped. They had turned on a flashlight literally every fifteen minutes through the night to see if Tom had regained consciousness.

Jean turned hers on again and aimed it near Tom's head. She saw that his eyes were open, and he appeared to be lucid.

"Do you know where you are?"

Tom made an attempt to talk, but his voice came out in a croak. Iris leaned over and lifted his head far enough for him to take a sip of water.

"Glad to see you back with us," she said.

Tom gave it a second try, and this time he was able to get the words out.

"I'm in a minor league baseball park. Wake me up when I've made it to the big leagues."

He shut his eyes again, and they thought he went to sleep until they saw the corner of his mouth stretch into a grin.

"Jerk," said Jean. "How about a big shot of sedative so you can really sleep? You can dream you got called up by the Braves."

He opened his eyes again and then tried to sit up on his own. The tarp was too low for him to manage it, so he settled for propping himself on his elbow.

"Where's everyone else?"

"Kathy, Hampton, Cass, Colleen, and Ed went out to scout the ballpark because we don't know how long we're going to be stuck here," said Iris. "That was last night, and they haven't come back."

Tom's eyes darted between the others in the tent and he did a mental roll call.

"You didn't mention the Chief. Is he...?"

"He's okay, or at least we think he is," said Jean. "He was hurt in the crash and made it all the way into the ballpark before he dropped over. He's a tough one."

Iris added, "He had a bump on his head the size of an egg, but when the others didn't come back he went to find them. Now we're worried because he hasn't come back either."

Tom could see the worry on their faces, but he also saw the way they were keeping their chins up. The last thing they needed was for Tom to react the way the Chief had after he regained consciousness. They knew there was no way to stop him from going, but they should have tried. Concussions could be a tricky business. The Chief may have found himself in a bad situation and passed out. Iris worried that she would never know.

The wind picked up and Sim grabbed at the edges of the tarp to hold it down.

"Wait a minute. Does anyone else hear that?" Iris had her head cocked to one side, listening to something. The steady thumping of rotors was a welcome sound.

Iris didn't know who else would be flying a helicopter near the baseball stadium, so she took a chance that it would be a Navy VH92A. Tom needed to be checked out at their hospital even though he was awake and more stable. It would be worth the risk even if it was someone else.

She threw back the tarp and squinted her eyes at the rain that sprayed her face. The familiar shape of one of their Navy helicopters was just beyond the left field wall. The pilot was hovering over the wreckage of the executive Sikorsky, and he was letting his aircraft rotate on its axis so they could search outward. Iris knew that you have a greater chance of being rescued after a crash if you stay near the wreckage and that any search grid would work outward from that spot.

She waved her arms in the air even before the helicopter was pointed straight at their location, and her heart almost leaped into her throat when the pilot stopped rotating. The nose dipped slightly downward, and he applied a small amount of power to nudge them the short distance to center field. The wind whipped the tarp too much to hold it in place, so Sim just tried to keep it over Tom.

There were a few infected falling over the railings from the stands in left field. Where they had been for the last day was anyone's guess, but it bothered Iris that the Chief was still out there if the infected were too. She tried to be positive by thinking that it was the infected that were at risk if the Chief was sneaking around the stadium, but one thing about being older was the way time helped to develop and refine gut feelings. She didn't feel like the Chief was out there. She didn't think the Chief would have abandoned them, but she didn't feel his presence anymore. She tried unsuccessfully to push that feeling back, but when her eyes met Jean's she saw the same thing Jean could see in hers.

The side door of the helicopter was open, and several soldiers dropped to the ground with a stretcher for Tom. He waved off the stretcher, but he was happy to let two of them get under each of his shoulders. Iris signaled for one of the other soldiers to come to her, and she asked him to shoot the infected. He yelled over the helicopter noise that they didn't need to, so she pulled him closer and told him the Chief was still out there somewhere. She didn't need to explain what she meant. If he was somewhere in the ballpark, there would be less infected for him to worry about.

As they lifted into the air, Iris leaned as far as she could from the door and tried her best to see anything at all that would tell her where the Chief had gone. She saw the pilot was waiting for her to give him a thumbs up, and Iris couldn't do it. Instead, she twirled her index finger in a circle, and the pilot gave her a nod. The pilot put the helicopter into a steep turn with the open door facing downward. He would give her one last chance to spot the Chief. She hoped it would be like one of those movies where the rescuer looks back one more time and sees the lost person waving. Nothing alive moved below.

******

Jed had never run so far and so fast as he did when the dam broke, but he knew the entire time that there was no way he would outrun it. The release of pressure sounded like a cannon or thunder rolling away from him. When he reached the thicker woods that hid their colony so well, he saw water between the trees long before he could see the hanging bridge, and if he guessed right, getting close to the water was a bad idea.

He stopped running and searched the floor of the forest for signs that he shouldn't go closer, and it didn't take long to see the milky webs already draping the trees like Spanish moss. If anyone survived the onslaught of the flood or infected that washed over the oxbow island, there was no way they would survive the spider bites. He listened and didn't hear any screaming, and in his heart he knew that it was all over for his friends.

Only a day ago they felt like they had finally gotten a break. Food, weapons, medical supplies, and real tents to live in, but best of all they had a place where they felt safe from the diseased creatures that had one goal. Now Jed didn't even know where to go. He was rooted to where he stood, unable to turn away, and definitely unable to go forward.

Anger started to build. At first it was blame. He blamed himself for not being there. He blamed himself for not realizing this could happen. He blamed himself for putting the colony in the path of certain death. He saw the faces of his friends, and then he saw them again as they would have been at the moment when they knew they were going to die. Over forty people, many of whom died from spider bites, and by now they were infected dead washing away with the river. The anger became his flood.

Someone had caused this, and he suddenly wanted to get even with them more than ever. He might never find out where the infection had started, but he suspected that the person who knew how to summon the infected might also know something about how it all began. Regardless, if they weren't calling the infected to them, the infected wouldn't have filled the Pinopolis Lock with bodies. The spiders wouldn't have found such a fertile breeding ground. Whoever was calling the infected should have to pay.

164

Jed backtracked out of the woods and decided to follow the infected to wherever it was they were going. He had seen them going south to southeast for long enough to guess they were going toward Charleston. Whether it was to Charleston or somewhere further down the coast, he wouldn't know until he got there.

When he had left for the Pinopolis Lock earlier in the day, he would have taken supplies with him if he had guessed that he would be leaving for Charleston.

"Hell," he said out loud, "I would've taken the whole colony with me."

The ringing in his ears was incessant, and even though he had known people who swore they listened to church bells or symphonies that weren't as loud as the ringing they had heard for years, Jed felt that it had gotten louder. It wasn't just him, and it wasn't just a normal case of something called tinnitus. It was a shrill sound that was coming from somewhere, and Jed wanted to know who was responsible for the deaths of his friends.

The anger and adrenaline made Jed push himself hard for the rest of the day. It was strange to travel so far away from the territory where the colony had lived for years. They weren't on the oxbow island for very long, but he had been in the woods above the Cooper River for his entire life. It was also strange to go so far without seeing any infected walking with him. His eyes moved left and right with every step. There were signs everywhere that showed the great horde had passed through before him, but he hadn't gained on them yet.

Jed heard a horn honking somewhere in the distance, but he didn't know if it was in front of him or behind him because he wasn't to a place where he could even see any roads. It was somewhere off to his right, but he was traveling as the crow flies, and not intending to just go west until he reached the interstate. After about an hour he could tell that he was closer and maybe not even as far away from the horn as he had thought. It was possibly a state road that he could use to walk the rest of the way to the interstate.

He found the state road only a few minutes later, and the car was sitting on a spot where the road crested a hill. Even from a distance he could see infected crowding up against the car on both sides. Whoever was inside the car honking the horn was probably hoping someone would hear it and come to their rescue. The problem was that the few infected remaining in the area were being called to the car too.

Jed checked behind him and didn't see anything following him, so he slowed his pace a little and stayed on the road. When he was only about a hundred yards from the car, he picked a tree that had plenty of big branches and climbed. As he went up, he checked for branches that would allow him to cross to other trees if he was spotted by the infected. If they ever got you up a tree, they wouldn't leave unless they were distracted by another victim or they couldn't see you anymore, so you had to be able to travel across the treetops.

He stopped climbing long enough to use his binoculars and saw there was definitely someone inside the car. What he couldn't tell was whether or not the person inside the car was alive or an infected. Then again, he didn't recall ever seeing an infected use the horn.

Ben had been fooled by that once on Highway 17. He thought he was rescuing someone who was trapped in a car because there were infected pawing at the windows. He learned the hard way that the infected were drawn to the movement inside the car, and that they didn't know the person inside the car was one of them.

Jed made his decision when he saw the person inside this car try to get out, only to desperately struggle to get back inside and close the door. It was a kid. Jed wasn't able to tell how old the kid was, but his guess was the kid couldn't have been more than a baby when the infection started. That was an awful way to start your life. This kid had never known a normal world.

It wasn't an impossible shot from where he was. He only had to be careful to hit his targets accurately and not have one of the bullets go through an infected. If it did, it might take out a window on the car. A broken window meant they could get inside, or even worse the kid could be hit. Jed decided to aim for the infected on the other side of the car first. There were four on that side, and most of the time he could only see their heads anyway.

His tripod was useless in a tree for keeping his rifle steady, but he used it anyway, and he was surprised that it helped with the weight of the AR-15. He exhaled slowly and squeezed the trigger. It was a better shot than he expected, and now there were three on each side of the car.

While Jed studied his targets for the next shot, an awful thought crossed his mind. The kid tried to get out of the car once. If he shot the infected on the other side, the kid might try to make a run for it. If he did, Jed wouldn't be able to cover him if he got too far from the other side of the car.

He realized he was thinking of the kid as a boy, but he wasn't sure why. He hadn't gotten a good enough look to tell if it was a boy or girl. The hair was long and shaggy, but kids didn't get a lot of haircuts anymore.

"Okay, kid. Let's see if I'm right about you being a runner."

Jed took aim at the head of an infected on the side of the car that faced his tree. His second shot was as good as the first, and he switched to another target. He was happy with the way he had sighted in the scope on the rifle because he easily switched to the remaining infected on the driver side of the car and disposed of it.

Just as he expected, the door flew open, and the kid hit the ground running. Jed smiled because he had been right, plus the kid was running straight at him. He was still a long way from him, but it meant the three infected on the other side of the car would chase the kid and be easier to hit. He dropped the first one before they reached the rear of the car. Then he checked on the progress of the kid and could see that there were no more infected waiting for the child to come their way. Not that the infected were capable of setting a trap by hiding, but the kid could always accidentally run into an infected that was following the sound of the honking horn. Not to mention the sound of his AR-15.

Jed sighted in on the last two as fast as possible and made it look easy. He climbed down as quickly as he could so he could intercept the child. He had just reached the bottom of the tree when he saw the brown mop of hair disappear into the ditch on the side of the road.

"Hey, kid."

Jed managed to call out to the child without making it sound like he was shouting at him. The last thing he wanted to do was chase him now that the infected were all down. He waited a moment before calling again, and for good measure he checked the surrounding area to be sure nothing else had arrived. He almost missed the child taking a peek at him from the tall grass by the ditch.

"It's okay. I heard the horn. You were smart to honk it like that."

Jed really hadn't thought it was a very smart person to be honking the horn, but now that it was done it wasn't going to help the kid to criticize.

He saw the head rise up just a little higher. More suddenly than he expected, the child bolted from the ditch and ran with spindly legs straight at him. It wasn't until the skinny little body collided with him that he saw the big wet eyes and knew that the child was crying. It was also a little girl.

She couldn't have been much more than six years old, and that meant she was born right about the time the infection started. Her pale white skin was such a contrast to Jed's own bare arms, but it somehow made her look that much more fragile against his brown muscles. Jed held her while she cried and was surprised to find that he was crying too. It was the release he had denied himself when he had felt nothing but anger.

They could have stayed like that for an hour. There was so much to let go. As the sobbing finally subsided and the tears dried up, Jed gently peeled her arms from his neck. He held her at arms length so he could take stock, and sadly to see if she had any bites.

"Did they hurt you, sweetie?"

She sniffed and ran the back of a shirt sleeve across her nose. Jed regretted that he didn't have a handkerchief or napkin. He hadn't ever carried a handkerchief that he could recall, but he had an all-purpose rag in his back pocket. It wasn't fit for a child's face, though. He had used it to wipe off too many things that he didn't want to think about. As a matter of fact he wondered for a moment why he was keeping it in his pocket. It had to smell ripe by now.

She shook her head from side to side, and Jed took that to mean she hadn't been bitten because that would have qualified as being hurt.

The little girl was wearing a pair of blue jeans that was a couple sizes too large and a faded, red plaid shirt. He was amazed at how quickly he was thinking like a parent because his first thought about the shirt was that he would have to replace it. For some reason he couldn't stand plaid. Her shoes were no-name sneakers that had worn thin a long time ago.

Her legs were as straight as two perfectly matched sticks, but Jed didn't think she was malnourished. Maybe a little underfed, but everyone was these days. Jed remembered the last of the candy bars in his backpack and knew beyond a doubt that it would be a hit. He let go of her shoulders, and she instinctively reached for him again.

"It's okay, sweetie. Jed has something he knows you're gonna like."

He peeled back the wrapper, and she eyed the chocolate suspiciously. She had never had a candy bar. He could tell by the way she regarded it as nothing more than something in a wrapper. It was hard to believe that a few years ago everything was made out of plastic, and his parents told him that candy bar wrappers had been made out of paper and wax paper when they were kids. Now a plastic wrapper was making a six year old cautious.

Jed knew just what to do. He held it out to her and smiled as big as he could.

"If you think this smells funny, I'll eat it."

She sniffed at it, ready to reject it, but her eyes got really wide. Her small hands came up together, slowly as if she thought he might pull it away at the last second, and she gratefully took a bite. Jed didn't bother to tell her to slow down. He was enjoying watching her eat it as fast as she could.

When she swallowed the last time, he saw her eyes dart toward the backpack, hoping there was another treat in there.

"Sorry, kid. That was the last one, but I would say it was almost as much fun watching you eat it as it would have been if I had eaten it myself."

That earned him a smile, and Jed felt like he had also earned a measure of trust. He hated to bring it up, but he needed to know what had happened to her parents just in case they were nearby.

"What's your name, young lady?"

"Matilda, but that's not what mommy and daddy call me. My mommy calls me Mattie, and my daddy calls me Squirt."

That caught Jed off guard, and he snorted. That seemed to be funny to Mattie, and Jed knew that kids liked to make big people laugh.

He hated to put a stop to her laughing, but maybe it was best to ask while she was happy.

"Where are your mommy and daddy, Squirt?"

Mattie turned to look in the direction of the car and pointed.

"Over there."

Jed saw that Mattie was already aware of people becoming infected. It was sad to think they could lose their innocence so young. It was even sadder that they could accept that a stranger just shot mommy and daddy, but the stranger wasn't a bad guy.

"Come show me, Mattie."

Jed didn't look forward to digging seven graves, but he didn't want her last memory of her parents to be the way they were. She could remember the grave instead of the snarling faces pushed up against the windows of the car.

He took her small hand in his and walked to the car. As soon as she pointed out her parents, he went over to cover their faces. The rag in his back pocket finally served a purpose. He thought maybe that was why he had carried it for so long.

Jed showed Mattie how to use his binoculars and gave her the job as lookout while he found a spot to dig that would have fewer tree roots. He was sweating and bone tired by the time he finished, but as he was throwing the last bit of dirt on the graves, he thought maybe this was what God had in mind for him. He had been so angry that he was going to run himself into the ground finding whoever was behind the sound that was calling the infected. If they were far enough away, he wouldn't have been able to do anything to punish them because he would have been dragging his rifle behind him. Mattie had been put in his path to slow him down and to make him think before he did something stupid.

When he finished, Jed brought Mattie over to the graves. He put wildflowers on four of them and gave two bundles to Mattie.

"Here, kid. This is how you can say goodbye to mommy and daddy. They loved you, and this is how you can tell them you understand that it was just the sickness that made them act like that toward you."

"I know about the 'fection," she said. "It makes people do bad things."

"That's right, Squirt. They were just sick."

Mattie put the flowers on each grave, and Jed asked her if she knew any prayers. He thought it was pretty appropriate when she began.

"Now I lay me down to sleep......"

******

Chief Joshua Barnes had never been the kind of man to just quit. If there was a way to do the impossible, he was determined to find it. Sometimes there wasn't a way, like the night Allison had died. That still haunted him, but surviving a bite from the infected was beyond impossible. This time there was only one way for him to keep from losing his friends.

When the pair of BATT-T armored personnel carriers pulled away from the bottom of the steps, the layout of the parking area flashed through his mind. He had been knocked out and maybe had a concussion, but before the helicopter crashed, he had scanned the parking areas around the stadium in search of the best place to crash. That was why they were at least alive. One of the places his mind had ruled out was the parking area on the side of the ballpark. It was far too congested, and there wasn't a straight path from the steps to the street. If he timed it just right, he could catch up with the personnel carriers.

It was a full sprint from the steps to the concourse that would take him to another exit from the ballpark, but it was also an obstacle course. The overturned vendor carts, the beer kegs, and the mountains of garbage meant he was facing the same challenges as the vehicles navigating the congested parking areas. It was only his determination that caused him to erase the advantage they already had on him.

When the Chief made the turn that put him at the top of a handicap ramp, he saw that he wasn't going to catch the first of the two personnel carriers, but it was the second one he was interested in. If the second one was full of soldiers, it might not be a good idea to jump onto the first one as it went by.

The ramp gave him even more speed, and he was able to approach the second vehicle without slowing down. It had to cross his path, and his only worry was that the driver or passenger in the front seat would see him coming. It was completely dark, and he could see the silhouette of the lumbering personnel carrier, but he was running through nothing but shadows. He had to take the risk, or he might never see his friends again.

The first carrier passed through the parking lot entrance and turned left, away from the Chief. Its headlights flooded the street but didn't reach the Chief. The lights were blinding and were likely to be just as bright to the people driving. They were having a hard enough time focusing their attention on the debris in the street, so they didn't pay attention to the sidewalks. If they did see him, there was at least a chance that they would think he was an infected, unless they saw enough of him to see he was running.

The second vehicle crossed the sidewalk, and the Chief felt the passenger's eyes as the man tried to focus them on the darkness. Maybe he had made the mistake of looking at the headlights of the vehicle in front as it made the left turn. The man's face stayed aimed at the sidewalk longer than the Chief wanted, and he was sure that he would react at any moment. Just as it seemed like the man saw him, an infected stepped in front of the personnel carrier from the other side. Its arms were stretched outward and upward as if it could grab the living people in the front. The huge vehicle rolled forward, and there was only a slight bump upward on the front left side, but the reaction of the driver was all the Chief needed to take the passenger's eyes off of him for a moment. By the time the man looked again, the Chief was behind the vehicle.

One good thing about BATT-T armored personnel carriers that

made the Chief give a silent thanks was the handholds. They were all over the back of the vehicle, and he was able to get a good grip before it got up to speed. He took care to make sure he wasn't going to be bounced from the back and surveyed the rear door for portals. He saw there were several gun ports, but he didn't see any cameras. If there had been one, they would already be stopping.

The Chief tried to remember the configuration of the BATT-T armored personnel carriers. He couldn't remember if the back was a separate cabin from the driver seat or if it was open all the way to the front. If he opened the rear door and the configuration was all one cabin, they could shoot him from the driver seat. Worse, he could cause his friends to be shot. He had to accept the fact that he was going for a ride, and rescuing the others would have to be put on hold until he was sure he could do it without risking their lives. At least he wasn't helplessly standing on the steps of the ballpark watching as the taillights faded into the darkness.

That reminded him. He had left four people behind. He had the satisfaction of knowing they were capable of taking care of themselves, but he was worried that they would try too hard to find him. He didn't want to think about them taking risks and searching the bowels of the rooms under the seats of the stadium. Iris would forgive him because she knew him, but that didn't mean she wouldn't worry.

The Chief shook off the thoughts about the others because he had bigger things to worry about. Iris and Jean were a force to be reckoned with, and Captain Miller would have his birds in the air searching for them at sunrise. The Sikorsky crash site was going to be easy to spot from the air. For now, the Chief knew he had to focus on where he was going, and what he was going to do when he got there.

He suspected that the captors driving the two vehicles were from Patriots Point. It wasn't likely that there was a third militia in the area. The biggest question on his mind was how the people planned to get from Charleston to Mt. Pleasant. The last time he saw the Arthur Ravenel Bridge over the Cooper River it was increasing its population of infected dead by hundreds of thousands. There was no way to drive there. The Don Holt Bridge over the Cooper River in North Charleston was probably wide open, but getting there from Charleston would be next to impossible for at least a few days because I-26 was packed with the biggest horde in the southeast and probably the world.

The Chief didn't have to wait long to find out. The personnel carriers navigated through the clogged streets but generally seemed to be finding their way to the Ashley River. Less than thirty minutes after leaving the ballpark, the vehicles both turned off their headlights. A quick glance around the side was all the Chief needed. They were at the city marina on Lockwood Blvd. Fort Sumter was visible in the distance, and if they were watching the dark city, they were sure to see headlights even from that far away.

He heard a boat engine start, and he knew they would be taking their prisoners away by boat in a couple of minutes. The Chief hated to do it, but if he weighed the odds against him, he knew someone he cared for would die if he tried to rescue them now. He had to be patient. At least they were taking his friends as prisoners. That was a good sign.

The Chief let go of the back of the vehicle and ran a short distance in a straight line before ducking under the cover of a boat on a trailer. There were plenty of boats for him to take, but the likelihood of one being able to start after so many years was zero. All he could do was watch as the back of the BATT-T was opened, and his friends were dragged out. He wished he could at least let them know they hadn't been abandoned.

14

Green Zone

Contagion Extinction Level Event - Day Two

Something didn't make sense to either of the Corrigans. Grace acted like she had been expecting someone all along. As a matter of fact she was calm, and there was something about the way everyone showed her respect...or was it deference? It was like she was the boss.

"Before we move, someone get the medics in here to check Alex out. Those civilians worked him over pretty hard," said Dr. Williams.

"Yes, Ma'am."

The uniformed men made room for a man with a Red Cross patch on his sleeve, but it had some letters around it in a circle that Phillip couldn't quite read. Something told him the man wasn't really from the Red Cross.

Alex protested the extra precautions, but Dr. Williams held up a hand.

"What if you have an internal injury and die while we're on the road? By the time we get there, you'll turn. We'll have to move you straight to the lab, where you'll be a useful subject, but I need you for other things."

Her tone made it sound like his health was only important to her if he didn't become an inconvenience.

Dr. Williams saw the way Alex glanced at the Corrigans. It was an unspoken warning not to say too much in front of them. She gave him a slight nod that let him know she understood, but she was also irritated.

Phillip caught the gesture and averted his eyes as if he didn't see anything. If they had secrets, it might be a good idea to act like he didn't notice. If he had heard her correctly, he was still stunned by the comment about Alex being taken to the lab.

The medic finished his examination and pronounced Alex fit to travel, but two of his fingers were broken by the kicks when he had covered his head. His ribs were going to be really sore, but none were broken.

"I guess I won't be playing the piano again," said Alex, holding up a hand and studying the splint applied by the medic.

"Can you pull a trigger?" asked one of the uniformed men. He was already holding out an automatic pistol.

As soon as Alex took the gun from him, he produced another and offered it to Phillip. Denise didn't seem like the kind of woman who could shoot anyone except for the unfortunate person standing too close to her when the gun went off. Phillip had some experience with a few different guns, and the first thing he did was check to see if there was a round in the chamber.

He faced Dr. Williams, but his eyes moved from her to Alex as he asked, "Is there something we should know before we go out that door? Not that we mind, but it appears that you two have some information about what's happening that you could share with us. I mean, those others that left here already didn't do so well."

"We'll tell you more later," she answered, "but for now, I'll tell you this much. Don't get bitten. If someone bites you, the best thing you can do is put a bullet in your own head. Don't even think about it or hope to live."

The medic was helping Alex up from the floor despite his protests that he could do it on his own. He felt like there was something else he should tell Phillip and Denise, but he didn't want to give away something that Marshall Sayer or Dr. Williams wanted to be kept under wraps for a bit longer.

There were at least a dozen uniformed security guards escorting them from the basement to the upper floor. They took the stairs because they couldn't risk the elevator going up to one of the floors that had been compromised. They also only had to go up two floors from the evidence room to the ground floor.

The ground floor had taken on the appearance of a war zone. What had been bright lights, shiny linoleum, clean glass, and modern furniture was now walls, floors, and ceilings filled with bullet holes and painted with blood. There were no bodies, but there were body parts. Grace took in the tragic scene and put two and two together.

"They didn't figure out that you have to shoot the infected in the head. Everyone that died has already walked out of here because none of them died from head wounds."

"Why do you know so much about this?" asked Denise. "How come you know that?"

She kept her voice low, just above a whisper.

Dr. Williams didn't answer. Denise knew she heard her, but Grace was obviously ignoring the question.

The bright, white walls that weren't splattered with blood stood out in stark contrast to the places where there had been the most shooting, but there weren't many walls that were completely untouched.

Without glass in some of the windows and doors there was nothing to keep the flies from coming in. Flies can smell meat from over four miles away, and there was plenty of meat and blood spread around the police station. Not all flies can make the four mile trip when they smell meat, but there was no shortage of flies in the immediate area, and the buzzing was almost as sickening as the smell.

Uniformed men went ahead of the small group of civilians to be sure the area outside the doors was safe. One stopped in the doorway and watched his comrades as they spread out in the parking lot. There were gunshots, and everyone instinctively ducked. The man in the doorway went to a knee as he held his palm out toward Dr. Williams signaling her to wait where she was. When he was sure she had obeyed the signal, he put his hand under his rifle to cradle it and took aim. There was a momentary pause before he pulled the trigger.

Phillip was just about to pull Denise back to the evidence room, but the uniformed man motioned rapidly for them to follow him. The sunlight was too bright as they rushed in a huddled group to follow the soldier, or whatever he was. They shielded their eyes against the glare, but when the full impact of the devastation outside came into view, the Corrigans were too stunned to follow Alex and Dr. Williams.

Vehicles had burned, and several were still smoldering. Heat waves shimmered off of scorched, blackened metal and even the melted plastic parts. The inside had smelled of blood, weapons fire, and human excrement. Outside the smell was like an auto salvage yard that had caught fire. Burning fuel, oil, and rubber released a toxic smell that made their eyes water before they even had to pass by the cars that still smoked. Even worse, there was the pervasive smell of cooked meat and scorched hair.

Even if the Corrigans hadn't stopped, frozen in their tracks, the overwhelming smell would have had the same effect. They didn't cover their noses and mouths soon enough, and they doubled over from the spasms that hit their stomachs and throats.

Alex covered his mouth and nose with his hand, but Grace hardly noticed the smell. She had spent so much time in labs and autopsy rooms that she had only smelled what she expected to.

Muffled by his hand, Alex sounded like he was speaking in a foreign language, and he regretted even trying to talk in the middle of the stench. As soon as he opened his mouth he felt like he could taste it as well as smell it.

"This is awful. I don't know how you can even stand to be around this stuff. How can you cut people up for a living?"

If looks could kill, Alex would have been spread around the parking lot in pieces just like dozens of other people.

"You make it sound so gruesome. You do understand it's a science, right? What I do for a living took years of education and years of practice, so I don't just cut people up."

The last few words were said very slowly and had a note of warning to them. Alex didn't know when to quit.

"You have to admit there must be a little ghoul in you for it not to bother you."

"I don't have to admit anything of that sort, and by the way, do you even know the definition of ghoul? I don't rob graves, and I certainly don't eat dead people. I have an idea, Alex. Why don't we leave you here so you can find out what a ghoul really is?"

He didn't think she was serious, and he missed the gesture Grace made toward one of the armed guards. Two of them closed on him from each side, and he was surprised when they pulled his arms back and slapped handcuffs on his wrists. Before he could protest the treatment, a gag was stuffed in his mouth, and a sack was pulled over his head.

In the middle of the tangle of vehicles in the parking lot, the doors opened on a military style vehicle. The guards virtually tossed Alex inside, and the roughness they showed was a contrast to the courtesy they showed the Corrigans. One of them politely extended his hand to Denise and offered to help her up the high step into the back of the vehicle. She eyed him closely, and he seemed genuine, but she and Phillip were both wondering who these people were that they were so organized and prepared in the face of such a strange disaster.

The ride wasn't what they considered comfortable. The vehicle's oversized tires bounced over things in the road, and the driver constantly changed directions. There were no windows they could use to be able to see where they were going or what they were driving through. The fact that they were moving at all was a miracle. Denise and Phillip weren't so distrusting that they didn't feel grateful to be alive. What little they had seen before getting inside the personnel carrier convinced them they were far luckier than most people. If someone told them they were the only people alive who had been sitting on the deck of the restaurant where they had eaten the night before, they would have believed it judging by the human remains scattered around the police station parking lot.

Thirty minutes after climbing into the personnel carrier they came to a stop, and a man dressed in body armor opened a panel that separated the front seats from the back.

"We'll be inside the Green Zone in a few minutes. When the door opens, proceed directly to the medical examination area. If you're bite free, you will be designated as a Survivor, Infection Free, and you will be escorted to the requisition center. Follow the signs that say SIF."

"How do we know if we're infection free?" asked Denise. "We weren't bitten?"

"That's correct, Ma'am. If you have been bitten, you won't be designated as a survivor. You will be designated as IDP."

"IDP," echoed Denise.

"Infected, Death Pending," answered the man.

The panel closed, and they waited in silence. Dr. Williams was reading something one of their escorts had given her. Alex was a heap in the corner under his burlap sack, and from time to time they could hear him mumble around the gag in his mouth something about doing as he was told. He sounded like he was praying and making promises. For some reason silence seemed like the right thing to both Phillip and Denise. One of the armed men had ridden in back with them, and he was off somewhere in a world of his own, totally disinterested in anything accept guarding Alex and escorting the Corrigans.

The vehicle rolled forward a few feet and stopped then did it again. They had the impression that they were in a line and moving closer to something.

Outside of the personnel carrier it was a long line of vehicles entering a compound. About forty of the same personnel carriers were passing through the main checkpoint of the Green Zone. They were already inside the Orange Zone which was heavily manned by guards. The Orange Zone wrapped in an arc around Patriots Point, and where there were no guards it was mined with explosive devices that were guaranteed to keep anything from getting in or out of the area. Beyond the Orange Zone on the outside was the Red Zone. The infected still wandered across the Red Zone in the direction of the convoy waiting to pass through the inspection area. Snipers were still shooting the infected when they came within a few feet of the end of the line.

Inside past the Orange Zone there was another buffer, but the guards had their rifle straps across their shoulders. Nothing was getting inside the Orange Zone that wasn't supposed to.

The line moved forward until their personnel carrier was surrounded by guards who slapped their palms against the sides to get them to climb out of the vehicle quickly. When they saw they had startled Dr. Williams, there were hasty apologies as the guards scurried to help her and Denise down from the high vehicle. A golf cart was brought up for her, and she hardly seemed to notice when Phillip and Denise were escorted into a tent. She rode away without saying a word. They received more courtesy than most people because they had come in with Dr. Williams, but after she was whisked away, their treatment became more indifferent as they were put into line with other refugees hoping to be admitted to the Green Zone.

They were helpless when it came to defending themselves from whatever it was that was about to happen, so there was nothing they could do for Alex. He was dragged from the personnel carrier and dropped along the fence to sit next to several other men who were hidden under burlap hoods.

Phillip leaned close to his wife's ear and whispered, "Are you believing all of this?"

"Who are these people?" she answered.

"That's what I mean. They aren't military, but they seem awfully prepared for this."

"I agree, but there's too much chaos. It's like they're some kind of private army."

Denise had been an Army brat when she was a child, so she had seen the crisp discipline of an Army base even under bad conditions. The men and women walking around in uniform were probably ex-military, but whoever was in command was more likely to be a civilian.

Shots rang out back at the end of the line of vehicles. Both of them jumped, and Phillip protectively put his body between his wife and the shooting. There were cheers from the Orange Zone because someone had apparently hit their target.

"See what I mean?" she said.

A guard at the entrance to the tent snapped his fingers impatiently, and the Corrigans saw a gap had formed in the line where the people ahead of them had moved forward. They closed the gap, but the man still kept an annoyed expression aimed at them.

"Sorry," mumbled Phillip as they moved forward into the tent.

Inside there were two rows of tables. Men and women sat at the tables and took down information from refugees who were answering questions. They saw that one row was processing men while the other processed women. The guard at the end of the women's table motioned for Denise to come forward. Phillip took one step to follow her, but he didn't get far.

"Hold up. You come over here."

It was the men's table, and they didn't like to be kept waiting.

Over the next fifteen minutes they were both asked a series of questions about who they were, where they were from, what happened to them the night before, and where they had been during the night. The biggest question was whether or not they had been bitten.

Both of them were taken behind curtains where they were told to get undressed. The serious faces of the doctors and nurses waiting to check them for bites left no doubt in their minds that they should comply without question. Denise was a bit shy about the whole thing, but until the night before she had never seen anything like the things she had seen, and this wasn't the worst thing that could happen to her.

Denise and Phillip finished dressing and stepped out of the curtained areas almost at the same time. Just as they saw each other there was some sort of commotion at the entrance of the tent. A man had turned around and attempted to get out of the line, and his movement was seen by the guards immediately. Apparently, he had entered the tent and seen that everyone ahead of him was being checked for bites, and he was nursing a bandaged arm.

Armed men grabbed the man and the trademark burlap bag seemed to come out of nowhere. Not being able to see tended to immobilize people, and it was quickly pulled over his head. He was lifted by his arms and legs and carried past the line of people who silently feared similar treatment. No one else wanted a bag over their head.

Phillip had a better view of the area beyond the inspection curtains, and he saw that the physical examination of the man only lasted a matter of seconds. Instead of coming out the way they had gone in, the man was carried through a door in the back of the tent. Phillip was receiving instructions from a processor at the last station when the guards came through the tent without the bitten man.

The processor pressed the backs of their hands with a rubber ink stamp and pointed at a side flap in the tent. Phillip led Denise through it without hesitation, eager to get away from the uncertainty inside the tent. The flap opened directly in front of a gate where a pair of guards glanced at their hands and then pointed toward a sign with SIF written on it in big letters. They felt some relief for the first time since the night before, and almost broke into a run in the direction indicated by the arrow on the sign.

******

In the initial days of the outbreak, millions of people were displaced, unable to even return to their homes a few miles away. The infection spread so quickly that the first survivors were people who were already at home, and they were smart enough to stay there. What drove many of them from the safety of their homes was the need for medical attention for family members, but no one knew there wasn't a cure. That knowledge would come later when it was too late.

A small number of people survived because they were in the right place at the right time. Even people who were close to Patriots Point were being slaughtered, so they ran blindly. Without knowing where they were going, some fled toward the maritime museum. They didn't know what they would find on the old World War II aircraft carrier, but it had to be better than what was happening in the streets. As people died around them, some fell into the safety net under Marshall Sayer.

Marshall Sayer had just enough advance notice to activate his emergency plan, and he flooded the area around Patriots Point with his operatives. Their primary goal was to save him and a small group of his essential personnel. In this case, medical staff were critical to survival, and they were whisked away from their medical centers and research institutes and deposited in locations around Charleston. The most versatile personnel carriers were then dispatched to round them up. Some never made it back, but the huge Stryker vehicles drove over cars and helpless people where they had to, and the overall plan was a success.

A second part of his plan was to gather up as many of the locals as he could without endangering his staff of doctors. He didn't know that they were dealing with a pathogen as relentless as this one would turn out to be, but he knew his doctors would need a good supply of test subjects. He didn't think of them as people trying to survive. He thought of them as subjects who ran in the right direction.

That part of the plan worked so well that most of his staff were in place before the Corrigans were processed. As a matter of fact, they were among the last of the civilians to be admitted, and they would have the good fortune to be given jobs instead of becoming test subjects. As they hurried up the ramp into the USS Yorktown, they would have been horrified to see what was happening behind them. They were met by an escort who welcomed them with a smile.

It was only noon when the orders were passed down the line to the processing tents inside the Orange Zone, and the entire screening process came to a halt. Personnel carriers in line at the gate turned around and drove back to the Red Zone. They drove straight through the infected dead that were stumbling along the road toward the sounds of the sharpshooters, and the drivers didn't try to avoid them. The roads were swept clear for the carriers that followed the ones in front.

The occupants of each vehicle became restless. They couldn't see where they were going accept for the limited view past the armed men in the front seats. They begged to know what was happening and why they were turning around, but they got no answers from the men who had seemingly brought them to safety. Now they followed closely behind the vehicles in front of them, and they traveled at a speed that made them sense the urgency.

In a few of the personnel carriers the passengers became defiant, but when they insisted on knowing where they were going, they were quick to obey when the guns were pointed at them. For those who weren't used to following orders, their behavior was changed as the guns were aimed at their families. In other carriers, the passengers hadn't given up hope. They believed that they were better off than the unlucky souls outside the vehicles, and they quietly waited for the drivers to take them to a new, safer destination.

Over an hour later the passengers heard gunfire in the distance, and it was obvious that they were driving toward the source. The convoy didn't slow down as it began weaving through a maze of wrecked cars. They passed a guardhouse that was manned by a large force of men who were busy engaging an unseen enemy. The passengers would have been right to assume they were firing at the infected, but not one of them could have conceived there were so many. The fields and trees around the entrance of the container terminal were flooded with the undead that were drawn toward the activity at the gate.

As the last of the vehicles passed through the opening, a large gate was rolled into place. The shooters withdrew from their positions and hastily joined ranks with a second group of uniformed men who were unloading trucks, setting up a new perimeter inside the original fence.

Marshall Sayer had insisted that contingency plans were needed for the wide variety of catastrophes that could occur. A zombie apocalypse had been a last minute addition to their list, and it turned out to be a good idea. It was only added after one of his spies had uncovered the list that had been used a long time ago by that crazy survivalist group that was being funded by the government to build shelters. He had laughed for hours after reading their list, but it had finally occurred to him the word 'zombie' could be used generically to mean any number of things, especially biohazards. Planning for a generic catastrophe was an entertaining endeavor for him, and one of his brainstorming sessions produced the suggestion that two fences were better than one.

The second fence was taking shape quickly. As the infected pressed their faces against the first fence, poles were raised and chainlink was stretched between them. Concertina wire was uncoiled to be strung along the top of the fence, but a quick thinking supervisor decided it would go to better use being stretched along the ground between the first and second fence. The wretched creatures clinging to the outside of the first fence didn't appear to be able to climb.

The cargo container storage area for the State Ports Authority terminal was capable of holding well over a hundred thousand containers at a time. It was only a small wonder that few people had ever noticed when certain containers never moved once they had arrived. When those few people inquired about the containers, they were simply told it was classified information. Military shipments came and went all the time, and occasionally some stayed longer than others. Even if it was a large number of containers, it was no concern to the operators of the shipyard because someone was paying for them to stay.

Now the special containers were open, and tons of supplies were being offloaded. The personnel carriers that had transported hundreds of survivors from Patriots Point across Mt. Pleasant to the State Ports backed up together and opened their rear doors. The bright sunlight and fresh air was a welcome sight, but instead of one processing tent serving a few people at a time, this area was set up to handle large numbers.

A whole row of tents similar to the ones at Patriots Point were between the carriers and the cargo containers, and within minutes people exited from the rear of the tents and were directed by armed guards to join the workers who were already unloading the containers. Families with children were allowed to send one parent of their choice with the children to a special processing area. Child care supervisors took over for as many parents as possible so that the parents were free to begin work preparing meals in the massive mess tents. The workforce grew rapidly, and in less than twenty-four hours after the start of the outbreak of the infection, the zombie apocalypse contingency was in operation.

If bite victims were discovered inside the row of tents, they were removed with as little fanfare as possible. There were some raised voices, and there was crying, but there were no gunshots other than those around the fence. Bite victims were taken away in the personnel carriers for a return trip to Patriots Point.

Some of the containers were stocked with supplies that were needed immediately, including the worker habitats. Crews were assembled and placed under the supervision of uniformed officers who carried manuals that contained instructions specific to their groups, and crews began constructing the habitats in a predetermined corner of the enclosed compound. Within two hours, the area took on the appearance of a refugee city complete with habitats for sleeping, cooking, dining, and latrines.

There was some resistance. As the personnel carriers released their passengers to be screened inside the medical tents, the angry voice of a new arrival carried far enough to gain the attention of everyone within the processing area.

"I'm not moving another step until I get to speak with someone in charge."

All eyes turned in the direction of a group of people just outside the entrance of a tent. A guard had taken hold of a man by the upper arm, and he had angrily spun his arm in a complete circle to break the guard's grip. Now he was face to face with the guard and leaning inward as he yelled. His hands were on his hips, which did nothing to protect his vulnerable solar plexus. The sensitive nerves in that area were a tempting target for the guard.

"Are you too stupid to understand what I'm saying?" shouted the refugee.

The man's voice was even louder in the silence that had descended on the processing area. It was a confrontation that would provide more useful information to the refugees than a formal orientation.

The guard's shoulders bunched, and his right fist shot upward into the soft spot below the man's sternum. The man collapsed onto the guard as he tried hard to catch his breath. When the guard stepped aside, the man fell to the ground. Before the man could successfully breathe, the lines were moving once again through the processing tents, and he was loaded back into a personnel carrier. When it left, no one asked where it went.

The sun set, but the work continued into the night. Crews erected gantries with work lights strung between them. As they worked they were followed around by their supervisors who consulted the manuals that were seen by many as a badge of authority. If you had a manual, you were important. The truth was that the disaster plans assumed the possibility that power might be interrupted, so the plans for the construction of the camp at the State Ports Authority would not rely on laptop computers or tablets. The people carrying the manuals needed them as much as everyone else.

One by one the containers were emptied of their contents. Some of the crates inside weren't unpacked, but they were placed in different locations around the compound. The people unloading them learned quickly that it was best not to be too curious about what was inside the crates, especially the ones that were loaded into trucks and delivered to the Green Zone at the aircraft carrier.

The second fence was finished by midnight, and construction began on guard towers. They bore an odd resemblance to prison towers, and the resemblance was intensified by guards who climbed into the finished towers and faced inward toward the workers. Some guards remained on duty at the fences to shoot the infected that slowly increased their numbers outside in the new Red Zone, and they opened fire from time to time in an effort to prevent concentrations in small areas.

Empty containers were lifted by special cranes that drove over them on both sides and the top. They were then driven to the docks along the river and assembled into a barrier. No one asked why it was necessary to make a barrier along the river, but apparently it would serve more than one purpose. When they were placed end to end with a second layer on top, the workers inside the complex could no longer see what was happening on the river. It was safe to assume the same could be said for anyone who might be on the other side. One by one they were emptied, carried, and stacked until the barrier was four containers high. The inside of the terminal took on the appearance of a fort, and the feeling of safety was an acceptable trade for the hard work.

A voice over a loudspeaker called for everyone to stop working shortly before sunrise and to gather at the mess tents. Tired men and women who had started their day by climbing into personnel carriers dragged their worn bodies and numb minds in the direction of the tents that had been erected in the center of the complex. They gave little thought to anything except for the fact that they had been told to stop working. Food was a good idea. Sleep was even better. As hungry as they were, they were almost too tired to eat.

They waited in line and barely had the energy to talk. Those who were still with someone they knew leaned on them to keep from falling down. Some even sat down in line, but they weren't on the ground long before someone told them to get up. It felt like prison, but the alternative was far worse.

The food turned out to be worth the wait, and the tired workers felt their spirits rise as they got to know fellow refugees gathered at the long rows of tables. It was contagious, and mealtime took on a celebratory mood. As they finished their meals they were surprised for a second time when they were given assignments for quarters. The tents housing the cots were crowded, but they were successfully partitioned to allow a small living space for families. It wasn't much, but it was far enough from the fences.

By the end of CEL Day Two as survivors climbed onto their cots for much needed sleep, the refugee city at the State Ports Authority was functional. Someone made a sign and hung it over the entrance to the quarters.

It said, "Welcome to the SPA."

15

Jed & Matilda

Contagion Extinction Level Event - Six Years Later

Jed was forced to travel slower now that he had Mattie to look after, but it didn't take long for him to realize his faith was still intact. He decided God had put Mattie in his path to slow him down. Also, he had to be serious about the way he approached the infected. He was so angry before that he might have gotten reckless. Keeping Mattie safe was a priority. He still planned to find out who was behind the strange thing that was calling the infected, but he could do that and protect Mattie too.

Mattie was good company, and she was good for his soul. The loss of the colony was unbelievable to Jed, and he kept thinking about the friends he had lost. Yes, God made him slow down, but he also made sure Jed didn't feel alone in the world. Mattie was a talker. She told Jed that her parents promised to take her to Dizzyworld when there were no more 'fected, as she called them. She asked him if he had ever been there, and he had to admit, he had grown up with the dream of going there himself. Of course it wasn't the infected that had prevented him from making the trip. If he could put the world back to the way it had been, he figured he would take Mattie to Dizzyworld.

It was comforting to hold Mattie's hand as they walked, and eventually he saw her stifle a yawn. He scooped her up, and she laid her head down in the curve of his neck. Her small arms circled his neck, and Jed experienced that remarkable feeling every parent had when they felt a child hug them. It made his heart swell to feel her breathing evenly as she drifted off to sleep.

There were several hours left in the day, and Jed wasn't nearly as tired as Mattie, so he decided to walk as long as he could. There was always the question of how far to go if you were on the move because you had to be thinking about shelter for the night before you were ready to stop. It was like the old days of traveling on the interstates. You always had to ask yourself if you needed to stop at that rest area, or could you wait until you came to the next one. Sooner or later you wished you had stopped at the last one.

Walking along the interstate since the first day of the infection had always been dangerous because the infected followed the path of least resistance. Then again, the wide open spaces made traveling faster, and Jed could spot trouble further away. If he saw any infected, they were going the same way, and he could avoid contact most of the time. He came to one overpass that had collapsed, and he wasn't sure what could make an overpass collapse, but it didn't appear to have been done with explosives. It looked more like it had been bulldozed.

Jed climbed over the rubble and stood at the top of the pile of debris. From his higher vantage point he could see the massive piles of vehicles where they had collided with each other years ago. Some had simply been abandoned as people either ran out of gas or became boxed in behind the wrecks.

He sat down and laid Mattie on a flat piece of asphalt. He slid his rolled up blanket from his backpack and gently placed it under her head. Sometimes Jed felt like he had to make some sense of it all, so he would sit down and study what he saw. What amazed him was the way everything looked the same on both sides of the interstate. On the day it all began, he imagined that people all felt like the best place to be was somewhere other than where they were, but no one really knew where they should be.

Jed checked behind him to be sure nothing was coming his way, and he thought about what was in that direction. About eighty miles away would be Columbia, and another fifteen miles along I-77 was Fort Jackson. If he had been on I-26 that day, there would have been some people surrounding him who were trying to reach the Army base, reasoning that it would have been the safest place to be. In his mind he pictured what it was like at the front gate of the base. The Army would have been frantically rushing civilians through the gate, and he doubted they would have realized that every car was a Trojan horse. The infection probably rode right in through the front gate, and by the time they learned of their mistake, the infection would have been spreading inside, already too far gone to stop. Eighty miles away there were still at least two living people trying to reach an already dangerous place to be.

In front of Jed was the road to that dangerous place......Charleston. One of the hottest tourist spots in the country, famous for its history, its food, and its friendly people. Refugees would have reasoned that the Navy base at Goose Creek and the Air Force base in North Charleston would have had enough power between them to stop the infected, and of course they would both have a way to escape. Less than thirty miles away, people frantically carrying injured family members to safety would be thinking that they would survive if they could reach the Navy base before all of the ships were full, and the Air Force must have been evacuating people to secure places in their huge C-17 transports. Thirty miles of people thinking the same thing. It was an obstacle that would lead to thousands of deaths.

The grass had grown tall in the years since that first day. It didn't take long for it to become a landscape of wrecked vehicles, and the only things moving were the infected that searched for more victims, occasionally finding someone who had hidden in a car or bus, and more often being drawn by the sounds of the big black birds that were feeding on a seemingly endless supply of food. Jed could still see the birds circling over something up ahead. That would probably go on for years. He had seen predator birds land on the infected and tear off strips of flesh before retreating to a tree branch.

When the horde had recently passed through, their numbers had been enough to flatten the tall grass, but here and there the green jungle that used to be a median maintained by the highway department was bouncing back again. A little rain was all it took to get the grass to stand up, and he thought it would only be a couple of weeks before there would be little evidence that the largest horde in the world had passed by.

Mattie stirred next to him, and her eyelids fluttered open. Jed felt so protective of her that for a moment he considered abandoning his quest to find out who had called the horde to them. He silently hoped it had been one of those times where the people behind the atrocity would pay for what they had wished for. How could they have not been overwhelmed by the response?

"Mr. Jed? I'm hungry."

Jed hadn't left the colony that morning with a lot of supplies, but he had put together a backpack the day before that was his idea of essentials. A few MREs, first aid kit, sleeping and cooking gear. He rummaged through the bag and made a show out of picking the right one. Mattie sat up as straight as she could and tried to catch a glimpse of the inside of the backpack. She was undoubtedly holding out some hope that another candy bar was hidden in between the MREs.

"Let me see. This one looks like it would be good for breakfast, and this one isn't something that kids like. It's something called pizza."

Mattie managed to catch a hold on his sleeve as he was putting the MRE back in with the other supplies.

"I think kids like pizza, Mr. Jed."

Every time she called him 'mister' he felt like telling her she could just call him Jed, but it sounded so funny that he kind of liked it. Not surprisingly, it reminded him of that TV show with the talking horse, and Jed realized hearing her call him Mr. Jed always made him think about a time before the infected dead. In the end he decided it wouldn't hurt a thing for her to keep calling him that.

"Kids like pizza?"

He put as much surprise in his voice as he could, and she laughed in that way kids laugh when they really know you're just kidding them.

Motion in the distance reminded Jed that they were still in a dangerous place. When it was quiet, and when you caught yourself doing something that made it feel like things were the way they used to be, it was easy to forget that you were always just a breath away from dying. It also reminded him of what he had lost back at the oxbow island, and he felt the sadness wash over him again. He was tired of death and tired of the dead.

"Don't worry, Mr. Jed. I'll let you have the pizza."

Mattie held the package out to him, mistaking the expression on his face as disappointment that she wanted the pizza.

"Oh, no Mattie. It's fine if you want the pizza. As a matter of fact, Mr. Jed was just teasing you. I was just thinking about my friends."

"I think about my mommy and daddy all the time, but I have you to worry about now, Mr. Jed."

Mattie had given Jed the wake up call he needed. If he didn't have her to help him keep things in perspective, he was likely to wallow in his own pity. She had never known a day in her life when she was free from danger. She had lost her parents just that morning, but she was trying to make him feel better.

Jed snapped himself out of the dark place he had slipped into, and helped Mattie heat up her pizza. His was labeled as pulled pork and sweet potato fries. He didn't think it would compare to the pulled pork his mother made for him his whole life, but it turned out to be close enough to satisfy his appetite.

The food lifted their spirits, and the movement he had seen in the distance stayed just far enough away to let them eat in peace. Jed also found himself doing what needed to be done. He thought about how far they had to go and what they would have to do when it was time to get some sleep. If they didn't find a place that guaranteed their safety while they slept, Jed would be forced to carry Mattie and move through the entire night.

Some of the anxiety that Jed had felt earlier returned as they continued their journey toward Charleston. The infected were still visible in the distance, but there were fewer than he could have hoped, so Jed patiently stalked them to find the easiest routes through the wrecked vehicles. From time to time they had to leave the highway and creep through the trees to avoid contact with infected that had become snagged on the twisted metal hanging from cars. If it was one or two, Jed would quickly dispose of them with his hatchet or a knife, but twice they approached within a few yards of infected that had become trapped only because they weren't capable of doing simple problem solving.

Keeping low behind cars and trucks, they crept past the groaning crowd of infected that had gone into a dead end formed by wreckage. If one of them found its way back out of the dead end, it would be completely by accident. They watched long enough to see that it was like the crab traps Jed had used to catch blue crabs. The cars were spread out over a wide area but slowly merged into one open lane that passed between them. There were no openings for the infected to stray outside of the lane to go around the roadblock ahead. That single lane gradually narrowed until it was the width of a sidewalk, and the infected continued to walk ahead in single file.

When they came to the two cars that were positioned with a gap between them barely wide enough for the infected to go through one at a time, they bumped into each other from behind, and the infected up front were pushed through. Once past the small gap, the path ahead widened enough for them to walk two abreast, so they picked up speed. With over two dozen of them squeezed into a cul-de-sac, they couldn't find their way back out, so they bumped against each other, fell down, and generally took on the appearance of a crowd at a heavy metal concert. It wasn't likely that they would ever find a way out of their trap.

Jed led Mattie through the trees, picking their way carefully past brackish pools of water. By the time Jed remembered what else lived in between those trees, Mattie was surprised by a snake that was upset by the intruders. It didn't strike, but its sideways motion told Jed it was about to. He snatched Mattie off the ground and rushed forward so fast that he almost walked both of their faces straight through a spider web.

That was enough for Jed. He decided he had to find a place for them to spend the night, and it had to be soon. He angled back toward the interstate and rushed up the shoulder into the open. If there were any infected, he planned to overwhelm them. He was so tired and so stressed from the long day that he almost ignored the truck with the bucket lift on it. The bucket dangled about eighteen or twenty feet in the air, and it wasn't likely to be capable of operating again, but Jed preferred it that way. As long as he could climb, it would be a perfect place to sleep. It had the added bonus of being a bucket with solid sides instead of rails, so nothing would be able to see them from the ground.

The bucket rocked slightly. Jed held a finger to his lips to keep Mattie from drawing the attention of whatever it was inside the bucket.

He said in a voice just above a whisper, "Somebody's sleeping in my bed."

Mattie put a hand over her mouth, and Jed mentally assessed whether or not he could shoot whatever it was in the bucket. He turned in a circle and searched the shoulder of the road for rocks. He picked up a bottle and was ready to throw it when it occurred to him that it would make enough noise to attract attention to their location.

Jed stashed Mattie on top of an SUV where he could keep an eye on her. It was almost under the bucket, but at least he could see her while he was figuring out how to reach the thing. He told her she was the lookout and draped the strap of his binoculars over her head.

He searched the SUV first and then several of the cars nearby. He figured the truck would have been picked over by now, but there were lots of cars to rummage through. He found some interesting but useless stuff, although he scored a cowboy hat that was a great fit. The sun was getting to the back of his neck, so he considered it to be a good find. He put it on and flashed a big smile at Mattie.

In the end, Jed decided he would have to check the truck, and he found what he needed had been there all along. A heavy rope was perfect and a large hammer to put some weight on the end. He tied it in place on the head of the hammer and climbed on top of the cab of the truck. He got his weight centered over his feet and started the hammer swinging in an easy arc at first, but as it picked up speed, he got it above his head until it was pulling on the rope. The rope was too heavy for Jed to play it out as far as he wanted, but he gave it everything he had. As it whistled through the air and came by behind him, he leaned as far as he could to the right and dropped his shoulder like he was throwing an uppercut punch.

Mattie was marveling at Jed's cowboy hat, but when he showed a talent for using a rope, he might as well have been a real cowboy to her. The hammer disappeared neatly into the bucket, and Mattie clapped her hands together and squealed.

Jed pulled the rope slowly until the hammer appeared at the lip of the bucket. The idea was to make the hammer come over the lip of the bucket from the bottom of the handle. Hopefully, it would fall with the claw facing backward so it would catch on the lip like a grappling hook. It worked like a charm until the bucket tilted much farther than he expected it to. There was something much heavier than the hammer and rope making it lean over.

The contents of the bucket did a somersault in midair and aimed for the top of the SUV where Jed had put Mattie. As it dropped from the bucket, Jed saw that it was an infected dead that was hardly more than bones held together by sinew and its clothes. Jed felt his heart stop, and the words 'look out' were stuck inside his speechless mouth. He couldn't do a thing to stop it from happening. The mouth of the infected was open and seemed to be opening even more as if it knew it was about to bite another victim.

Mattie had grown up with the infected in her life in much the same way that children in Australia had been raised to understand that crocodiles waited in the shallow water. She didn't try to understand them. She knew that they were just part of life, and even though it was hard for her to accept that her parents had become infected, she had remembered it wouldn't be the last time it would happen. That didn't mean she would let it happen to her.

The infected skeleton might have been nothing more than a rotted corpse, but neither Mattie nor Jed could tell. The bucket had moved on its own before, so they expected the worst. Jed couldn't help, but Mattie knew how to somersault too.

Her right arm tucked down across her body, and she went head first toward the hood. Her dad had taught her to let her body follow her head and then to look at her feet. She didn't realize that she would roll so fast because she had learned on flat ground, but by the time she reached the end of the hood, her feet were ahead of her. Mattie let her rear end slide, and she landed neatly on her feet.

Behind her the brittle bones of the infected flew apart with the impact. The clothing that still clung to the wasted frame of the body kept the bones from flying in all directions, but there was nothing to keep the head attached. It bounced like a basketball.

The words managed to finally get past Jed's lips, not when the infected skeleton fell, but when the head bounced. He saw the angle of the bounce and knew that it was going to follow Mattie.

"Look out for the head," he yelled.

Mattie knew what she was rolling away from, and another thing she learned in her short life was that the infected kept following you. It never occurred to her that it would only be part of one.

The head made its second bounce on the cracked windshield of the SUV, and the slope of the glass combined with the forward momentum made it spin as it flew toward Mattie. She ducked and heard the loud thump as it met with the fender of another car behind her. Jed was amazed at how well Mattie understood this new world, because it wasn't enough for her to somersault from the roof of a car, and it wasn't enough for her to duck when the head bounced by. She also ran.

As soon as she heard the thump behind her she took off for the gap between two cars to her right and was behind one of them before the head came to a stop right where she had been standing. She peered at it around the rear of the car, and Jed stared at it from up above. The empty eye sockets stared back at him as the jaws worked at the air one final time.

"That worked," said Mattie.

Jed felt like a spectator at some kind of ridiculous competition, and between the two of them, they had scored enough points to win. All he could think of to say that seemed to fit with what Mattie said was something that caused Mattie to get an expression on her face that was out of place on a six year old.

"Just like I planned it," said Jed.

During the acrobatics by the infected and the equally impressive moves of the six year old, Jed unconsciously kept his grip on the rope. The bucket was tilted to one side, but it wasn't moving anymore. It was doubtful that there were any more surprises waiting inside it, but Jed wanted Mattie safe with him before making his next move. He kept tension on the rope but carefully climbed down from the cab into the back of the truck and held out one hand to her. She ran over and took it, and he smoothly lifted her up with him. He pulled her in and gave her a big hug, as much for himself as for her.

The hydraulic arm that lifted the bucket into the air had long ago lost the ability to be raised or lowered. Jed inspected the hoses that supplied the hydraulic pressure and saw the stains where the rubber had aged and cracked. Years of exposure to the harsh southern sunlight and disuse had taken a toll on the entire system. He doubted that there was anything he could fix even though he understood enough about mechanics and hydraulics from working on cars.

Jed guessed the bucket was only about eighteen to twenty feet above the ground, but that was high enough for their purposes. He had seen 'cherry pickers' as they were called, that went as high as two hundred feet. Jed was glad he wouldn't have to climb that high. He tied the end of the rope around Mattie's waist, and for good measure he also fastened it through his belt. If the hammer came loose from the bucket, she would still be connected to him.

"Do you know how to ride piggy-back?"

Mattie grinned as she circled around behind Jed and stepped onto a toolbox to get a little height before climbing onto Jed's back. She circled her arms around his neck and held on tightly without putting him in a chokehold.

"Of course you do," he added.

Jed felt more like himself as he made the climb to the bucket. It seemed like he hadn't been in control anymore even though he had rescued a little girl from certain death. The weight on his back as he climbed was nothing compared to the weight he felt from losing the colony, but he wanted her weight to replace the other. He couldn't do anything to change what had happened to his friends at the colony, but he could keep Mattie alive and do whatever he could to get even with whoever it was who had been calling the infected.

When they reached the top of the arm that held the bucket, Jed held Mattie back a moment longer to be sure there were no surprises waiting inside. He was glad he did. There wasn't another infected, but the last thing Jed wanted to see was another spider. Jed was seriously angry with himself for not thinking of it before carrying Mattie up to the bucket. It wasn't the messy web of the brown recluse, but all spiders had become offensive to him.

Jed checked the position of the sun and knew he had to deal with the problem quickly. It would be dark in less than a half hour. He restrained himself from using language in front of Mattie that he normally would have used, but he climbed back down to do what he had to do if they were going to be safe by dark.

He untied Mattie and jumped down from the truck. A dry branch with plenty of leaves was all he needed. Jed made the climb a second time, and pushed the branch into the bucket. The last thing he wanted to do was melt the bucket, but he had to create enough smoke to make the spiders evacuate if they didn't die. For once, he felt like things were going his way. When he held a match to the dry leaves, it blossomed orange for just a moment before it sent up a plume of smoke, but then the flames died down, and the smoke did its job. Strands of filament descended from the bucket as spiders dropped to the ground below. Even from twenty feet above, he saw them running across the roof of the SUV.

The sun was much lower, but Jed had one more chore to take care of. He had seen blankets in a car he had searched. They would be useful to line the inside of the bucket. Otherwise, they were going to be covered in black soot within minutes after climbing into the bucket.

It only took another fifteen minutes to clear the debris out of the bucket and drape the blankets in place. He had to admit, it was going to be one of the safest places he was likely to find if not the most comfortable. He went back for Mattie and carried her up for a second time. She wrinkled her nose at the smell of burnt plastic, but the blankets helped some, and a light breeze would make it tolerable.

As they settled down in the cramped space at the bottom of the bucket, Mattie curled up against Jed and went to sleep so quickly that Jed hadn't even found the best way to get comfortable himself. With walls around him to keep them safe, it didn't take him long to adjust his long legs and find a way to make it work. The sun dropped below the trees, and Jed drifted off to sleep.

Sometimes silence is louder than noise, and Jed woke with a start. He checked to see if Mattie had been awakened when he jerked, but her breathing was still even. He slid out from under her and eased himself up to the edge of the bucket until he could see the dark shapes of the cars below.

Shadows moved between the cars, and a faint scraping sound like the rustling of paper drifted up to him along with the smell of decay. Jed realized that he hadn't believed there were more hordes behind them now that the massive horde had been called to Charleston. He should have thought about smaller hordes that had been trapped in places like the wrecked cars a couple of miles back. He didn't know if they had gotten free from their 'crab trap' or if this was a different group. What he did realize was that they would have been done for if they hadn't gotten off the ground for the night. He stayed where he was until he couldn't hear the rustling below and then slowly lowered himself into a sitting position for the night.

It was during those long hours that Jed had a revelation. He had been gazing up at the stars and wondering if there were still people up there at the International Space Station. He hadn't seen anything in the sky for so long that it was hard to believe man had ever been able to break the bonds of gravity. There were people who had claimed to have seen planes and helicopters, but he had never seen them himself. He was willing to believe someone had survived and still had the technology to stay alive, but he had always wondered what kind of people they were.

The revelation came to him when he remembered the booming sounds that rolled like thunder from the direction of Charleston. Someone said they may have been sonic booms from a jet aircraft, and some people thought they were they sounds caused by earthquakes, but most of them, Jed included, thought they were explosions. In the darkness and solitude of the bucket, it came to him that someone was doing something about the infected. He didn't think it made sense to try to blow them up. That would take a lot of explosives because there was no way to get enough of them into one small area and blow them up. Jed didn't know what they were blowing up, but it had to have something to do with the infected.

The main thing was that there were people at work trying to take back the world. He wondered if they were the people responsible for the ringing in his ears and for the infected being called to Charleston. If so, maybe they were just trying to do something about the infected, but they were going about it the wrong way. Then came the revelation that maybe there were the people who were calling the infected to Charleston, but the explosions were done by someone else.

"Why should I assume the same people are doing everything?" he asked himself out loud. "Maybe I could get the people with the explosives to blow up the people who called the infected and got the colony killed."

16

Yorktown

Contagion Extinction Level - Day Three

From the moment Phillip and Denise walked up the ramp and through the big door of the Yorktown they felt like outsiders. It was an odd feeling. They weren't outside where it was dangerous. They didn't see crazed people trying to bite other people. They didn't feel the threat of death, but they also didn't feel like they were where they were welcome or supposed to be.

There was activity everywhere. Forklifts were carrying crates to and from elevators that descended to lower decks. The strange uniforms outnumbered people in street clothes, and almost everyone carried a weapon. The Corrigans didn't know what to do next.

Behind them the big steel doors were closed, and the wide open area where they stood took on the feel of an underground city with all of the hustle and bustle of traffic and pedestrians. Everyone except Phillip and Denise seemed like they had a job to do or at least knew where they were going.

"They let more of you in?"

It was so noisy that they didn't know the question was directed at them.

"I said, did someone just let you in from the processing tents?"

The voice came from a matronly woman who had a sour expression on her face. She had her hair pulled back in a tight bun, and she wore a business suit that had been in style around 1950. The appearance of the Corrigans was clearly a problem for her, and at the moment they didn't feel like being a bother to anyone.

"Well, they could've told me. I'll have to open everything back up and check you in. Names?"

Denise never wanted to wind up like the lady with the sour look on her face, and she had known plenty of women like her in the workplace. She was so used to being pushed around by people in higher positions that she couldn't resist pushing around everyone else.

"We're Denise and Phillip Corrigan. We came in with Dr. Williams," said Denise.

That seemed to stop the woman in her tracks. The difference between the sour expression and the sweet appearance she put on were as much in contrast as night and day.

"Oh, my. If you're friends of Dr. Williams then I'm sure she will want to know that you're satisfied with your accommodations. Please follow me."

The woman spun on her heels and literally scurried away, wanting to make up for the inconveniences endured by friends of Dr. Williams.

"Did you see that?" asked Denise.

"The way Dr. Williams dumped us back at the processing tents, I'm not so sure it was a good idea to pretend to be friends of hers."

"I didn't say we were friends of hers. I just said we came in with her."

Phillip regarded Denise with his 'don't give me that' look. She tried to act innocent, but they both knew she had at least led the woman to think they had friends in high places. They picked up their pace and caught up with the woman at an elevator.

The woman continued talking as if they had been by her side all along.

"You were very lucky to get in when you did. The order to draw down had just gone out."

"Draw down?"

Phillip didn't want to sound like they didn't know anything at all, but he felt like they had to know what was happening, or they just might get into trouble.

"Yes, you know, become inconspicuous...invisible if possible. Within an hour there won't be a trace left of us out there. If anyone else shows up, the Yorktown will be closed up like a big oyster. No lights, no noise, and no way in."

"How long will we stay like that?" asked Denise.

"That's above my pay grade. We have everything we need, but the best part is that we aren't out there. You're lucky you made it inside when you did."

Now that they had gotten the woman to talk, Denise took the risk of asking her another question.

"What happened to the people who were behind us in line?"

"Oh, they're okay, but they'll have it a little harder than you. They'll get to do a bit of hard work to earn their keep."

The elevator door opened, and they followed her inside. She could have been taking them to a jail cell or worse, but it didn't seem like it. Besides, if they refused to follow, it appeared that they wouldn't be asked to do anything. It was more likely that they would be forced to.

When the door opened they were in a narrow corridor that was in a completely renovated part of the ship. The cabin doors were more like the doors on hotel rooms than a World War II warship. They followed her down the corridor until she stopped in front of one and produced a magnetic keycard. She slid it into the lock and pushed the door open for them. She stepped politely out of the way and handed the key to Phillip.

"You should find everything you need in your room. Be sure to check the schedule for galley hours so you can get something to eat. I'll be sure to let Dr. Williams know which room you're in."

They wished they could have told the woman not to bother with her last promise, but that would have been worse than hoping she would forget. They surveyed the small room, and despite the feeling of uncertainty, they could have been in a worse place. There was a double bed and nightstand with one chair in the corner. The bathroom was just big enough for one person, but a toilet, sink, and a shower were more than they had the night before.

"How did we go from a beautiful hotel room with a view to this in such a short time?" asked Phillip.

It was obviously a rhetorical question because either of them could have asked it. Denise turned on the water at the sink as if she didn't really expect it to work.

She said, "Somehow I don't think this cabin or this part of the Yorktown is mentioned in the tourist brochures."

"What's that mean?"

"It's something secret. I mean, who knew that there would be a zombie outbreak, and the Yorktown would be used as a zombie shelter?"

Something about saying it out loud gave it confirmation. It was really happening, and no matter what you called it, people were behaving exactly the way they did in zombie movies. People had died right in front of them. They had gotten back up, and they had bitten the nearest person they could.

"Zombies?" asked Phillip.

Denise raised an eyebrow at Phillip and said, "If it looks like a duck and quacks like a duck."

"It's probably a duck," Phillip finished for her. "What do you think we should do?"

"Fit in the best we can. Let's start with that galley schedule."

The schedule was posted on the back of the cabin door, and they saw there was a meal service in progress. Directions to the galley were on a crude map below the schedule. Aside from that there wasn't much information, and they both were in need of food, so they decided to give it a try.

They followed the directions until they came to a large dining room with a serving line along one wall. It had the appearance of a real ship's galley, complete with benches and tables that were bolted to the floor. They followed the lead of a few others who looked as lost as they felt, and they got in line for their food. They pulled trays from a large stack and Phillip handed Denise a set of silverware rolled up in a napkin.

"Cabin number."

The uniformed man behind the counter didn't even look up from his clipboard.

Denise felt like she was going to panic, but Phillip answered evenly.

"F-22."

The man made a note without changing his bored expression.

"When did you get the cabin number?"

Phillip flipped the keycard up between two fingers, and she saw the big cabin number on it.

"You could've saved me from a heart attack back there."

"I didn't know they were going to ask for it. It's just lucky that I saw the number when 'Ms. Personality' gave it to me."

They were handed plates of food, and they looked around for a place to sit, hoping they would find a spot relatively free of other people. They settled for a table with a few people who were sitting at the other end. They also appeared to be keeping to themselves, content to eat in silence.

The Corrigans unrolled their forks and eyed the food. There was no shortage of starches on the plate, and there was some kind of meat patty covered in lumpy gravy. Despite the appearance of the food, it satisfied their hunger.

"Right about now is when the waiter attacks the customers," said Denise.

"What waiter?" asked Phillip.

They both laughed despite their circumstances which drew stares from the people at the end of the table. They weren't quite angry, but the message was clear.

It was plain to see that there wasn't anything they could learn by hanging around the galley, so they decided to eat their meals and get back to the cabin as soon as possible. The only thing they managed to pick up were some hushed whispers behind them between a couple of men in uniform.

It seemed that the matronly lady was right about draw down. They heard one of the men say it was going to be a boring month, and he was glad he had plenty of books to read. The other one grumbled that he didn't know why they had to close the place up for a month. He quit grumbling when the first man asked him if he would like a transfer to the State Ports. He could shoot the infected if he was bored, or he could shoot the workers that wouldn't listen.

They realized someone else at their table was looking at them, so they stopped talking. Phillip didn't want people to think they were hanging around too long, so he ate quickly and hinted to Denise to do the same.

Back in their cabin, they had a moment of panic because they realized everyone else had some sort of role to play, and their presence was somewhat of an accident. They didn't feel like they were supposed to be there, and it wouldn't be long before someone found out.

They had a sleepless night despite the comfortable bed. It was just way too quiet, and it had a feel to it like someone would be kicking in their cabin door at any moment. It wasn't kicked in, but the knock arrived early.

Phillip checked his watch and saw it was only six o'clock, so he knew it wasn't a breakfast reminder. He opened the door and found a well groomed man in his thirties with a big smile on his face. Something about him almost screamed politics. Phillip felt like the man was looking for campaign contributions.

"Ted Atwater, at your service."

The man held out his hand in such a cheerful manner that Phillip had to shake it.

"And you are Phillip Corrigan?"

The man advanced toward Phillip, still gripping his hand, so Phillip had to back up into the room.

"Mr. Corrigan, I understand that you came here to the Yorktown with our own Dr. Williams. I wanted to personally welcome you and assure you that your stay will be comfortable. I only ask that you limit your movements throughout the ship to the galley and your room for the first month. We'll make you aware when it's time for you to move more freely."

Denise stepped up behind Phillip and leaned around him to speak before Phillip had the chance. She knew her husband well enough to know that he wasn't buying the Mr. Nice Guy routine from this man, whoever he was.

"Mr. Atwater, that's very nice of you, and it's certainly not a problem. We appreciate the hospitality. If there's anything we can do to repay you, please let us know. Oh, and if it's not a big problem, could we possibly have some books and maybe a deck of cards?"

A month was a long time to be stuck inside with nowhere to go but the galley. Denise didn't know what they had done to deserve a room inside this operation, but the other cabins had to be occupied by people who at least had something to do.

"Of course, Mrs. Corrigan. That wouldn't be a problem at all."

Just as quickly as he had taken Phillip's hand he switched to hers.

"I'll have someone drop them by within the hour. Just let me know if you need anything else."

Mr. Atwater was already out the door before Denise could stop him, so she had to catch up with him in the corridor.

"How will I do that Mr. Atwater? How will I contact you?"

She could tell he was used to being put on the spot because he recovered nicely.

"That won't be necessary, Mrs. Corrigan. It's my job to ensure your needs are met, so I'll be checking in with you daily."

******

On the way back to the stateroom occupied by Marshall Sayer, Ted marveled at how different the Yorktown had become under his supervision. In one hour the place had gone from being a beehive of activity to being as quiet as a tomb.

The fences outside were gone, as were the guard posts that separated the red, orange, and green zones. All personnel had been brought inside, and the ship had been sealed. The only unfortunate situation had been the families. Some had arrived with injured family members, mostly with bites. The contagion had a one hundred percent mortality rate, so they couldn't afford to bring them inside. Ted had his usual flash of brilliance and gave orders for those families to be taken to the World War II destroyer that was docked at the stern of the aircraft carrier. He hastily had his medical staff set up a hospital ward, and after a second flash of brilliance he settled the issue of staffing the hospital.

As a condition of admittance, the families would have to care for the wounded. Atwater selected a few of the husbands, wives, and parents who had an authoritative bearing and put them in charge. He had them dressed in white hospital coats and even hung stethoscopes around their necks. In no time they were acting like they had played doctors and nurses on TV. It also became so crowded that arrivals accepted the newly appointed hospital staff without question. Atwater gave the order for them to begin disposing of new bite victims at the processing tents.

At first they were discreet about it. Adults not accompanied by family members were easily escorted away because there was no one to protest or question what was going to happen with them. Once they were quarantined, it was easy to give them a sedative strong enough to put them to sleep. They were taken away and injected with a combination of adenosine and lidocaine. None of them felt pain, but none of them woke up.

Their mistake became obvious within a half hour when the first to be euthanized sat up under their sheets and put their feet on the floor of the makeshift morgue. Guards carrying another body into the tent were met by a dozen of the infected that hadn't suffered bodily damage, and they were capable of overwhelming a few armed men.

Chaos spilled over into the processing area as the guards tried to regroup, and eventually someone opened fire. It probably saved lives. Once it was discovered that head trauma was the only way to prevent the dead from reanimating, the people placed in quarantine were sedated and then executed by a sharp knife pushed into the soft spot on the back of the head. No one wanted the job, but then again, no one wanted to have it done to them.

Families were the real problem. Separating them was guaranteed to cause a disturbance, and at first they were immediately sent to the hospital on the destroyer, but after the first wave of arrivals, more families arrived together than before. The decision was made to dispose of entire families if the bite victims were hard to separate from their relatives. The decision wasn't well received by the people working in the processing tents, and there were signs that discipline was about to dissolve.

Atwater was able to rationalize the choice. There was no way they could provide for everyone who came to their gates. They had supplies, but not enough for the kind of crowd that was coming their way. They were never intended to be a shelter for the general public. He knew that the operation would be forced to take in some refugees, but they didn't have an open door policy. The problem was that he could rationalize the choice all he wanted, and it wasn't going to change what was happening at the gates. His job was to keep problems from reaching Marshall Sayer, so he decided it was time to begin phase two even if it was ahead of schedule.

The tower of the Yorktown gave Atwater a good view of the surrounding terrain. The Green Zone was a stark contrast to the Red Zone. In one, guards smoked cigarettes. In the other, sharpshooters were trying hard to keep the horde out of the Orange Zone. Every shot dropped another, but there was an endless supply. They were stumbling down the main road from the entrance to Patriots Point, but they were emerging from the trees and even from the marshes. The sun was on its way down, and the long shadows across the infected made it appear to be more of them than there were, but Atwater couldn't afford to be wrong about when to start phase two. He gave the order and sat back to watch.

Everything came to a stop down at the processing tents, and the sharpshooters withdrew from the fence along the border to the Orange Zone. The last he saw of them was as they disappeared into the passenger seats of the personnel carriers. The guards at the tents reversed the crowds of people that had gotten into the long lines. There were bound to be some complaints, but those people who had seen what was happening in the Red Zone were glad to get back into the vehicles.

The vehicles that hadn't even unloaded their refugees turned right where they were and became the front of the convoy. Their drivers had a good view of what was approaching and were ready to go before they were ordered to move. If they did, they ran the risk of getting swamped by the growing horde. The success of a convoy of small vehicles would lie in their ability to stay together, but for added insurance, Atwater ordered a Stryker to escort the smaller personnel carriers. The oversized tires on the Strykers would make a path on the road by crushing the infected. It would make for a bumpy ride in the personnel carriers, but they weren't likely to be stopped.

It was amazing to see how quickly the tents were abandoned. Before the convoy was completely in motion the doctors and nurses were already at the ramp of the Yorktown inside the Green Zone. Before the last vehicle in the convoy accelerated to stay on the tail of the personnel carrier ahead of it, the ramp was withdrawn, and the Yorktown was sealed.

As the taillights of the long convoy disappeared beyond the entrance to Patriots Point, Ted Atwater leaned as far as he could from the window of the tower. He viewed everything laid out in front of him as if it was his domain. The three zones that would very shortly become one and the abandoned processing tents that stood just inside the open gates. There was no need to close them, and he had no intention of locking himself inside until he got to see what the horde would do. It was spreading out below, but it would converge on the gates. With nothing to stop them, they would march forward until they reached the ships.

Most of them would probably walk into the water of the Cooper River, but enough of them would discover that the destroyer was also occupied. No one would warn them to pull their ramp in, and they wouldn't know to do so until at least a few of the infected made it on board. Then again, the patients on the destroyer would start dying, and when they did, the living would be trying to get off the ship. Atwater hoped to see how that worked out.

The flaps of the tents swayed in the breeze and got the attention of the infected that swarmed into the Orange Zone. They went inside the tents as if they would find someone who had been left behind, and Atwater watched the tents sag as the infected walked into the cloth walls. They also must have walked into the poles because the roofs collapsed quickly. The infected outside were momentarily drawn to the lumps that struggled to stand under the heavy tents. They couldn't tell if there were living people under the material, and they were at least momentarily delayed from entering the Green Zone.

The horde pushed forward, and a steady stream formed on the road that crossed the wide pier along the starboard side of the carrier. Atwater was delighted to see how many walked right to the edge and dropped over. The splashes sounded far away, but they were straight below his window. Some had their heads raised as if they could see him, and it was possible that they could. That was fine with him as long as they kept coming.

That reminded him. Not all of them were coming straight toward the carrier because no one had told the people in the destroyer hospital to stay quiet. Sound carried at night, and as the darkness fell on Patriots Point the lights and sounds coming from the Navy destroyer were like an open invitation to the infected.

The sun set on the Charleston side of the Yorktown, and the shadow of the great ship crossed over the pier. There were less splashes from below, and Atwater knew why. There were hundreds of infected now, and they were following the dead up front. They saw the lights and heard the shouts from people inside as they dealt with a bite victim. The conscripted medical staff was disorganized, and more than one had quit, but they would find it wasn't a job they could just walk away from.

A plump woman whose husband had been bitten had just gotten her first bite from a young man who had been fine earlier. As a matter of fact, he was wearing scrubs and helping as a nurse. Apparently, he had been bitten but kept the information to himself. The woman's husband had slipped into unconsciousness, and she had seen enough to know what came next. When she was bitten, she had taken the stethoscope from her neck and thrown it at the man who had assumed the role of chief medical officer. She forced her way past him despite his insistence that she couldn't quit and found her way topside to the aft ramp to the pier. That was where she was bitten the second time... and third.

They boarded the destroyer as if they were a solid line of tourists, and as they filled the open deck at the stern, they were drawn to the lights and sounds inside. When the plump woman had stormed out through the steel door she would have bought the people inside a few more minutes if she had at least swung it shut, but it was an inviting sight to the infected dead.

The doors on ships that travel in high seas have thresholds that sit higher than the deck, and even the living tend to trip and fall head first through doors until they get used to lifting their feet high enough. It wasn't strange to see the infected do the same, but their falls were more spectacular since they didn't reflexively throw their hands out in front of themselves to break their fall. Before the first one could recover from the fall, a second one fell through and landed on top of the first. The newly appointed doctors and nurses rushed to help them to their feet and were greeted with snapping teeth that found plenty of targets. The screams drew more of the infected through the open door, and even though they were falling down at an impressive rate, there was no way to get away from them.

A few quick thinkers went up the ladders at the back of the large compartment and managed to open the doors that led to higher decks. It was amazing that they had felt so safe in the Green Zone earlier, and now it was as bad inside the destroyer as it was in the Red Zone. The people who went up the ladders slammed the heavy steel doors into place and spun the locking mechanisms. They were safe for the moment. All they had to do was make sure there were no other entrances to their higher decks. They would worry about food and water later.

Atwater could hear the screams and knew it was just a matter of time. There were no supplies on the destroyer, and he had dealt with the bite victims without arousing any suspicions or fears from the people safely enclosed within the steel walls and doors of the aircraft carrier. What they didn't know wasn't going to be a problem for him. He reached across to a panel of circuit breakers and without hesitation flipped one to the off position, plunging the destroyer in total darkness. He saw the change outside in his peripheral vision and knew that the screams would be louder for the next few minutes.

He shut off the lights behind him so the infected wouldn't be drawn to him and leaned out the window in the direction of the destroyer. The dark silhouette of the ship was visible but the moment he had turned off the power to the lights that had blazed brightly, it had become a mass of shadows. It was as if the ship was being eaten by a dark cloud, and he could no longer make out details. He was right about the screams, though.

Below him the shadow that was the new Red Zone moved from side to side as it turned toward the screams. It would move like that as long as there were screams that called to it. Atwater decided that he had seen enough. He slid the glass window shut and blocked out the noise. He had also become aware of the smell. Before the gates were abandoned to the throngs of infected that came through, there was the ever-present smell of the marshes. The locals called it 'pluff mud', and it had a distinctive odor. Now it was masked by the smell of decay and human excrement. He didn't think he would ever get used to the smell of the mud, but he knew he would never get used to that other smell.

He descended from the tower into the enclosed warship, and the difference could only be known to someone who had been outside watching what the world had become. A messenger approached and told him that Marshall Sayer had been trying to find him, and that he should meet with him in the labs. He wanted to be sure that the next phase of their operation inside the Yorktown was completed by the time their operatives were finished at the State Ports Authority.

It was only a matter of good timing that made the two men run into each other on the way to the labs. Sayer never really had an expression on his face that could be described as happy, but there were times when it came close to a look of satisfaction. This was one of those times, and it was because Sayer had shown more interest in what was happening outside than Atwater had known. While he had watched from the lofty protection of the tower, Sayer had gone to the stern observation deck in the fantail and watched from a much closer vantage point. He was so close that he was practically able to understand what people were saying onboard the destroyer. The stern of the carrier protruded out over the dock that ran along the side of the destroyer, and Sayer could even see what was happening when the lights were turned off. He was glad that Atwater had found a way to keep the contagion off of his ship.

Sayer had started calling the Yorktown his ship almost as soon as he arrived. When he greeted the Mayor of Mt. Pleasant, he had said proudly, "Welcome to my ship." The Mayor had bristled visibly and pointed out that the Patriots Point Maritime Museum didn't belong to the federal government. Sayer had simply nodded and said under his breath, "We'll see."

"You outdid yourself, Ted. Nice job with containment. What's the good word from the State Ports?"

Compliments were so rare that Atwater was momentarily caught at a loss for words.

"They made it to the compound and got sufficient protection in place before it got bad. The personnel carriers can transport more people, but the Strykers made the difference."

Atwater had actually stolen the idea of using Strykers from the people who had planned the exfiltration of the President from Washington DC. His intelligence reports made him aware of the number of contingency plans that could be met with Strykers as opposed to most armored carriers, and the oversized tires made them excellent for off road use, but the best part was how easily they rolled over the crowds of infected.

They passed the decks where the civilians had all been given rooms without being stopped by someone who would want a bath drawn for them. Sayer didn't feel like dealing with any of the local dignitaries and was glad to escape their attention.

"No one important saw what happened outside, did they?"

That was a question Ted was hoping wouldn't come up, and he almost said no one had noticed, but it would be easy to get caught in that lie if Sayer asked enough people.

"The last couple to come aboard may have seen the beginning of the draw down, but they didn't say much. They came in with Dr. Williams."

Sayer lost his satisfied expression at the mention of her name.

"Why did she have to bring in civilians? Did we have space for them?"

"Apparently she dumped a local guy who we had in place at the Mt. Pleasant Police Department. He had a big mouth and he made her mad enough to give this couple his ticket to safety?"

"What did she do with the local guy?"

Atwater knew that Sayer didn't really care what Dr. Williams had done to the big mouth. He was just curious about how ruthless she could be. It was a talent that was in short supply, and Sayer wanted to be sure there was enough of that talent on his staff. He didn't even notice that Atwater didn't answer his question.

They arrived at the level where the lab was hidden beyond a strong sea door, and the area outside the lab had been purposely neglected to keep outsiders from suspecting there was something important on that level.

"Tell someone that they did a good job with the renovation of my ship, Atwater, but tell them they took the realism just a little too far." He pushed aside a sticky mass of milky spider webs that crisscrossed the door to the labs. "Tell them to clean this stuff up and stop pretending it's Halloween."

17

Infiltration

Present Day

There was more activity around the boats when several more BATT-T armored personnel carriers rolled into the marina. The Chief had wondered if the people who had captured his friends had gone to the site of the helicopter crash or if they had been in the area. Apparently the patrol had been one of several.

One of the drivers was a big guy, and the Chief absently wondered if he was an ex-SEAL or a pro football player. The big guy shouted some orders and then disappeared into the marina. It was obvious that most of the men were 'grunts' while some were in charge. By the way the big guy acted, the Chief assumed he wasn't a grunt, but as soon as the man disappeared, he heard the others complain.

"Who is that guy, Lieutenant? Is he in charge now?"

"He just transferred in from the ship, and no, he's not in charge."

"Why's he giving orders then?"

"Just shut up and do your job. Let me worry about him."

"This could be my lucky day," the Chief mumbled half out loud. Discipline was essential to any unit, but one bad attitude could cost lives. The Chief knew he could use that to his advantage. Plus, the guy was a bully, so the other grunts would probably avoid him.

He accidentally walked up on the man where he was sitting on the rail of a small sailboat that was half submerged right where its owner had left it years ago. He had expected to find the man wanted a little privacy to take care of a matter of a personal nature, but instead he was enjoying a home rolled cigarette. Judging by the length of time he held the smoke after he inhaled, it wasn't regular tobacco. The man was so relaxed he didn't even flinch.

The Chief couldn't believe the physical similarities between himself and the other guy. He had a dark baseball cap pulled down over his head, and he liked to wear it with the bill pulled even lower. He had to look upward to be able to see straight ahead.

"Mind if I join you?"

The Chief saw the man's forearm as he held out the joint, and the tattoo was all he needed to see to know he was in for a fight. The guy had been trained by the same people who had trained the Chief, and the SEAL Trident was proof. Not just anyone was allowed to wear that tattoo. He wasn't happy to fight a brother, but this one was on the wrong side.

He reached for the joint, but instead of accepting it from the man, he reached past it and grabbed his wrist. Maybe it was the surprise, and maybe it was the pot, but the former SEAL did the opposite of his training. He pulled back on his arm.

Every bit of training the Chief had ever gotten was still a part of him. He had never let himself become soft, complacent, or undisciplined. If someone grabbed him by the wrist, he moved toward them. Pulling back would only bring his opponent closer to him, while moving inward put him on the attack.

The man pulled hard, expecting resistance, especially because a big man was holding onto him. The Chief's sucker punch arrived before he could move his head. There was no doubt about the sound and the point of contact. It would be a long time before he woke up.

The Chief studied his left fist and wondered what would have happened if he hadn't used his offhand.

Despite the fact that the man was on the wrong side, the Chief decided to leave him a fighting chance at survival. There was no shortage of rope in a marina, and the synthetic stuff was going to take years to deteriorate. He found enough to tie the unconscious man up inside the cabin of a small boat and left him a fish cleaning knife that was also as common as fish hooks in a marina. His clothes weren't something he would need anymore, but the Chief's sense of fair play made him leave his own clothes for the man.

He took a moment to go through the pockets of the clothes he stole, and he took another moment to admire the fit. It had been the man's bad luck that he was the Chief's size…and that he smoked pot. There was some kind of ID in the pocket of the shirt, and he sounded out the name so he would be ready to use it. David Clemenza. He looked like a David but not a Dave. More likely than not he went by his last name like most military people.

"Well, Clemenza, we could've been friends, but you're with the bad guys."

From what the Chief had seen, the uniformed men from the Yorktown were individually trained but not as a unit. They were loosely knit at best, and if he could mix in with the right group, they might not realize he was a replacement. Normally his big size would have been a problem, but he thought he might just be able to pull it off. He sniffed at his shirt and realized for once it was a good thing that it smelled bad, and the added aroma of pot was part of the disguise.

The Chief was careful not to walk straight up with his shoulders back. Not many people would do that if they were high. He also pulled the bill of the baseball cap down the same way Clemenza had been wearing it. He got back to the activity around the boats just as everyone was loading up, and the boats seemed to be bobbing in black ink where the moon reflected from the water. He drifted toward the boats that were carrying prisoners, but there were far more than he expected. He could tell who some of them were, and he was glad to see they were okay even though they were bagged and had been tossed around. He just had to spot his moment, and it wasn't going to be easy. The Chief almost always had a plan, but this time his only plan was to mix in.

Someone barked, "Clemenza."

It was the voice of authority. He had heard it many times during his active duty, and he had used that tone to terrify new guys. He also recognized the voice was young and maybe overcompensating a bit.

A sideways glance at the source of the voice confirmed his thinking. Young officers always tried to sound tough with the big guys.

"Sir?"

He put just the slightest amount of edge on his response, so the officer would hear one thing but understand another. The real answer was, "Don't mess with me too much, or I'll show you up."

"Tucker needs someone to ride shotgun."

The Chief was stuck for a moment because he didn't have a clue who Tucker might be. He put an expression on his face that conveyed his best look that asked, "Do I have to ride with Tucker?"

It worked better than he could have hoped because Tucker moaned, "Aw, man. Do I have to ride with Clemenza? He's not even from America. He's from some place called Utica."

The Chief answered, "Utica blood is red, white, and blue, Tucker. You want everyone to see what color yours is?"

That earned Tucker a few laughs and cat calls, but it told the Chief which boat to get into. It also meant he was riding with only one other person. The Chief took note of what the other boat crews were doing. The rest of them all had at least three uniformed people in them, except the officer's and his, so there was less chance of someone discovering that he wasn't Clemenza. The problem was that his friends were spread out. From what he could tell, they were in three different boats. The best he could hope for was to stay near them.

Tucker had a bow rider idling in a slip, and the prisoners had already been loaded. He didn't want to get too close to Tucker or he would have to explain why Tucker fell overboard on the way to wherever they were going. He climbed in back with the prisoners and shoved one off the bench seat that he was sure was Kathy.

"Hey, what'd ya do that for?" she screamed through the burlap bag on her head.

"This seat's taken, Lady. You got a problem with that?"

He didn't want to say too much, but he had to say enough for her to wonder if she had heard what she thought she did. He saw the hesitation.

"Yeah, you heard me right, Lady, and you know I'm not somebody you want to mess with."

"I know your type, and you're all alike. You can dish it out, but you can't take it. Untie me and take this bag off my head, and I'll make short work out of you."

The Chief couldn't help himself, and he let out the laugh she would recognize anywhere. He had to be careful because a lot of people were turned toward his boat, but he was sure he saw four other hostages tilt their heads as if they were listening closely.

All six boats pulled away from the slips and headed toward the harbor. They didn't form up or get in line behind each other. That was another sign that they lacked discipline. The only reason they could have survived for so long was their numbers, and they had probably seen their share of losses over the years.

He thought they were going to the Yorktown, but instead of circling around to the other side of Castle Pinckney, they made the closer turn into the channel that crossed between the old island fort and the city of Charleston. They were much closer to the city than was advisable because the massive horde trying to cross the Ravenel Bridge was spilling over into the river like a lava flow. They couldn't all get onto the bridge at the same time because there were far too many.

The Chief could only guess at the numbers, but all lanes on the bridge were packed, and hundreds or thousands were still being forced to fall into the river at the foot of the bridge. Most of the infected got caught in the current and were dragged under, but there were so many that some stayed on the surface and bobbed like driftwood. It was a bad move, but the lead boat planned to go right through them.

The rest of the boats hung back a bit and started to drift to the starboard side of the lead boat. The Chief could see that the young lieutenant was in the lead boat, and he was standing up straight on his seat like a general riding into battle. The best guess was that the young man had recently been promoted, and he didn't have much experience. In the world since the infected dead arrived, experience usually meant you had the sense to avoid dying.

The boats were almost at full throttle because they were approaching the bridge, and for once he was glad his five friends couldn't see what was coming. The worst part was that he hadn't been able to tell for sure if any of them were in the boat with the officer. There were four hostages riding behind the driver and the foolish officer, and they were about to have a terrifying experience. Bound, blind, unable to fight back or swim, and facing the possibility of an infected landing in the boat with them. If the Chief could do it, he would shoot them before it happened.

One of the boat drivers pointed toward the marshes that sat in the curve formed by the retaining wall at the base of the bridge. There were at least thirty or forty of the infected standing knee deep in the water. The officer had ignored his driver when he had pointed at the same place. The other boats all veered to the starboard to avoid what was about to happen because they all realized what the driver with the officer had been trying to say. The channel marker that warned of shallow water was gone, and their boat was racing into a spot that wasn't more than two feet deep.

Things happen in slow motion in memories. That's the way the Chief would remember what he saw. The boat hit the shallow mud bank at the leading edge of the marshes, and all six passengers from the boat were launched through the air toward the infected dead that had been standing shin deep in the mud, unable to leave the spot where they had fallen in.

The officer flew the farthest, and because of the way he had been standing as tall as he could and holding the top of the windshield with both hands, he was practically aerodynamic. He was saved the worst fate by virtue of the fact that he flew far enough to make solid impact with the retaining wall behind the infected, and he was most likely unconscious when he hit the ground. He bounced backward as much as a human body could and landed on top of the trapped group of infected.

The other people in the boat were luckier because none of them flew out of the boat without hitting something else first. Two of the hostages hit the backs of the front seats. The driver and the remaining hostages all hit the windshield. The driver got there first and took out most of it, but he left enough for the others. They probably all died from broken necks. The sick feeling in the pit of the Chief's stomach was not knowing who they were. One of them looked too much like Hampton.

The Chief turned toward each of the other boats to see if he could tell for sure where his friends were, but they were moving too fast and bouncing too much over the choppy water. They were approaching the bridge, and somehow the infected were managing to get over the tall side barriers to make the long fall into the Cooper River.

The Chief watched as an infected did a perfect head first landing into the boat farthest away from him. With four more hostages and three crewmen in each boat, he could only hope the slim odds were good enough. When the infected dead hit the boat, the impact drove the boat deeper into the water just as they hit a small wave. The driver overcompensated, turned the wheel too far, and flipped the boat.

There were still four boats left with a total of sixteen hooded passengers, so the Chief was determined to will the odds to be in their favor if he had to. He was the kind of guy who leaned left or right when watching a football game and someone was kicking a field goal, so he felt like they would all be in the remaining boats if he just believed it.

Even though he felt like he had witnessed the tragedies in slow motion, everything happened so fast that they were past the Yorktown and past the bridge before he could think again about where they were going. Up ahead on the starboard side he could see the tall cranes at the State Ports Authority. Over the last six years he had flown over the area and passed it on the river, but he could never tell if there was any activity. Of course there had been at the beginning because there was activity everywhere, but the cargo containers were stacked so high and so close together that he couldn't see past them from the water. When he had flown over them, all he saw was long rows of tents but never anyone out in the open. He had flown over once at night, and he thought he had seen a light inside a tent, but when he went back for a second look, the light was gone.

The lead boat was heading straight for a small boat ramp at the State Ports, and the driver of the Chief's boat fell in line behind the others. The Chief knew this would be the true test of his ability to rescue his friends, because he needed to buy some time. Whatever these people had planned for their hostages, it most likely included interrogation. That meant separating them, so he had to keep track of where they were and form a rescue plan based on changing information. He considered that to be a moving target.

Something was happening at the first boat, and the Chief couldn't tell if it was good or bad. Someone was sorting the prisoners. Two of them were pulled off to the side and two were led away by a guard. The Chief realized he had been thinking of them as hostages which implied they had trading value, although he didn't know what they would be traded for.

Something about the way one of the sorted prisoners was standing seemed familiar. Military demeanor never leaves some people because it becomes a part of them, and that prisoner was standing like a soldier who had spent some time at sea. It had to be Cassandra, and the other one was a slender man who he had watched develop from couch potato to lean and quick. Ed could be lethal if he had to be, and at the moment the Chief felt like he was looking at a coiled spring ready to release its energy.

The other boats were empty by the time they tied up, and the sorting only lasted a short while before the man in charge separated Hampton, Colleen, and Kathy from the rest of the hostages. They were all shoved off to one side while the others were rushed away beyond the containers. Tucker came up next to him.

"What do you suppose that's all about?"

In an unfriendly voice the Chief answered, "I don't care. If we mind our own business maybe we're done for the day."

"You two."

The man doing the sorting clearly pointed at Tucker and the Chief.

"Get a BATT-T and take these prisoners to the ship. The boss wants to talk with them."

The Chief grumbled at Tucker like it was his fault they were chosen, but he saw his chance laid out in front of him like the yellow brick road. He had undoubtedly been picked because of his size, and Tucker just happened to be standing next to him.

Tucker said something about sending one BATT-T without an armed escort, and the Chief had to stop him from making the suggestion to the man in charge. He caught Tucker by his collar and pulled him close to his face.

"How well do you know me, Tucker?"

Tucker looked up into the Chief's face with wide eyes and said, "I don't. I don't know you at all except for what I've heard."

He sounded like he was ready to cry. The Chief had a way of doing that to people when he needed, but apparently the man he was impersonating was somewhat of a legendary threat to the health of anyone he didn't like, so the Chief didn't have to do anything except play the part.

"Do you know what I did before CEL Day?"

The Chief was using the opportunity to get Tucker in line and to get something useful about his new identity if he had to use it later.

"I heard that after you got out of the service you delivered pizza in Utica."

Tucker's voice was shaking, but the Chief had gotten something at least, so he let Tucker go and told him he was going to get the BATT-T. The man in charge asked if everything was okay as he went by, and he gave him a quick nod.

"Just taking care of some personal differences."

The Chief knew exactly which BATT-T he was trying to find. There were two models. He wanted the one that had the wall separating the driver and passenger seats from the back of the vehicle. That way he could ride in back under the pretense of keeping a closer watch on the prisoners. They were lined up at the gates to the State Ports, and it didn't take long to find the right one. The keys were in the ignition, and he guessed there weren't many car thieves around a place like this.

While he selected the right vehicle, the Chief didn't miss out on his opportunity to study his surroundings. He thought back to the times when he had passed the area on the water and in the air and could see the measures they had taken to prevent outsiders from knowing what went on inside the cargo container compound. There were thousands of containers, and only a fraction of them were needed to create a barrier around the entire compound. It was a good plan that had to have been made before the infection began, so the Chief had to wonder who would've had that kind of power. He didn't doubt the possibility that this was another government operation separate from the one that Ed had fallen into through his inheritance.

Some of the containers stood open, and he saw that some were empty while some were in the process of being unloaded. Since there were tens of thousands to begin with, he imagined that they must've had enough packed with supplies to last for years. Maybe even more than his people had in the shelters.

Empty containers had also been converted to buildings. The containers that were stacked on top had windows cut in the sides, so the perimeter was well protected. If he and his friends had ever tried to infiltrate the ports from the water, they would have been spotted well in advance. He thought back to those times when the Mud Island Family had talked about sending someone in to see what, if anything, was going on here, and he could tell it would have been a one way mission. The only way into this place was the way he had gotten in, and that was disguised as one of them.

Everything was going his way so far, so the Chief didn't press his luck by taking too long. Even though he had gathered some useful intelligence, he couldn't wait to get his friends into the personnel carrier and get on the road. He started the engine and pulled the vehicle out of line. It didn't take more than a minute to drive back, and as he got out of the driver seat, he tossed the keys high in the air in Tucker's direction.

Tucker was caught off guard and dropped his M4 rifle. He was so excited about the opportunity to drive that he didn't really care. The Chief felt sorry for Tucker. He wasn't meant for the way the world had become, and the Chief could see a bad day in the man's future. It was going to be far too easy to overcome him on the road.

"You drive, Tucker. I'll ride in back with the prisoners."

"Why can't you ride shotgun, man? What if I come up on a crowd of those things?"

"You need me to hold your hand too?"

The menace in the Chief's tone of voice was enough to keep Tucker from asking twice. He went around the vehicle and climbed into the front. The Chief took advantage of the opportunity and leaned closer to the prisoners as he opened the rear door.

"Five more minutes, and we're home free. Everyone just climb in and leave it to me. No heroics."

"I knew it," said Kathy.

The Chief gave her upper arm a little squeeze as he guided her into the BATT-T. He climbed in behind her and pulled the door closed. He slapped the wall between the front seats and the back two times, and the truck lurched forward. The Chief kept his balance and immediately pulled the bag off Kathy's head.

Kathy blinked against the light, but she was almost breathless when she saw it really was the Chief. It had seemed too good to be true with the bag over her head even as he had spoken to them behind the open doors, but now that she could see him, she was overjoyed beyond words.

"How? I mean, you were unconscious the last time I saw you, how'd you get here?"

"Long story for another time. Let's get everyone untied."

******

Ed

There isn't much that makes someone feel more helpless that taking away their ability to see, and from the moment the bags were pulled over our heads to the moment they were removed by the Chief, it had been terrifying. The bumpy ride in the back of some kind of truck had us all feeling sick to our stomachs and sore with bruises, but it was nothing compared to the boats. We knew they were boats, of course, but from what we could hear, the luck of the draw for some hostages was that they were in the wrong boat.

When I heard the Chief laugh, I finally began to hope for the best, but I don't think I started feeling physically better until I could see again. It was either the light, even in the back of a truck, or it was the Chief's smiling face. He was all business, but he couldn't keep the smile off his face.

I felt like I wanted to hug him, but I left that to the ladies and settled for a knuckle bump. Still, it was the best knuckle bump I ever had.

"I can't wait to hear the rest of your plan, Chief. So far it's as good as it gets."

"Thanks, Ed, but you've seen all my cards. If you have any suggestions, I'd be happy to hear them."

"Well, to start with, you have a gun. We have that guy up front to get by, but I think we have him outnumbered. What more does the plan need?"

The smile faded from the Chief's face, and his eyes became unfocused, like he could see something in the distance. Cassandra, Hampton, and Colleen were the picture of restraint. They had all been freed and their hoods removed, but the expression on the Chief's face made everyone postpone the celebration. The anticipation hung in the air like smoke, but we were five people who knew the Chief well enough to know when not to interrupt his thoughts.

"You're right," said the Chief. "This has all been too easy. I was okay with running into an ex-SEAL who was my size. That was good luck, and I believe in luck. But getting you guys all together in a safe vehicle and given the chance to escape, that's too much. Someone wanted us together in here."

The Chief tried the lock on the back door. He wasn't really expecting it to unlock, but he had to know for sure. It didn't budge, and it wasn't the kind of door he could expect to kick open. The entire vehicle was armored, and the door looked like it belonged on a bank vault. In the center was a rearview window with a sliding panel that was in the closed position. To the left and right sides of the door were two more windows with the same sliding panels that were also closed. He slid the one on the door to the open position.

"I just walked right into a trap."

Behind them were two more personnel carriers that were matching their speed. Their headlights shone brightly through the tiny window. He had to admit, someone had been a quick thinker. If they had tried to take him as soon as the boats were unloaded, there's no telling how many people would have died. They let him think he was escaping and caught him without firing a shot. He still had his M4 and a sidearm, but they weren't going to just open the door and let him shoot them.

"Ever feel like a fly stuck in a spider web?" asked the Chief as he unloaded his weapons and piled them up by the door.

With nothing else that could be done, we all just sat back on our seats and waited for the inevitable...whatever that was.

******

* * *

By late morning Jed and Mattie caught up with the back of the horde a few miles from Charleston. Mattie was too young to understand what was happening, but Jed knew. When the horde got so big that it couldn't stop moving once it got started, it was like some kind of perpetual motion machine. When an infected stumbled and fell, it wasn't like the ones behind it were going to lend a hand to help it keep from being trampled. They got stepped on, they were crushed, and they tripped more of them as if they were getting even at the ones that tripped them. At first they spotted a few infected crawling on their bellies. They dragged their legs behind them, and they weren't making much progress, but they all crawled in the same direction.

Jed steered Mattie away from them and wondered what had produced this phenomenon. It wasn't readily apparent what had happened, and he mentally worried about it the way a dog worked on a bone. He knew there had to be an explanation, especially since there were more and more 'crawlers' as they got closer to Charleston. At first there were a few, then dozens, then hundreds. They were unable to walk because they were too damaged, but they fought to move forward with their sick will to bite another victim or to answer the summons of whatever was calling to them.

At first he thought the horde was dying…really dying. He actually began to hope that whatever it was that had reanimated the dead had run its course. After more than six years of misery the apocalypse was over. The thought made his heart pound as he believed he was witnessing the real death of the infected. Something was killing them. He even went so far as to say it out loud once, and as he saw more and more of them crawling instead of walking, he became convinced. His elation almost walked them right into more of them than they could avoid, even though they were crawling. Jed had to lift Mattie from the asphalt and focus his attention on where to put his feet. Stepping away from one was the same as stepping toward another.

His disappointment came when he stood near the junction with I-526. There were so many infected crawling on the road that they climbed over each other. The ones that weren't crawling weren't moving at all, and there was a logjam across the interstate. He wasn't sure how they were going to get around the mass of writhing bodies, but he could tell that whatever it was that was making the infected crawl toward Charleston, it was still doing the job. For what must have been the thousandth time, he tilted his head to one side and listened, hoping he would hear whatever it was that was calling to them.

A wet slap on his foot made him jump, and he saw one of the crawling dead had reached for him. He was lucky it hadn't been more patient and waited to make a grab after getting closer. There were too many for him to stand still, and there were too many for him to keep going forward. His only choice would be to work his way to the Cooper River and then find a boat.

Still carrying Mattie, Jed backtracked across the lanes of infected that reached for him as he went by. That was when he noticed that many of the infected that weren't moving at all had head wounds that were obviously the result of being shot with bullets. As a matter of fact, there were more of them at the spot where the logjam began. From his higher elevation, he could see down into the place where the interstate lanes branched left and right forming figure eights cut in half by exit ramps. The interchange that formed the connection between I-26 and I-526 must have been the place where shooters had taken a stand and greeted the horde as it came over the crest of the hill where he now stood. He imagined it must have been quite a thing to see.

The exit for Remount Road was right behind him, and Jed decided that would be the best place for him to begin working his way to the east. If he could find a road that was free of the infected, he would try to turn toward Charleston again, but if he couldn't, at least he could find a boat that would get him across the Cooper River where the horde had to be thinner.

That was what he assumed, but he was worried that there was a flaw in his own thinking. He was hoping that the years had been plenty of time for the population of infected to have dwindled on the Mt. Pleasant side of the Cooper River. His reasoning was based on geography. There was the Francis Marion Forest on one side, the Atlantic Ocean on another side, and the Cooper River on the other. There were plenty of living people in between those geographical barriers when the infection began, but as the infected were eliminated there wouldn't be a steady supply of replacements.

"If I'm wrong, I guess I'll find out," he said to Mattie as if she had been part of his mental conversation. She wrinkled her nose at him because she knew he was teasing her, but she didn't know how.

It didn't take long to reach the Remount Road exit, but he saw immediately that there was no way he was going to use Rivers Avenue to reach Charleston. It ran parallel to the interstate all the way to the city, but it was littered with bodies just like the interstate had been. He worked his way down Rivers for a few blocks, stepping over bodies that weren't moving while examining them for the head wounds he thought he would find. Strangely, there were none, but what he learned was that the overflow from the main horde had used Rivers Avenue to get around the logjam created by all of the infected that had been shot. That was bad luck for him because it wouldn't be long before he caught up with the infected that could still walk. His only choice was to find a way to cross the Cooper River.

18

Loyalties

Contagion Extinction Level - Day Thirty

The routine alone was almost enough to drive Phillip Corrigan insane. Denise had found it easier to cope with the boredom, and she had kept reminding Phillip that they could have wound up getting stuck in any number of places less hospitable. At least they were safe while they were bored.

They weren't given much in the way of information, but what they managed to learn from listening in on conversations and from the few people they had a chance to talk with, the strategy of whoever was in charge of the Yorktown was for the ship to appear to be unoccupied. It had been sealed up so tight that no one would know there were survivors on board. Not so much as a single lightbulb could be seen from the outside. No sounds were generated inside that could be heard above deck, and it would remain like that for a month.

During that time they were allowed to go to the dining area and their cabin but nowhere else. When they needed more books, they told Ted Atwater in advance, and he managed to get the ones from popular authors. A month is a long time, but they were safe.

The ban on movement was lifted at the end of the month, as promised. They learned the good news when they went to breakfast. They got their trays and stood in line as they had been doing for a month. There was a menu board by the silverware, and this morning it had an announcement in bold letters that said, "CEL Day Plus 30. You are now free to move about the ship."

Over breakfast there was excited chatter at the tables as people talked among their groups about what they planned to do. The general preference was to tour the ship. People wanted to see anything except the insides of their cabins, and it was no surprise to find there were crowds everywhere.

On busy days before CEL Day the Yorktown was jammed with tourists, and on the first day they were allowed to explore the ship, it was just like the tourists had returned. One other thing was the same as it used to be. There were signs that said there was no admittance allowed beyond some of the closed doors. Ropes were draped between poles with signs hung on them that said RESTRICTED AREA, but the serious looking armed guards by the doors made the signs unnecessary.

"I feel like a tourist," whispered Denise. "Do you think we're going to be allowed to see anything worth seeing?"

"That would be defined as anything except our rooms."

"What about tomorrow? Once we see everything today, are we going to keep looking at everything until we get as tired of it as we are our rooms?"

"What're you getting at?"

Denise leaned in closer, and for effect she gave her husband a smile that others might interpret as affectionate.

"This is a big ship. There has to be a way to get past the guards into some of the places not meant for everyone. I have an idea. Just follow my lead."

Denise casually walked a few steps faster and fell into line behind a small group of people who were obviously part of the establishment. She didn't know what they did on the ship, but they were dressed like they worked in a hospital or some kind of lab. They were all wearing white lab coats over a mixture of civilian clothes and uniforms. The main thing about them was that they were part of a group, and they were leaving the main concourse through one of the doors that was guarded. The guard stepped aside as they approached and held the door open for them.

The natural way Denise smiled into the face of the guard as she thanked him caused the man to do what he had been taught to do his whole life. He returned her smile and wished her a good day. Phillip almost made it. The guard on the other side of the door caught him by the elbow.

"Sorry, Sir. This is a restricted area."

If Denise had kept going, she would have made it into the stairwell with the rest of the group, but she glanced back over her shoulder, and the light behind her made her visible to the man standing behind Phillip.

Marshall Sayer had his eye on the Corrigans from the start. They fit the profile that he needed. No children or immediate family ties, good careers, intelligence, and recommended by Dr. Grace Williams. Sayer had visited her to ask why she had adopted the Corrigans in place of the local agent who had helped them with logistics at the municipal center. Dr. Williams had explained that they were a natural fit for them to use on a special project. When she explained why, he had decided to see for himself, but he waited until the end of the mandatory month of tedium. If he drove them a little crazy with boredom, it might soften them up when he offered them some excitement down the road.

"Denise, Phillip. We're going this way."

Sayer held one hand out to indicate which way they were going as if the Corrigans were making a wrong turn. Denise stepped back through the door and apologized to everyone. If she and Phillip were confused about who the man was, they didn't show it. The important thing was that he knew them, and the guards had snapped to attention at his appearance.

Marshall liked the way she kept her cool, and he saw what Dr. Williams had meant.

They knew they were caught, but they didn't try to offer an explanation to the man for making a wrong turn through a door that was clearly off limits. They exchanged smiles and walked away with him as if they were old friends.

That was what he liked most about them. He saw that they recovered quickly even when they didn't know who he was. This was a time to take advantage of the situation and to gain their confidence.

"Are you enjoying your freedom today? I imagine the routine over the last month left much to be desired."

"It was boring," said Denise, "but you aren't going to hear any complaints out of us."

Phillip added, "I'll second that. We're grateful for the hospitality. You didn't have to take us in, and I'm sure there were people out there who would be glad to trade places with us."

"There's something I think you should see. Let's go topside for a bit.

I imagine you could use some fresh air."

"Topside," said Denise. "I've forgotten what the sun looks like."

Marshall led the way to a staircase that was guarded, but the man removed the barrier chain and held it aside for them.

"I should warn you. There are still visible scars on the city. It was a bad first day, and it didn't get any better over the first few weeks. It's going to be a long time before people live in Charleston again."

They came to a steel door at the top of the staircase, and Marshall paused for dramatic effect. He pulled the big lever that unlocked the door and swung it out of the way. Bright sunlight flooded the landing, and the Corrigans had to shield their eyes. He held out a hand to Denise and helped her to step over the sill.

The smell of saltwater assaulted them, but there was another smell. Things had burned, and a month wasn't enough time for the weather to wash away the stain of that first week. The seagulls surprised them both. There were more seagulls than they had ever seen anywhere, and they were feeding on an endless supply of twisted heaps on every visible piece of shoreline around the harbor. The heaps were everywhere, and even though they were unrecognizable, there was no mistaking what they were. The smell of rot washed across them with the next breeze and it easily masked the other smells. Denise gagged, and Marshall was quick to produce a handkerchief.

"I'm sorry, Denise. Are you okay?"

Denise had one hand over her mouth and one hand held her stomach where a cramp had made her double over. She took her hand away from her face and tried hard to reassure Marshall and Phillip.

"I'm fine. I want to see."

There was a bitter taste at the back of her throat, but she really did want to see. As a survivor, it was her duty to witness for those who didn't survive.

With a little help from her husband and the handkerchief over her mouth and nose, they walked across the flight deck of the old aircraft carrier. A safety railing had been added for tourists, and Denise was grateful to have it there. She leaned heavily on the top rail and stared with wide eyes across the harbor toward Charleston.

She didn't know where to start. Her eyes were drawn toward each anomaly as if it was the main thing. There were so many bodies. Even from a distance she could tell they were piled deep across the granite boulders of the battery.

The cruise ship terminal had been where a horde of infected had attempted to reach the frightened passengers who were trying to board their ship. The infected had fallen over the side of the dock by the hundreds, and the tides hadn't been able to wash away their bodies.

They could see the small island in the Cooper River that sat halfway between the carrier and Charleston, and even from a distance they could see the blue crabs scurrying from one victim to the next. They were normally a favorite meal of the seagulls, but today the birds and crabs dined together.

"I'll never eat crab dip again," said Phillip.

"I wouldn't recommend it," said Marshall. "Our preliminary test results indicate the infection can be passed along by the crabs. The shrimp are most likely contaminated too, as well as anything that eats shrimp."

"The city," said Denise. "It was so beautiful. So many of the buildings are burned."

"We estimate sixty percent of the historic section suffered damage. On the first day the firemen who responded to the fires were among the first to die. They were attacked by the infected, and as they died they turned on their fellow first responders. The bravest among us ran straight toward their own deaths, and within hours no one was putting out the fires."

As he described the first day, he pointed at the landmarks. The bodies on the small island were the people who had gone into the water from both sides of the river and reached Castle Pinckney. He explained that the tourists at Patriots Point were jumping from the deck of the carrier and from the docks in the marina. Boats were everywhere in the harbor, but there weren't enough to pick up all of the people in the water. There was also the problem of the people who had been bitten. He described the way some people tried to help others, only to be bitten by people they pulled into their boats.

"Did anyone else survive?" asked Phillip.

"There was a cruise ship right over there."

Marshall pointed at the cruise ship terminal.

"I saw it leave, and it looked like it was full. It cruised out of here with about five thousand people on board. We heard they didn't get far. There were reports that the infection broke out on the ship after they were at sea, and everyone was lost."

The Corrigans stood shoulder to shoulder and silently surveyed the changed city. Smoke still drifted from small fires in the downtown area, and despite the fact that there were bodies everywhere, it was the sight of so many infected walking around in plain view that stunned them the most. The Battery at White Point Gardens was as populated as it would have been on a summer day at the height of tourist season, but those weren't tourists. No traffic moved, but there were so many abandoned vehicles along the street that bordered the water that it resembled a typical traffic jam.

Marshall continued his description of that first day.

"When the cruise ship left the dock, the harbor was literally jammed with small boats. Everyone who could get into a boat tried to, even if it wasn't theirs. People were shooting each other to either protect their boats or to steal someone else's."

He pointed at Fort Sumter and told them the chaos that followed when the cruise ship had gone by the Civil War fort. People shot at the passengers for no reason other than the fact that they were escaping with their lives.

"Hundreds of boats made it to Fort Sumter, but it wasn't the best place to go. The first people to arrive there decided the fort belonged to them. They didn't want to allow anyone else to join them because the boats were carrying victims with bite marks. So, they shot whole boat loads of new arrivals. Even the kids. Judging by everything else that happened on the first day, there were undoubtedly bite victims inside already, and they were doing as much of the shooting as anyone else."

"Is that why you didn't let more people in?" asked Denise.

The question was blunt, and there was an edge to her voice that asked if he thought he was any better than the people at Fort Sumter.

"We work for the government," he said, "so we had some advance information about the infection. Not much more time than everyone else, but enough. We had been studying an infection that was carried back to the US from South America by a researcher, and it was surprising that we got as much warning as we did. The infection he carried was so bad that every test showed a one hundred percent mortality rate. If it had spread as fast as we expected, we wouldn't have been able to save as many people as we did. Now we have to stop it from killing the rest of the world. That's why we're here. As for letting more people in, we did what we could."

Phillip reacted as if he had been reminded of something.

"By the rest of the world, are you saying this is just happening in the United States? I've been asking the guards for periodicals. We haven't seen a newspaper or magazine in a month, and you know as well as anyone that there's no cell service. That quit a long time ago. It would be great to see the internet again."

Marshall shook his head. "No, that's not what I meant. I should've chosen my words better. What I should've said was that we have to stop the infection from killing everyone left in the world, but this has happened everywhere. Not a single city in the world was spared. Billions have died, and the rest of humanity is clinging to little places like the Yorktown and Fort Sumter."

Denise was startled but hopeful at the same time. "There are still survivors at Fort Sumter? We should help them."

Phillip was in agreement with Denise as soon as she said it. "We need to contact them. Find out how many people they have over there. Do they have medicine or food? How hard would it be to get there?"

Marshal showed extraordinary patience with the Corrigans. From what he could see, they were exactly as Dr. Williams had described. His friends in the intelligence services had talked about how they recruited couples to be spies, and it was a long process. It often took years of grooming before sending them on a mission, and time was something they had in large supply. He could work with their empathy and sense of what was right. If they weren't good people with a sense of right and wrong, they wouldn't be what he needed.

A flock of seagulls swirled around them, and they ducked with their hands over their heads. An air horn blasted the deck of the ship. The seagulls scattered in all directions and flew into each other in panic, but they were scared away.

"We have people in the control tower whenever someone comes up on deck. We have to keep the seagulls away from them because they've been eating the infected dead, and we don't know if they can transmit the infection to the living. The air horn was the best idea we could come up with to keep them away. Are you ready to go back in?"

"No," said Denise. "I want to know more. What's going to happen to us?"

Marshall Sayer was the consummate salesman, and he knew better than to jump right on the opportunity that was in front of him. He had to work carefully to close the deal, and he didn't want to lose the Corrigans by being over anxious. He lowered his eyes for dramatic effect and paused before he answered.

"What is it?" asked Phillip. "We're going to be allowed to stay, aren't we?"

That was exactly the worry Marshall had hoped would cross their minds. It didn't need to exist for long, but if it crossed their minds at all, it would make them receptive to the alternatives.

"I don't see why not," said Marshall. "I can tell I can count on you, and I might have an important job for you at a future date."

"Anything," said Phillip. "I'm sure we can be useful at something. Denise would be great in your medical center, or if you have plans for a school for the kids, she could do that. I can do anything you want. Just give us a chance to earn our keep."

Marshall put on his reassuring face and used his best fatherly voice.

"Oh, I'm sorry. I didn't mean to make it sound like there was even a chance you weren't staying. I have something in mind for you. Something special that not just anyone could do."

"Name it," said Phillip.

"In due time, Phillip. For now I can use you both in a supervisory capacity. Take some time to get used to things. Get to know your way around the ship and get to know the people. When we're ready, we'll begin talking about your mission."

That one word was both ominous and uplifting. Marshall had something big in mind for them, and they were going to do more than survive. They were going to be protected, and they were going to play a big part in their own survival. They didn't know what part that would be, but Marshall knew what it was, and for now that was enough.

******

What had started out as a little spying by the Corrigans turned into a place for them to be. A place where they fit in with the rest of the people working for this unusual organization. They hadn't known it was USAMRIID until they were officially given an orientation by Marshall. It seemed that Marshall Sayer had taken them under his wing. For whatever reason, he included them in his plans and made them feel like part of the family. Ted Atwater saw to it that everything they needed was theirs for the asking, and one of the rarest of commodities was news from the outside. They were far better informed than most of the people in the Yorktown.

In the early days, there wasn't much news that was good, and that wouldn't get better with time. There would just be less news. Any good news they heard was likely to be nothing more than a rumor. Before the Internet disappeared completely, they read more than once that a cure had been discovered and that the military was defeating the infected dead.

Locally, there was a report of the Navy evacuating the Naval Weapons Station at Goose Creek. A couple of Navy ships cruised into the harbor. One was a transport ship. The second was its escort, and Ted had identified it as an Arleigh Burke class destroyer. Ted told them it was like the business end of a rifle. You didn't want one of them targeting you.

The two ships would normally have entered the harbor much more slowly, and they would have been accompanied by a harbor pilot. Denise asked Ted why they weren't signaling the ships to let them know they were in the Yorktown. It just made sense for the military and USAMRIID to coordinate disaster relief efforts. He had explained that marshal law was in effect, and the country was essentially at war. The military knew they were there at Patriots Point, and if they needed anything from them, the Navy would let them know.

The ships showed no interest in the survivors on the Yorktown, and they appeared to be in a hurry. They used the channel on the other side of Castle Pinckney and cruised up the Cooper River past the former Charleston Navy Base. Ted told them that the base at Goose Creek had been overrun by the infected, and the Navy was pulling out while they could. The next morning the ships returned in a convoy with two other surface ships and a really big submarine.

The convoy was just passing Fort Sumter when someone opened fire from the old Civil War fort. The response was breathtaking. It had probably been one person with an M4 or an AR15 in the fort. The Arleigh Burke destroyer didn't waste ammunition because it only needed to make its point. It responded with a short burst from one of its Phalanx 20 mm Vulcan cannons. The brick and mortar defenses of Fort Sumter disappeared in a cloud of dust where the shots had originated.

The only other shots that were fired were random rifle shots from the Marines stationed along the decks of the Navy ships. They couldn't be blamed for losing their cool as they passed by the Battery. The infected leaned against the railings and stretched their hands out toward the living people who lined the decks of the ships. It was an insult to the proud Marines who wanted to personally strike back against a new kind of enemy.

When the news was discussed within the inner circles of the Yorktown, there was little doubt that the people of Fort Sumter were worth avoiding. There had already been guards posted at the stern of the Yorktown to give early warning if anyone from Fort Sumter crossed the harbor toward Patriots Point.

So it seemed the battle lines were drawn around the harbor. On one side was the city. It was ruled by the infected dead and the occasional people who ventured into a territory that was so dangerous that it was unlikely they survived their quests to locate supplies. On another side was Patriots Point. A safe haven to a small group of loyal citizens who had an equally small chance of saving the country for all Americans. They were willing to sacrifice comfort in order to stay alive long enough to find a cure for the infection. It was well known throughout the ship that the labs in the decks below them were close to that cure on the very first day. They just needed a little luck.

The other side of the harbor was Fort Sumter, and it became known as the enemy. Whoever they were, and no one ever knew for sure, they were ruthless and cared little for anything beyond their own survival. Fires burned at night, and according to people who knew for sure, there was almost always someone being sacrificed as the occupants of Fort Sumter lived out their lawless fantasies.

There was a rumor about a helicopter crash early in the first month before any of them had been allowed to go topside, but no one knew anyone who actually witnessed the crash. One part of the rumor was that it had been a presidential helicopter from the Marine-1 fleet, but neither Ted nor Marshall could confirm it.

The weeks passed slowly at first until time began passing in months. Routines became modified as supplies arrived from the depot USAMRIID had established at the State Ports Authority. A supply route between the port and Patriots Point had been established. The infected still arrived in large enough numbers to require an armed escort with every convoy of supplies, but gradually the USAMRIID compound at the port became the garrison it needed to be for the real mission to begin. The containers were emptied of their precious cargo, and plans were revealed about how they intended to strike back at the infected.

It was a three part plan, and every inhabitant of Patriots Point knew that each part had to work or the entire plan would fail. Part one was to eliminate all threats around the Yorktown. That included the infected dead and the living who would interfere with their endgame. The second part was the beacon. The beacon was discovered and developed in the labs of the Yorktown. When the discovery was made, the news spread like wildfire through the ship, and the survivors who lived and worked on board were allowed to celebrate for two full days. The beacon was essential to the third part of the plan. It would call the infected dead from hundreds of miles away, and they would stop at nothing to answer the beacon. Then, when all of the infected were within a few miles of the source of the beacon, the heroes on the Yorktown would release an agent that would destroy them all.

The agent was developed in the same laboratory where the beacon was discovered. Only a few members of the crew could go there, but everyone knew who was behind the work. The man responsible for the breakthrough that would save the remainder of mankind was Anton Mikhailov. The Corrigans were introduced to him once at a meeting, but the man remained aloof and distant from his fellow survivors. They were told he was a genius and to expect him to look down his nose at them. As far as they were concerned, he was entitled to be a snob. If he saved mankind, he deserved to be made king.

At the end of the first year, Denise and Phillip found themselves to be content with the way things had developed for them. They couldn't believe the rest of the world had died around them while they had become part of the organization that would take back the planet. They strolled along the deck of the Yorktown enjoying the night air and discussing the meeting earlier in the day. Marshall had unveiled the plans, and they were excited to be playing their part, but the timeline was hard to accept. They were ready to go now, but they had been told to expect it to take another five years, and that was without more delays.

There had been setbacks. Parts of the plan were dependent upon goals that were somehow in place before the outbreak of the infection, and that had bothered the Corrigans. They only spoke about it when they were alone on their nightly walks, and it had been hard to wait. They were both solidly behind the plans, but they hadn't been part of the political establishment before the infection, and they didn't just accept things on blind faith.

Phillip asked, "How could they have a plan for this so far in advance?"

"I asked Ted about that, and he said they had a list of possible disasters. One of them was a pandemic."

"I'm sure they did," he said, "but a pandemic that created zombies?"

"I saw the list, and it was on there, but Ted said they didn't actually think there would be a zombie disaster. Ted said that planning for one would make them ready for a lot of things they hadn't included on the list. He called it a generic plan."

Phillip wasn't totally sold, and Denise wasn't either, but one thing they could agree on was that their doubts about their hosts didn't change the world. They would still wake up tomorrow in a world dominated by zombies, but at least they would wake up.

******

Shootings became a nightly event at Fort Sumter, and many of the survivors in the Yorktown sat in the dark and watched as if they were at a drive-in theater. Firefights became so spectacular that it sounded like armies were waging war. It was a piece of real estate that had very little value because it was so difficult to resupply, but it was a place where the infected couldn't go. The fighting escalated one night until there was a prolonged battle that was followed by total silence. It seemed that someone had won.

The official report given by Marshall Sayer was that two well armed gangs had fought over the fort and that the winners had somehow dug in and would be hard to dig out. He made a point to everyone that it wouldn't change their plans. It just meant they would have to be watchful.

It seemed that the conflicts at Fort Sumter were not quite over as a convoy of Cuban gunboats attacked Fort Sumter at night. For the survivors on the Yorktown it was one thing to watch rival gangs fight for sovereignty over the little island, but it was still US soil, and the flag that flew on the gunboats wasn't the stars and stripes.

Marshall Sayer surprised everyone when he wouldn't allow his men to intervene. Patriots Point didn't have the weapons it needed for a prolonged battle, but there were RPGs in the armory that could eliminate the gunboats with ease. Even Ted Atwater urged him to use the weapons, but Marshall told them he didn't want to show their hand so soon. When the Coast Guard ship arrived to defend the fort, the spectators at Patriots Point had cheered for their fellow Americans, but Marshall ordered the Yorktown to go into lockdown just like it had for the first month.

Anger and frustration set in among the survivors at Patriots Point just as it appeared there was a celebration at Fort Sumter. Only Ted Atwater seemed to understand what was happening with his boss, but he didn't share what he knew. All he would say was to be patient. When the helicopters arrived, everyone could see that Marshall was the last person who could be called patient, but Ted knew better than to say it to Marshall.

Phillip and Denise were as close to Marshall Sayer as anyone could be with the exception of his two old friends, Ted Atwater and Dr. Grace Williams, but the helicopters made him unapproachable for weeks. When he finally came out of his shell, he said he was better because he still had a plan. He called together his senior staff and told them he had hoped to use the helicopters in the final phase of his plan to stop the infection, but there was only one way to get them back. He announced that he wasn't prepared to tell them how they would get the helicopters, but there was plenty of time over the next five years for that part of the plan.

19

Discovery

Contagion Extinction Level - Six Years Later

Somehow the years had gone by, and their beliefs had never wavered. Still, these people of Fort Sumter weren't what they had expected. Everywhere Denise and Phillip went, all they saw were friendly smiles. There had been children at first, but for some reason they had left Fort Sumter. When Denise had asked where they had gone, an unassuming young lady had told her they were taken somewhere safer. There had been no attempt in the pleasant response to hide the truth, although the lady hadn't volunteered why they were safer somewhere else.

There was an undercurrent of seriousness around the shelter that hadn't been there before. They were still allowed to go almost anywhere, and they still felt like they were being watched, but part of that could easily have been their imaginations. After all, they were on a mission.

It had been easy to allow themselves to be found by a patrol from Fort Sumter. There was a small runway on Johns Island that was overgrown with weeds pushing themselves up through the asphalt, and it was a bumpy landing they would prefer not to repeat. The pilot assured them it was routine, and he had done it plenty of times. They were willing to take his word for it but glad they would only have to do it once.

From there they only had to avoid the infected while staying in the open, but in their briefings they had been shown maps of the flight paths most often flown by the helicopters. It was obvious that the helicopters were avoiding the Yorktown and their landing strip on the fairway of the golf course at Patriots Point. Johns Island was southwest of Fort Sumter and directly away from the Yorktown.

When the plane came to a teeth jarring stop in the tall grass, they barely had time to get clear of its wings before it was circling away and lining up for take off. The patrols from Fort Sumter had undoubtedly spotted the crushed grass from previous landings and knew that the Yorktown was using the small airport. They could have laid a trap for them, so the plan was to land and get some distance between themselves and any evidence that they were somehow connected with the airport.

Phillip had doubts about the plan when they saw how many infected were in the area. At first they thought the infected were drawn to the sound of the plane, but soon enough they saw the infected were all moving in one direction. The beacon was doing its job. These particular infected were never going to reach the source of the beacon, but they didn't know where they were going or why. The irony wasn't lost on the Corrigans that they were going in the same direction as the infected.

They found a barn that had been used for heavy machinery, and the ground was packed hard and bare in a large area around the front. It gave them some cover where they could hide from the infected while they waited for the sound of a Fort Sumter patrol.

Just as they hoped, it was only three hours before the unmistakable thumping of helicopter rotors pounded the air. They were moving quickly, and it seemed they would go right past them before they could even get out of the barn. When they came into the open with their arms waving over their heads, they didn't count on finding over a dozen of the infected standing in the open area where they had hoped to be seen.

Denise turned to run back into the barn, but it was too late. They had practically knocked over several infected that were right outside the barn door, and the dead had already moved into position behind her. Phillip didn't know if he should wave his arms at the advancing helicopters or try to help Denise. That was when they understood how helpless they had been. Neither of them had focused their training on hand to hand combat with the infected, and it showed. Denise was pushed over backward onto the ground and resorted to kicking frantically at the infected. Phillip was busy trying to get an infected to let go of his shirt. As he fought with the groaning creature's rotten fingers, it advanced on him with its mouth stretched open.

Phillip went down when he backed straight into the infected that had caught Denise by her right foot. His weight all but crushed the fragile infected into the ground. He found himself on his back, and Denise was kicking the infected that was on his legs in the side of its head. They hadn't been this close to something trying to bite them since the first day, and when her kick snapped the head of the infected off of its shoulders, it landed squarely in Phillip's outstretched hands. He caught it out of reflex and cradled it just like he had caught a football.

The teeth closed with an audible clack on the front of his shirt, and he felt the searing pain on his chest. Denise was on her feet and had jumped across the bodies to catch a handful of hair on the back of the creature's head. She pulled the head backward and threw it in one motion, and Phillip screamed at the pain again.

Both of them had been so busy with their mistake that they weren't aware of the heavy wind and the sound of urgent voices shouting instructions. Someone scooped up Denise from behind and practically carried her through the reaching arms of the infected that were drawn into the fray.

Two uniformed men had Phillip and were escorting him through, and several others were expertly clearing a path with machetes. The helicopter lifted away from the ground like a high speed elevator, and the Corrigans felt themselves being pulled to the floor by the force of gravity.

Denise saw the big red splash of crimson across the front of her husband's shirt and immediately screamed because it was a death sentence. She tried to go to him, but there were still arms holding her back. Someone slid the door shut and the wind that had buffeted at them was gone, but she still couldn't go to Phillip because another group of men had pinned him to the floor on his back.

What happened next had been so confusing and so out of place. While they held him down, one of the men gripped Phillip's shirt in both hands and ripped it wide apart. Buttons flew away and Phillip screamed for them to stop. Denise just generally screamed with every ounce of energy she could muster.

Just as suddenly as it started, the man who tore open the shirt was laughing, and the other men joined in. One of them had a red cross on an armband, and he was examining Phillip's chest closely. He sat back on his heels and grabbed Phillip by his forearm. Phillip was yanked into a sitting position, and incredibly he was laughing along with the men.

Denise took a swing at one of them, and he easily ducked it. Through the noise of the helicopter's rotors she finally heard the medic telling her something.

"He's going to be fine. The infected bit his shirt and missed his skin, but when you yanked the head off of his chest, it ripped out a bunch of his chest hair. There's no bite mark, just a big bald patch that looks like it got a hot wax."

She didn't know if she wanted to kiss Phillip or slap him, but he was ready for it and deflected her swing.

"Why're you hitting me?" he yelled.

"You were screaming so much I thought you were going to die."

She was angry, and the tears were streaming down her cheeks.

"I never had my chest hair ripped out before."

That was supposed to be enough for her, but instead it was enough to send the uniformed men into hysterics. To a man, they all told her Phillip had a right to scream if he wanted to.

The medic cleaned the area where Phillip had been bleeding and inspected it closely. He pronounced it as being non-terminal but painful and put a bandage over it. As he worked, the pilot came down from the cockpit and introduced herself to Denise. She pulled a curtain across the inside of the helicopter and privately inspected her for bite marks. Denise liked her, and she liked the way the uniformed woman made her feel at ease. She caught herself forgetting that these people were the enemy and wondered for the first time what it had been that made her dangerous.

The woman asked her a few questions, and Denise stuck to the script. They expected to be asked how they had come to be in that part of Johns Island and where they had been before that, but the script had a flaw. She had to stick with it because she knew Phillip would be asked the same questions, but she saw the expression of doubt on the woman's face when she answered that they had been on Mount Pleasant when the infection had started. There's no way Denise could have known it, but the helicopter crews had rescued dozens of people, and they were the first to have been in Mount Pleasant on the first day of the infection. They were just going to need to be convincing when they told their story.

Mount Pleasant had been cut off from Charleston, and if they had gone over land to get from Mount Pleasant to Johns Island, they would have been forced to cross the city. The only other way would have been a forty to fifty mile journey across several bridges, through West Ashley, and finally onto James Island at yet another bridge. Denise and Phillip gave the same answer when questioned separately, and as improbable as it sounded, they made it convincing.

As they explained it, they escaped from Mount Pleasant on a small boat and managed to get past the jetties at the mouth of the Charleston harbor. From there the current pulled them south past Morris Island and Folly Beach until they came to the mouth of the Stono River. They used the river to travel far enough inland until they were away from the metropolitan areas. They almost made it safely out of the areas where the infected were concentrated, but they had been forced backward by advancing hordes.

When the pilot filed her report, Captain Miller assigned some personnel to watch them more closely than usual, but their story was possible. She also told him she didn't know how they had survived so long, because they were almost clumsy when they defended themselves. Then she amended it to say they weren't almost clumsy. They were clumsy, and it was a miracle they had survived so long.

As the helicopters lined up to make their descent for landing at Fort Sumter, Denise whispered to her husband, "Why was our cover story so impossible? Why couldn't we just say we've been surviving on Johns Island?"

"Marshall said these people have probably rescued a lot of survivors from Johns Island. If we said we had been over here for six years, they would have wondered how they hadn't come across us sooner. Just stick to the script. They have to believe it, and we can't change it now."

They watched through the windows as the walls of the fort came up on the sides. The landing area was small, so the helicopters landed in the open and were towed to a parking spot after the rotors stopped. It meant they wouldn't be able to take off at the same time, but they could see by the efficiency of the flight crews that this group was as practiced as a pit crew at a stock car race. One helicopter wasn't in the air long before the next one would join it.

There was a crew of maintenance workers standing by with their equipment, and one of the pilots was talking with them about changes they were making. From what Denise overheard, they were sealing the entrances to the shelter, and the helicopters were supposed to land at the back entrance.

"What do you make of that?" she whispered to Phillip.

"I didn't know Fort Sumter has a basement," he answered.

"Not only a basement but a back door. There must be a tunnel from here to somewhere else, but it would be underwater."

After six years of living on the Yorktown, their perception of life at Fort Sumter had to be something along the lines of living in a hot, humid, sand flea infested mud hut. There was brick and mortar, but from what they could see, living in the ship was like living in a five star hotel compared to Fort Sumter.

One of the crew handed each of them an ice cold bottle of water, and the real surprise was that the bottles still had their original seals. Another helicopter was hovering a short distance away, so the landing crew had to get everyone clear of the first one to land. The Corrigans were escorted away from the aircraft toward a door, and before they could mentally absorb what they saw in front of them when the door opened, they were slipped into harnesses that buckled around their chests and waists.

"These are just a safety precaution," said one of the soldiers. "We don't want you to make it this far only to slip and fall down a ladder. It's a long climb. If you fall, we've got you."

They had stepped through the door onto a landing that was perched at the top of a deep shaft. A ladder descended into the brightly lit shaft, and for the first time either of them could recall, they were glad to use a safety harness and rope to climb down a ladder.

"How deep is this place?" asked Denise.

For some reason the soldiers thought her question was funny.

"This is just the entrance shaft, Ma'am. The elevators will take us down the rest of the way."

"Elevators?"

One of the soldiers went first while the second took Denise by the arm and guided her into position. The rope slipped through a winch system that would feed her line out at an even pace as long as she didn't fall. If she did, it would pull her to an abrupt stop. Phillip was urged forward as Denise climbed down, and from his view above her, it looked like they were going down the inside of the world's biggest aluminum can.

If they thought the view was spectacular from the top, it was nothing compared with the view from the bottom. They stood next to each other with their heads leaned backward as the soldiers untied their harnesses. The ladder shrank into the distance above them until it disappeared through the platform, but the surprises didn't end there. A polished metal door that seamlessly followed the curve of the wall slid open, and they were escorted into a carpeted hallway that rivaled anything they had seen in the Charleston hotel where they had stayed six years ago.

From there they entered an elevator and their guide pressed a button that took them down six floors. Phillip stared at the lit elevator button as if he had never seen one before. He was trying to understand how they could be going down six floors after already climbing down that ladder. The soldier with him had seen that reaction before and offered some understanding advice.

"Don't let it overwhelm you. After everything you've been through it's hard to accept that something like this even exists, but it's real. You're going to be okay now. Just let it all soak in."

The second soldier added, "We're going to drop you off at the mess hall. You'll be able to smell it before we get there. The cooks have this special dish they like to make for newcomers, and we radioed ahead to let them know you were coming. It's all kinds of meat and cheese baked in a crust. After you're finished eating there'll be some people who will get you settled in your quarters."

The door of the elevator opened, and the man had been telling the truth. The aroma of freshly baked food made their stomachs growl.

"Welcome to Fort Sumter," said a pleasant lady with a big smile. She was short and had dark hair that was also short. "You're in for a real treat. If you don't mind, I'll join you. My name is Jean." She gestured toward the room where people were lining up for supper.

******

Dr. Grace Williams could remember a time when she had patients, and they mattered to her. Things changed when they started to matter too much. When it was her own husband who became sick, and she watched the treatment take the life out of him, she forgot the rest of her patients. She neglected her practice until it went broke, and she eventually found herself in the silence of a forensic pathology lab. She didn't think of the people in the drawers of the lab as patients. She didn't think of them at all.

Her cold indifference toward men and women both made people

avoid her, and she liked it that way. Just like her feelings toward patients, her feelings toward friends dwindled away until her work was the only thing that mattered to her. That was why she was a perfect lab partner for Anton Mikhailov. His disposition was as abrasive as sandpaper toward everyone except Dr. Williams, but together they studied the virus and made discoveries beyond their wildest expectations.

The simple fact that it could reanimate dead people was startling enough, but their Holy Grail was the way it worked. How did it reproduce? How did it cause muscles to move in something that appeared to be voluntary action? Like when the infected heard a sound and decided to investigate? There was clearly something more at work than what anyone had ever seen in common viruses. Their best guess was that there were genetic and environmental influences, and if that was true, the virus became even more frightening because it meant it had the capacity to learn. As a matter of fact, before the news networks completely disappeared the French had labeled it as the "Learning Virus".

While the rest of the ship had suffered through the first thirty days inside their cabins, the two scientists had unraveled the infection as if it had been gift wrapped and delivered to them. Despite the insufferable American politician, they found a common cause that needed the attention of their talents. Marshall Sayer needed this success to validate his worth, and Ted Atwater got them anything they needed to keep his boss happy. Anything.

******

When the doors had been sealed on the Yorktown, there were over five hundred people inside the ship, and most of them didn't need to know what went on in the laboratory. Grace and her Russian counterpart gave Marshall a list of things they needed to begin their work, and the initial stages were going to be too hard to hide, so he ordered Ted to manufacture an explanation everyone could live with. Thirty days of silence was a brilliant idea.

While everyone else was restricted to their quarters and the dining facilities, the lab and its support facilities were brought into full operation. Ted often asked himself what the rest of the people on the ship would do if they knew about the experiments being conducted in the lower levels, but he doubted they would like the idea of bringing the infected dead into the ship, even if it might lead to a cure.

Six years ago Ted would have been willing to bet any amount of money that the infection couldn't be contained in the special rooms attached to the labs. He visited the area in the early days to ensure the work was being done, but watching the infected rot in their sealed rooms wasn't something he could stomach. He could tell that Grace and Anton enjoyed his squeamishness, and it would give them satisfaction if he stayed away, but he wasn't stubborn enough to win that battle. They could have their dungeon as long as they got results, and if he didn't go down there, he didn't have to pretend to ignore what they were doing when they crossed ethical boundaries. He wasn't so sure their work would pass the 'smell test' literally or figuratively.

One of the biggest surprises came when Marshall visited the labs and learned that Grace and Anton had accidentally discovered that the infected could hear sounds that humans couldn't. It was a simple matter of frequencies, and everyone knew that many animals had better hearing than humans. Somehow the virus improved the hearing of its victims.

Anton was focusing his work on the virus, while Grace was studying the infected. They had separate biohazard labs, but they kept up with each other's work religiously. Both were excited about everything they learned, but it wasn't until the third year had passed until the biggest discoveries were made. Anton was examining samples inside his lab when he heard the rapping on the glass. He looked up and saw Grace waving frantically for him to join her in her lab. That meant he would need to decontaminate and put on a fresh biohazard suit. They were self-contained when they needed to be and had their own oxygen supplies when they knew they wouldn't be inside very long. If they needed to work longer, they could connect to the oxygen and cooling systems inside the lab.

It took Anton a half hour to decontaminate and swap suits, but whatever had Grace so excited, it was still going to be there because she was positively ecstatic. She was standing in front of a row of ten rooms that were the holding cells for infected they used as subjects. At the moment they held twenty of the creatures, two per room. Anton didn't know how she could handle the smell that seemed to defeat the air purifying system on his hazmat suit. The smell of the entire lab had begun to assault his senses by the end of the second year, and he knew what he was smelling was likely to be the smell he remembered rather than what was really there.

He stepped over to her and saw she was holding an audiometer. She was tapping one of the displays that read ten thousand hertz. A dial was set at minus five decibels, and as Grace turned it to minus fifteen decibels the infected dead in each room became more animated. They had already been drawn to their presence and pressed up against the glass enclosures, but they doubled their efforts when she applied power to the audiometer.

Anton could see that Grace was smiling. Something she rarely did. She turned inside the awkward biohazard suit to better see his face. He couldn't help returning the smile, but he didn't completely grasp why she was so excited. It was an interesting anomaly, but what made it cause for celebration?

She saw his hesitation, but it didn't deflate her excitement just yet.

"Don't you see, Anton? Don't you see what it does to them?"

"Yes, yes I do, but we have to prove there isn't another cause for their behavior, and even if we prove they are able to hear frequencies we can't, what good will that do us?"

"It will be easy to prove, but don't you see? If they are drawn to the sound we can summon them, and that frequency is one that can be transmitted a great distance."

Anton understood but was still uncertain about her reason for summoning the infected. His blank stare was enough for her to know he was too focused on the microbiology.

She said, "Before you can kill flying insects on the wires of a bug lamp, you have to draw them to the wires. You do that with light. We can use sound to bring them to us and then use some form of mass destruction."

"But we haven't discovered a way to kill the virus other than blunt force trauma to the head."

Grace regarded Anton for a long moment. He was a brilliant scientist, but he could get stuck on the simplest form of practical application. She could tell he had been thinking only about finding a cure.

"Anton, what are we trying to do here? Are we only trying to find a cure?"

When put in the simplest terms, he realized as much as he despised his American partners in this venture, he was only doing what he had been told. He hadn't tried to go beyond his instructions. Marshall Sayer had told him to find a cure, so that's what he was doing.

She could see the realization dawn on his face.

"That's it, my friend. You can see it now. We should be finding a cure so we can stop the spread of this virus, but we have millions...no, billions of carriers to deal with. What are we going to do about them? If we want to exterminate them, we need to find a way to do it all at once, and that means we need for them to come to us."

It made sense, and he was nodding. They could spend a lifetime hunting the infected down and shooting them in the head, but did they have enough bullets? They could use knives or clubs, but did they have enough people to use their arms to stab at them or swing at them? They could burn them to destroy their ability to walk, but everyone knew the infected were still dangerous even when they were a pile of ashes. He and Grace had performed an autopsy on one that had burned, and they marveled at how little tissue was left, yet it still snapped its teeth at them. Even reduced to charred flesh it focused its attempts to spread the infection to them.

"How do you plan to prove it's the sound they are attracted to?"

"That's simple. I'll set it up, but instead of focusing all of your attention on finding a cure, you need to divide your time to devote your work to something that will kill them other than blunt force trauma."

It was a new phase in their work. As a virologist, of course he was interested in more than just the cure in one host. His focus was too narrow in that it was aimed at producing a vaccine that would prevent healthy people from contracting the disease if they were bitten. That was an essential goal when developing a vaccine for any disease. To prevent measles, people get a vaccination against measles. That doesn't mean they won't ever be exposed to measles. It just means exposure won't cause the disease to spread. The same was true for this infection. If he developed a vaccine, getting the vaccination wouldn't prevent you from being bitten.

His new way of thinking had actually been the way early medicine had approached the problem. Find the source, and decontaminate it, rather than provide potential victims with a vaccine. Now he just had to find a way to decontaminate the planet.

Grace could hear Anton laughing inside his biohazard suit as he went through the door into decontamination, and she knew he was laughing about something ironic and would have to ask him later what it was. That was what made Anton smile the most, and she knew it was his cynical nature that humor had to be dark, but she understood it better than the other kind of laughter that came from happiness.

It didn't take more than two hours for Grace to set up the lab containment rooms to test her theory about the sound, and most of that time was spent decontaminating while making several trips inside. When she was finished, Anton saw that he shouldn't have been surprised at how easy it was to control for other variables. She had simply limited their senses to hearing. The thought of putting a blindfold on each of the infected gave him his second laugh of the day, but Grace had just turned off the lights.

There were already cameras in the containment areas, but Grace had never needed the rooms to be dark. Night vision cameras were set up to view all ten rooms, and the audiometer had been equipped with WiFi controls. They were able to operate the audiometer and monitor the cameras remotely, so the lab technicians were all sent to their quarters. Anton and Grace used strict experimental paradigms, so they began recording, logged the times, and initiated the frequency from the audiometer for exact bursts in duration. The results were unquestionable.

With the labs totally dark, the infected inside the containment rooms began milling around with no specific interest in anything. Most of them stood still, but it was noted in the documentation which directions each of them faced, and it was agreed they were sufficiently varied to be called random. Then Grace initiated a burst of sound at a frequency unheard by human ears. All twenty subjects turned in the direction of the audiometer and reached toward the source as if they could touch it. When their hands met the glass, they pushed their wet faces against it and snapped their teeth.

The smiles were real this time, and Grace knew she had a new goal. She would talk with Marshall and Ted to locate the engineers among their survivors. Hopefully, there were some talented people who could design the equipment needed to amplify the sound and broadcast it over a long distance. The other hope would be that Anton could develop the weapon they needed to be able to exterminate the infected in large numbers.

There was one other hurdle, though. Marshall and Ted could see that they were on the brink of a discovery that would change the entire landscape of the apocalypse, but while the scientists were singularly focused on the resolution, the two bureaucrats saw the human implications. There were still living people out there.

The two scientists met with Marshall and Ted in the stateroom. They felt uncomfortable, not because of the expensive decor but because they had spent years rarely leaving the lower decks. They didn't care to associate with people who didn't think like them, so they didn't see much point in visiting the other parts of the ship.

When the idea was placed on the table, the first reaction was mixed. Just as Anton hadn't seen what was so important about the discovery, the bureaucrats didn't see what it meant to the big picture. They might as well have discovered that the infected preferred the taste of chicken. It was an interesting idea, but what was it good for?

Expecting no less, Grace explained that they could make the rest of the world safer by exterminating more infected at one time. She told them they would begin work on a weapon that would kill more infected at one time now that they had the ability to call them together.

Ted was the first to put the impact into words, but it wasn't out of concern for the living. It was born out of his natural tendency to make a joke out of something serious. The class clown was often a source of words of wisdom.

"I'd hate to get in the way of all those infected headed in the same direction."

There was a palpable silence as the words sank in.

The expression on the face of Dr. Grace Williams was as if she had just been criticized for doing something wrong, and she was prepared to defend herself.

Anton Mikhailov grinned and appeared to be seeing something beyond the walls of the ship. Undoubtedly he was seeing people running helplessly ahead of a slowly moving horde. Women were carrying children as men sacrificed themselves in a futile attempt to slow the horde. No, he wouldn't have a problem with it.

Ted was as easy to read as a comic book. He realized what he said as he said it, and he was deciding whether it was a good thing or a bad thing. He hadn't really decided it would cause harm to people in the way. After all, if they were in the way, all they had to do was move out of the way.

Marshall studied each expression, and it may have been partially out of concern for voters, but at least he saw it in terms of human loss and suffering.

"There's no way to warn everyone. People could get out of the way if they were warned, but what kind of range are we talking about? For every mile that thing can broadcast, how many more infected will it summon? I'll give you an idea. Think in terms of cities. How far to the next one? You summon everything stumbling around between here and Columbia. That's likely to be at least a million of those things."

As he spoke, he became more animated, and his voice got louder.

"Remember we aren't just talking about how many people there were on the last census. We're talking about how many people were on I-95 when CEL Day One happened. Everyone passing through the state died. There are pockets of people out there, and if we drag every infected down here, they're going to have a lot of people joining their ranks by the time they get here."

There was no argument that would convince Marshall that they should use it, but there was one that convinced him to build it. As far as they knew, there was no one else who had discovered it. They would be famous for at least coming up with something no one else did, and fame was the motivation Marshall lived for.

The final decision that came out of the meeting was that they would build it as a means of self-defense. It could control the creatures, so they could use it as a short range weapon if they ever needed to. Marshall ordered them to proceed with their research to develop a weapon and to learn anything else they could about it, and like all other infectious diseases stored at USAMRIID, he told them to find a way to weaponize it. Not for their own use, of course, but just in case someone else did.

******

It was dark in the deepest corners of the old ship. There was no need for lights, and the wide variety of insects liked it that way. The spiders were largely unaffected by the chemicals that were occasionally dumped into the damp compartments, but over the years those chemicals hadn't arrived, and nothing stopped the insects from seeking new corners where they could breed.

When the sound came, the one that caused a prickly sensation across their nervous systems, it also caused them to become aggressive. Not all of the spiders...just the ones that really mattered. Instead of hiding in their milky webs, they searched for the cracks and holes in the bulkheads that would allow them to get closer to the sound.

20

River's End

Contagion Extinction Level - Six Years Later

Jed and Mattie almost gave up on reaching Charleston. By the time they had dodged swarms of infected that materialized from practically every street, every building that was open, and every corner where they had been deposited by the massive horde that had crashed through the surrounding area, Jed felt like it would be enough to just take Mattie somewhere safe and keep her alive.

The decision was made for them to some extent when they were cut off from the only escape route that would take them back the way they had come. Every time they tried to move in a direction away from Mt. Pleasant, they were forced to detour. It was like the old days when moving traffic jammed the highways. If you got stuck in the wrong lane, sometimes you just had to go where the flow took you.

What Jed found to be even more disturbing than their inability to escape from the press of the infected into the Lowcountry was the fact that they weren't alone. It was obvious that animals were being pressed to move ahead of the infected just as they were, but the cats and dogs of this new world order had adapted their own survival instincts to include immediate flight when the infected were nearby. Their scent was different from living people, and the heightened senses of animals helped them to slip through gaps in the ever-shrinking cordon around them.

But it wasn't animals or people that accompanied them on their journey to find the source of the sound that summoned the dead. It was spiders. When Jed had come upon the massive web in the Pinopolis lock, it was certainly unusual to find the dirty and dangerous tangle of sticky silk, but out in the country surrounded by trees wasn't as unusual as finding thousands of them draped across buildings. He also knew that an estimation of thousands was likely to be low. They were everywhere.

Jed had been so busy navigating away from the infected that he hadn't really paid much attention to the webs. It wasn't until Mattie commented that she hated spiders that Jed saw how they were swallowing territory that had belonged to man. When she brought it to his attention, he realized that the collapse of the Pinopolis lock had done more than destroy the colony and his entire circle of friends. The water had carried a deadly cargo of brown recluse spiders and deposited them along every square inch of the riverbanks. He took Mattie by the hand and increased their pace.

The river wasn't too far away from the road he was traveling, and he didn't know how much he would be able to see from the Don Holt bridge, but he had to know how bad it had become. He was already within view of the highway that began the long climb to the top of the bridge, and he could see entire parking lots full of cars covered by a dusty brown blanket that had to be home to millions of spiders. It looked liked someone had emptied the lint screen of a giant clothes dryer onto the city.

Jed scooped Mattie up and ran to the top of the bridge, and he saw that it was far worse than he could have imagined. Both banks of the river came into view, and as far as the eye could see there were immense pillows of recluse webs on the trees, boats, docks, and houses that lined the river. He stopped and stared, wondering how there could be so many over so many miles. It didn't take long for Jed to realize he had misunderstood the impact of the collapse of the lock. He couldn't do the math, but he could guess. He guessed billions of baby brown recluse spiders had washed downriver toward the city of Charleston, and as they were deposited along the shore on the backs of the bodies where they had bred, they built their homes and multiplied even more.

He eventually reached the highest span of the bridge, and the panoramic view of the Cooper and Wando Rivers, the cities of North Charleston, Charleston, and Mt. Pleasant, and the harbor were all stretched out in front of him. From above it reminded him of the trip he had made to New York when he was a boy. It was the only time in his life when he had flown in an airplane, and he would never forget the realization that he was above the clouds instead of under them. He had squinted his eyes at the little window and pretended that the world was upside down, but when he opened them he found it was more fun not to pretend. This time it wasn't fun. Inside these dirty clouds were eight legged creatures that were feeding on human flesh. Infected human flesh.

Downriver was the Arthur Ravenel bridge and the Yorktown. The bridge didn't look right to him. Once again he squinted his eyes above the clouds, but this time it wasn't to pretend, it was against the glare of the light reflecting from the webs that shrouded everything for miles. Jed wondered how he would be able to cross Mt. Pleasant without becoming food for this new threat.

There was something on the bridge. Something had been built on the deck from the road up, and from what he could tell without binoculars it appeared that the road had been walled off to prevent anything from crossing it. There was also something that he had never seen on the top of the highest part of the bridge where the big, steel cables were attached. It was small at this distance, but it had the familiar shape of a satellite dish. Jed searched his memories for anything that told him otherwise, but he could find nothing that said this thing had been there before the infection. It had to be the source of the sound that was calling out to the infected, and from where he stood on the Don Holt Bridge, the barrier on the Ravenel bridge reminded him of a walled castle. Those walls wrapped like protective arms around the Yorktown.

Jed couldn't imagine the kind of power and resources behind such an operation. Someone had fortified the bridge and then put up a protective barrier around Patriots Point. Whoever they were, they were responsible for the deaths of a lot of people. Jed wondered if they knew.

"I don't like it here, Mr. Jed."

Mattie's voice was shaking, and he became aware of his own when he answered her.

"We're not staying here, but I think we have to go there."

He pointed at the carrier and the bridge that seemed so out of place.

"Why?"

Mattie's question wasn't the typical beginning of a string of 'whys' that kids could use to annoy their parents. She really wanted to know why they had to go there. Maybe because it looked like a place that they should avoid. Before Jed could answer she followed with a more direct question.

"Can the spiders go there?"

Jed had been carrying Mattie, and he put her down as he turned in a circle at the top of the bridge. Behind them and to their left the webs blanketed enough of the landscape for him to know they could never go back that way. Ahead of them the webs still had a large amount of forested countryside to cross, and trees slowed the progress of the spiders more than the remnants of mankind. Buildings, cars, and roads made it easier for them.

Their choices were obvious because they didn't have many. They could go forward, or they could stay where they were, and that would have been the same as giving up. Mattie pointed back the way they had come, and Jed saw a small horde of the infected emerge from the billowing webs between two tractor trailers.

Jed remembered a zombie movie he had laughed at along with his friends when they were kids. A bunch of zombies lurched out of a graveyard that just happened to be shrouded in fog, and as they stumbled toward a group of teenagers who didn't have the sense to run, the fog had swirled around them.

Jed and his friends yelled insults at the teenagers and threats at the zombies, but mostly they laughed at the bad special effects. Years later as he stood on the top of this bridge he remembered those special effects and thought how much better they looked than the real things.

At least eight of the infected had come into view as if they came out of a tunnel underneath the web, but each of them had filaments, threads, and even bundles of the sticky webs stretched out behind them. It didn't swirl around them the way the fog had in the movie. The infected dragged it with them and helped it to spread over new territory. Jed imagined the brown recluse spiders reacting the same way they had when he had encountered their webs as a kid. They would become agitated as if they were angry, and they would eventually attack. The infected walked as if nothing was happening, but they were undoubtedly being bitten from head to toe.

At the pace the infected walked, it would take them close to an hour to walk up the bridge to where Jed and Mattie stood, but in one hour their choice would be narrowed to one of their two options. There was no reason to hang around. Besides, the big holes in the webs were closing even as they watched. By the time another horde came through, there would be more web for them to drag along with them.

Jed scooped Mattie up again, not because she was tired but because Jed suddenly felt the need to expand his options. He didn't think he could travel fast enough to circle around the menace that was coming from the north, but he didn't plan to let it catch up with him. That thought made him turn his eyes to the north again as he descended the other side of the Don Holt bridge toward Mt. Pleasant. He couldn't see it from the bridge, but somewhere beyond the forests was Highway 17, and a small part of him wondered if it was at all possible that he could reach it before the spider webs. If he could, he felt like he knew the area well enough to dodge the infected that were coming south in answer to the call of the contraption on the Arthur Ravenel Bridge.

Highway 17 had been the main stomping grounds of his colony. They were all born and raised in the area, so he knew where it was safe to travel. He knew the bridges were gone near Georgetown, but there were still boats that could be salvaged from marinas, and he could use the Intracoastal Waterway to go far enough around the infected and the spiders.

Jed felt energized by the thought and let the slope of the bridge build up his speed to a trot. He kept a watchful eye on the rusting hulks of the cars and trucks that jammed the road and wondered why there were no infected up ahead. As a matter of fact, there were as many vehicles as he would have expected, but there was something about the way they were spread out in some places that made him wonder if they had moved recently.

His suspicions were partly confirmed when he came to a wide gap between vehicles. He almost missed it because there were so many piles of rusty junk in every lane, but one tractor trailer was missing the rig. The trailer had been detached and left where it was, and the rig had apparently been driven away. Cars had been moved aside on the left and the right in a zigzag pattern up ahead, and Jed knew someone had used the bridge since the infection began.

It wasn't exactly a straight path, but it gave Jed the ability to see a longer distance up ahead, and he could spot any unwanted company. The good news was that he made better time than he had on the interstate, and he was able to put more distance between himself and the expanding spider web. It was nice to see trees with Spanish moss hanging from them instead of the stuff that resembled Halloween decorations.

By nightfall they had made such good time that they reached the intersection with Highway 17. He had considered using a shortcut at Longpoint Road that would have saved him a few miles of travel, but it didn't take long to see that it would become a deathtrap. From the overpass on the exit he counted over forty of the infected wandering in his direction. Some of them were already passing directly below him when he peered over the side. None of them were draped in spider webs, which meant the webs hadn't made it that far yet, but the number of infected meant he would have to use buildings as cover to follow the shortcut.

One thing he had learned in six years of survival was that some buildings had been closed since the beginning, and opening them meant letting out the infected trapped inside. Sometimes you could see them pressed up against glass or hear them making that awful moaning, but most of the time you didn't know they were there until it was too late. Buildings were great shelter, but you could also get trapped inside them. A rule he had followed was to always be sure there was a back door.

Jed decided that moving from one building to the next in the opposite direction of the infected was a bad idea, so they passed the shortcut and went straight for Highway 17. He was hoping that the infected were taking the shortcut onto Longpoint Road in larger numbers. If they were, he could make up the time he had lost by skipping the shortcut himself. Jed didn't know how fast that spider web was spreading, but he knew he had to be north of it before he got boxed in.

Judging by the view from the top of the next overpass, Jed could tell life wasn't going to get any easier. There was a steady stream of the infected going south and passing right under him and Mattie.

"What do you think, Mattie? Can you stay really quiet for me? I think we have to go to the same place where all of these infected are going."

Before Mattie could answer, they heard a sound they hadn't heard in a long time. They instinctively ducked lower next to the overpass railing. The sound got louder and was obviously coming in their direction. Mattie lifted her head high enough to see what it was, and Jed pulled her down again. He put his finger over his lips and motioned for her to follow him to the other side of the overpass. If he guessed right, the vehicle would pass below them on Highway 17, and they could see it after it went by. If anyone saw them, they would just think they were infected.

Jed remembered to sit his rifle down on the pavement, but he stood up just in time to see three large vehicles lumber by on the highway below.

"Personnel carriers," he said in a surprised voice.

Mattie turned from the vehicles back to Jed and then to the vehicles again.

"You mean like buses?"

"Yeah, sort of like buses."

"Buses carry persons," said Mattie.

Despite himself, Jed was amused by Mattie's connection between persons and personnel, but it didn't pull him away from the moment. Personnel carriers driving down the road were like seeing civilization arriving.

Jed was too surprised to do more than stare with his mouth hanging open. The three vehicles weaved between the old wrecks that lined the road, and when they came to an infected that was wandering down the centerline, they just ran straight over it. It didn't appear that they even slowed down, and they were so heavy that they hardly even bounced. He shook his head from side to side.

"I wonder what they will do if they come across any of those big spider webs. Let's go, Mattie. We have to move fast so we can find out where those things are going."

It was dusk before Jed and Mattie got close enough to the Yorktown to see that he was correct about where they had gone. There had been a few of the infected for them to avoid, but he had reasoned they would also be going more in the direction of the bridge than Patriots Point. They spotted a fire engine that had a ladder extended to the roof of a building, and he could imagine the scene had been fairly common across the country as people scrambled for the safety of rooftops. It was far better to be trapped on a rooftop than trapped on the ground, and quick thinking firemen had hustled as many people up the ladders as they could. Years later it was helping someone again.

He had only driven past Patriots Point when he was a kid. The last time was when he was in high school, and his football team traveled all the way to Charleston for a game against one of the big high schools. They had been beaten badly, but not so bad that they didn't have fun. The sight of the big bridge and the World War II aircraft carrier was enough to make them feel like they had made it to the championship.

The ship was sinking into the shadows now, and a barrier had been built around Patriots Point by hundreds of containers from the State Ports. The sun was going down on the other side of the ship, and it was getting dark fast, but there was still enough light for Jed to tell where the gate was. All of the containers were placed end to end except one, and it was larger than the others. As a matter of fact, it still had a large sign on it that said it was an oversized load. It was positioned perfectly with its doors facing outward, and Jed didn't doubt there were doors at the other end that he couldn't see.

To their right the containers were stacked in a curving line all the way to the bridge. He studied the layout and would have bet anything that the ends of the containers were all open so people could walk through them in safety. The whole thing resembled a freight train that was sitting still on the railroad tracks.

If Jed didn't have Mattie with him, he would probably be far less cautious, and he would have just gone straight for his target. He wanted to find whoever it was that had gotten his friends killed by building that thing that called the infected dead to come to it. That reminded him. He had far more to worry about now than he had before.

In front of him was an unknown enemy with obvious power. Enough power to defend themselves against the infected, and to some extent the power to control them. They obviously had something in mind for dealing with the infected, but so far they hadn't revealed what that might be. All around Jed were the infected that had been summoned to the bridge. They would attack him and Mattie if they were spotted, but they were so distracted by the invisible pull of the thing on the bridge that they walked with their heads aimed slightly higher than normal, as if they were being called to their creator.

The thought made Jed get an involuntary shiver. What if these people knew how to call the infected to them because they had something to do with the infection in the first place. If he found out they did, he couldn't imagine anything stopping him from letting loose the anger he would feel.

Behind Jed was an even more insidious threat that made Jed realize his options had been narrowed to one, but he was the kind of person who always wanted to know what was beyond the last option. He had to go forward. He had to find out what was happening on the Yorktown, but after the Yorktown secrets were exposed, what was going to stop the billions of spiders that were consuming the remnants of civilization? As total darkness fell around him, Jed felt himself ready to give in to the inevitable.

He gave one more thought to what might lay beyond the Yorktown, and he knew it would depend on what happened on the ship. He wondered if they would treat him and Mattie well in return for warning them about the new threat. He mentally filed the thought away as something to try if they were caught by the people in the Yorktown.

If Jed had been stunned by the sight of the personnel carriers, it was a mild reaction compared to how he felt the next time he turned to face the Yorktown. He was just thinking about whether he should sneak past the barrier of containers or if he should try a more direct approach when he saw something beyond the Yorktown. He hadn't seen any guards yet, but if he could find one and get his attention without getting shot, it might be the best way to at least get away from two of the threats on his side of the barricade, but what he saw made him forget what he had been thinking.

Without regard for being seen by anyone he stood to his full height on the edge of the building and watched the blinking red light descend toward the coast. It was too dark to see where it was going, but from Jed's position it looked like it went straight into the water. Then he remembered what was over there. It was Fort Sumter, and that red flashing light could only have been one thing.

Mattie saw it too, but she hadn't grown up in a world with lights moving through the sky. When Jed stood up, she assumed it was safe to do the same thing, and she saw his reaction to the light.

"Is that a star, Mr. Jed? It's moving, and it's the wrong color."

"No, Mattie, it's something Mr. Jed hasn't seen in a long time."

The loud creak of the hinges on the oversized cargo container tore through the silence of the night. Jed wrapped an arm around Mattie's waist and pulled her back from the edge of the building. He told her to stay put and then crawled just as quickly back to where they had been standing.

Three personnel carriers were driving through the open doors with their headlights brightly illuminating the container. They were either the same ones he had seen or three different ones. There was no way to tell for sure in the low light. He had assumed they had gotten here before nightfall, but he had taken a different route from them. The noise of their engines were enough to distract the infected from the 'zombie-call' on the bridge for at least a few minutes, and if they got delayed by a detour, Jed would have been forced to find a safe hiding place while the infected converged on the area. He figured they would get to Patriots Point long before him, so he chose to cross Mt. Pleasant and use Coleman Blvd.

The doors swung shut as soon as the third personnel carrier was through the opening, and Jed saw why when the crowd of infected emerged from the darkness and pushed up against the container. Whether they were the same vehicles or different ones, Jed saw that he had been right about the attention they would attract. At least fifty of the infected pressed up against the metal doors as if they could see people inside.

On the other side of the wall of containers, the doors were just as loud as they had been on the outside. Jed muttered to himself that the people in charge didn't pay attention to details, and that was a sign that they weren't afraid of much. Maybe they would be more afraid of spiders.

The headlight of the personnel carriers lit up a contingent of guards that Jed hadn't seen before. They were all carrying military style rifles, and Jed wondered what they would have done if he had been seen when he stood up. He told himself not to be stupid again. Then he chuckled when he considered that practically everything he was doing was stupid.

The sound of the engines faded as the vehicles drove toward the Yorktown, and the only noise came from the crowd of infected. They were still hanging around the door, but they were beginning to lose interest in the quiet metal. Jed watched them turn, one by one, and lift their heads in the direction of the bridge.

Jed said out loud in a low voice, "Okay, everyone go home. Nothing to see here."

"I was just thinking the same thing."

The voice had come from somewhere behind him, and Jed was sure he had time to turn, find his target, and shoot, but Mattie was behind him too.

"Take your finger away from that trigger if you want the kid to live," said the voice.

Jed immediately lifted his right hand free of his rifle and held his hand above his head.

"Please just let us go, man. We didn't mean no harm. We're just passing through, trying to stay alive like everyone else."

"Sure you are. I'm sure you'll forgive me if I don't want to get knocked out twice in the same day. Is there anybody else up here with you?"

Jed took a chance and turned his head to face the man as he answered.

"No. It's just me and Mattie."

Jed had heard once that strangers were less likely to hurt you if they knew your name.

"I'm Jed. And that's Mattie."

The man behind Mattie seemed impossibly huge. He was holding a hand gun of some kind loosely aimed toward Mattie.

Jed opened his mouth to say something again, but the man only had to say two words. They were said in a way that made Jed understand the consequences of not obeying.

"Stop talking."

Jed decided that he needed to keep the big guy from overreacting, so he held out one hand toward him palm first. With his other hand he gently pushed the rifle further away. Then he scooted his body across the rough surface of the roof away from the rifle.

"Smart man. You want to live? You need to keep being that smart."

The big man motioned toward the side of the building where the ladder was, and Jed put his hands in front of him as he took a step in that direction. He kept his eyes on the man but held one hand out toward Mattie. The man gave Mattie a slight nudge forward, and she gratefully ran to Jed, wrapping her arms around his leg. There was enough light behind the man that Jed saw he wasn't wearing a uniform.

They crossed the rooftop and climbed down the ladder without talking, and when they reached the fire engine Jed just pulled Mattie off to one side with him. It was quiet except for the sound of the infected that were walking toward the bridge. For some reason Jed could hear the ringing in his ears better, and he wondered if it was because they were so close to the bridge.

Jed saw that the man had taken a moment to pick up his rifle before following them to the ladder. He had it strapped across his back and still had the handgun where he could use it in a hurry if he had to. The man surveyed the area around the truck and motioned for Jed to climb down.

"Nice weapon you got here. Looks like military issue. You don't mind if I keep it, do you?"

Jed didn't bother to answer. He just kept following the silent orders of the big man until they found themselves outside the container doors he had watched the personnel carriers drive through.

The man rapped twice on the door and asked in a loud voice, "Who's on watch tonight?"

It sounded like someone fell down inside the container. It was probably someone who didn't expect to hear a voice outside the door.

"Who wants to know?"

The voice that answered was higher than normal, and the big man seemed to enjoy it.

"Clemenza."

There were hushed voices on the other side of the door as if people were arguing in whispers.

"Prove it," yelled the high voice.

"How about I start pumping lead through this door at you? I'll bet a bullet would ricochet all over in there and get more than one of you."

New sounds came out of the darkness around them as the noise had drawn a few of the infected away from the call of the thing on the bridge.

"It's getting crowded out here. Open the door and you'll see it's me, but if I get bit, I'm coming after everyone who didn't let me in."

His reputation was apparently enough, because the door opened only a few seconds later. Jed and Mattie went through fast, but he still felt a big hand give him a shove. Jed felt the strength in that arm and knew he had done the right thing by not resisting the big guy.

When the guards saw the man, they were openly surprised, and they started talking all at once. A light turned on, and Jed picked Mattie up from the floor. She held tightly to him with both arms and buried her face in his neck. The guards didn't pay much attention to them because they were too busy with Clemenza.

They had learned when the personnel carriers arrived about how Clemenza had disappeared on a trip out to the city and how some guy had come back pretending to be him. Clemenza wasn't amused until he heard that they had the guy in custody on the Yorktown. Jed didn't have a clue what they were talking about, but he decided it was a good time to act innocent. The other guys told Clemenza the rumor was that he had been jumped by at least six people. He asked if there was any proof, and one of the guys said they found the bodies of three people. At least that's what he heard from a friend who knew someone who had been there.

"Someone get me a ride. Tell them I'm coming in with two guests."

A personnel carrier showed up a few minutes later. Someone had shown Clemenza a measure of respect by sending a uniform, and he had plans for the guy who left him tied up in that marina.

Jed and Mattie were escorted from the vehicle into the ship, and he did his best to reassure Mattie when they separated them. He had expected they wouldn't know what to think of them other than the fact that they were lucky to be alive. He knew they would interview them separately, and since Mattie didn't know much about him, she would just tell them the truth. Her parents were bitten, they became infected, and Jed rescued her. They would ask if there was anyone else with them and if they came from a camp. She would tell the truth. He would tell the same story, and their captors would decide they were harmless.

Maybe it would have gone like that if they hadn't thrown him in a cell with Chief Barnes.

21

Sabotage

Contagion Extinction Level - Present Day

The population of Fort Sumter had swollen over the years, but Iris knew every face and every name. It was like back in her days as the mayor of the shelter under Ambassadors Island, and it had just become a habit to pay attention when she was introduced to someone. She couldn't turn a corner without seeing someone she knew, so the shelter felt particularly empty knowing that she wasn't going to see her family when she turned the next one. She would feel better if she knew the Chief had found the rest of the group. At least they would have each other's backs.

She was thinking of Jean as she walked around the next corner. She seemed to be the most worried because her husband was missing, but she was determined to have Kathy come back to find Tom on his feet, so Jean kept herself busy by nursing his wounds. It was like Iris didn't have her eyes focused on things close to her as she thought about people far away, so she didn't even try to stop as she walked straight into someone going in the opposite direction. The couple Iris ran into seemed almost frightened by the collision with her, but she recalled they had just been brought in a few days ago. Maybe they were still jumpy from being out in the open for so many years.

Iris made her apologies, and they did the same. Everyone said they weren't watching where they were going. Then they excused themselves and went their separate ways. It had happened every day back when the world was normal, so she wondered why it was bothering her now.

She shook it off and continued on her way to the command center in the communications room. She was checking again to see if anyone had anything new to report. A radio call, a sighting by a search party, anything that would give them a clue. The only news they had in the last few days was about the wrecked boat that had appeared on the same morning the helicopter had picked them up at the ballpark.

A wrecked boat was only news if it was a wreck they didn't already know about. There were wrecks everywhere, but the Army had sufficient resources to monitor changes around the harbor. This one had a bright red hull that stood out in the morning sun, and it had to have wrecked during the night. Iris couldn't think of how it might be connected to the Chief, but he was somehow bigger than life, and she felt like he was involved in everything that changed if there was no other explanation.

Captain Miller saw her come in and walked toward her. It gave him the opportunity to make eye contact and answer her question before she asked him. He was at a loss for words that could make Iris or anyone else feel better. He had all of the helicopters in the air, and there was so much happening where the horde was making contact with the bridge that he needed to have at least one of them monitoring the situation.

He was just about to give her his best 'good news bad news' report when Sim appeared behind Iris. Iris had been so intent on her thoughts that she not only ran over those people in the corridor, she hadn't heard Sim calling out to her.

Sim had his forehead so furrowed that it looked like someone had drawn lines across his face with a paint brush. He obviously had something on his mind other than asking for updates about Cassandra, which was what Captain Miller would have expected if not for his expression.

"Do you know those people? The ones you ran over back there?"

He hooked a thumb back in the direction of the hallway.

Iris almost shook her head, but the names came to her just as they always did.

"Just their names," she said. "They were picked up on Johns Island a few days ago. Why?"

Sim shook his head and asked, "How long have I been here at Fort

Sumter?"

Iris and Captain Miller were both confused by the way the questions went from one thing to another, and Sim appeared to be just as confused.

"Slow down," said Captain Miller. "What's up? What's that couple have to do with how long you've been here?"

Sim shrugged his shoulders and said, "How come I never knew that a Senator had died here, but they did?"

The death of Senator Thornton wasn't exactly a topic of conversation around the dinner table, especially because his actual death had happened before they had come to Fort Sumter, but mostly because it was accompanied by the death of one of the kids being watched over by the Mud Island Family. It was painful to lose anyone, but the kids were beyond comprehension. Whitney and Olivia didn't need for it to be a topic of conversation around Fort Sumter, but Captain Miller was confused about how the topic connected with the newcomers. He couldn't have made his voice sound more deadly when he got Sim to stop talking.

"Don't ask me about that again, Sim, but I need to know in as few words as possible what they said."

Between the expression on his face and his choice of words, Sim knew he had walked into a minefield, and he did what almost anyone would do. He stopped talking and stared into Captain Miller's eyes. What he saw was something dangerous.

He hesitated as he searched for the right words, and he knew his friend wanted him to cut out everything extra and get to the bottom line. They had said something about the Senator who died at Fort Sumter.

"They asked me if I knew when the Senator died, or how long ago he died. Something like that."

Sim wanted to ask Captain Miller why the question had him ready to self-detonate, but he could see his answer didn't make him any happier.

Iris had never learned the details. She only knew enough to know the Chief considered it to be one of his biggest failures, and there was nothing she could do to make him feel better about it. It was just left alone as one of the tragic losses that came along with the infection. She put a hand on Captain Miller's forearm, and he looked down at it like he had forgotten she was standing there. He also didn't realize that he was squeezing Sim's wrist so hard it had to hurt.

"Sorry," he muttered and seemed to shake something off. "Sim, I'm sorry, I have no right to do that to anyone."

Sim could see something new in the Captain's eyes, and he wasn't sure what to say, but he didn't need an apology.

"Jim, I'm sorry, man. There's obviously more to this than I realized."

Captain Miller held up his hand in a gesture they had used on patrol together when he wanted to let everyone know it wasn't safe, and he swiveled his head to see who might be close enough to hear. Sim stopped talking and leaned closer to Captain Miller and Iris so the Captain could speak in a lower voice.

"This is very important, Sim, so I want you to think about your conversation with them. Did it sound like they knew it was a long time ago?"

When Sim thought about it, he knew exactly what his impression had been at the time.

"No, as a matter of fact, I felt like they thought I had actually known the Senator here at the shelter. I got to meet the President up in Ohio, but I didn't know anything about no Senator."

Captain Miller was about to say something else, but it was Iris who signaled for quiet this time.

"I know what's been bothering me about those two," she said. "Forget the obvious clues like the condition of their clothing and shoes, their recent haircuts. The man didn't need a shave when we found them, and he didn't have a used razor in his backpack. All of those things can be explained away, even the fact that they don't appear to be starved. But one thing is different about them than anyone else we've brought in. They ask the wrong questions."

"How did they react when you said you didn't know about the Senator?" asked Captain Miller.

"Now that you mention it, they suddenly remembered they had to be somewhere," said Sim.

"Who processed them?"

This time the question was to both Sim and Iris, but they both answered together.

"Jean."

******

The third phase of the plan to destroy as many of the infected as possible had turned out to be the most difficult despite the fact that the construction of the container wall on the bridge and the installation of the huge dish required the most manpower. Finding something that would eliminate them, besides blunt force trauma, was hard enough, but once it was discovered there was the question of the delivery vehicle. Dispersing it in a way that would make it reach enough of the infected would require ingenuity, because they didn't have the luxury of finding and testing their weapon on a large enough population of the infected.

If they had discovered a sound wave that summoned the infected and then destroyed them, they would have done so from the start, but the only thing Anton Mikhailov could isolate was a nerve agent that worked the same way on the living as it did the infected. One microscopic grain of the toxic powder was enough to turn the brain to jelly. When he demonstrated it for Marshall Sayer and Ted Atwater, they weren't impressed. As a matter of fact, they told him the only reason the Russians didn't know the US already had that nerve agent in their possession was because it was an illegal weapon. Mikhailov was fairly sure the Russians already had it in their arsenal too.

The problem wasn't just dispersal in combat. It was safe handling and storage of the agent. A few ounces were enough to contaminate a million gallons of drinking water, and Marshall wasn't too happy to have it on his ship. He told the scientists to find another way to eliminate the infected.

Several weeks of research on the tissue extracted from the bodies of the infected always led back to the same conclusions. The brain tissues were producing neurotransmitters that shouldn't be produced in a dead person, and muscles were responding that shouldn't be. Those were not conclusions that could be used to eliminate them, and the first of the infected to respond to the summons were already arriving. The camp at the SPA reported that the infected that usually hung on their fence had left, presumably in the direction of the Yorktown. As they arrived, most of them found their way into the current of the river, but many stumbled up the Arthur Ravenel Bridge and pushed against the steel walls of the containers.

The infected pushed on the containers and Marshall Sayer pushed at Anton and Dr. Williams, but the scientists were as immovable as the steel walls. Their problem wasn't a lack of understanding. It was a lack of time, and they told their boss he had to either get on board with helping them find a way to disperse the agent, or he could get himself a hammer and go back to blunt force trauma. It was Ted who persuaded him not to feed them to the infected. For one thing, they needed the doctors, and for another, Ted knew he was likely to be the next one in line after the doctors were gone, probably being blamed for not stopping Marshall from killing the doctors.

Marshall finally gave in and met with them to talk about what would work, and they explained their best plan. The agent would be effective over a large area even if it was windy. It was so potent that it could be dispersed as a fine spray that the victim wouldn't feel it on the skin. The brain would be destroyed in seconds. The problem with spreading such a potent agent was that the persons given responsibility for spreading it wouldn't know if they were being contaminated until they began dropping over, so they had to be wearing protective gear, and hopefully dispersing the agent from above the infected in order to maximize coverage.

The picture began to become clearer that the scientists were talking about using something Fort Sumter had but they didn't. They needed the helicopters, and getting them wasn't going to be as simple as asking for them.

******

Captain Miller had been a career military man, and he wasn't one to sit around and wait for the next bad thing to happen. He didn't realize how much he had depended on the Chief's input until he didn't have him to share his thoughts with. The Chief was able to balance the military and civilian needs so well that Captain Miller was able to focus on the military logistics. Right now he was torn between those needs, but he knew he had to move fast. He didn't know exactly what he was dealing with, but he didn't have time to worry about feelings being hurt.

His first order went out through the entire shelter, and he commanded all civilian personnel to remain exactly where they were. The stunned population stood in silence as they listened to his very stern warning that any civilian moving within the shelter would be considered an enemy combatant and shot on sight. The soldiers on duty were armed, and the second command was directed to them to draw their weapons and hold all civilians in place. Off duty personnel were to arm themselves immediately and assemble with on duty soldiers.

Not in the entire existence of the colony inside the Fort Sumter shelter had there been such orders, but that was likely to be the reason why it worked so well. Everyone knew that something extraordinary had happened to cause such an event. Throughout the shelter the soldiers did their jobs, and the civilians who had come to know the soldiers as their protectors were frightened.

Captain Miller desperately wanted to key the microphone and offer assurances to the people who were hearing his voice. He didn't have to see their faces to know that they reflected their fear, but most of all the betrayal. As a struggling outpost of humanity, relationships had grown between the two groups. There were marriages, and some of the older civilians had practically become parent figures to the youngest soldiers. It was a close knit community, and right now they looked at each other with suspicion. The worst part was that they didn't even know why.

Captain Miller continued his announcement with instructions for the medical staff, military and civilian, to evacuate the shelter. It was painful to single out anyone to survive while leaving others to die, but Captain Miller knew one of the first rules of engagement with an unknown enemy was to ensure your medical support system was in place to minimize the extent of casualties. As he finished that part of the order he lifted his eyes to the clock in the command center and wondered how much time he had, or if he was already too late.

The next order that was broadcast over the shelter's intercom system was given with the fear that he might already be too late. Everyone could tell he was out of breath when he spoke.

"Effective immediately, do not eat or drink anything. I repeat, do not eat or drink anything. If you have something in your hands that can be consumed, put it down."

He probably didn't need to say more, but for added effect he yelled, "NOW."

There were plenty of people in the mess hall being watched by armed guards, but they had already stopped eating when their appetites had disappeared with the first order. The people waiting for further orders behind the serving lines backed away from the food as if it was going to attack them. Throughout the shelter, there were similar reactions, but the gravity of those first orders had largely stopped people from doing anything that involved movement of their hands.

An hour earlier he had his revealing conversation with Sim and Iris, but he had moved quickly in sixty minutes. He located Jean and the team of processors assigned to monitor the couple that had been brought in from Johns Island. They all agreed the Corrigans had walked a fine line between suspicion and believability. They were smart enough to have survived, but they had failed some of the tests that were given to survivors at times when they didn't even know they were being tested.

It was easy to catch someone off guard with a test because there were so many jobs being performed around the shelter at any given time. All new people were given small chores on their first day, and everyone who had already been processed knew about the tests.

Denise had been given kitchen duty and because they were found on Johns Island, the processors knew exactly which test to give her. All smiles and trying to fit in with the rest of the survivors, she had arrived in the kitchen and tied a crisp white apron around her waist. Expecting to open a can and prepare food from storage, she was handed a rabbit that had been trapped that morning. Anyone who had survived six years in an area with dwindling supplies would have had the opportunity to clean a fresh kill. She stared at the rabbit as if she didn't know which end was which. One of the other women stepped up and showed her how it was done, but her revulsion wasn't something she could hide.

The processors notified Jean, and she added the information to their profile folder. Jean had just received the report about a similar test given to Phillip. Captain Miller found her in the infirmary, and she was scanning the report. It said Phillip Corrigan was taken on a routine run with a boat because their story said they had escaped from Mt. Pleasant by boat. He had failed every aspect of safe boating, and if it had been a normal world he would not have survived as a recreational boater. When Captain Miller appeared at her door, she somehow knew why.

"How bad is it?" she asked.

"I don't know yet. It depends on one thing. Did you read their property inventory?"

Jean realized she had glanced at it, but maybe things had gotten too easy for them since they had returned from New Orleans. She should have viewed everything as a potential threat, but unlike the time she had risked her life trying to disarm an explosive device on a dock, she hadn't listened to any silent alarms that should have rung when they brought in the Corrigans. She thought about their inventory and heard the alarms now.

Every survivor they found had something personal they clung to as a token of their former lives. A picture, a cross, a wristwatch, a pocket knife, or anything else that had played a part in their survival. There was always something, but the Corrigans had nothing of sentimental value. Some people still had their wallets with their drivers license in it, but the main thing was there was always something that meant they had clung to humanity, clung to their survival.

Jean slipped the list out of the folder and held it where she and Captain Miller could both see it together. The Corrigans had both been carrying backpacks, and there were the expected survival items everyone tried to find, but the processors who listed the items had done a good job making notes in the margins, and several things were obvious. Jean was embarrassed to have ignored them.

Each backpack had contained a box of matches, and the Sergeant who itemized the inventory had taken the time to note that each box was labeled to hold fifty matches, and each box contained exactly fifty matches. The odds against having two unused boxes of matches were unquestionably high.

Jean scanned ahead on the list, her eyes searching for one thing. She found it and checked the note next to it.

"Why didn't I see this?" she asked as she put her finger on the note.

Captain Miller saw that she had found they carried a bottle of aspirin. A survivor in the infected world would treat aspirin like gold because there were so many bad things that could happen without it. The note said the bottle still had its original plastic seal around the top.

"This list reads like their backpacks were issued to them before they were dropped off in the field," said Captain Miller. "What else was unusual?"

"Remember that kid who was found last year who still had a candy bar in his pocket that his mom had given him for his birthday?" asked Jean. "He finally ate it, but when he unwrapped it we learned to check chocolate if any was carried in with survivors. It's almost always ashy in color or melted into a new shape. It says here they had a fresh candy bar."

The backpacks had been like most survivors in many ways because things took on a new value when you didn't know if you would ever need it again. Ziplock bags were precious because they kept things dry, and the match boxes were bagged. There were dry socks that were old and worn, a manual can opener, tweezers, toothbrushes with a partially used tube of toothpaste, and dental floss with a fish hook tied to it. Captain Miller pointed out that it was a nice touch and that it wasn't the first one he had found in a survivor's backpack.

Captain Miller held the list at an angle to let the light hit it better.

"There aren't any notes next to these things. It looks like the pen was running out of ink, and someone made a scribble over here to get more ink to come out, but they didn't finish. What happened to the containers of powdered milk and the bottles of water?"

Jean turned pale.

"I think someone started to write that it was new. That looks like an 'N' where the pen ran out of ink."

All survivors carried water bottles in their backpacks. There was never going to be a shortage of plastic even now that no more of it was being made, but typically it was noted on the inventory sheet that it had been disposed of. The same was true of the powdered milk. The shelter had enough powdered milk to last until the next century, and survivors seldom had enough of it that made it worth keeping, but if it was still in a sealed container, it might have been sent to the supply rooms.

The shelter remained at a complete standstill with one exception. Denise Corrigan was under armed guard in the laundry room, ironically where the Senator had wandered after his death. There was no way she could slip out and escape without being seen because there was a guard at each door. It was a bit hot in the room, but she was sweating more than the other workers. She only hoped Phillip hadn't done his part of the assignment yet. If he had, then they were as good as dead along with everyone else in the shelter.

******

Chief Barnes knew what effect he had on people when they first saw him, but this one was new. The man who was tossed into the cell with him was fairly large, too, but his reaction was like he had just seen a ghost. He pointed an index finger at the Chief, and then he looked back down the hallway to the steel door to the cell block. For some reason he pointed his finger at the door, but he seemed to be at a loss for words. The Chief decided to help him out by speaking first.

"Joshua Barnes, but my friends call me Chief."

He held out a large hand to the confused African American by the door.

"Not Clemenza?" the man managed to squeak out in a higher than normal voice.

The Chief had an awful thought and for the first time realized letting someone live might have been a mistake.

"No, but that explains the look on your face. Did you see a big guy out there who looked a little like me?"

"More than a little like you. Are you sure you aren't brothers?"

"We should be."

He saw that didn't help the new guy understand so he added, "We were both Navy SEALs, so we should behave like brothers, but it looks like he was recruited by the other side."

"Jed Ambrose," he said as he shook the Chief's extended hand. "Do you know what's happening here? I mean, are these people using that thing on the bridge to call those dead things?"

"That's my best guess, but why they're doing it, I don't know. I've seen it from above, and if I told you how many of those things are out there, you wouldn't believe it."

"Try me. I've been on the ground with them, and believe me when I tell you it's hard to go anywhere around here without running into them. Whatever it is they have in mind, I doubt that they know what they started."

Something about the way Jed said it made the Chief feel like they weren't talking about the same thing anymore, and Jed had taken a seat on the bench that ran along one wall and buried his face in his hands.

"You don't think that barrier on the bridge will hold?" asked the Chief.

Jed didn't answer immediately, and the Chief was just about to ask him again when Jed said, "What they did to us just wasn't fair. They had no right. We've been doin' all right on our own, and we were just about to have things better, but they couldn't leave it alone. I mean, what right do they have to decide who lives and dies?"

"You and family were on this side of the horde?"

"Horde?"

Jed had to think about it a second. Now that he was actually in the place with the people who created that thing on the bridge, he knew that he hadn't really thought about what he was going to do when he got here. He had killing on his mind. He wanted revenge, but it never occurred to him that the people behind the deaths of everyone in the path of the horde might be hard to beat. Then he remembered.

"You can forget about the horde, man. At least you can see them coming and hit them in the head. You can't hit no bug in the head."

The Chief hadn't been having one of his best days, to say the least. He had fallen for a trap when he got into the back of the BATT-T with his friends, but he wasn't licking his wounds. It was a smart trap, and he had to hand it to whoever it was who thought of it. When the vehicle stopped next to the aircraft carrier he wasn't too surprised to find out it was the unknown group from the Yorktown that had captured his friends. How they were treated was going to decide for him how to deal with the people. He didn't plan to make enemies of them if he didn't have to. For all he knew, they were just paranoid of him and his friends at Fort Sumter.

A rattling at the door of the cell block made the Chief forget for the moment what Jed had said. It still registered, but he thought the man might just be ranting about something that had driven him crazy over the last six years.

For a second time the Chief was amazed that he had never come across Clemenza in the Navy, but in different light he saw the man was much younger than him. He had probably become a SEAL after the Chief had retired. Now he was standing on the other side of the bars, and the Chief didn't like the way he was flexing his fist.

"Well, can you believe this? What were the odds that we'd see each other again?"

The Chief was never afraid to exchange smart comments, and he always had one ready.

"I would say far better than they would have been if I hadn't given you a break."

"We'll see if we can't go over that little meeting a second time, old man. The boss wants to see you or we'd be taking care of that question right now. You're lucky he told me not to hurt you....yet."

The Chief knew there was a time to fight and a time to get answers, and this was not a time to fight. He walked up to the bars and squeezed both hands through together. Clemenza shook his head but didn't say anything, so the Chief turned around with his back to the bars and pushed his hands through again. He felt the cuffs close on his wrists.

"You know those things aren't really necessary as long as you have my friends locked up around here somewhere."

Clemenza apparently didn't think much of his bosses because something really amused him.

"You got away with pretending to be me once already. You could walk into the boss's office and pull it off again. Not gonna happen,

Chief."

Clemenza didn't bother to put a bag over the Chief's head. He explained that he didn't want to spend all day walking him up to officer's country and having to warn him every time he was ready to trip or bang his head on something. Of course the Chief thanked him in his most sincere voice.

If nothing else, it was an opportunity for him to learn enough of the ship to think about his escape plan. With a little luck someone would give him an idea of where his friends were so he wouldn't have to search when he made his break.

People gave them a wide berth as they crossed what had been the main hangar deck of the old warship. Restored aircraft still occupied a corner, but the current occupants of the Yorktown had little if no concern for history, and they had dismantled some of the planes to make space. They had squeezed more people into the ship at the beginning of the infection than they had planned, and most of the hangar deck was partitioned as a huge set of barracks.

When they passed through corridors, people going the other way changed directions when they saw them coming. He couldn't say he blamed them. Eventually there were less people, and it was quieter, and the Chief knew they were close. A man stepped into their path, and instead of moving out of the way, his mouth broke into a huge smile.

"Well, what do we have here?"

Ted Atwater had always wanted to meet this man. If they hadn't seen him at a distance, they wouldn't have believed he was as large as his legends.

"I would shake your hand, Mr. Barnes, if it wasn't tied behind your back. You deserve some credit for surviving this long without a plan."

That struck a nerve with the Chief. He believed in plans, but he didn't believe you could plan for everything. He just didn't like having this little man who was so obviously a politician acting like he had a better plan. The fact was, they had both survived from the beginning, and the Chief felt like he had done all right. He also didn't like being called Mr. Barnes.

Atwater opened the door to the stateroom and stepped in ahead of the Chief. Clemenza followed as they walked into the sitting area in front of the big desk. Marshall Sayer leaned back and studied the Chief. Atwater motioned for Clemenza to remove the handcuffs, a move that he clearly disagreed with. He reluctantly gave into the icy glare from both of his superiors, but he was surprised a second time when he was told to wait outside.

The Chief kept his expression neutral and considered the likelihood that there would be an easy escape from this room. His conclusion was that it was more likely to be yet another trap, so he decided it was a time to behave. Besides, he didn't have to like these people to strike a deal with them.

The Chief rubbed his wrists, and for good measure he gave Clemenza a wink as he was leaving. The look he got back said volumes about what their next fight would be like, if there was one.

Marshall said, "Chief Barnes, welcome to the Yorktown."

He motioned to one of the chairs while Ted Atwater took the other one.

"I would offer you refreshments, but we are pressed for time and need to get down to business. I understand you still have at least three helicopters at Fort Sumter. I don't have the luxury of time to beat around the bush, so I'll just come right out and say it. I need for you to have the helicopters delivered to me immediately."

The Chief didn't know why the man was in such a hurry. As a matter of fact, he had expected them to at least entertain him with some kind of agreement or court him to see if he would consider changing sides, but this man was acting like there was a fuse burning somewhere. The man in the other chair still wore the broad smile on his face, but he was so motionless that the Chief felt like the man was afraid of delaying the Chief's answer.

"The helicopters don't belong to me, they belong to the Army. Well, one of them kind of belonged to me, but I crashed it."

Marshall Sayer didn't show the slightest hesitation when he answered.

"The Army works for me. As the head of the joint agency I control, I carry the rank of General, so I am ordering that they be turned over to me."

The Chief didn't have a clue why the man thought he could order Captain Miller to do anything, but something told him he needed answers. Maybe it was because he doubted the man's sanity.

"I must have missed something, Mr. Sayer, but what agency are you?"

"I am the director of USAMRIID, and if you don't give us those helicopters, we'll be forced to take them."

There was something about this man that told the Chief that it

280

didn't matter if he held the rank of General or not, only that he believed he was a General. He also felt like he had just been threatened by a poker player who was holding a royal flush. In other words, if he said he was going to take the helicopters, he had in mind a way to do it.

"You can't have the helicopters. Final answer."

The Chief didn't know Clemenza had come back into the room, so he didn't have a chance to brace himself against the punch. Added to the effects of the helicopter crash only a couple of days earlier, the punch was enough to knock him out. When he woke up the next time, he didn't know where he was, only that it was totally dark, and he didn't have much room to move. There was also the faint smell of diesel fuel.

22

Venom

Contagion Extinction Level - Present Day

The container fort at the State Ports Authority had no reason to feel like they weren't safe. After six years of resisting every horde to come their way, it didn't matter that every infected dead on the east coast that was close enough to hear the call was coming this time. Most of them were coming from the other side of the Cooper River, and those that managed to wash up along the docks of the SPA were so water logged they couldn't stand up. The smell was the part that got to the occupants of the fort.

It had taken over a year for the infected to start arriving in large numbers, and it was another three months before they started washing up along the docks, but the smell didn't take a day to arrive after the bodies started to pile up. Then there was a day when so many washed up against the docks that they threatened to dam the Wando River where it joined with the Cooper River. The fort sat on a small peninsula where the two rivers met, and as long as the bodies washed by in the Cooper River, it wasn't a threat to the base. The officers in charge of the Yorktown's land base were afraid for the first time, because a dam across the Wando River would cause water to flow over the walls of the docks and across the entire camp.

Crews were sent out in rubber hip waders to break up the log jam of bodies, sending them back into the current of the river, but it was clear within a few hours that more bodies were arriving than leaving. The water continued to rise and splash over the concrete platforms where dock workers used to unload the containers, and even though the containers had been stacked end to end around the entire perimeter of the fort that faced the rivers, they weren't waterproof. Foul smelling water ran under and between the containers across the camp, and hundreds of workers and guards tried to find higher ground.

As the water rose, the bodies of the infected were pushed over the walls and began to pile up against the containers. As bad as the smell had become, everyone was surprised to see the water draining across the camp into the marshes. For some reason the camp wasn't flooding anymore. It was ironic, but the bodies were stacked so deep against the container wall that they were acting like sand bags. The water rose a few more feet, but the wall of bodies held.

The reprieve was short. The water receded until the camp was dry, but the only warning the people of the SPA got was from the seagulls, and they didn't understand the message. The seagull population had exploded after the infection, and even though it seemed to have at least leveled off, it had never decreased. If you didn't wear a hat or a raincoat, you had no one to blame but yourself, but on this day hats and raincoats weren't enough protection.

The workers in hip waders were standing on top of the containers along the docks using long poles to push bodies far enough away to get caught in the current. When the seagulls began to fall out of the air, the workers were amused at first and stopped to watch. For some reason the birds would land on the bodies and rip away a piece of flesh, rise into the air, but then fall with flapping wings. The first seagull to fly over the camp before falling, bounced off of an armed guard who immediately started screaming and spinning in circles. He pulled the trigger on his rifle as he spun and sent bursts of bullets into the spectators who had emerged from their tents. Then it seemed like the sky fell in as more and more birds spun in the air and crashed into the camp.

The people in the open were the first to realize what was happening to them because they saw it happening to others before they themselves were hit. When they felt the impact of a bird against their own bodies, they knew that the burning pain that followed was from the hundreds of spiders that seemed to explode like confetti over everything. They screamed, they ran, they fell in the mud, and they even tried to reach the river that was already packed full of bodies.

The people in the tents were fighting over the few hazmat suits that were kept at the fort, and the only person to get inside one in time was shot. People from the outside ran into the tents and collided with the people inside. The collisions threw the tiny spiders on everything, and it wasn't long before people were running outside to escape.

Groups of people who ran inside the containers and pulled the doors shut sat in the darkness and waited. They could hear the screaming outside and didn't really understand what was happening until the first screams began inside with them. Unseen in the darkness it was somehow more terrifying, and people who weren't being bitten were screaming in fear. In their fright they forced the doors open and exposed everyone to the crawling death.

The last people to feel the stinging pain of the spider venom were those who reached the personnel carriers. The vehicles were designed to protect the occupants from short term exposure to gas and smoke, so they were the last safe places to be breached. The people who sealed themselves inside weren't the trained operators of the vehicles, though, and none of them knew the protocol for making them airtight. They sat and waited for death to come without knowing that it was crawling in through the simplest place. If anyone had started the engines and pressed the one button that controlled air circulation, they could have driven the vehicles away. Eventually the occupants of the BATT-T personnel carriers flung open their doors and rolled out onto the ground.

The birds continued to fall over the camp that had stood longer than military bases around the world. They fell until the base was almost completely covered with the white feathered bodies that flapped in pain over the backs of the people who had lived in the camp. Before sunset the swollen bodies of the people who had died from spider bites began to stir, and where they could get their feet under them, they managed to stand. By morning the former occupants of the camp were still standing, but they were covered by a milky white blanket, and the spiders moved from one body to the next reaping the harvest of an endless food source.

Sometimes nature manages to do things that man couldn't do, and it seems to do it with less effort. Outside the perimeter of the camp the water pressure against the dam of bodies finally grew until the dam moved. It moved a little at first. It shifted at one end as a great mound of bodies was pushed aside. The water from the Wando River forced its way into the Cooper River carrying tons of bloated bodies downriver toward the harbor.

******

The designers of Patriots Point wanted the maritime museum to feature different kinds of ships, and while the Yorktown was the showpiece, plenty of tourists wanted the opportunity to see the inside of an old diesel submarine. A tour of the USS Clamagore gave people an appreciation for the brave sailors who served on her.

At a length equal to a football field, its size was deceptive because only a small portion of it could be seen above water. Despite its size, it was packed with machinery, weapons, and all of the systems necessary to support a crew of eighty men, so space was a luxury. The crew had to become adept at movement throughout the cramped spaces, but they managed to do so with efficiency. It wasn't meant for men the size of the Chief.

There was no light when he opened his eyes. None seeped through cracks or under doors. It was silent and cool, but it had a familiar feel to it. Not knowing what surrounded him, the Chief stayed motionless. As far as he knew, any movement could be deadly, and he wasn't the kind of person who would panic just because he was disoriented.

That faint smell of diesel fuel was what made him sense familiar surroundings. He had spent enough time on ships to remember waking up to that smell. His first impression was that he was in an engine room, but there were other smells masking the scent of diesel. Fresh paint. Cleaning products. New lubricants. When he processed all of the information it came back as only one possibility. He was inside a ship that had its history scrubbed away as it was restored to new condition.

The Chief thought about the different ships at Patriots Point and which one would fit the profile described by his senses. He could be in any one of them, because they had all gotten facelifts before the public was allowed to see them. The air was breathable, so suffocating wasn't his first concern. To most people the pitch black darkness would be suffocating, but the Chief was intent upon sensing another clue.

The silence would have also made the average person call out into the void to learn if they were alone, but the Chief didn't want to find out that his isolation was shared with the infected. Instead, he listened for the slightest of sounds, and that included breathing. Somewhere in the darkness, someone was trying to hold down fear, but the breathing would be the hardest thing to hide. They would hold their breath for as long as they could, but eventually it would come out faster than they wanted, and they would clasp a hand across their mouth. The attempts to quiet their breathing made it that much more ragged.

The Chief didn't want someone to panic in the darkness because someone could get hurt. If they were armed, they could shoot at the first thing they heard. The Chief lifted one hand and almost delicately explored his surroundings. He began with the surface he was on. Someone had deposited him in a sitting position with his back against a wall. He found the floor and felt the cool raised patten of metal decking that allowed sailors to keep a grip with their feet even when a ship was pitching at sea.

After a minute of searching with one hand, he felt comfortable with using the other, and even though he had never been in a compartment exactly like this one, he was remembering a training exercise when he had made an exit from a submerged submarine. The thought crossed his mind that he would be fine with the idea of being inside one now unless there was an infected inside with him. He had to find a way not to scare the other person to death and to protect himself at the same time, but he had been thoroughly searched on the Yorktown, and anything useful had been taken. He decided he only had one choice, so he lowered a hand to the metal deck, aimed a fingernail downward and tapped.

Part of their survival had been the shelters, and part of it had been what they taught each other. Morse code had been one of their most entertaining classes, and they even had days designated when all communications had to be in code. Not everyone caught on, but not everyone was as serious about survival as the Mud Island Family. The Chief decided to use a prosign, or an abbreviated form of a word that would allow him to say more with just a few taps. He tapped, "dash dot dash dot dash," the one word that meant a message was about to be sent, 'ATTENTION'.

He didn't expect it, but he heard someone relax and exhale. As a matter of fact, more than one person exhaled. A dim battery powered light turned on, and the Chief was amazed to be in a compartment with so many people. He was also overjoyed to recognize their faces, and he wanted to hug all of them. They were just as eager as he was to get in a neck hug, and it was generally a lot of bumping of heads in the confined space. They exchanged hugs and a few kisses, and managed to each get in a few words of welcome. When it all began to settle down, the Chief noticed in the middle of it all there was an extra little person who he didn't know, and she was clinging to Cassandra.

"We have a problem," said Kathy. "Besides the obvious, things are worse than we thought."

"I picked up some of it before they knocked me out," said the Chief, "but I get a feeling you have worse news than mine."

******

Ed

When the Chief had shown up out of nowhere back at the boats, it wasn't as if we didn't expect him to rescue us. He always did. This time it felt wrong, and just a little too easy. The boat ride across the harbor had been the worst ride of our lives, and we were all bumped and bruised by the time we were manhandled out of the boats. We still had hope, though, because having him there was better than not knowing where he was.

After we discovered it had been a trap, we knew we had no choice but to go along with whatever our captors had in mind, and it seemed inevitable that we would make contact with the people on the Yorktown sooner or later anyway. We had hoped it would be under better circumstances, but that ship had sailed.

We were split up as soon as we arrived at the carrier, and we were all questioned separately by Ted Atwater. He got right to the point with what they wanted from us, but it was clear to him that we weren't going to be able to make it happen. There wasn't much sense in guarding secrets they probably already knew about, so we answered his questions. If anything, it seemed to be more in our favor for them to know that we really did have as much power at Fort Sumter as they suspected. The bright side, if there was one, was that Mr. Atwater was the kind of person who didn't like to be intimidated, so he was also free with his information.

The 'bell' was what they had been calling the device at the top of the bridge. I told him we called it the 'zombie-whistle', and I thought he wouldn't quit laughing. He thought it was too funny for my tastes, so I chose that moment to call him a murderer because of the survivors who had probably been overrun by the horde they had created. His laughing turned to a sneer, but then he actually expressed regret and attempted to explain why it was for the greater good.

Atwater told me how USAMRIID had come to possess the

Yorktown, and in his mind, who was better able to deal with this infection than them? They had all of the resources they needed to summon the infected to come closer so they could be exterminated. All they needed was the aerosol delivery system, and we had the helicopters. He explained that they planned to release an agent that would produce death in seconds after contact with an infected, and the agent was effective in such a small amount that there would be enough to eradicate the entire population. The minor problem was that it would have the same effect on living people as it did on the infected.

When I challenged their right to kill the living in order to eliminate the infected, he tried to assure me that once they had eliminated enough of the infected, they would be able to more selectively control who they sprayed. He envisioned a time when living people could walk around with aerosol spray cans targeting the infected. Yes, there would always be collateral damage, but it was also a humane way to die. Atwater was practically excited at the implications when he explained it.

"Imagine it, Mr. Jackson. We could even use it after the infection is over. When someone would die of natural causes, we wouldn't need to use blunt force trauma to ensure they stayed dead. We would simply spray them with the agent."

Listening to him had been like sitting in the front row of a theater during a B rated movie. At least it was until he got down to business about how we were going to give them the helicopters, or we were going to watch them go to Fort Sumter and take them from our dead friends. That was when I knew we had a worse problem than we had known. He told me they had someone inside Fort Sumter who was ready to release the agent, and it would kill everyone within minutes. I thought about Jean, and I was numb from head to toe at the thought that I couldn't do anything to warn her.

I was blindfolded again and practically carried to my new prison. When they dropped me down through the hatch and closed it behind me, I was glad to find Cassandra and Colleen were already waiting with our new addition, Matilda. She said to call her Mattie, but it felt too much like I had Molly here with me.

Cassandra and Colleen had learned the same things I had, but Atwater had given a little more information about his people inside Fort Sumter. He had laughed about how he and his cohorts had skillfully brainwashed an everyday couple into becoming deadly spies, and about how the Corrigans believed the people of Fort Sumter were the real bad guys. If they were asked, they believed us to be nothing more than brutal savages living off of what we took from other survivors. The very proof was evident by the fact that we had their helicopters.

Hampton and Kathy showed up next. Kathy was the most furious of the group because Ted Atwater found her so attractive he thought he could seduce her into helping them. She was untied and her blindfold removed to find he had arranged a hot bath complete with soap bubbles. She said there was an ice bucket with champagne chilling next to the tub, but the worst part was that there were two glasses. We considered it remarkable that he had survived the interview, but Kathy got some satisfaction out of describing it.

Despite our situation the encounter between Kathy and Atwater added some levity for a brief time. It lifted our spirits until Mattie told us she was worried about Mr. Jed. We listened intently as she explained through a child's eyes how her parents had gotten sick and tried to hurt her. Mr. Jed saved her, and they were trying to find the bad people who had made the machine that was making the spiders crazy. Then she added, "Oh, and the 'fected."

My first thought was how much I hated the word spiders, let alone the way they seemed to crawl out of nowhere. Out of reflex my eyes glanced around at the maze of pipes and overhead conduits that snaked through the submarine, and I aimed one of the battery powered lights we had found mounted to the walls in each compartment toward a dark corner.

"Easy, Ed," said Kathy. "The inside of this thing couldn't be cleaner. Go on, Mattie."

Mattie explained that Mr. Jed had noticed the spiders were angry everywhere, and he had pointed out the 'white stuff' that was hanging from trees and buildings. We had all noticed the abundance of webs but had chalked it up to a natural explosion of the insect population. More dead people meant more bugs. More bugs meant more things that ate bugs, and that was spiders. More spiders meant more spider webs. We had seen the same thing happen with rats, so we had expected it to happen with insects. What we didn't count on was the theory from Mattie's friend, Mr. Jed, that the zombie-whistle was also making the spiders crazy.

As a native of Georgetown, Hampton had spent enough time in the woods to learn the dangers of camping in the wrong place. He asked Mattie to describe the webs, and he heard enough to confirm that they were the most deadly species found in the area. He gave us a general description of their bodies and the violin shape on their backs, but he said you could almost always recognize them by their narrow legs. He gave us the bad news that it appeared they were the next population explosion as a result of the infection, and they probably would have kept to themselves until the population adjustment occurred if they hadn't been disturbed by the zombie-whistle.

Out of instinct, we scrambled away from the compartment we were in when we heard it being unlocked. We turned off the lights and waited quietly. It was dark outside, so all we saw was a shape lowered then dropped into the compartment with us. We shrank into our corners and waited because we all thought the same thing. They had dropped an infected inside with us because we hadn't cooperated, and they were using it as a way to get the Chief to give in. It might have worked on me even though I couldn't have given them the helicopters if I had wanted to.

When we all heard the Morse Code prosign alerting us to an incoming message, I think we all thought it came from Kathy for a split second, but the collective sigh of relief from the group was the joint realization that we were back together again. We weren't better off than we had been, but we had our most potent weapon assembled when there were enough of the parts present. We started working on a plan.

******

A flare from the Yorktown was supposed to tell Phillip and Denise whether or not to release the agent, but if they couldn't be at a place where they could see a flare, they were instructed to release it no later than noon of their fifteenth day inside. The lockdown had taken away any opportunity they may have found to watch for a flare.

Going in on the first day they had learned that the outer doors were being sealed, and people wouldn't be allowed to exit to the surface. They would be allowed to go outside through a tunnel that came out somewhere on Morris Island, but they had not reached that level of shelter access yet. They were given the opportunity to watch televised events on the harbor, but the televisions were only on for a few minutes at a time, and it wasn't likely they would just so happen to be watching when a flare was sent up. They were told the broadcasts were only done as a way of keeping people happy with the confines of the shelter. Being underground could get to you after a while, but it was easier to accept when you were reminded of the situation outside.

The broadcasts were less frequent because they were so disturbing, and it was hard to watch as thousands more infected plunged over the edge of the bridge into the river. So, the Corrigans had counted the days. On the day of the planned release, they had anxiously worked on permission to get some fresh air outside, and the best they could do was hours behind schedule. That meant they would need to finish their shifts in the shelter, release the agents, and get out before it spread throughout the shelter complex. There were also far more people living in Fort Sumter than they had expected, and they hadn't been the barbarians they were made out to be. They had their doubts, but they were set to carry out the plan until the announcement that had everyone frozen in place.

A detail of soldiers came into the laundry, and she wasn't really surprised when they walked directly to her. She had already heard more than one person say that they had never seen the shelter go on lockdown before, and it had to be someone new they were looking for. They all knew she was the most recent addition to their work crew.

Denise was taken to the elevators and escorted directly to the command center. She had never spoken with Captain Miller, but she knew who he was. The tall, gray haired woman next to him was somewhat of a folk hero because she was part of the inner circle that ran the shelter, but she couldn't remember her name.

"Where's your zombie-whistle?"

The question was delivered without preamble or courtesies, and she knew that they had found out about their plan. She also knew that Phillip was probably in position to release the agent and had only delayed because he didn't know if Denise would make it out of the shelter in time.

As for Phillip, he knew that he wouldn't. With an order for everyone to remain in place or be shot, he could still release the agent, but he couldn't possibly make it from the shelter power plant to the tunnel without being seen. He could hear the soldiers not far from him. They were at the only exit to this part of the ventilation system. If he released the package of powder into the central air ducts in front of him, it would reach every room within the hour. Marshall Sayer had explained that there might be only one chance to destroy millions of the infected, and the lives of a few people were a small sacrifice. He wondered how it had come to this.

* * *

******

Jed didn't need to see more than one of the spiders to understand what was about to happen. As he told the people at the picnic table so long ago, where you find one, you'll find more. It had set up house in the corner of his cell, and for some reason it had crossed the confined space in the middle of the floor. Jed knew brown recluse spiders didn't do that. He backed up to the door and screamed for someone to let him out, but if the spider hadn't kept going, he would've stepped on it.

A guard appeared and immediately teased Jed about being afraid of little bug, but the man could see he was beyond afraid. He didn't think he had ever seen a grown man become so frantic, but he was screaming that more were coming. The guard was in the process of getting the prisoner to calm down when he saw it for himself.

Even though the cells were dimly lit, he could see something moving on the back wall of the corner cell. Until recently the doctors had kept the cells full of the infected, and there was never a reason to go in or out of the cell block unless it had to do with getting another of the vile smelling creatures for an experiment. He couldn't see the web that filled the corner of the dark cell, but when the spiders erupted from the hole in the floor where it met the rusty bulkhead, their movement made it look like one animal climbing the wall. He shined his flashlight on it, and what he saw made him scream along with Jed.

"Don't try anything," he yelled at Jed as he fumbled with the keys.

"I don't plan to, man. Just let me outta here. I don't wanna die like this."

As soon as the lock opened, Jed was out the door and headed for the passageway out of the cell block. The guard was right behind him, but he was less concerned about guarding Jed and kept looking back over his shoulder as they ran. He could swear there were already spiders coming out of the cell he had just opened and running between the cells after them. Jed was going too slow for him and he decided no one would know that he had let him out of the cell. At the next turn Jed went straight, but the guard made a right and disappeared. Jed didn't know, and he didn't really care where the guard had gone. The guard made the mistake of going down a flight of stairs, and when he saw what was already filling that deck, he went back the way he had come, searching for a fire alarm pull station.

Jed came to a door that he figured might be a way to the upper decks because it was so heavy, but when he pulled it open, he felt like he had gone into a different world. The lab was brightly lit with overhead fluorescent lights, and people worked at microscopes and other equipment he wouldn't have recognized. In the far back corner he could see the isolation chambers, and behind the thick glass were rooms full of the infected. The lab technicians paused from their work and stared in his direction.

"I think I saw this movie. First spiders, and now this. I'm on the wrong floor."

Jed didn't even bother to close the heavy door, and this time he decided he would only go through doors that took him up. The main elevator opened as soon as he pressed the button, and he jumped inside. He furiously punched at the button that was supposed to close the door, and when it did and the elevator lurched upward, he backed into the far corner as if it would be safer there.

Alarms sounded throughout the ship, and everyone did what they usually do. They turned to the person nearest to them for an explanation. The fact was, the security personnel on the ship never had drills, so they assumed it was either a fire drill or there were infected trying to board the ship. Either threat seemed to call for the same response, so everyone headed for the main flight deck. When the elevator doors opened, Jed came out of an unguarded elevator and joined in with the mass exodus to the outside.

Below decks hundreds of people were already cut off by the spiders that were attacking instead of running. Their filaments trailed out behind them as they made their assault on the screaming people who were furiously running their hands through their hair to comb out the creatures that bit with such fiery pain. Within minutes the stairwells were blocked and the millions of spiders that had been breeding in the lower levels came out for food.

Anton was inside an isolation chamber with Dr. Williams, and they didn't hear the chaos in the lab until the alarm sounded and the revolving lights turned red. Through the glass they saw their assistants in their white coats slapping at their faces and inexplicably pulling out their hair by the roots. They watched from the safety of their hazmat suits and the closed isolation chambers as the people fell to the floor writhing in agony.

They could stay inside the chamber indefinitely, but that was a bleak future at best. The spiders covered the lab personnel with webs so quickly that the room was blanketed in minutes. It was the fluorescent lights. The spiders didn't like the lights, so they were building their webs to block out the light. It wasn't long before the two doctors couldn't see through the milky webs that covered their windows, but they could see all too well what moved inside them.

23

All Good Plans

Contagion Extinction Level - Present Day

None of us expected the submarine to move, but it was such a sudden lurch that we tripped or fell toward one side. It happened after we decided the answer to our escape had to be somewhere inside the boat. What if the people who restored her considered the possibility of someone being trapped inside? Stranger things could happen. When we talked about it, we realized what an insanely understated comment that had been considering the work was done on the sub before the infection. We agreed there had to be something onboard that would be useful, and we began our search.

Two hours had turned up some interesting items that would come in handy later, like a hand operated generator with a solar panel. It would make a welcome addition to a survival pack, but considering the equipment we had in the shelters, it was like finding a book of matches. What we were hoping to find was an instruction manual labeled 'In Case of Emergency'.

We were spread out in the ship to keep from searching the same compartments as someone else, and we had found the sub to be much bigger than we had thought. We reported back periodically, but I think we were hoping to find someone had found the ultimate can opener. Once we regained our footing we all stopped and listened. There was nothing.

We all made our way back to the control room under the hatch as if we expected the door to open next.

"How much force would it take to make a ship this size move like that?" I asked.

Cassandra and the Chief had the most experience with big ships, so we all looked expectantly at them for the answer. Cassandra shook her head, but it wasn't because she didn't know. It was because she couldn't believe it had happened.

She said, "I can't think of anything that could have used that much force against the hull. At least not anything that could be out there."

"This thing weighs about fifteen hundred tons," said the Chief. "The only thing I can think of that could move another ship like that would be a tugboat."

The Chief made his comment and directed it at Cassandra for confirmation. Her eyebrows went up.

******

Jed worked his way free from the crush of bodies trying to get to the flight deck. There were too many people trying to get outside at the same time, and he had a different idea. He didn't just want to get outside. He wanted to get off of the ship. The people climbing the stairs to the outside didn't know what was chasing them, and they didn't know it was already inside the ship with them.

Everyone else was going up, so Jed chose to go to the back of the ship. There were still signs for tourists that pointed toward restrooms and gift shops or food courts, but for some reason he thought the one that said FANTAIL was the best choice. He was surprised to find himself outside on the back of the ship with the flight deck extended out over his head. The best part was the thick, two inch mooring line that was tied to the back of the fantail and extended all the way to the dock next to the old submarine parked behind the Yorktown. It didn't matter that the two inch line had been added as decoration. It was something he could climb down.

Jed had one leg over the railing and was reaching for the line when he was yanked back by the skin on the back of his neck.

"Goin' somewhere?" asked Clemenza. "How did you know I put that little girl in there?"

He motioned with his head in the direction of the submarine, and Jed realized Clemenza thought he knew where Mattie was and planned to climb down the rope to rescue her.

"You wouldn't have anything to do with the alarms being tripped, would you?"

Jed felt helpless, and at the moment he felt like everything was going right and wrong at the same time. He had no clue Mattie was in the submarine until Clemenza told him, but he had no way to help her with Clemenza holding onto the back of his neck. He had a rope that would take him right to her, but unless he started climbing really soon, he was going to die with the rest of these people.

As if he needed confirmation, screams carried out to the fantail from the hangar deck. The big ex-SEAL didn't put Jed down before he walked across the fantail and looked back inside. His eyes narrowed as he watched people falling where they were, fighting an invisible enemy. Comprehension dawned on his face, and he walked back to where he had caught Jed climbing over the railing. He put his face in front of Jed's.

"Can you swim, man?"

Jed barely had the opportunity to answer before Clemenza threw him over the railing.

"Whatever," said Clemenza. "Not enough time to climb the rope."

Jed managed to get his feet under him so that he wouldn't hit the water at an awkward angle, and as soon as he popped to the surface he was stroking toward the submarine. The big splash behind him announced the arrival of Clemenza, and Jed was willing to bet the big man would swim past him in seconds. When he didn't appear on either side, Jed turned in the water and searched for him. He was already twenty yards away and swimming out of the cove reserved for Patriots Point. The area of water beyond the end of the dock where the submarine was parked was a marina and then the open harbor.

It didn't make sense, but Jed had other things to worry about. He wasn't the fastest swimmer, but it gave him plenty of time to think about how he was going to get into the submarine. He didn't have a clue if the doors were easy to open or not.

On the fantail behind him, the railing collapsed under the weight of the people climbing over it. A group of at least thirty fell together, and most of them were either knocked unconscious, drowned, or were too badly bitten by spiders to recover. Those who were still alive thrashed wildly at the tiny creatures that were clinging to their skin. There was no more room for people to cross the fantail and make the jump, so they piled up through the doorway into the hangar deck.

Jed climbed a ladder onto the dock at the bow of the submarine and turned back in time to see they were beginning to fall from even higher. The spiders had reached the flight deck, and despite the size of the ship, they came from all directions. Hundreds of people who had lived in relative comfort for six years made the jump, but none would survive.

High above the flight deck in the tower that had become Ted Atwater's favorite place to get away from it all, he was trying to get away one last time. He had never brought his boss to his private place, preferring to keep it all to himself, but this time he had led Marshall Sayer to safety. Always one to rely on favors, he was sure his boss would never forget this one.

"Spiders, Ted. Why are there spiders on my ship?" Marshall couldn't believe all they needed for this multimillion dollar operation was a better exterminator, and he had been giving Ted a lecture all the way to the tower.

Ted assured him that he would look into it as soon as they all went away, but Marshall cut him off in the middle of his sentence when he got a sharp pain on his hand. He cursed and smashed the eight legged spider into a sticky mess right where it bit him. Ted was quick with a handkerchief to wipe it away, but Marshall screamed and pulled his arm away as if there were flames on it. The poison from the bite didn't always hurt, but sometimes it was excruciating, and this was one of those times. Ted helped his boss the last few steps to get inside the tower then shut the door.

He got Marshall into a chair and then opened a window facing the deck of the carrier. The screams made them both lean over the opening to watch, and they saw one of the people they had caught the night before. He was standing on the deck of the submarine, and for some reason the submarine was moving.

******

Jed had been right about the hatch on the bow of the submarine. It was dogged shut so tight that he wasn't getting it to budge, and he was running out of time. The cove between the Yorktown and the submarine was already half full of bodies, and if more people chose to fall off the stern of the Yorktown, the spiders would be climbing the sides of the Clamagore in no time. He kept throwing his weight into it as hard as he could, and when the submarine moved under him, he thought he had made it move. He fell over the hatch and stared at the dock. The distance between the submarine and the dock was two feet wider than it had been.

The second time the submarine lurched, he fell over the hatch again, but when he turned his head toward the dock, the distance was still increasing. It was increasing, and so was the speed that the sub was moving away from it. Jed couldn't believe his eyes, but the old submarine was sliding quietly out of the opening with the marina, leaving the bodies in the water behind.

Jed picked himself up from the top of the hatch and got his balance. The submarine was moving slowly and smoothly, but it still bobbed a little and made him slide toward the sides. He wanted to see why the submarine had pulled away from its dock, but every time he tried to see past the sail, he started to slide again. He finally gave up and went back to work on the hatch. He laid his body over the wheel and gave it everything he had while he watched the distance between him and the Yorktown grow.

He was past Castle Pinckney in the middle of the harbor when he felt the wind and spray begin to pelt him, and the water around the submarine began washing against the sub like he had entered a storm. He lifted his head and shielded his eyes against the stinging saltwater only to find himself staring at a helicopter only a few feet above him. Two men in Army uniforms were already lowering themselves toward him, and his first thought was how similar it was to the way the spiders dropped in from above.

One of the soldiers fastened a harness under Jed's arms, but he managed to communicate over the noise that there was someone inside the submarine who needed help. As far as he knew it was Mattie he was trying to rescue. He saw that they understood, and as he was raised into the helicopter, two more soldiers dropped by ropes to replace him. He cheered when he saw the three men use their combined strength to loosen the big wheel on the hatch and give it a spin. The hatch popped open, and he saw someone hand Mattie out to the first man. Then he watched as she was followed by a woman with flaming red hair. He didn't have a clue who she was, but he hardly had a chance to wonder about her as she was followed closely by five more people. The last one he knew as soon as he saw his size, but Jed was on top of the world to know they had been saved.

As the helicopter leaned toward Fort Sumter, Jed got one last glimpse of the Yorktown, and the unmistakable walk of the infected dead from the stern of the flight deck toward the bow was all he needed to see to know the fate of everyone on board. They were already walking over the bow as they tried to reach the beacon that called to them from the tower above the bridge.

******

Ed

There were only a few minutes for introductions in the helicopter, and we were already circling to make our landing on the back of Morris Island before we understood how we had escaped. We still didn't understand why, but the crew of the helicopter at least knew how.

Sergeant Graham told us they were still conducting searches for us even though there were problems at Fort Sumter. They spotted the USS Clamagore being towed toward the Ashley River by a tugboat, and there was one man on the deck of the submarine trying to open the hatch. They had seen plenty of unusual things in the last six years, but a diesel boat on the surface being towed was worth investigating. Besides, it was coming from the Yorktown and things were taking a turn for the worse over there from what they could see.

When they dropped lower over the submarine, the operator of the tugboat cut the line and increased his speed up river. They didn't understand why he did it, but it was obvious that the man on the bow of the submarine needed their help, so they stayed behind to help him. They were happy to see all of us, but they were really surprised when the Chief came out of the submarine, because up to that point they all thought the Chief was the man in the tugboat. If he would have had time to explain it he would have, but the Chief had an idea why Clemenza had done it, and it was enough for him. Once a SEAL, always a SEAL.

As the doors opened to let us out of the helicopter, Jean was the first one there, and I couldn't believe we had survived to be together again. We had seen so many things and faced death so many times, but this was one time when we wouldn't have made it without help. We had been together long enough for me to recognize that the expression on her face was a mixture of happiness to see me alive and sadness over something I didn't know yet.

The Chief was standing near the entrance to the tunnel that led to the back door of Fort Sumter, and judging by the way his shoulders dropped, we could tell he was getting bad news from the soldiers gathered at the door. I saw one of them point toward the other two helicopters as they were coming in for a landing, and as soon as they touched down he was sprinting their way. Iris dropped down from one and threw herself into his arms.

I heard Kathy saying a quiet prayer of thanks that Iris had made it out too. Jean told us quickly that Tom was already at Mud Island because Captain Miller had her evacuate the patients and medical personnel first. Then he pretended to keep the shelter on lockdown and stalled Phillip Corrigan while everyone else got out. He learned from Denise Corrigan that he was going to release the packages of powdered agent into the air circulation system, and that it would take less than an hour to contaminate everything. Jim Miller couldn't broadcast to everyone that the shelter was evacuating, or Mr. Corrigan would have released the agent sooner, but he wouldn't let anyone else go in with him while he got people out. He got everyone out except twelve of his men and two dozen civilians, but he saved hundreds of people.

"He would never have forgiven himself for losing the few that didn't make it," she added.

******

It took a week to make all of the arrangements, but there was a lot to do. After the loss of our good friend everyone gave the Chief his space except Iris, and when he came out to us it was with a whole new plan.

While we waited for the Chief to take the time he needed, Kathy and I talked about what needed to be done. Fort Sumter wasn't habitable. We didn't know how long the agent would be active, but we learned enough about it from Denise Corrigan to know that we couldn't test it. Well, maybe we could if we wanted to push a few of the infected inside and see if they came back out. Human test trials weren't really our thing, though, and we agreed in the Chief's absence to seal the shelter. It was a shame to lose the shelter and the supplies, but we still had Mud Island, Guntersville, Ambassadors Island, and even Columbus if we needed to ship in supplies.

We decided to take all of the civilians to Guntersville because the shelter was bigger and safer. There was also the functional community living in the village above the shelter, and we could continue to support them if needed. The helicopters had already carried most of them there by the time the Chief returned to us. Jed and Mattie had left on the first flight. He said he wanted to stay in the south, but he heard good things about Guntersville. You could go back into the woods because the terrain was a bit harder for the infected to navigate, but he really liked the idea about mild winters that still got cold enough to keep the spider population down. He was interested in hearing more about Sim's friends living across the border in Canada, but he figured they could try Guntersville first.

Lt. Harrelson was next in line for command, and she had the respect of the soldiers because they knew Captain Miller had respected her. The other officers agreed that it wasn't usual for an officer to promote themselves, but they believed she should assume the rank of Captain for the sake of continuity. They all supported a decision for them to maintain a small base at Mud Island where they could resupply when needed, but there was a new threat to the area because of the population explosion of the spiders, and it would take time for the population to balance itself the way the rats did. In the meantime, the Army decided to patrol the lowcountry by air to ensure no one else stumbled into those massive webs. Not to mention the thousands of infected that were added to the area.

We had no intention of going to the Yorktown for the supply of the agent they had produced. According to Denise Corrigan, they had enough of it made that we could probably use it to destroy the horde of infected and the horde of spiders. Besides the obvious risk of going to the Yorktown, we weren't willing to risk the possibility of collateral damage caused by the agent. It wasn't safe to handle, and it never would be because she didn't know how long it would remain active even out in the open.

We did, however, bring to an end the source of the ringing in our ears. It had already done its damage by killing so many innocent people whose only mistake was to be in the wrong place when the thing was turned on. A Navy helicopter delivered one of our missiles into the big dish at the top of the bridge and silenced it forever.

So, the Army had a new plan. Our old plan was to fight back and to regain what had been taken from us, but we had lost too much in this battle, and we had made too little progress. The Army's new plan was to keep people out of the lowcountry, sort of like Russia's old plan for Chernobyl, but at least Russia knew what was there. If we all abandoned Charleston and someone else tried to reclaim it, they would fall prey to things they didn't expect. We hoped it would work out for the Army because we all felt responsible for what we were leaving behind. Charleston was under quarantine and would be for years.

Our new plan was the Chief's idea, but we were all in favor because we still wanted to fight back. We just had to know more about what was out there, and that had been our biggest mistake. We had gotten too comfortable in one place with a big threat in our own back yard. Now we were going to go out and find what was out there, who was out there, and what was being done to stop the infected from killing the rest of civilization.

After the Army was situated at Mud Island with a small force in Guntersville, we finished our preparations. Jean and I felt like bad parents already, so after some convincing by the Chief and Kathy, we agreed to stay behind. Actually, they ganged up on us, and they could lay a pretty good guilt trip on us when they wanted to. Besides, once word got around that we would be staying in Guntersville, I was elected mayor before the rest of the gang could even leave.

Winter was spent in the shelter at Guntersville while preparations were made. At the beginning of Spring as the last of the snow disappeared at the edge of the Appalachian Mountains, the official First Mud Island Expeditionary Force was ready to depart. Lined up on the road in front of the village above the shelter were four, specially equipped and modified Polaris RZR XP 4 Turbocharged all terrain vehicles. Needless to say the stock models didn't come with the additional armor or weapons.

The Chief circled the vehicles with me and Jean and rattled off a list of their capabilities. Each one was originally a four-seater with the backseats removed for cargo and extra fuel. He proudly announced that they were all wheel or two wheel drive with one hundred and sixty-eight horsepower. At a few inches longer than five feet, they could go places cars couldn't go easier and faster, and with the added safety features they could maneuver out of tight spots. If I didn't know better, I would have thought the Chief was stalling because it was hard to say goodbye. When we got to the driver side of his vehicle, Iris was waiting patiently with an understanding expression.

We finally got the Chief into a seat that fit him remarkably well for his size, and I reached past him to start the engine. He thought I was coming in for a hug and caught me off guard with one of his own. He wouldn't let me see that his eyes were wet.

As the engines roared to life, and the tires crunched on the dirt road, we watched our friends roll by. Kathy and Tom were in the second RZR, and Jean yelled that Molly was in good hands. Cassandra and Sim were in the next one, and even though it wasn't warm enough to really appreciate it, he thanked us for the Carolina iced tea we had made just for him. Hampton and Colleen drove past in their RZR, and Colleen yelled something about Hampton being into speed dating.

"What did she mean by that?" asked Jean.

"They met while fighting a big horde. To hear Colleen tell it, Hampton wanted to say something to make an impression, and it came out as a pick up line. I guess you can ask her the next time we see them."